FALL

FALL

Kai Maristed

 RANDOM HOUSE NEW YORK

JUN 1 7 1996

AUTHOR'S NOTE

This is a work of fiction. With the exception of Tommy Burns and the Browns, all characters in this novel exist solely in the writer's and readers' imagination.

Copyright © 1996 by Kai Maristed

Library of Congress Cataloging-in-Publication data is available.

ISBN 0-679-44409-2

Random House website address: http://www.randomhouse.com/

Printed in the United States of America on acid-free paper.

98765432

First Edition

Book design by Caroline Cunningham

To my son Sascha

Don't give your son money, give him horses. No one ever came to grief—except honorable grief—through riding horses. No hour of life is lost that is spent in the saddle.

Young men have often been ruined through owning horses, but never through riding them—unless, of course, they break their necks, which taken at a gallop is a very good way to die.

—WINSTON CHURCHILL

I didn't want everybody knowing how to do it, I'd be out of business. . . . My motive for killing horses was to make money. For the owners, it was just rotten cheapness at its worst.

—TOMMY BURNS, awaiting sentencing, as quoted in
Sports Illustrated, November 16, 1992

Acknowledgments

The author wishes to thank generous friends for their encouragement by word and deed, and shared professional expertise: Dr. Sandra Pratt, DVM; Christine Roth; Barbara Stevens; Lauren Stevens; Leslie Wheeler; Alexandra Broyard; Mike Mee; Andre Dubus; and the kids out there riding; as well as my editor, S. Samuel Vaughan, and agent, William B. Goodman. Lastly, thanks and love to the home boys—Costya, Nico, Sascha, Gregory, and Sweet Pepper.

PART 1

The "A" Circuit

Deerfield, Massachusetts, August 17

H<small>E FOUND</small> 164 <small>MIDWAY DOWN A DIM FLESH-TONED CORRIDOR</small>, and because the Mohawk Motor Inn didn't look like a place where things worked smoothly he was surprised when his key turned the lock, first try. The room was dark and felt narrow and smelled indefinably awful. He dropped his travel bag and then pulled back a wallful of plastic curtain for a view onto parked cars and semis, and highway arching over the neon sunset.

The window gave with a tearing sound, as if it had never been opened.

A concave bed draped in a passionflower print took up most of the room. The surrounding green carpet was scarred with cigarette burns like stunned brown caterpillars, and grayish in corners where a vacuum hadn't reached. Above the bureau a large slice of mirror was bolted flat to the wall. It held his too-familiar lanky self, slope-shouldered by the habit of height, the down-tugged lack of expression caught unawares. Fresh dirt-crusted T-shirt, denim jacket, jeans. He rubbed his palm over bristly silver-tinged hair that in a mysterious reprieve had stopped receding four years ago, when he turned forty, and over the black silky growth of a week's beard. He debated whether to shave. She hadn't said whether she liked the beard or not.

Turning sideways to the mirror, he forced the hunch out of his back. Shower, dig out clean clothes . . .

He did nothing. He was waiting for the phone to ring.

The box jammed in his breast pocket weighed it out of shape. Like wearing a pacemaker. The beeper made him feel awkward and falsely important. From the day it was issued to him it had stayed mute. No alarm, no midnight high jinks or theft or catastrophe. Maybe a dummy. He'd intended to buy a belt to hook the beeper on, but the job kept him moving and he didn't know these towns; he steered past rural scrubfield malls of furniture outlets, gun shops, and craft boutiques, wondering where country people went for food and clothes.

And more and more his spare moments—whether she could slip free or not, whether or not he would see her, alone—were for her. For waiting, now.

He tugged the box out. "HorseGuard International. Unauthorized Use—": the threat had been torn off. He frowned at the tape gun misprint of his name: "A. Heely." The company could get nothing right: witness hiring him. A month ago, lease and unemployment bennies both running out, he'd followed a seductively vague ad ("Supervisor Wanted, Flexible, Immediate") to one brief upbeat interview aimed, like Army recruiting, at denying any stumbling block to enlistment. In fact, "A. Heely" knew zilch about horses except that sheer size plus dumb equals dangerous, and about security only what he'd experienced at seventeen in Deer Island Correctional: one of those rattlesnake memories he tended to sidestep.

Healey, for what it was worth: his Irish side, the bad side. Usually he gave the *A* as standing for Alexander, but he'd begun as Alessandro, for the side of his mother. At home still Mama's Zandro, and Zandro still to a few mellowed ex-hoods left in the old bars and streets. In his real job—the job he'd built from volunteering in an after-school sports program into the full-time security of thirty-two K a year, the job the tax axers had sliced to shreds and which he was suing to resurrect with enraged conviction but a lot less hope—there, he was plain Healey. Or Lex, to the little kids. To Janice he'd been "Dyslex," when she was in her hopped-up, aren't-I-adorably-witty mood. . . .

He stopped, queasy at the betrayal. Because he had adored her. Quips like "Dyslex" had made him laugh. How could all the tenderness threaten to curdle down into cheap bitter shots? She'd had her reasons for walking out with implacable finality after six years of shared work, jokes, Celtics passes, and respective beds (weekends her place, Wednesday nights his). Janice was not unkind. It hurt *her* to hurt, she wanted only the best for two people who had separate selves to actualize. *You're afraid to share your essential self, Lex. I'm not a control freak. I've finally confronted my codependent fantasy of "rescuing" you.* Growth entailed pain—healthy pain. Someday he would thank her, for taking the lead, having the courage to see. . . .

What he saw, for the next months at work, was her empty desk with a single rose in a bottle. The rose blackened but kept its petals; only when it had shriveled and gone crumbly as ash did he finally allow one of the kids to toss it out. If he hadn't been so drunk on shock and loneliness, he might have seen the political axe whizzing closer. Might have somehow deflected it. Maybe not. Janice's timing was unbeatable, almost nature's warning. Rats do not go down with the ship.

The phone rang and because he'd been waiting he jumped, then he hesitated, balanced the beeper on the bureau. A third ring blasted Janice and all miserable memory to oblivion as he belly flopped across the bed to reach the receiver.

"Hello?" Grinning like a bozo.

"It's me."

"It's *you*."

"I just got in. What a dump . . ." Her voice was pitched low.

He realized she might not be alone. On the road, to save money, she often roomed with one of the grooms. Though not when her husband and Farah, the baby golden retriever, were driving out to stay the night: keeping the family together. "How's the—what? Mohawk?"

"Usual highway gothic. You wonder why they send probes to Venus when there's places like this to explore."

She puffed through her nose, amused. Then silence. He rolled over, gazed at the frosted ceiling fixture, and fought his sudden betraying shyness. *Speak.* He wanted to say some astonishing thing she would always remember.

"What a shitty-run show!" Her voice exploded in his ear. "That jumper ring's a maze. Footing like granite. Deerfield always is. Then last minute they call a trainers' meeting to tell us tomorrow's schedule is totally switched around. So now I've got to somehow . . . Hello? Lex?"

"You're alone. You said my name."

"Wow. A *real* detective." He could hear her smile. He could see her—still in britches and boots, sleeves rolled high up tanned muscular arms. Her square white teeth, because she never smiled halfway, couldn't do anything halfway. . . . Her sun-reddened nose and cheeks. Her eyes, wide with listening, bluer than all the skies she'd ever stared into. She would wedge the phone against her left shoulder and run a hand through straight blunt pecan-brown hair that was still sweaty at the nape and brow. Lying on beds a lot like this one he had watched her telephone, to others.

"Erica? Hey."

"Well, look, you sound kind of . . . the day ran forever, you must be tired—"

"No!" He felt her fading, eluding him, and in panic he jerked bolt upright on the edge of the bed. "I'm *not* too tired. Did you eat yet? You, of course not. No time. Look, we'll meet somewhere, we can drive somewhere a few towns out where no one you know will be, you can relax—"

"Or I could come to you."

"Yes. You could." He drew a breath, looked straight into the last of the smoldering sunset. "I'd like that."

"Now?"

He pulled the key from his pocket to make sure. "It's the Mohawk. Not far. Nothing's far. Room one-six-four."

In the shower he opened with "I Concentrate on You," and then began to dance—not out of joy but because the plastic regulator flipped between frigid and scalding according to unpredictable whims. He escaped into blinding steam and began to blot his body with paper-thin cloth strips that reminded him that a real towel was another road-life investment he'd promised himself. A fan set in the waterlogged, sagging ceiling blasted his own steam back at him.

" 'Whenever skies look gray to me, and trouble begins to brew . . .' "

He popped the cellophane bag around a disposable razor. His electric had quit on him three stops ago, in Fairfield, Connecticut. That was the only stop he'd made without Erica. Otherwise, in the twenty-eight days since their first meeting, their separate schedules had kept them traveling in parallel, as if—he'd said one night, holding her, gazing up at constellations, the red eye of Arcturus—as if Someone with time on his hands was taking an interest down here. Christ, she'd said, it's not like competing on the New England circuit leaves a lot of choices. This time of year everyone's chasing hunter points or equitation medals—you either ship from one big A show to the next or you bag it and stay home.

Please don't stay home.

" 'Whenever the blues . . . become my only song—' " He was in great voice, lathering up, under the roar of the vent. Risky, though, to sing while shaving. He pulled one cheek taut so the skin wrinkled beside a leering eye, and drew the razor down into the soapy beard, where it became immediately tangled.

"Oh *shit*." The wrong approach. No way out but forward. After rinsing the razor clean he looked up into a blank, completely refogged mirror. Rubbed clear, it showed the white-stippled rectangle that doomed the rest of his beard. Again the razor scraped and stuck, like a hand lawn mower plowed into a thicket of weeds.

From her motel to his would be less than fifteen minutes down the main drag. His hand twitched, scraping. No . . . she would shower first too. But Erica showered and dressed faster than anyone he'd ever known. Her idea of evening makeup was a smear of Vaseline on chapped lips. Thirty, twenty minutes?

A nick oozed up into the lather, rosy red.

He dumped the first razor and wrestled the slippery bag off a fresh one. He commanded himself to relax, act more his age and less like a high school dork. After all—as Erica pointed out—they had already, by some combination of miracle and reckless ingenuity, hoarded more hours together than most married couples managed in a year. But his nervousness before seeing her again persisted. Intensified. He reminded himself that the moment he heard her knock at the door his heart might stop completely, but would then resume—for a while at least—its normal beat.

That had happened, the first time he saw her. He put love at first sight in the same category as papal indulgences, hadn't given it a thought that afternoon either, but after his heart regained its rhythm he found himself walking behind her. Not asking why. She wore the uniform—narrow-waisted white shirt, beige britches. Even in knee-high black boots her stride was relaxed and supple; following, he was surprised at the ground it covered. Her hair (brown except for bleached wisps at the temples) was pulled back that day in a little-kid dime-store barrette lettered ERICA, but she was no little kid: when she turned to greet a passing rider, deep laugh lines sprang across her face. He followed her, at least with his eyes, through the crowd of contestants and horses, from ring to stabling tent and back, until it was dusk and the show was packed up and she banged the door shut on a two-tone Bronco and with expressive acceleration pulled away.

That had been on his fourth day. That very morning—before he saw her—he had decided to stuff the job. The job was a crock:

boring and physically hazardous and underpaid even for a stopgap. He had a badge and time sheets on each horse and a Mace gun and the beeper. He "supervised" three seasoned illegal Hispanics and found little to do but keep out of the boys' way and make believe he wasn't edgy around large animals.

At sunrise the next day he saw her again. The planes of her face glowed silver and peach as she strode by. He stepped forward, but was speechless, and for a second her gaze went through him as if he weren't there. He realized then what he was, in this job, within the hierarchy of the show world: invisible.

He had hoped his boys (though Jesus was about his own age, probably a grandfather already) might know who she was. Gravely, they shrugged. Next, he barged into the show secretary's office, stumbled over the description, and was told that the trainer he might be looking for was Erica Hablicht. "With the 'ch' . . . Well, now since she married, I'd like to say Hablicht-Pettit, but *she* doesn't, so. Young women are awfully, you know, aren't they these days? They commit but they don't, if you catch my drift. By the way, I know what you're after but forget it. She can't be talked into it. You're not the first fellow to try."

"Excuse me?"

"You are the HorseGuard manager, aren't you? Well. *She* never signs up for the service. Do-it-yourselfer. Penny-wise, pound-foolish in my opinion, given the awful things happening recently. It's not like it was, don't you agree, back when George and Frank and Bert were everyone's heroes, winning the Olympics every year and setting the standards back here at home? Nowadays look at the riffraff! No one has a notion how to braid a tail anymore, and you see ladies riding hunt seat in such funny-colored jackets. . . . And not to mention the brutalities—horrible, horrible, it's as if everything's going downhill at once. If you believe half what you hear, she is *certainly* penny-wise, pound-foolish. Of course her thingamajig farm, Stoneacre, isn't one of your top *top* if you know what I mean. Nothing against her reputation! It's a hard business. So competitive. Erica Hablicht . . . Should I page her?"

No! he'd said. Please don't bother.

Swabbing the mirror he saw that his beard had been replaced by its ghost: a livid nakedness below the cheekline of tan.

Erica, Erica . . . For once, she was late. Perversely, this fact calmed him. Then, as he hitched the wet scrap of towel tighter around his waist, a sudden memory of her body against his, the full dizzying depth of an embrace, stunned him like a blow.

He opened the door to drier, stale air. A chance she was waiting already, in the hall. "Erica?" No answering single knock. Her knock was always one syllable, like his name.

The room had turned uniform gray except for the luminous blue window. He crouched down to rummage in his bag. Fresh khakis. His last clean T-shirt read, 3RD STREET KIDPOWER. LEND US A HAND. His kids' purple handprints stenciled all over. Pulling on the shirt he flipped a light and this time had to grin, abashed, at the joker caught in the mirror. His jaw glowed fiery and abused, and touch made the sting worse. He studied his watch, bit his lip, then stared over at the phone. At that moment a toylike siren filled the room: the shrilling of the beeper.

THE SHOWGROUNDS WERE SET ON THE DECOROUS ROLLING fields of a boarding school, three miles north on Route 6. This country's running out of *grass,* Erica had complained; when I was a little girl there used to be major shows right outside the city. Now every square inch is malled over and we're lucky to find space in Boonieville, on some corn-stubble acre already perked for the developer. So thank heaven for private schools. This Pioneer Valley circuit, for instance, they've organized three A-rated shows almost back-to-back: after Deerfield we move to Haydenville, then Greenfield. The preppy trinity. Noblesse oblige. I mean, a show rips lawn to shreds so the schools dread us—but the parents twist arms. It's their kids who *ride,* after all—

Lex had pictured the kind of schools he knew. Using the same word for both types of institution went beyond convenient abstraction. He figured the chances of a 3rd Street KidPower alumnus ever riding horseback at maybe one in ten million.

He wheeled his Escort, pseudo-official blue with the Horse-Guard company logo, through the clapboard compound of dorms and halls, all but one donated office deserted and padlocked for the summer. Ahead, white poles and standards in two ribboned-off rings glowed phosphorescent under a vibrant depth of stars. Lex felt alien, under this country sky. The Escort bumped over grass hummocks and hoses, between manure heaps and empty listing trailers, to a stop. There were lights on in the stabling tent. He saw no one. No other cars.

Pino ran out and without a word grabbed his elbow, leading. Pino, who barely reached Lex's shoulder, had the horseman's steel grip. "*Vivo. Vivo, Señor Alejandro, un poco mas rápido*—" They sprinted past horses locked in the rickety portable stalls, all disturbed by some unexpected night commotion and gazing down the aisle. Somewhere a radio was playing Bob Dylan. "Hurricane Carter." Lex felt an uneasy cousinship with Dylan that had nothing to do with liking. The guy was a zombie; if he had any sense of style he would be retired, or dead.

"Are you all right?"

"*¡Si!*" Pino wiped one side of his mustache so it lay up his lip, skewed. All the boys understood English, but only Jesus would speak a word.

"Is it one of our—" As they rounded a corner Pino's grip saved Lex from skidding on the slick hard-trodden ground. Before them lay a massive reddish orange horse, larger somehow for being down. The horse shuddered and gave a moan that came from some deep place. Its shoulders heaved, but it made no other attempt to rise. In the shadows of the dim rigged lights Lex took a full second to notice that the animal's right front knee was torn open like a flap of thick felt, revealing white tendon and bone. The wetness on the ground was blood.

"Put—you better put a halter on him." Lex had a vision of the horse rising, careening out into the night. "Just in case."

Pino threw Lex an impenetrable look. His eyes were solid polished black, like stones in a game of Go.

At night, the aisles were normally left squared away, a drill sergeant's delight. Now Lex scanned a scattered mess of overturned wash buckets, brush boxes, whips, and hard hats knocked off hooks and racks. Havoc. How had the animal broken loose? Nearby, one stall gate hung open. All the other stalls were double latched from the outside. As Pino knelt to slip a halter over the stretched, unresisting muzzle, Lex said firmly, "I have to get a vet here. And I've got to reach the owners—" He slapped at his empty pockets, aware of putting on a useless act. In his mind's eye the HorseGuard logbook lay on the floor of his car. The only phone was in the show office, up the hill: Pino must have sprinted like a demon, torn between staying with the injured horse and notifying the boss, who would deal with all that had to be done. Lex backed a step. Poised to take off, escape to that office. Anywhere away.

Pino was stroking the horse's head, its hairy plate jaw. He pointed toward the wound, forcing Lex to return, to bend lower, to smell the sour horse odor and the new sweetness of blood. The edges of the wound pulsed, seeping a continuous, unsteady trickle. Before leaving, Lex had jammed his bare feet into leather boat shoes; now he noticed the yellow soles dyed rust brown. His toes felt slippery, inside. He wondered how much blood a horse could lose without dying. People could lose an amazing amount and survive, he knew: or rather, he knew that the volume always looks deceptively greater than it is. On a man's leg, someone would have wrapped a tourniquet by now. Lex knew how to do that.

His job was to protect property. The wound, if bad enough, or the blood loss alone, threatened to wipe out an investment worth at least fifty thousand. Maybe three times that. According to his book nothing came cheaper, under this tent.

"Gad lag!" Pino said.

Lex frowned and then followed Pino's nod toward the open stall gate. From this angle the brass plate was visible: CRIMSON CADILLAC. Gad lag? Cadillac, okay. It was not a name he recalled from his roster.

"This one—so he's not ours?"

Pino shook his head no.

Lex waited for a sense of relief that didn't come. "Christ, Pino, why did you—? I'm not a vet!"

Pino rose, making a gesture with arms and spread palms like Atlas lifting the earth. "*Us* get him up? How? Don't be ridiculous."

"*¡Si! Necesidad. Fatalidad, señor—*"

Part of the duty guard's job was to record the minutes a horse spent lying down at night. Why, he had asked Erica once, do horses sleep standing up? Because otherwise after a few hours their whole circulation starts shutting down. That's why you always want a sick one on its feet. Same thing.

"Okay, Pino. We'll try, okay? Only . . . wait a sec, hold on—" Lex snatched a long rolled leg wrap from the nearest tack box. He approached the horse again, this time forced to crouch well inside the range of polished sharp-shod hooves. "Good boy," he said, swallowing dry. He slid the wrap under the warm upper foreleg where a main artery bulged. The horse flicked its ears and then twitched everywhere as if attacked by gnats, and Lex shied back. "*Good* boy, now . . ." He finished the knot. He liked the wrap material, elastic but firm. "Okay?"

"*Excelente.*"

Pino's lips were pressed tight together below his mustache as he shoved and threaded a pair of ropes under the orange neck and barrel. The horse whipped its tail, breath whistling. Pino positioned himself next to Lex holding the ends of one rope loop. Lex accepted the other. "*Sirvase, señor. Uno, dos, tres—*"

Together, they hauled. Shocked into movement the horse scrambled, three good legs churning the ground. "*Rock* him," Lex shouted, and Pino grimaced agreement; they leaned away with backs and thighs straining, shoes slipping and digging in. The horse pitched and whinnied and then from one instant to the next was swaying upright, threatening to fall forward on the dangling right leg before Pino lunged to support its chest with both hands braced.

"*Christ . . .*"

Pino shifted, balancing the horse, head hanging. Sweat dripped from his long black hair. He nodded at the ground. *"Vamos, señor,"* he said.

Lex's memory was literal rather than deductive; it worked like a camera. He could see, for instance, where some missing object— a certain pair of socks, say, or a once devastating letter—lay in a drawer, and could see clearly the shapes and colors surrounding it. He might be less sure which drawer, in whose apartment, which city. Now he was right to have trusted memory: hunched in the car, holding the journal up to light, he found no Crimson Cadillac on his current list. But the name resonated. He flipped back a week, and then another, all the way to the first stop. "Crimson Cadillac. Ch. m., 9 yrs. Star, hind socks. Jumper/equitation, in-sured Am Bankers 120K, owners Sarah and Russell Morton." So. At the height of show season, its owners for some reason had can-celed HorseGuard protection. Perfect timing—from his company's point of view.

The address and phone number were in Vermont.

He shoved the car into drive and roared up the long grassy black hill.

The office, an ell off a main building, was dark and shuttered, but the door gave at his touch. He was vaguely aware of traffic on the road behind him as he entered, and then of headlights veering in, and he turned and waved then, probably invisible but glad of any insomniac horse lover who was about to discover Pino, and stand by him.

He ran his hand along the wall. Fluorescent light sprang on. The cluttered room still held the heat of the day. He dialed the vet's number and reached a sleepy protective husband who, before Lex had half explained, was replaced by Dr. Ianuzzi's crisp voice. "I hear you," she barked, "I hear you. Be there in ten."

He dropped the phone and stretched back in the show secre-tary's chair, flexing cramped fingers that had begun to tremble a lit-

tle. No surprise. He had lived with these lousy nerves since childhood. Shakes. Treacherous bursts of tears over next to nothing. Big
Tom Healey, before splitting for good, had done his paternal best
to whack the sissy streak out of his boy. With the father gone Lex
himself took over: first by joining the Vito gang, and then, after
Deer Island showed him a fast-forward of one future, by switching
to amateur boxing at the Y. Then stock-car racing, white-water
runs, 'chute jumping . . . The night-shift job in a halfway house for
recovering addicts probably figured here, too.

He counted seventeen fractures, five dislocations, two concus-
sions, three sprains. (Dys, you're *bragging,* Janice had once exclaimed. Ick. Like some welfare mom boasting how often she's
been knocked up. What do you want, the Purple Heart?) He was
minus a toe joint and various cartilage and most of the hearing in
his left ear—but the lousy nerves stayed intact, unchanged. Something he had finally learned to make private allowances for.

He snatched up the phone again and then paused, staring up at
a sepia portrait of the school's muttonchopped founder. Seeing
Erica. He never stopped seeing Erica. Sometimes she moved just at
the periphery of his vision. Now her face was close enough to
touch and the dour founder, the office, everything real, faded
under the sheen of her cheek, the inquiry in her eyes, the curved
shadow of her lips. His chest tightened. He had never felt haunted
before.

Nine-fifty, by his watch . . . Just over an hour since he'd left the
Mohawk. What had she thought, when she knocked and waited in
vain, as the minutes ticked by? Would she have risked going to the
motel clerk, asking in bright light where show people were coming and going, for a message from Mr. Healey? It was a small, in-
terlocked world, he'd learned, riddled with innuendo and feuds
and simmering obsessions. He'd left no message. Could he risk calling her?

She would remind him of his duty—personal, not official—to
these Mortons, in Vermont. He envisioned a gray-haired farm
couple, innocent of their loss. The horse would be a homebred, its

hopeful young rider here, their daughter . . . He stopped himself. He had this maudlin streak.

The phone rang six times, muffled by distance, before a cool female voice came on.

"Mrs. Morton?"

"One of them, yes."

"I'm calling in regard to your horse. Crimson Cadillac?"

"Oh Christ. Just don't tell me a problem's cropped up at *this* stage of the game."

"Well—I'm afraid there's been an accident. I can't say exactly how serious yet, but the vet's on her way over and—" Despite voices raised in the background he plowed ahead.

"Who the hell are *you*?" the woman interrupted.

"I'm with HorseGuard International. I'm the, uh, supervisor in charge here."

"Well, Mr. HorseGuard. Evidently your company's records are as sloppy as ever or you'd be aware that Morton Enterprises sold Cadillac to Suzy DiSenza three weeks ago. In fact I just ran a full pager in the *Chronicle of the Horse,* congratulating the new owner. Two hundred bucks. Which is more cash than I've seen from the buyers yet! But we wrote a contract tighter than a terrier's tush, and if they think for one single—"

"Mrs. Morton?"

"What?"

"Could I trouble you for their phone number?"

"Oh, why not. Though I'm probably making some goddamned legal boo-boo. But why *not.*" He heard papers rustling as the woman went on to say, "I wish you joy with Suzy. Though it's not so much the girl, she's your basic catatonic teenager, or even her nutsy mother who screwed us, but her trainer. *Boyd.* That flaming swish! These trainers have their mitts in everything, they control all the deals, but of course it's never *their* money! The only asking price offer we had, from Texas, I *know* he torpedoed. Believe me, we didn't get forty cents back on the dollar for Cadillac. But we will *get* it. And then, I tell you, I am out of the horse biz. Promises,

promises. They sucker you into buying an Olympic prospect for a silly little hundred grand, and turns out you bought a fifteen-year-old with the chronic heaves. Think I'm joking? Shipping bikinis to Tehran makes a better investment." She paused. "You still want this number?"

"Please." He jotted it down. A 413 area code. Local. Western Mass.

"Listen. One thing—"

"Yes?"

"When you talk to little Suzy. Just tell her I'm, well . . . not *sorry*. Sympathetic."

"I'm no expert, but I guess there's a good chance the horse can still—"

"I don't want to *know* about the horse! God. I *loathe* horses. Listen. On second thought. Better not pass anything direct from me to Suzy after all. I've got my rear end to cover." With that, Mrs. Morton hung up.

Lex punched in the 413 number and closed his eyes, suddenly weary, listening to a long, empty ring.

When he looked up Erica stood framed in the open door. The uncertain smile she sent in his direction was one he hadn't seen before, and her eyes were wide and shining with the look of someone absorbing a sudden loss. "I saw it," she said. "Went to the stable area. Just to check. To find you. I stayed to help until the vet—Christ. I just never can get used . . . It's . . . horrible. When they suffer. Lex. Why do things *happen*?"

"I—" He shrugged, felt the simultaneous downward tug of his mouth. "I at least found the owners, I think."

"Good." Pause. In the same dull, indifferent tone she said, "You were there. You saw. There was nothing you saw . . . unusual, right? That injury had to be an accident."

"Of course. What else, for heaven's sake? And with any luck there'll be a rapid recovery and zero aftereffects, and in a few weeks, given how fast things move on at the shows, we'll both have practically forgotten tonight. Now, you come here."

Erica scuffed toward him like a child. She wore a plaid blouse, new white sneakers, new stiff indigo jeans. He reached to touch her wrist. "You found me. Tracked me down. Pretty smart."

"Hey, if you want I can get lost—maybe you were expecting someone else at this hour—" She tried to grin but pressed her lower lip to stop it from trembling. She frowned, focusing closely. "Oh God. Lex, what did you do awful to yourself. You shaved."

"Come here," he said again. He drew her down to his lap, felt the distinct weight of her narrow legs settle across his.

"Maybe we're both too scrawny for this," she whispered.

"Maybe."

"You're not, not trying to *comfort* me. . . ."

"No. Never." Her breath warmed his skin and it was the easiest, the only answer: to kiss her. Lightly, to comfort. Between her lips he tasted a trace of peppermint, and the salt of sadness. Erica gave a low moan and her arms tightened suddenly around him, binding, as if in the tide of a kiss he could be swept away.

Haydenville, Massachusetts, August 20

Ruthie steered her golf cart up over the lip of the grassy plateau where the practice jumps stood and parked just out of range of the gallop lines. The cart, poison-apple red and jeweled by the light drizzle, was a customized model with extrasmooth suspension and rubber-grip hand levers for accelerator and brake. Expensive—but after her accident Ruthie could have bought a fleet, the whole factory. She didn't want a factory. To try to think of anything worth wanting tired and irritated her. Then and now she would have thrown the settlement back at them, would have paid all 1.8 million for one hour face-to-face with the man who had left her on the road, unconscious, crushed and bleeding. In the courtroom she would have stripped down her easy-on sweatpants so he could stare at her gouged, twisted legs. The pearly hairless sheen of scar tissue that cannot tan or blush. *There. Look. Come close to me now!* But then she'd still been "underage," and in the hazy agonizing months of surgery, lawyers and her parents had made all decisions for her. *Better we all focus on the future, Ruthie. One step at a time. You have your whole life ahead of you still. . . .*

Now Ruthie elbowed her crutches out of the way and prodded her wasted thighs inch by inch sideways until she sat with a clear view of the show rings, below.

Here on the rise the grass was slick and treacherous and only a fool, thought Ruthie, would risk cantering so much as ground rail. The lone fool who occasionally crossed her line of vision, anonymous in hooded rain cape and riding a horse disguised by sea-foam sweat, was jumping four-foot-high poles. Ruthie felt comfortably shaken by the crescendo and diminuendo of the gallop just behind her.

Owen Goodchild's fruity drawl drifted up from the loudspeakers, announcing the first of the afternoon's advanced equitation classes: Open, Age 15–18. Ruthie leaned forward. Despite distance and rain dripping off the visor of her slicker she could follow the action better from up here than at ringside, where she would be wedged among spectators and horses and frustrated by fence boards at her eye level.

The depression she'd felt all morning, which had nothing to do with buffeting crowds or the nasty change in weather, was about to end.

Down below, number forty-nine posted into the ring, splashing muck. Ruthie's pulse quickened almost as if she were that girl. Probably she *had* worn the number forty-nine, somewhere. Maybe won?

The rider attacked the first line—brick wall to a two-stride—with aggressive control. Spur. Release. Check. Spur.

Ruthie's bare hands gripped the golf cart's cold metal. This was what she had come for. To lose herself out on the course. To forget, for at least the next few hours, the trapped crippled thing she had become. The Open, essentially a warm-up round without much at stake, would be followed by the Medal class, then the Maclay, and finally the toughest, highest course, the USET. These were the respective qualifying classes for the three final nationwide competitions in the fall. A rider hoping to qualify for all three finals before the end of the season—and who didn't?—would need three

wins each in Medal and Maclay, four in the USET. While the rule
book set no limit on USET wins, once qualified for "M/M" a
competitor was "finished" until the respective finals. For that reason, although by August time was running out for dozens of average desperate "eq" kids milling near the in-gate below, Ruthie
knew that certain riders, the confident stars on superstar horses, had
held back from completing their wins at earlier, lesser shows in
order to triumph here. There would be real prizes: the grand prix
saddle and bridle, and real cash—the envelope palmed like a discreet afterthought to the champion's trainer. Today at Haydenville
Ruthie anticipated some sizzling rides, in the cold misting rain.

Forty-nine dropped a rail in front of the water jump. *Aaws* of
sympathy wafted up from spectators, huddled under a striped
awning. Ruthie leaned back, stricken by momentary disgust.

"Too bad. That one always tries her heart out."

Ruthie's heart contracted as if touched by a hot wire. She knew
the voice. Coco Beale. Coco—her first trainer—had all along been
the anonymous rider galloping behind her back.

Ruthie didn't turn around. She shut her eyes, heard Coco's
mount gasping like a beached fish, and said, "You know that kid?"

"Get real, Ruthie. Don Deluna's been pulling every string he
ever strung, promoting that girl. Laura . . . ? Laura Whatsis.
Where've *you* been?"

Ruthie looked at her former teacher.

"Honey! I didn't mean that like it—"

"Okay. Okay."

The next rider had entered the ring, but Coco's heaving, lath-
ered horse blocked the view. Coco pulled her hood back to shake
loose billowing champagne hair. Her mobile mouth was redder
than the golf cart, lacquered with a lipstick neither sweat nor rain
could dilute. But the feature that always drew Ruthie's attention
was her ex-trainer's nose: narrow and small, with a defiant arch
below the bridge. Permanently flared nostrils. A younger Ruthie
had been fascinated by that nose.

"I mean I just assumed you knew. Since you *rode* a while with

Don." There was no rancor in Coco's soaring nasal tone, the Beacon Hill blend of vinegar and molasses. Six years ago, when she was
sixteen, Ruthie had broken up with Coco for good—after a weeping, screaming binge of no-holds-barred recriminations out in a
snowy field where they and their horses were the only living
things. The quarrel had ostensibly started over Ruthie's refusal to
jump a five-foot iced-over ditch. Now, with two years' head-
shrinking to draw on (not that she had ever mentioned Coco in
therapy, but between all the bullshitting a few facts did emerge),
Ruthie realized she had been in love with Coco, so fiercely and
desperately enthralled that the breakup was inevitable. Her deser-
tion to Don's barn had left Coco minus the two-thou-per-month
board on two good eq horses, but Coco, born into the trust fund
of Beale Pharmaceuticals, could shrug. She looked down her ex-
otic nose at the bootlicking and client nabbing of her colleagues.
What she *had* minded a lot was losing a promising rider. What she
minded absolutely was disloyalty. Cowardice. Betrayal.

"Don and I don't talk much anymore," Ruthie heard herself
admit. She bit her tongue and pitched sideways to see the ring. Her
true reason for avoiding Deluna was: he acted too kind. Kindness
made her physically sick now, gave her hot flashes. . . . Psychoso-
matic. But knowing didn't help.

"On the outs?" Coco reined her horse back a step. Saliva from
its bit dripped on the golf cart. "You should bury the hatchet,
honey. Don's good people—especially compared to some scum-
bags." She gestured downhill with her chin. "Old soldiers never
die, that's Don. Straight and narrow. A gentleman wop . . ." Coco
laughed. "Although, Christ, look where *straight* got him, three
brats to put through college, plus the wife can't stay off the sauce.
In and out of the detox spa, revolving door. Decades, think she'd
be dead by now, but isn't it awful how alcoholics hang on? Don't
his eyes tell you what a drain that's been? I *hate* looking in Don's
eyes. Don't you?"

Go away, prayed Ruthie. *Go away.*

"So, I guess, if he wants to promote that girl, let him. Shoot the moon. Rots of ruck. I wouldn't. *You* could've ridden rings around her."

Ruthie felt the prickle of a flush.

"Never forget how glad I was for you when you decided to go on with Don. Good choice."

Ruthie glanced up through the drizzle, blinking. A patter of clapping like damp rustling leaves rose from below.

"Now, that was a lucky long shot! One of Erica's kids," Coco volunteered. "The boy."

The boy whose ride Ruthie had missed posted out of the ring, shoulders bowed against rain he must have been numb to while pounding over the jumps moments before. Ruthie still knew that pitch of terror and exaltation, how once on course you will finish no matter what, even with a broken leg or lightning striking all around . . . not with two legs gone, however. No one could do that.

"How was the round?" she had to ask.

"So-so. Chipped at the picket though not as bad as Laura. He won't *win*. He's a total unknown at this exalted level, and so is his horse. Technically Erica's an ace but would you risk sending a kid to her? Kiss of death. Can't deal with the politics so she pretends none of the crap exists."

"Sounds like you." Though Ruthie managed to make her tone snide, Coco looked pleased.

"Yeah? Well there're certain differences. Know what they're calling Erica these days? Never mind. Not nice. Come to think, how many friends has she got down there?" Coco held up a closed fist, to indicate zero, and laughed. Her full laugh trumpeted like the cry of some large aggressive bird. Ruthie knew what she meant: judging eq is subjective, a matter of art, vision, and experience, and there are judges insecure enough to be swayed in their scoring by hefty applause.

"Don't *you* have any kids in this?" Ruthie narrowed her eyes. It would be pure Coco to leave a student stranded at the in-gate, wondering where in hell her trainer was, up to the last moment.

Coco understood as much about jitters as a falling rock knows about physics.

"Not this class. My girls only came up here to collect USETs. We're all qualified." Coco smiled benignly. "You know I never 'save' for these big shows. Too much can go wrong at the last minute."

Ruthie nodded. Once you'd won your three Medals, and Maclays, those classes were closed to you, but in USET you could keep competing. Ten U.S. Equestrian Team wins earned a silver cup, twenty bought the gold. A huge deal: USET gold meant a once-over from the Olympic Committee, just like a win at the finals would. But the horses took a rough beating along the way. How many USET wins had Coco's two girls already collected? Ruthie knew them only by sight: both uncommonly tall and slim hipped, icicle-sleek. Coco could afford to pick and choose, in her image.

"Hallelujah," said Coco. "Good-bye, rain!"

Ruthie held her palm up to the sky. It was true. A fresher breeze was blowing. But when she tried to concentrate on the ring nothing made sense, it didn't *work,* the horse and rider ticking from jump to jump seemed aimless windup toys, and she felt her depression snug tight around her: foggy, opaque. *Go away.*

She squinted at her former trainer. "Your horse is shivering."

"Wimpie here? Oh, he's not cold. . . ." But Coco spurred into a walk, then a trot, calling back over her shoulder, "He's just petrified! He *knows* he's got the jumper course ahead!"

Under the wet, heavy slicker Ruthie clawed her pockets for her pills.

By the early rounds of the Medal class the Flexeril had kicked in to relax and warm her. Gratitude toward a tiny brown diamond-shaped pill struck her as both funny and normal. Now that her vision was clearing again Coco was nowhere in sight—unless she was the pin-dot contestant negotiating the monster jumper stakes course down in ring 2.

Yes, funny—to suddenly picture all the drugs circulating in the show scene, as if in one connected body. All horses on daily doses of bute to preempt pain, kids' equitation horses on Acepromazine to tranquilize their spirits, jumpers on testosterone for supernatural courage. Grooms nodding off on weed. Adult grand prix stars so thrilled with nose candy, the way it banished the jitters, that they even slipped it to certain favorite eq kids. Or so she'd heard. No one ever made the mistake of offering dope to Ruthie Pryor. Ruthie was *not that kind.* But now . . . But now, so *funny* . . .

Other riders had straggled up the hill to use the practice area; they cantered close around her, flailing mud. A thought about moving her golf cart floated like a soap bubble through Ruthie's mind. Overhead, the wind had torn a jagged blue hole in the sky.

The eq ring belonged to number forty-nine again. Gallop on, you—Lorna or Laurie whoever you are. Go *get* 'em. . . .

In some respects the Medal had been Ruthie's favorite class: not as technically demanding as the USET, but suspenseful because at the end the top four contestants would be called back according to a ranking known only to the judges, to ride a new jump-off course kept secret till the last moment.

Clean through the triple combination. *Yes.*

Planted at the in-gate was the stocky, bow-kneed and booted figure of Don Deluna. His sideburns flaring beneath the old brown velvet hard hat. His right fist socking hard into his left hand after each successfully negotiated fence. *Yes!*

Good luck, down there. Ruthie knew even better than Coco how badly Don needed a sweep. Three years back it had been Ruthie who was supposed to save him; she was the one who had wandered into the back office, to find her trainer tear-smeared and shameless, turning the pages of a cobwebby scrapbook that nobody else ever took off the shelf. In '81 his star student, Ranger Boyd, had swept the finals; now the up-and-coming talent flocked to young honchos like Boyd, no glory for Deluna since. She'd thought it was that. "It's fucking *money,*" he'd cried, hurling the book to smash wide open against a wall. "Maria and Joseph, what would a kid like *you* know?" She had never before seen him angry.

His eyes, the pouchy sad brown eyes Coco avoided, had burned like the devil's in the *Exorcist* movie: furnace red. "Just . . . you ride out there, come finals, and win. You're the one. *Ride* for me, Ruthie," he'd said.

Remembering now, she was repelled. But not then. Then, the summer before the accident, she had been someone else.

She had been the one with a chance. Until this new girl, the only bettable chance he'd had in years. She wondered how Don had managed to stay afloat, the years between.

And she did not, deep down, wish him or anyone else good luck. When the kid with the cardboard number forty-nine flapping on her back misjudged the distance and crashed through the last jump, tumbling a wing standard and scattering pots of chrysanthemums, Ruthie heard her own low moan of relief. The ride had come too close to perfect. She loved the moment-to-moment uncertainty on course, the risk, the detonating chain of split-second decisions. But she did not enjoy watching winners: their egg-smooth complacency. In Ruthie's ideal world the jumps would go on and on, and no one would ever win.

"Well, *hello*. Little Miss Muffet on her tuffet? Better yet, it's Ruthie Pryor, keeping an eye on us all! She does turn up everywhere, this season. . . ."

Towering over her on a massive dappled gray, outlined by gilt sky, was Ranger Boyd. He held his grin in unwavering control, a mask of friendliness. Despite the Flexeril Ruthie felt a shivery spasm. Boyd was someone she had no desire to see, or listen to. Her hands squeezed the levers of the golf cart. Her eyes flicked over the shifting confusion of riders behind him, willing any of them, even Coco, to ride up and take Ranger Boyd away.

Boyd asked pleasantly, "Are you alone up here?"

She swallowed. Her palms were slick and cold.

"Now, let's see, Ruthie. I noticed you up at Stowe. And Worcester before that? And Deerfield yesterday, no? And now—my goodness, Ruth. Dedicated! You ought to apply for your judge's card."

He wants the cart moved is all, Ruthie guessed. Her throat stuck. "Yah. Sure."

"Seriously. Vast improvement over *these* myopic cows. You always had a fantastic eye for distances. By the way, I don't suppose you happened to catch the Open here? I was late. I just now tacked up." In winking apology, he ran his fingers through sideswept golden curls.

"Some boy of Erica's won."

"Oh no kidding! Young Ned . . . We'll have to watch out for him now."

Ruthie couldn't tell whether Ranger's grin, which never faded entirely, now expressed generosity or derision.

Her hand tightened again on the brake release. "If you want the cart moved—"

"Oh not on my account, Ruth!"

"Yah. Well, anyway, I'll just—"

"My best student had to scratch," he said, blocking her. "So it's a light day for me. One jumper class. I suppose you know why—I mean, you must have heard. What happened to us, at Deerfield."

Ruthie nodded. The barrier in her throat was like a fist.

"Suzy's in pieces. That I can understand, but my other students are riding like such pigs that I took them out too. For today. Call it punishment if you will. Can you please explain to me why hysteria is so *catching* among adolescent girls? They've all wasted two nights' sleep on a weeping jag." He reined his horse back a few steps, kicked it up again. "It was an awful accident. Awful. But they have to learn that no matter what happens, you go on! You simply have to *ride forward*."

Ruthie's gaze rested on the broad chest of the jumper. He hadn't been worked yet; the coat was still dry, white satin. Suddenly something snapped inside her, she was listing, and then falling forward, the stiff slicker squeaking as her head bumped low against the steering wheel and her arms jerked up around her ears.

Yes. I know what happened to that mare—

She might have whispered, or made no sound at all. In the

blackness she heard her own blood rushing in its hidden channels. She saw the chestnut with its crooked blaze, and long reddish lashes twinned in the brown eye, and the flayed, wrecked knee, exposed to the bone.

She knew. The whole world knew that after the vet had cleaned and stitched the wound, Crimson Cadillac was left bandaged up and tranquilized to the feasible limit in her stall, supported by a sling, on three legs. Ruthie had once looked in, seen the dazed, dangling mare and seen but not spoken to Suzy DiSenza, who had stayed most of the night on watch. In the morning, outside on the dew-fresh showgrounds, all the mothers pitied poor Suzy. The devastated child. Sheet white. Basically in shock. She refused to eat breakfast. It was self-destructive not to eat, the mothers agreed.

In their sympathetic murmur Ruthie heard the threads of suppressed optimism. Whether or not the mare pulled through, for this season at least one serious competitor appeared eliminated. Their own kids' chances suddenly that much improved.

But during that day, something happened to the mare. Either the pain pierced its mind, or else the medication was too much. Crimson flipped out, battering the jerry-built walls of the temporary stall before losing balance forever and crumpling, a ton of flesh bearing down on the weak leg, ripping new stitches, hemorrhaging—there was nothing those who came running could do to stanch the new flow of blood. Suzy had screamed. To Ruthie, at that moment a quarter mile distant by the Deerfield eq ring, the screams sounded like jagged bursts of song.

And only last night, at dusk—after the eighteen-wheeler vans heavy with horses had pulled out for the trek to nearby Haydenville and the grounds lay half dismantled—Ruthie had seen a huge backhoe rock slowly down to the stabling tent to pick up and dispose of the carcass of the chestnut mare.

"Hello? Earth to Ruth? Everything all right in there?" Ranger Boyd, far away above her.

"No." She raised her head. His grin was unclouded. The blank

incandescence of Boyd's face reminded her of a comic book char-
acter from her childhood, a hero whose sketchy ideal features remain unchanged from panel to panel no matter what kind of
mayhem the background depicts.

"You take care of yourself," he said, surprising her. "Show days
can be so exhausting. Whether one rides or not." His horse sidled
closer. Ruthie found herself momentarily impressed by the overtrained bulge of Boyd's thigh muscles, straining the seams of tight
white britches.

"There's nothing *wrong*." She heard her words echo and
choked a laugh. "Except I don't understand. Wasn't it only the
knee, only a cut? A deep cut, I know, but why did she—"

"This sport isn't always fun and games, is it?" Ranger bowed his
head, rubbed at an invisible spot on his leather gloves. "Well.
Come to think, it's been a rough summer all around. . . ."

He might have been referring to Becky Hedgepeth, Ruthie
guessed, whose mount had spooked during an indoor warm-up
and thrown her headfirst against the arena wall. A poor-fitting saddle, the know-alls said; that horse had sore withers. Now Becky
was back in a new saddle, starting from scratch, but going to a special school because she still couldn't form her words right.

Or Boyd might have remembered Coco Beale's fancy black
mare. Storming the hunter divisions until one mist-shrouded April
morning a groom led her off the trailer and she dropped stone dead.
Heart attack. That one hadn't suffered.

Certainly he had to be thinking of the Sandman. Ruthie
thought about the Sandman much more often than she wanted to;
she pictured him crawling through the stables at night, silent as a
crab on the seafloor, unseen by humans and unremarkable to his
prey. Recently other predators had appeared, mutilators rather than
killers, but these could be dismissed as crazed outsiders, their attacks
vicious and deranged. The Sandman lived inside. He was the Dr.
Hyde for all the Jekylls in the show world, she thought, he was the
moon side of their sun-drenched life. Officially of course the Sandman had been rendered harmless, pulled into the light and identi-

fied and placed under arrest, but still no one mentioned him out loud. Deny, at any cost, the canker in the apple?

Boyd toyed with his horse's mane. "I'm not as worried as I pretend. I've known Suzie since she rode in pet pony. She'll bounce back. My problem now—" his eyebrows rose while his voice dropped "—is to find her a good, new horse. Any tips, Ruth?"

She shook her head. A new mount would mean commission to the trainer. Ten or, depending how Boyd finagled the pressure on Suzy's parents, even twenty percent. Ruthie asked with sharp interest, "Can her people afford it? Was Crimson Cadillac insured?"

"Goodness. Of course! Don't give me nightmares. . . . Listen—you are looking fabulous, Ruth! Wonderful to see you! But I'd better stop chattering and put this boy to work now, hmm?"

"Yes. You'd better," Ruthie said.

She stared away hard at the ring again, heard Owen announcing a standby list for the Medal test, and drew a deep, shaky breath as Ranger Boyd moved off to join the galloping circling blur of his rivals.

Erica's boy had made the standby, along with another Stoneacre entry, a skinny, black-haired girl called Mick. And Ruthie recognized another kid down ringside, excitedly hugging her reins to her chest, someone who rode on a shoestring, trailering around the circuit with her mom in a battered tagalong. So this judge favored the underdogs. At the rail a pair of New York supertrainers, hundred-per-hour men, were shaking their heads in disagreement. One spat.

The next rider cantered stiffly to the first jump, where her horse stopped hard. Three refusals, and "Thank you, the rider is dismissed." Nod to the judge, bawling inside. Bye-bye.

Despite the Flexeril a pain like a small hot coal had begun to burn low in Ruthie's back, snaking flares down her left leg—the smaller, more twisted leg, the one that dangled like a dead branch and received no messages from outside at all. The Flexeril kept her head floating above the pain but didn't wipe it out. The stuff that would was back in her hotel room. She imagined breaking off now, the stages of getting back: finding someone strong enough to help her from golf cart to van, driving to the Holiday Inn, then crawling, sweating, inside the van from seat to wheelchair, to lurch down the ramp. Then into the lobby past thumb-sucking bug-eyed children huddled against the sturdy legs of parents who would *shh!* and turn away at Ruthie's approach, as though courtesy required feigned blindness. And then the room itself, humming with loneliness, cheerily abstract despite its homey personal touches—the Rockwell print, foil chocolates on the pillow—touches repeated identically through two hundred rooms around and above her.

She would swallow the stuff normally reserved for nighttime and lie back lost as a pin on the honeymoon-sized bed, facing the flickering colors of the TV. . . .

Ruthie grated her teeth. She didn't want to leave yet. Quitting now would mean the day was no good—just didn't count, didn't matter enough—and if the day didn't matter then this show didn't, not this one or the next, or any of the twenty-some shows she'd managed to get herself to since the season began. The summer, her whole idea of it, would be wrong. "You'll be wasting all that precious *time,*" her parents had said. "And traveling all alone? Even if—no. For a young girl, alone just isn't healthy." Ruthie had loved *that.* "I'm twenty-two," she had replied. "I am well, and I'm going." She had stopped trying to explain that everything was already wasted, and nothing was healthy anymore, least of all her effort to become a student like all the rest at Skinner College. Where she couldn't concentrate on the lines of text, where in the middle of lectures her tears would leak in silent irrelevance as she gazed through the window at cloud horses, sunny-barred cloud jumps. When she wheeled out surrounded by her classmates what she saw of them was their tight-jeaned butts, their belt buckles, crotches, nostrils, and knees. Sometimes she felt like a helpless child, sometimes like an old woman who could see in them the seeds of all their future compromises, disappointments, losses. In fact the time-skid was not so long. Only four years ago, in this month of August, she had been fully qualified for what Deluna had promised, and she had believed, would be a triumphant sweep of the finals.

Her teeth made a sound of pebbles scrubbed together. The grinding would enrage her dentist. Between the operations, during that first lost year, he'd had to fit cap after cap.

She shook out another Flexeril, trying to convince herself this would be the answer. If the pain would only settle somewhere, steadier, she could separate the rest of herself. She knew how to do that. The pill though tiny resisted her swallowing. No saliva. This drug dehydrated; at least it helped her put off the hell of going to the bathroom. She craved a drink. She licked at rainwater pooled in a fold of her slicker. She remembered how at the end of a demanding round she would ride out the gate unable to moisten gummy lips with her tongue, her mouth completely dry as if it had been swabbed with acid.

"Will the following entries please return to the ring." Owen Goodchild's voice boomed heavy as stewed prunes. An expectant hush spread over the showgrounds. The warm-up riders, who now included Medal kids sharpening their horses in the hope of being called back, pulled up to listen. "Number eight. Number two-forty-two. Sixty-eight. Fifteen. Please ride in and line up facing the judge to hear your test. I'll repeat your numbers: eight, two-forty-two . . ."

This judge had reshuffled the deck. The only rider left in from the first standby was the boy. Novice luck, thought Ruthie. He'll crack in the test. Glancing toward the practice area she saw the boy and three girls break rank to trot down the hill, their tightly jacketed backs stiff with excitement. The boy was all knobby joints and long bones; black hair poked from under his velvet show cap; down smudged his long upper lip. His cheeks were pale despite the long summer, while the girls were all butternut tan.

Trainers dashed after this quartet on foot, yelling last-minute advice. Only Erica Hablicht sauntered down with a rolling stride, folded arms, taking her time. The wind played licks of brown hair across her profile. Her expression was impassive, almost grim.

If Ruthie came near to liking anyone here, it was Erica.

She didn't *know* Erica Hablicht. Had known her merely as one of the enemy trainers. But from what she'd seen, Erica believed in perfection. She cared too deeply about winning, Ruthie suspected, to ever let on. Hard on her few students but fair. Ruthie vaguely recalled a spate of raunchy jokes having sprouted around the news of Erica's recent marriage. *Her high school cherry popper. After all these years she couldn't land something better? Go figure. Guess the lock was getting rusty.* Ruthie didn't listen to crud like that. Now she found herself imagining that instead of moving to Deluna's barn she'd chosen Stoneacre Farm instead. She pictured the map: to get to Erica Hablicht's farm she would have driven northwest each day, instead of south. A hot flush coursed through her—to go to her regular lesson she would have merged with the flow of traffic on Route 2, instead of hurtling down 128 to the exit leading toward Deluna's place, the exit where—Four years ago there'd have been no Ruthie Pryor on that strip of road, and today she would be—

Stop.

The four Medal riders stood lined up in close formation, fidgeting surreptitiously with their reins as the fences of the new course were tape-measured and set. This was eternity. The wait before the jump-off turned your gut to jelly. Ruthie squirmed to lean forward out of the golf cart. She was smiling. She had moved as far away from the pain as she could.

"Heads up! Watch out! Oh my *God*—" A girl's voice rang shrill and terrified. Grabbing the cart's wheel, Ruthie wrenched herself around to face danger. For an instant she found nothing out of the ordinary in the fast-moving chaos swirling across the practice jumps. Then, in midair over the four-foot pole, with a sickening dull crack, two jumpers collided.

As if a switch had been thrown the other riders jerked to a stop.

Ruthie set the golf cart in gear and swung it around, edging closer. She saw a mud-caked gray horse stagger to its feet and amble away, dazed. The second horse, a bay, rolled back and forth for leverage in the tangle of jump poles and fallen riders. With a splash and heave the bay shot up. Dismounting riders grabbed at dangling reins.

"Where's the medic? For Chrissake will one of you kids go for the *medic?*"

Two riders kicked into action and sprinted down the hill.

"Don't anybody try and move them."

"Ranger, you hurt?"

"Ranger, easy, you don't have to *prove* anything—"

"How's the girl look?"

"She's conscious—she's crying . . ."

"C'mon, honey. You're all right. Hey, you're lucky, huh? Could've been worse—"

Ruthie surveyed the two trembling riderless horses. She saw no obvious signs of injury, but you couldn't be certain. Riders and spectators were surging up the hill now; down in the ring the four Medal contestants sat bewildered and forgotten, half turned in their saddles.

Things like this happen, Ruthie thought. Under the slicker her heart was vibrating like a hummingbird's. Things happen like this, *stupidly,* by accident and by carelessness, to people who've gotten away with it for too long.

Through the shifting crowd she saw a chubby medic kneeling in the mud. He hauled the fallen girl across his canvas stretcher. He had snapped a plastic brace on her neck but was not moving her the way he should, Ruthie knew. By the way the girl yelped and pleaded, she knew too. Beneath the smeared contorted face Ruthie recognized one of Coco Beale's stars. Her tailored britches were split wide from hip to boot top. A long laceration stood out bright red and lavender along her white thigh.

The crowd closed in. Though the sun was shining, pulling steam from the ground, everything Ruthie looked at directly darkened, as if she were wearing a day-for-night filter over her eyes.

Junkies, she thought. All high on a daily fix of close calls, so sure nothing can happen to them.

Haydenville, Massachusetts, August 21

"Am I a slut?"

He leaned away from her. The tired springs of the motel bed creaked. "*No.* And if you ever ask me that again, I'll—I'll whack you."

She squinted at him in the curtained gloom, then nodded, content. Her hand curled into his. "Sorry. It's just that I don't know what I'm doing."

"Ah, well. If that's all—"

"Before, I could always see my life as a story. Maybe a crazy story—not much like other people's—but at least there was a kind of line that made sense. If I made a mess of things I could still look back and see what led to what. A *story.* Now I can't see. It's gone."

He stroked her hip, and felt her skin tighten beneath the palm of his hand. He feared failing her, by not completely understanding—but he had never found any kind of story in his life.

"Lex? What is going to happen to us? I mean, after the season's over?"

He started to answer, but no words came. The walls and floor melted away, and as the room opened up into blue twilight he rolled his face into the thin plastic-wrapped pillow. Biting the pillow to break his fall. Then she moved close behind him, clasped herself around his back, to ride with him through the fall.

"Erica?" She was everywhere, diffuse, a shadow in his eye. "I'm wondering. Maybe we've both been around the block too often to hang a story together."

"Speak for yourself." Indulgence in her voice.

"Or maybe there's more than one, and they are all tangled in a knot like a nest of snakes, and we're better off like this. Not knowing more than we do now about where the other came from, how we each got here—"

"Where I came from . . . ?" The mattress dipped as she swayed up on one elbow. "My mother was what she termed a homemaker. My father was what he termed an investment counselor. I was their only child. My first pet was a box turtle named Nora who stowed away in bed with me some nights. Let's see. We all lived in a safe sanitary suburb near—"

"Stop! You don't sound like you. Hey. I *like* being strangers. Remember how telling someone about your past, the great confession, used to take a few hours? Maybe one night?" He laughed. "But when we were in our twenties, what was to tell?"

"Lots," she said. "Except that in my twenties, I didn't do stuff like this."

"Come on. Never?"

"Well. Not like *this*." She fell on him, full weight. Her lips were swollen and bruised from kissing. "You still turn me on. Why? I mean, even now. Even after we . . ."

Her tongue tip touched his. He saw a sliver of white glimmer below her iris. The sign of a faint. Or, like her gift of speaking with animals, or her sweet breath, sweet even after sleep (but this was all some hoary superstition, where did he learn it?), the sign of a spirit, a natural witch.

• • •

Lex prodded the plastic curtains. Morning sun stabbed and vanished.

"Don't. Please? No daylight yet." Erica in the center of his bed,
cross-legged. Her clothes on the floor, her wedding ring shoved
under a pillow, her watch on the night table. He used to think only
dancers could sit so tall. The sheet, drawn across her lap, cradled an
Egg McMuffin carton. She licked both her thumbs, peering at him
through the spill of her hair. "Late, Lex. Come back and finish
breakfast?"

"Can't."

"You don't eat enough. I eat twice—"

"You *work* twice as much. I don't for example this morning
have six horses to ride."

She reached for the quart of o.j. from the table, arched back,
and drank. He watched the swallow-pulse run in her throat. In the
dim light her torso shone like quartz, isolated by the deep farmer's
tan of her arms, face, and neck. Below her firm shoulders and pec-
toral muscles, the soft scoop of her breasts was like a helpless confession.

"What are you thinking?"

"About—" He blushed, safe in the gloom. "Oh. Well. Maybe
about how I adore you?"

"No. I mean, *really.*"

"Well—okay, then. *Really,* I was thinking about my uncle Leo's
garden. Leo was—is maybe still—the mover and shaker of the neighborhood. He owns his own triple-decker and collects two rents. He
grows the prize tomatoes. When I was a kid, Leo's rose bushes
bloomed into November. Every other scuzzy yard on the block had
the same old chipped Virgin in a blue shell, but not Leo's. . . ."

"So?"

"Leo had Venus. The *Venus de Milo.*" He saw the statue: in
slanted distant contemplation. Broad white planes of her armless
shoulders, and narrow buttocks dappled by tomato vines. Forever
and ever, amen.

Erica smiled. "Your uncle was a pagan."

"Maybe that's why my religious education came unglued."

"Mine too. . . . Lucky for us both, right now, huh?"

"Yeah. Lucky us."

She replaced the orange juice with exaggerated care, then lifted her arms. "Lex? It's not so late. Come back?"

Outside, he waited. Straddling a tiny stagnant pool filled with his own cigarette butts. The jutting air conditioners of the motel units buzzed like the hives of giant wasps. This time he was smoking what she called a stinker, Old Dutch Corona, heady enough to disorient any insect, but it gave him no pleasure. *Shit!* He jabbed the stinker out against the rough concrete wall and scraped it down to shreds.

She was inside, telephoning. Calling "home." They had a signal—when the curtains inched open, Lex could return to his room. There'd be just time to watch her pull on britches, polo shirt, paddock boots, and leave.

Lex, don't make it even harder. Please, what do you want me to tell him: to stay away another week? Before—if I had a show anywhere in striking distance he used to come every weekend, drive three, four hours. This isn't his fault. He's already packed, he said—the dog misses me like crazy, he says—

Lex stood ten feet away from the window, beyond hearing. Nothing, nothing could make him want to hear her words right now.

HE. HIM. *ROLAND.* ROLAND PETTIT. THEIR NOT SPEAKING THE name couldn't stop it from echoing in Lex's head. He lounged in the shade of tent 6b on a bag of shavings, drinking the morning's third can of cola, scanning the hazy sodden heat-shimmering showgrounds, and laying his cards down to Jesus.

Jesus swapped a diamond for the jack of hearts. "Tino's taking today off. Not feeling good." Tino was the Colombian. Pino was Argentine, Jesus Mexican. Lex called them the OAS.

"Hungover, you mean."

"Alejandro, don't worry. I work his shift, okay? So remember, you pay *me.*" Jesus dumped a low club. "Gin."

"Three gins in a row? I flipping don't believe it. Your deal."

The figures in the distance all appeared to be women. Not that Lex could always tell with riders—but there was no rider's swagger in his single stored impression of Roland Pettit. That glimpse was from nearly a month ago—the afternoon before the first night. That afternoon, watching a burly stranger boost a reluctant blond dog into the back of a rusty pickup, Lex had had no idea of the change the night would bring.

Years, you slide through, knowing too well who you are today and who you will be tomorrow. Same as yesterday, same as ten years before, except for some stiffening of the joints and the funny bone, which you generally ignore, and flashes of apprehension when the old reliable highs—such as a Bruins play-off or the Democratic primaries or the magnolias on Comm. Ave. in May—don't seem to do it for you anymore—

And never imagine you could wake up some morning reborn, innocent as a fighter emerging from coma, hardly able to remember who you'd been or what you'd felt, even the afternoon before. What had he felt on that afternoon? A butterscotch dog had thumped its tail. Beside the truck, taking his time, a man had smooched his wife good-bye. Watching from a distance, Lex had felt heartsick. The fool's despair. Wrenched by the loss of something he'd never had.

Roland Pettit was strictly earthbound: a bullnecked mezomorph, with curly thinning hair and a raw-fish complexion. Lex overlaid his image on all of them—grooms, riders, spectators, trainers—just in case. A glove only one hand could fit. Every time the fit showed promise, a swift sickening chill ran through him.

"On the lookout," Jesus noted. "You got it bad, man."

"What are you yakking about? Come on, play your cards."

"Alejandro, you should trust me more. Maybe I can do you a favor." Jesus' down-slanted brown eyes held only sympathy, and curiosity. He had been with HorseGuard over two years (not that any record existed, the illegals were paid off book, in cash) and had worked with horses all his life. There wasn't much he missed. "Alejandro. Probably I can tell you where she is."

"I know where she is. Ring three. I'm not *looking* for her."

Jesus pouted ironically, scratching sparse pepper-and-salt whiskers, dropping two cards Lex had no use for. "Who then?"

"A guy. Nobody. So—" Lex held the tepid cola in his mouth, stifled an urge to spew it out, finally swallowed "—quiet night for a change? No more trouble? Christ, but that was a hell of a somersault some kid took up in the practice area yesterday. Whoever started the idea of this being a sport for little girls?"

"Last night, no problems. But not *quiet*. Every animal moving around, moving." Jesus' hand waggled, mimicking restless horses. "That new hay, it's totally shit."

"Too bad." But not our responsibility, thought Lex.

"That little girl . . ."

"Not so little, in fact."

"No, man!" His free hand indicated her extravagant height. "She is called Vivvy. Vivvy Sherpin. Nice kid. Very very rich but even so she washes down her own horse, walks him cool—"

"Her horse—is he on *our* list?" Lex didn't think so, but in his distraction, or the torpor induced by having so little to do in this job, he hadn't checked.

"Not as per yesterday. Maybe soon? Fine horse, though. I checked, he's looking primo as ever. That poor Vivvy, though. No more riding, probably, this summer." Jesus leaned forward, folding his cards. "Alejandro," he hissed, "you have a very excellent chance, right today. Pick up some new business, yes? Owners are nervous. So much scary talk going around." Stretching back he added, in a more public voice, "Okay? Get what I mean? Raise you five."

"Greedy. I can read bluff written all over you." A dust-cloaked pickup jumped along the rutted track between the tents. Invisible driver. Suddenly Lex thought: if Pettit does turn up today, I am gone. Out of here. Tell Jesus I'm sick. He might give me that look, but he'll keep his trap shut.

The thought lifted him. He was used to running, he was good at it, he believed running was an underrated solution to a wide range of problems.

"Gin," announced Jesus.

It was the cola, he thought. Those four words, over and over. He squatted, racked by gut cramps, in the 120-degree heat and rotten-sweet filth of a Porta-John. The sun's heat trapped to boiling point in a green plastic box. Sweat pouring down his ribs, back, thighs. But the core of him chilled and quaking. A thoroughly used tampon on the damp floor beside his foot, and scrawled on the door inches from his face the messages "suck me" and "I luv Ranger Boyd 4ever." A crazed, imprisoned fly buzzing and banging the close green walls. Hell. *Hurts.* Abyss of anonymous shit beneath him, afloat in blue disinfectant. Always they set these boxes in a godforsaken field, shadeless, in the blistering sun. Stand-up coffins. Sweatboxes. Like in Vietnam. 4-F. He'd bawled when he got the 4-F. Wimp. Deaf in one ear. He hadn't even realized, but when the doc told him, he guessed why. Pettit had made it over there, though. Hero. Nobody's a hero. Hell. All the same. Croak in here, just the same. It was the cola. . . .

And heat, and an abusive diet, and a nocturnal activity level that would do credit to a sailor on shore leave . . . And today, maybe, bad nerves . . . The spring-loaded door banged shut behind him as he stumbled into the freshness of noon—barely ninety degrees.

An apple red golf cart was rocking slowly toward the row of Porta-Johns over the hummocks of dry grass. He had noticed this flashy vehicle around shows before, and its driver: a woman with a translucent complexion and lustrous, nearly waist-length black hair. Her aluminum crutches jutted up like flagpoles. He turned away (the horizon jigged like a torn filmstrip) in the denial that is polite between people seeking the privacy of a toilet.

She pulled in front of him and stopped. The black hair was bound in a brown print bandanna. She wore dense Ray-Bans. Though his vision was skipping he had the impression that close up, she was younger than he had assumed.

"Um, I wouldn't go in that one, Miss."

"I can't. Not yet." She made no effort to return his attempted grin of apology. "I have to wait till someone comes by. Female, that is."

"Someone—Oh. Oh, I see." Lex considered her predicament. The sun beat straight down, splashing off aluminum and chrome. The field, acres broad, was empty. Tiny applause, a sound like crumpling paper, drifted over from the show rings. He took a step away, then stopped. How long would she have to wait here, alone? For some obscure reason he thought of his mother. *The strong are gifted to help the weak.*

The girl, lifting her chin, sighted down her bold, handsome nose. "I've seen you before. You're the security person."

He touched the beeper in his breast pocket. "I guess. I'm Lex Healey. Hi—" His hand moved forward, then fell.

"Ruth Pryor. I rode equitation. Not anymore, obviously." She glanced back over her shoulder, with some anxiety, he thought.

"Um, look—" He saw the lie open up and rushed into it. "Miss Pryor? I also happen to be a medic, you know? EMT? I mean, if I can lend a hand—it's no big deal, is it, absolutely not to me—better than you having to wait around here for—"

Her sunglasses flashed at him. "I'm quite capable of waiting. No thank you."

He flushed. A gluelike misery kept him rooted. They both scanned the empty field, looking for rescue.

"It was *you,*" she said suddenly. "Weren't you on duty the night Crimson, that chestnut, Suzy's mount—?"

"Um. The horse broke loose. Injured itself." He was hearing Jesus' remark about "scared talk." The business prospects didn't entice him. Lex had seen how rumor, running out of control, could literally set a neighborhood on fire. The horse show world was just one close-knit neighborhood that moved from place to place.

"Must have been terrible, seeing that. And nothing you could do." Her tone was detached.

"No. Not much."

"So, are you investigating now? Did you find out how the horse got loose? Because I heard—"

"Look, Miss—Ruth, right?—the horse ripped himself up *in the stall*. On this huge damn nail, I *saw* it, sticking out under the feed bucket—" Lex stopped himself, realizing there was nothing unreasonable about her question.

"That's actually possible. Crimson was a knee banger. Banging the bucket? Some of them do that, to demand food. Bad habit. I'd call it a vice. But you're not actually all that much into horses, are you?"

"What makes you think that?"

"*Her*self. Tore *her*self. Don't you know Crimson was a mare?"

He'd assumed the letter *m,* in his book, stood for male. "A mare . . ." Lex blinked. The frown between Ruth Pryor's long black brows was carved in the shape of a lyre.

"Mr. Healey? I won't get any points for saying this, but you look—honestly—really awful. You're not sick, are you?"

In the distance behind her a dot appeared, was growing, bifurcating into legs, then arms: with any mercy of fate, a female form. His smile steadied. "I was feeling sort of rocky, few minutes ago," he admitted.

"I could tell." She nodded toward the booted woman marching toward them. "That's why I decided to wait. It's not that I'm hypermodest. I'm not. I was simply afraid you'd drop me."

He gave the food truck a wide berth. Riders in shirtsleeves, incandescent with sweat, stood around wolfing hot dogs, guzzling soda, batting at the hornets zeroing in on lunch. Lex, recalling his own long-ago life in training—the vitamin packs, carb stokes, debates

over steroids and electrolytes—couldn't fathom how these athletes
kept going, on the junk they ate. They *were* athletes, he was now
forced to concede. Kids who could be lolling on the beach chose
instead to pilot a ton of live galloping flesh over tricky hurdles three
to four feet high. And for the adults—Lost Boys and Girls who
wouldn't dream of leaving this never-never land—there was the
ultimate thrill of open jumper courses, culminating in grand prix:
obstacles over five feet, with widths to match. Merely holding the
jumper horses—frothing maniacs—took considerable strength and
nerve. Lex noticed a gang of wiry, bandy-legged guys standing in
the food line. Their presence signaled a grand prix today.

He veered toward the shady oasis of the sponsors' tent. Normally, this time of day, he would duck out and catch a nap, before
his evening rounds, before—somehow, by some last-minute whispered possibility he'd begun to count on as certain—meeting her.
Short nights . . . He smiled, remembering his alertness and joy at
five A.M. that morning, when her single knock woke him. She'd
been gone only six hours. But she needed these spaces of time
alone, she explained, away even from him, otherwise she'd start
feeling jittery, as if she were losing herself. It was just the way she
was. What she never seemed to need, Lex had remarked, was sleep.
Maybe you're right, Erica told him. *Counting down to the finals is like
a steady IV of adrenaline. But once it's all over—in December, January,
February—those months I'll sleep. Like a bear. Straight through till
springtime.*

His smile faded when he realized how long and empty tonight
would be, if Pettit came. No call. No tap on his door, near dawn.

And it was the question of whether and when Pettit would arrive that kept him prowling the showgrounds. He couldn't return
to the motel, to his empty air-conditioned cubicle, and pretend to
rest.

The first night, after witnessing Roland's good-bye, he had given
up pretending. He'd lain on the bed aching, open-eyed, paint-

ing her against the dark. For six days he'd gone on watching and following her with the hungry optimism of a street dog who's adopted a busy, oblivious stranger. He'd discovered what she looked like in every shade of daylight, he studied the barometry of her moods. Twice, briefly, they had spoken. *Yes, thank you. Excuse me. Oh no, you go first.*

That evening, there had been a party—"Exhibitors' Gala Reception." Wine and a deejay, under the tents. The adolescent girls in bare-shouldered dresses shuffled self-consciously to music—restless because they overwhelmingly outnumbered the few boy riders. Lex had borrowed a fine embroidered shirt from Jesus, too short in the sleeves.

Erica was drinking wine from a plastic cup. Her hair was braided high. She wore something smooth, straight and white, like a slip. In cold desperation he spoke her name, and the first glance she gave him was startled and wary. The thought occurred to him that she wasn't one who frightened easily, but maybe she'd sensed him following her all along, and now was apprehensive. He told her he hadn't danced since tenth grade. She said: So, sure, let's try, give these kids something to laugh about. . . . She had curved against him in a way that made it nearly easy. The deejay switched to oldies: "Baby Love," and "Hey Jude." She kicked off her white sandals. Aroused, sweating through Jesus' shirt, he tried to hold her at a considerate distance. She grinned and tapped his cheek like a sister, then pressed close again.

They talked about nothing. Five hours later, lying alone in his room, he could replay every word.

No sleep. Heat thunder rumbled after midnight. The ache of desire numbed other senses. His arms and hands were leaden—something prevented him from touching himself, from even that relief. He remembered the small soft V-fold of flesh where her arm joined her shoulder. Shallow hollows of her knees. No sleep. It seemed possible to hate her.

At two-fourteen the telephone rang.

Lex?

Good Lord. Hello.
Did I wake you?
No! I haven't slept. Where are you?
Here. I couldn't sleep, either. I'm right here, downstairs. . . .

"Heads up, there!"

The ground quivered. Lex scrambled sideways as a trotting piston brushed past him. The horse's swishing tail stung his arm. Its rider pivoted in her stirrups to shout, "Sleepwalking, mister? Need your ears cleaned? I *said,* heads up!"

Lex stared at the platinum bun and black jacket of Coco Beale, posting away toward the in-gate. He bent down for a stone but stifled the impulse to lob it at her horse's rump.

Strange vocabulary they had. "Heads up." "Washed out." "Psyched." "Fried." "Tight fence, long fence, killer fence, dream fence . . ." Eskimos had umpteen words for snow; this tribe specialized in words for fence. He'd learned "oxer" (a double set of rails jumped as one), "Swedish oxer" (ditto, only set zigzag), "Liverpool" (dreaded, involving water); also, "panel," "crossrail," "in-and-out," "bounce," "vertical," "rolltop," "table," "picket," "coffin" . . .

The sponsor's tent was open on three sides, for an unobstructed view of the ring. He ducked under its roof fringe, hoping maturity would imply a right to shade. Those who had paid for the privilege, seated here at linen-draped tables, happened to be wearing outfits distinctly dressier than his.

"This free?" He sat, gingerly, on a folding chair. The trio at the opposite end of the table granted brief, crimped smiles, their eyes sweeping away to affirm his nonexistence.

He noted club sandwiches and a high-piled fruitbowl, beyond reach. Iced bottles of beer.

"*Forward,* Mickie! Don't *ever* let him get away with that crap!" A hoarse cry from near the ring made Lex spring to his feet again, jarring the table, to look for her.

"*Murder* him, Mick! That was only a scaredy-cat tickle—take your stick in the *left* hand! Hit him! He's got to *believe* you!"

Less than ten yards away, in the space between the tent's corner pole and the in-gate, Lex saw a sun flash of brown hair. As bystanders and riders backed off, Erica, hoisting a long businesslike whip, lunged at the haunches of a snorting dappled gray. The whip cracked, the horse kicked violently rearward, Erica dodged but kept coming. The horse rose on its hind legs and pawed air. The small girl on board dug skinny knees into its big barrel, her teeth clenched in fear. "Excuse us," Erica spoke calmly, to the world in general. Then she yelled "Harghh!", attacked again, and the gray suddenly dropped back down, swiveling in a pirouette. Erica ran splayed fingers through her hair. "Okay. He's such a pea-brained dumbblood. You got it. *Keep* it." The girl cantered a small circle, gaining confidence, her heart-shaped face beginning to unfreeze.

Lex laughed out loud. Disapproval wafted across the table, but the laugh felt good. No one in the crowd remotely resembled Roland Pettit.

Erica grabbed the gray's bridle, and turned her attention to the ring. An irritatingly handsome fellow on horseback leaned down to her. "Good job, sweetie. Rule number one: keep these kids more afraid of their trainer than of the rankest beast."

"Thanks, Ranger, for sharing your philosophy."

The announcer called number fourteen. With a dazed lack of expression, as if she could fall off at a standstill, the girl called Mickie rode into the ring. Lex saw tension gather in Erica's squared shoulders.

From across the table, an opened can of beer hissed seductively.

"Sadists." The man opposite Lex smacked thin lips, tilting beer into glass. He was fiftyish. Strips of pewter hair pasted across his dome alternated with a magenta sunburn. "*Tomorrow,* I expect to see Vivian signed up at the Racquet Club. Got that? I am profoundly disgusted. In fact I'm damn glad you dragged me here! When these trainers aren't brainwashing kids into suicidal risks, they're torturing the goddamn—"

"How will Vivvy play tennis," inquired the woman next to him, "on one leg?"

"*Don't* get funny with me." The man drank. Lex was aware of a scratchiness in his own throat, as if he'd chewed rock salt for breakfast.

In the ring, small Mickie on the massive gray was cruising over fence after fence. This trip's on autopilot, thought Lex, it's in the bag.

He leaned forward. "Mrs. Sherpin?" Her mascara fluttered— he'd guessed right, these were the parents of the Vivian who'd been injured in a fluke collision, only the day before. "Which class are they on?"

"The medal, of course. *We're* all qualified—thank God, under the circumstances." She couldn't help sparing him these few proud words.

"I said, *forget* finals," Mr. Sherpin said. "The financial hemorrhage stops here. Four K a month—you realize that's more than most guys shell out in *alimony*?"

Lex shared the man's outrage, though from a different angle. Did these hooked-on-a-dream parents all cough up that much? For *what*? Thousands of kids competing each year, but only three—at most—could win a national title. And *then* what? Riding didn't pay off like varsity football, say. No college come-ons offered for this sport. No Cinderella contracts for the rookie of the year.

What happens to these kids, he wondered, after the high?

He glanced around at the men and women in the shaded tent-grotto, scoring rides on their programs. These were the leaders, managers, stockholders of the nation. These were the devotees of trickle-down—granted, he and Jesus and the boys were catching the trickle, but he couldn't help imagining what 3rd Street Kid-Power could do on four grand a *month*.

"Plus," the man added, "what you're skimming off the grocery funds. I am well aware of your shell games, doll. Plus an animal that cost—"

"Better investment than some I won't mention. At least Thanks to Daddy is *insured*." She shot him a not-in-front-of-the-staff glare. Her chins twitched toward Lex.

Lex said, "Kid out there's looking pretty good, huh?"

Mrs. Sherpin's smirk could have wilted all the flowers of summer. "If you like the kamikaze death grip on reins. *I* don't."

"Oh." He nodded. Mickie was steaming down to the triple: three close-spaced jumps of ascending height.

A second woman, apparently indifferent till now, studied her fingernails—inch-long mauve trowels. "Nobody heard me say this, but if that girl wins today I'll know the fix is in."

The wife said, "*Tell*."

Clear, through the triple.

"She's with Stoneacre Farm? That Erica person? *You* know." The voice dropped. "One of the local second-stringers. Erica Hablicht's been around for quite a few seasons without ever quite making the grade—"

Lex stiffened.

"Well," the voice rolled on, "the word is she's having a *torrid* fling on the side. No, darling, I haven't turned prudish. I mean, all these trainers live by different rules anyway, don't they? *No* rules, to call a spade a spade. Except *this* bit on the side is very hush-hush. Well, considering that she's just married her childhood sweetheart—"

Mrs. Sherpin coughed. "Why bother?"

"I know. Like eating leftovers. But frankly, I would *love* to know who the new mystery man is."

Mr. Sherpin said, "A bunch of real charmers. Our daughter's broad choice of role models in her chosen hobby: a roundheels or a dyke."

Lex had a swift vision of sinking a punch into Sherpin's quicksand gut.

The wife said, "Oh. If Vivvy ever—if *Coco* ever heard you—oh. You're drunk, aren't you? Nasty drunk." She shifted her bosom toward the other woman. "Are you implying, one of the *judges*—"

"I imply *nothing*. Merely one of life's little puzzles . . . What I find curious is, she's here with a measly two students? Backyard riders. Complete unknowns. But you recall who won the Open yesterday? *And* yesterday's Medal?"

With a virtuous quaver Mrs. Sherpin said, "At that moment I just happened to be sitting in the ambulance."

"Erica's boy! Which clinched her the trainer's award, by the by. Shh. They're standing right over there."

Heads turned as a full-throated wolf call broke out. Erica's victory howl. Followed by scattered applause. The gray, drenched in sweat, came trotting out of the gate. Small Mickie grinning. From the ground, Ned pumped her elbow in excited congratulation. Erica began sternly to point out Mickie's errors and narrow escapes, but with a glow in her eyes that said: I loved it, kid. Stand by for the jump-off. Super trip.

Just outside the tent, on a sunlit path, a pair of striking matched blondes strolled by. Coco Beale, the shorter and older of the two, supported her willowy companion, whose left leg, below brief tennis shorts, was swathed hip to knee in a fresh compress bandage.

Chairs scraped. Suddenly the Sherpins were leaving. Lex watched their retreat between the scattered tables with interested antipathy. Mrs. Sherpin was stumbling backward, begging her husband to slow down and calm down, to think twice, while she pushed in vain against his heaving chest.

Sherpin grabbed his daughter's long tanned arm, pulling her off balance. She bumped against him, while catching Coco's shoulder with her free hand, and hung suspended between them, graceful and precarious, like a one-legged bird.

Sherpin roared, "I ordered you to stay away from her!" He glared first at Vivvy, then the trainer. "*You*. I want the name of your attorney."

"Now, let's cool it for just a moment, Sherpin—"

Vivvy pleaded, "Dad, this is awful. Let go. You are totally embarrassing me!"

"Oh God," drawled Coco. "I get it. Is somebody's brittle male ego upset? Oh quick, call for the lawyers. Wah wah."

"Why, you silly, arrogant—I intend to expose you, Beale. My lawyers will *strip* you. You can thank Vivvy here. Hah! She's let quite a few things drop she clearly doesn't grasp the full significance of—"

"I cannot imagine what you're hallucinating about."

"You damn well don't have to imagine."

"Daddy, I told you, it was an *accident*. Stuff happens! If anyone it was Ranger who—Dad, Coco wasn't even *around* when I crashed."

"*Right. She wasn't there*. Listen: the Sherpin family's relationship with this person is severed, you understand? I make that clear? You will not *see* her, you will not *speak* to her, you will not—" He squeezed his eyes as if in pain. His third emphatic shake of his daughter's arm tipped her weight onto the bandaged leg. Vivvy yelped. Coco swung her fist with the speed of a bantamweight into Sherpin's ample jowl.

The little crowd under the tent sighed, as if watching a jump crumble.

Mrs. Sherpin hid her face behind ringed fingers.

Coco leaned up to kiss Vivvy's cheek. "Be good, kid. Keep the leg iced." She spun on her boot heel. "So sue me, Sherpin," she said, and walked crisply away.

Jesus plunged into the tent. His brown eyes bore down on Lex, who waved with the beer he had managed to hook. "Hey man, take the load off awhile. You just missed the action."

"I am running everyplace. I call the motel. Alejandro, maybe you could say where you are going when, more!"

"Okay." Lex flicked a wasp off the sandwich tray. "Here. Help yourself. What's up?"

"That guy you been looking out for? That guy, he is *here*, waiting over an hour. No more patience, this guy. He wants you for a talk. *Private*, he says. Right now."

• • •

From a distance, the visitor was a plump city pigeon, roosting on a hay bale in the fly-ridden shade of tent 6b. As Lex slowed his jog, he saw that the pigeon was decked out in a straw hat, pearly polyester suit, lavender tie.

Not-Roland.

Rising, the man stuck out a fleshy hand. Rimless glasses wedged in glistening cheeks magnified his eyes to a look of drowsy amazement. "You Heller?"

"Healey. H-E-A—"

"Fine." The fat hand waved. "Similar difference." The hand sloped inside the gray jacket, searching. "I was about to give up on you. I'm steaming here worse than a quahog at low tide. I *don't* give up, though. Here, have a look at my card."

Wiggled, the card flashed like a gem. The visitor's holo-grammed head winked lifelike from inside a silver globe, beside more conventional print: "Global Insurance, Whitman Whitaker, Claims Adjuster."

"Crazy, man." Jesus plucked the card, admiring it.

"It's the new thing," said Whitaker. "The new edge. You're about to see it everywhere, I guarantee."

A golden retriever loped around the tent, ownerless.

"Mr. Whitaker—"

"Whit."

"We're flat out here today," said Lex. "Short staffed. So if you tell me briefly what this is in regard to—"

"Regard to that horse we lost. Crimson Cadillac. Three nights ago."

"I didn't lose any horse."

"Manner of speaking. However . . . It's a sensitive situation. . . ." Whitaker looked pointedly at Jesus, who caught the look with exaggerated blankness, before drifting into the shadowed aisle of the tent. "Darn it," said Whitaker. "That foreign guy stole my card."

"Stole . . ." Lex slumped on a hay bale. "A minute ago, did you see a dog run by?"

"Absolutely not. No dog. Healey, my interest here is a horse. Now, even if it wasn't under your outfit's supervision, I'd sure appreciate your professional cooperation. Now, I understand it was you who found—"

"Wrong. Whitaker, all I can tell you is this: my employee beepered me. I drove out. I notified the vet, and *she* came out. By the time I left the grounds, the horse was stitched up and . . . definitely alive. From then on I was never *in* that barn. And next day—but I assume you've got the vet report?"

Whitaker grunted. He was scribbling in a four-inch spiral notebook.

"*She* have any problem with the death?"

"Nope."

"Look, what's the life expectancy on these animals, anyway? Fifteen, twenty years? I can't believe it's your company policy to personally check out every one that—"

"Are you kidding, Healey?" Whitaker flipped his notebook shut. "Didn't *used* to be the policy. Used to be *my* call: to figure the trade-off between chasing down a possible faked cause, against the cost of the chase, understand? Only that's all changed, since the Sandman. Come on, Healey, the *Sandman*. Tommy Burns? Where's your memory? Two-bit punk, nabbed down on the Florida circuit for cracking a horse's foreleg with a crowbar? Who meanwhile confessed to killing nobody knows yet how many horses? This scum is devastating livestock insurance. It's an industry nightmare. See, once your actuary starts thinking death is organized by human agency, there are no affordable risks in this world! You ever stop to think what kind of planet this would be without insurance? We'd all be savages. But—for the moment—I'm here."

The Sandman. A hired hit for horses. Niche business. Age of specialization. Lex shivered as he lifted the lid of the Styrofoam cooler. "Thirsty?"

"Not for that stuff. Gives me the runs. Now, that boy who stole my card—he the one who found Crimson Cadillac?"

"Nope." Lex popped the can open and scrutinized Whitaker over cola fizz. "So this Burns guy is in jail?"

"Well, house arrest. Some kind of custody. Probably for his own protection . . . Because this sleaze is naming names of his alleged clients faster than cuckoos lay eggs. Get it, Healey? If nothing else he's feeding the D.A. more suspects, to buy down his time! Plenty of folks must be itching to get their hands around his neck. I'm not referring just to the animal rights freaks. Burns has pointed the finger at some extremely respectable and wealthy individuals. . . ."

Your clients too, Lex thought. "So what damage can he do, Whitaker, from inside a cell? No offense, but you coming here today seems a little like closing the barn door, after."

Whitaker spread his round shiny thighs apart in order to lean closer. "We're practically colleagues, Healey. You tell me."

"Maybe the guy had accomplices?"

"Two, in Florida. But they were strictly gofers. About as much brains as a pair of bowling balls. Burns is more the entrepreneur type, proud of going it alone."

A rusty Ford truck rattled along between the manure mounds. Massachusetts plates. Lex held his breath, until the truck turned out of sight. "You're thinking someone could pick up on the opportunity? That the Sandman now has competition?"

Whitaker wheezed, sucking air through small gray teeth. "There you go," he said.

Marion, Massachusetts, September 5

A RING OF BARNACLED ROCKS, BLACK AND TALL AS DRUIDS, protected their sand hollow from ocean wind. Lex could hear but not see the constant crashing and clattering withdrawal of waves from the beach.

"Sun smear?" Erica gave a supplicating shrug of bare shoulders. The top of her blue cotton bikini was untied; the bottom had faded to twin white patches.

As Lex dribbled dabs of hot oil down her backbone he felt a twinge of remorselessness—like a transformed echo of the pain of missing her for all but one night of the past two weeks.

The oil smelled of coconut and tangerine, fragrant as penny candy. He smoothed it across her skin with steady pressure, probing up into the tendrils at the nape of her neck, down the shallow grooves between her ribs. He was surprised by how much of her body his hand covered at any given moment. How small she was, after all.

"Ah." Her back arched. Between the dimples of her haunches lay a glint of down. "Expert touch. You've done this before."

"Sure." Except that he wasn't sure. In Charlestown there were no beaches, only docks and the Navy yards, and the oily sloshing depths of Boston Harbor, teeming with phosphorescent jellyfish. For townie kids, the dune playgrounds of the North Shore and the Cape lay a lifetime or two away. Lex tried to recall one specific beach trip, one specific girl. Or was this powerful image—boy massaging sunscreen into a complacent girl's pliant back—simply an archetypal American memory, a subliminal celluloid dream?

He wasn't a beach type anyway. He found the shore broiling and gritty, the Atlantic too deep and too cold. Glancing down at his chest, which except for its pattern of sweaty hair was pale as the underside of a seagull, he was just as glad she kept her eyes covered.

Voices, shrieking and laughing, mixed in with the gulls' cries.

"Something's changed." What happened at home? he wanted to ask. Has he guessed? Did you tell him? "You act like you could care less—" he curled down to kiss her upper thigh, sea-salt tang, before applying more oil. "Suddenly you don't care if anyone sees us?"

"They can't. This is the secret hideout. We're invisible." Her voice blurred into the sand.

"Don't bet on it. The kiddie clambake must be letting out. Kids are swarming down from the hill already. Hear them?"

"Swimming? Why not? They deserve, nice . . . One day off . . ."

Talking in your sleep, he thought. Why not? You can sleep, baby. It was her day off too. She'd shipped in driving a six-horse gooseneck three nights before, had worked dawn to sundown coaching riders and schooling horses, and in the evenings had been dragged off to restaurant parties to which he was not invited, before finally disappearing—remote as a debutante—into her guest room at the "Big House." This show was an anomaly: not run by any of the official clubs but hosted by the family Urbach: fortune-blessed owners of Seacrest Farm (a hundred acres of green waves rolling to the Atlantic) and parents of sixteen-year-old Ned. If Bruce and Helen Urbach seemed at times baffled by their gawky somber son, they obviously revered his trainer. Their hovering attention made Erica lift her chin with a self-possessed smile he'd never seen before. Their open admiration left Lex uneasy, as if trespassers had invaded his own secret place.

What place? He had hardly dared wander in her direction. They had hardly spoken. It was as if nothing but his imagination connected them—as if time had spun them back to the beginning.

She had left early from Haydenville after a rushed telephoned good-bye. *I have to go home. The horses are all lame,* she said. *All the horses need a rest.* He had tried to believe that. By pure chance he had seen the Stoneacre trailer rattle out of the showgrounds, with a dusty pickup truck bringing up the rear.

Since then, their orbits had crossed only once—at Killington. A star-studded grand prix event. But he could remember only one night, and stars pinwheeling close to the mountain, and his body cleaving to hers. Since then he'd lost his sense of time, as addicts do. All that had carried him through was the vision of time together, here. And now she lay beside him, an almost stranger, drifting into sleep. Exhausted. Another man's wife. Her dreams pieced out of a real life he couldn't enter or imagine. Lex trickled sand on her waist, then stopped. He pitied her. He was angry. Who could he blame?

In the surf kids splashed each other, whooping, letting loose with their prep school swears.

He stared inland, across shell mounds and driftwood and marsh and pasture, at the reddening sun that hung over deserted hilltop show rings, like a spotlight someone had forgotten to turn off. The rocks had tossed shadow blankets over Erica's sleep. *Monday's Labor Day. Time off. I'll have the whole day free,* she had promised. *I can invent some excuse, skip the dumb parties—*

Labor Day. Seacrest was actually two shows, divided by this holiday break. Seacrest, according to Erica, was an annual godsend, an Urbach tradition. As close as most riders came to a summer vacation, and also a relaxed brush up before the cutthroat competition of regionals and finals. Not that the competition here wasn't genuine—but the perspective's different, she explained, when going up over a jump, suddenly it's as if you're suspended over the planet, all around below you see cornfields waving and the beach curved like a sword and the ocean sparkling out to the edge of sky. . . .

A gust from inland carried smells of sunbaked hay and honeysuckle. Through the rock chink he watched the athletic children charging back barefoot on the marsh paths, shrieking their gull-laughs. Explorers in paradise. Already, it hurt Lex to think of leaving. What would it cost, to live here? What would a person give? His breathing relaxed and deepened. This place could change anyone. Its perfection was solid and seamless. All the perspective money can buy.

"What are you doing?" She rolled over. Grains of mica clung to her skin.

"Covering you." He smoothed the towel.

"Why?"

"Because you are cold. Because believe it or not summer is over, and I don't want—"

"Kiss?" Her arms linked around his neck. He was kneeling, and then lying, his whole length covering her cool body, in the long exploration of the kiss. She moved beneath him and his eyes closed against a surge that was strong as pain, a blissful welcome pain.

"Shh," he whispered. "Shh . . ." Sliding his fingers under the loose bikini top. Cold nubs of her nipples. Was it because she'd never had a child that her nipples were still full and pink and childish? With his other hand he brushed back her hair as if he could soothe her to sleep again.

"You're so warm." She smiled. "I'll freeze you, Lex."

"I doubt that." He reached low between them, to tug the blue bikini down her thighs. "But try. There, yes . . . Keep trying."

When he looked up one long high cloud, an exclamation mark streaked violet and gold, floated in the sapphire afternoon sky. Silhouetted against this cloud stood a riderless horse.

The horse passed by. A little boy's voice called, "See? Cherry-bomb trusts me if I go first!"

Lex rose up on his knees and roughly arranged his towel again over Erica. Her eyes were wide and still shining. "Stay *down*," he said.

Through a chink between rocks he viewed the long curve of beach. Everywhere, in a second invasion from the marshland toward the surf, were children on ponies and horses—mounted bareback, steering only with halters and ropes. Their legs, dangling from shorts or bathing suits, flashed like fish against the horses' sides. A few animals balked and wheeled. Lex could feel the hoof-beats, a soundless vibration through the sand.

The boy who had called out stood below on the wave-hardened shingle, holding his pony by its rope. He was short and chubby, in contrast to the rangy pony, which faced the surf with legs braced and splayed in eloquent terror. "Won't anybody give me a lead in?" the boy shouted, and a dapple gray galloped past, plunging with its rider through the breaking spray. The little one grabbed mane and vaulted up, booting his pony out of its paralysis, into the sea.

"Come here," whispered Lex. "Risk it. You *have* to see this."

He glanced sideways as Erica pressed against him. Her hair was crusted with sand. Her bikini was approximately in place. She was grinning. "Those jerks! Hotshots . . . If they knew I was here, I'd have to kill them."

Seagulls rose skyward screaming as the main phalanx cantered into the surf. The first horses had already breached the breakers and were bobbing in the choppy waves beyond. The sea—a broad gold sun path flanked by shifting purple and jade and turquoise waves— was filling fast with horses that metamorphosed to legless centaurs as riders clutched their undulating necks. They all moved with a certain purpose, circling or striking a straight line, leaving a bubbling wake. The noise of whinnies drowned the gulls' cries. A few riders leaned toward each other, in an effort to link hands.

"*Sea* horses," said Lex. "I never realized—"

"Oh, they can swim. It's instinct. Most love to swim. Not

something a fancy show horse usually gets to try, though. These critters must think they've died and gone to heaven."

"They're damn far from shore—" Farther than he would swim, let alone on horseback.

"Hmm . . ." The squint lines above her cheekbones sharpened. "How many would you guess, out there? Fifteen? Sixteen? Oh look, there's Mickie. That figures . . . And there's Laura, Don's kid—see her?" She pointed. To Lex, the faces were blurs.

"Laura. That's the girl who's leasing Vivvy Sherpin's horse, right? Her trainer's Don Deluna. Just signed up with me." The urge to impress her—not with the expansion of HorseGuard's clientele, but with his expanded knowledge of these names, in her world.

"Laura on T.D. Great match. Good move for old Don. I think they could be the pair to beat from now on. Ranger is *fried,* he wanted the mount for his DiSenza kid but Daddy Sherpin told him to go screw. Poor Suzy. Trying to lease a top eq horse is hell, this time of year. Money's no object."

"How much is no object? Let's say, to lease Vivvy's horse."

"Ten K a month? Wouldn't surprise me. Plus trainer's commission."

Lex whistled. "Score one for Sherpin."

"Okay, to you it's blackmail. But when a kid makes it this far, especially in their last junior year—plenty of parents remortgage the house—or put off their kid's college. They find ways of borrowing they never dreamed of before. But that's the game, they can take it or leave it."

"And now Don can lease out Laura's old horse? Musical horses . . ."

"Look—Don and me are only the pros. Hired advice. It's these owners who insist on pounding on their horses' legs all summer, chasing Medals and racking up USET cups; they're devastated when right before finals the critters come up lame. Lex? That's why I had to take our horses home for a while. You understand—you didn't think there was some other reason, did you?"

He shook his head, avoiding her. At this moment he was more concerned about the herd of centaurs drifting in the open ocean. One pair of animals appeared to be fighting; the sea horses snaked and struck. The kids on board hauled on their halter ropes and yelled shrill commands.

His stomach flip-flopped. "Maybe we should— *Erica,* those two kids are in trouble." A vision of himself swimming out through churning waves and churning horses made him swallow hard.

"Nah. It's all show. The beasts can't kick. Way too deep out there." Suddenly she gave a low laugh. The flush in her cheeks might come from sun, or lovemaking, or excitement shared now with the riders in the sea. She said, "I used to do stuff like this."

"I believe you."

"I had this rank pigheaded quarter horse. He had a criminal mind."

"Whatever you two did was all his idea?"

"Sure. But I got the hidings."

He brushed over her hair, releasing a brief shower of sand. She wore what he called her judge's look, and was biting her lip. In another woman he might have suspected a rush of nostalgic self-pity, but Erica was no more able to feel sorry for herself than to flatter a loser, or forgive a quitter. All her rough sympathy went to the horses, and to the kids who gave their best—not necessarily her own kids. He thought, You're more worried for them than you admit.

At night, when he lay hot and miserable and alone, it was these discoveries about her that shifted in his mind like mosaic chips, when he moaned to himself: Why?

She was smiling again. The fight had dissolved, and horses and riders were struggling up out of the surf, streaming water. The black-haired boy led. Lean and graceful in a warrior's bareback slouch, he circled his fist in the air. "Ned looks relaxed for once, huh? Know what holds that boy back? Trying to *control* everything. You can't *win* in the big league by keeping your head down and planning every move. I told him yesterday: there'll be situations where you have to forget all I ever taught you and ride by the seat of your britches—loosen up and *trust*—"

She made a sweeping gesture. Lex touched her shoulder; it was cool as stone. He reached back for the bits of her clothes. "Put these on, hm? Else you'll be shivering."

"I don't shiver. I don't have the nerve that tells when I'm cold." She kissed him, holding the clothes in her lap. Some question nagged at him, a fraction below consciousness, but he couldn't capture it in words.

They watched the last rider cross into the marsh. Erica said something into the wind about rinsing off and he nodded gloomily, anticipating the salty cold trickle of shower in his cabin. Next moment, she was flying down the beach. Again, sounding long alarmed mews, the gulls scattered. Erica crashed into the surf with arms held high. The sky was blazing with sunset circus streamers, but the sea was asphalt, the beach gray, the marsh almost black. Only the hilltop field, a mile away above terraced, stone-walled pasture, glowed greenish gold in the late light.

After she had toweled off they set out single file, bare feet sucking into tidal mud. Now and then Erica zigzagged, to avoid the razor-edged eelgrass.

She said, "You know there's a party up at the Big House tonight."

"Ah." He felt a door slam.

"Free food. Booze. Helen and Bruce are incredibly generous."

"Incredibly."

She shaded her eyes. "They've hung lanterns out, see?"

He glanced uphill to where the four-chimneyed colonial should be, winged by oaks and arborvitae. "Not from this far off, no. Not all of us mortals have your superhero vision."

"What's wrong?"

"Nothing. Great day."

"It *was* a great day." She hugged his arm, then bowed her head against him, quick as a cat.

So what was wrong? Where was his elation, the dazzled conviction he had each time, lasting hours after their lovemaking, that there were no obstacles in the world more than two inches high, that he could leap tall buildings, maybe even learn to jump a horse?

His feet stung from a few dozen cuts of eelgrass and submerged shells. Did her mention of another party tonight imply that she planned to go? Why didn't he *ask* her? Why couldn't he ask her *anything,* straight out? He was acting like a sulky son of a bitch. She still leaned against him, and he touched her neck, hesitantly. Try. Change the subject. Find something to say.

"Erica? Tell me about the Sandman."

She pulled away and stopped. "What on earth inspired you to bring that up?" Her face was as gray as the sea.

"Well, I—"

"Don't you read newspapers?"

"On occasion. Yes. But not the horsey magazines—"

"The *Times*? *Sports Illustrated*? There was a long, snide, sanctimonious write-up in *Sports Illustrated*—"

"Sorry. Guess I missed that."

"Look, Lex, I'd rather not even *think* about that scum, okay? The whole story, about all these people being involved—it's all wild accusations at this point, isn't it? Nothing's been proved. Rumors—well, *you* hear all the rumors that fly around the show scene. At least everyone's finally stopped talking about this one. I guess we're all waiting. When you think of the good riders he's implicated—people we all compete with, we eat and sleep in the same places, they're *friends,* or they were— Jesus. Why *would* they? Most of these people are rich, they don't need—"

"Like your friends the Urbachs?"

Erica frowned. "Richer. No comparison."

Lex caught a glimpse of a hierarchy of wealth, usually as invisible from where he stood as a clan of self-absorbed gods would be, above the cloud cover.

"Tommy Burns is a dumb, loudmouth loser. Who'd *trust* him?" She was walking again, and Lex followed. "The grain of truth in the whole story is, he talked too much in a bar, and then the cops caught him in Florida—cracking a horse's leg with a crowbar! My God. My God." She stopped, then walked faster. "The horse was named Streetwise. He belonged to Donna Brown, who's married to Buddy Brown, who up to now was everybody's favorite grand prix rider, used to be on the Team. Burns claims Donna Brown paid him to do it, but even if, that's *one* crime, not a whole conspiracy! I think it's more likely that this thug Tommy Burns—or whoever his publicity agent is—is simply out to wreck a few careers, for the splash it'll make. Or even this whole sport?" She shot a glance backward. "So who's been talking to *you*?"

"No one you know. Let's drop it."

"Who?"

"Look, Erica, I'd nearly forgotten—must have been the beach reminded me, you know, 'Sandman'?" She wouldn't laugh. "*Nobody*. This insurance pusher I talked to, couple weeks back at Haydenville . . ." Not a good association.

"Whitman Whitaker?"

Why was he not surprised? "Yes."

"Whit is not a salesman. He's an adjuster, investigator. . . ."

"I misspoke. Could we walk a little slower?"

"So what did he want? Who—what was he snooping about?"

"Mainly, about that Crimson Cadillac horse."

"Ah." Silence.

"Not that I could add zip to what he had already. Basically, I think they were trying to decide whether to do an autopsy."

"Do a— On Crimson? Oh, Jesus. What's the *point*?"

"Some insurance wrangle, is my guess. I remember when I talked to the owner—ex-owner—ah, what was that woman's name?" The ground was rising from slick marsh bottom to a steep path through thick pasture. Lex was panting, but saw relief ahead— a level mown terrace where horse trailers were parked, overlooking the beach. "Martin? *Morton.* Something she mentioned, way back that night—"

"Yah. August . . . A couple of weeks does seem like forever ago. Well, why didn't Whit talk to *me*? I was there."

Lex said gently, "He might have wanted to. Only, you ditched the show, remember? It was that same afternoon—when you disappeared. Went home."

"I had no choice!"

He caught her arm. "Slow down. God, you're cold. I shouldn't have let you go back in the water—"

"I am not cold." Her voice echoed, obscured, because he was holding her close. The hillside lay in deep shadow. Above on the grassy terrace the long aluminum horse trailers glinted, peacefully deserted, like a giant's scattered silver blocks. Erica said, "I'm okay. Let go."

"Not yet."

"Lex. What happened to Crimson has nothing remotely to do with the damned Sandman."

"Good."

"Burns is simply insane. He *boasts* about how he killed horses for pay. *Dozens*. Any horse. No questions. His favorite method was to electrocute them—easy?—a clamp on the ear. And one on the rectum. You plug the wires into the nearest socket—and they spasm instantly. Afterward, you see, it looks like colic, and ninety percent of things that go wrong with horses end up in colic anyway, it's the commonest cause of—but these were all perfectly healthy—"

"Okay. Hey, it's okay . . ."

" 'Streetwise.' Poor thing. He wasn't at all, was he? Let himself be haltered by strangers, and led. . . . Burns says Streetwise had to be clubbed because the insurance didn't cover colic. There are supposed to be witnesses—grooms—who say it was common knowledge. . . . That Burns would march into the showgrounds carrying his gear in a satchel and we all said, well well here comes the Sandman, and laid bets on which horse is going to snuff it—"

"Easy."

"You think riders are all a bunch of head cases. And you're probably right. Screwballs whose whole lives are wrapped up in these animals—but that's *why*. No one who *rides*—no real horse-man—could ask for a horse to be killed. Lex? Tommy Burns is no rider. And I *never* saw any Sandman. I don't think. Unless I'm blind."

"You're not blind. And I believe you."

She sighed. The path was leveling out. He welcomed the weight of her arm when it circled his waist; they walked hip against hip. With Janice, any attempt at this sort of walking embrace had turned into a slapstick tangle. Now, looking down at the even, matched stride of four glimmering legs, he felt initiated into the secret of motion. He could hardly remember his anger—was it anger? At *what*?

This is what happened, he realized. When Erica was with him, his moods tumbled and changed like a white-water river. Multiple personality disorder. There was no one particular Lex but a shifting crew, each convinced for the moment of his watch that he was the true Lex. They traded places like tossed dice. He—the "he" of this moment, blitzed on the spell of this walk in the twilight—felt eerily unresponsible. There was even a Lex who still stood alone and apart, taking notes from a stubborn distance but not giving a plugged nickel for the chances of the rest of the Lexes, nor for Erica, just waiting for it all to crash. Poor bastard. Looking ahead, across the twilit promontory where the trailers were parked, he imagined he could see that isolated figure, huddled and indistinct, facing out to sea.

"Wait," he whispered.

"Why?"

He kissed her. The kiss deepened to an afterwave of desire; he traced her smile with his tongue. Erica leaned away with a small laugh. She held his hand, along the slight path that skirted the trailers. They heard the sleepy nickering and bumping of a few horses whose owners couldn't get stalls in the main barn.

Her grip tightened. "Lex, up ahead there—who *is* that?"

No one, he almost said. Just my imagination.

She pulled him along quickly, thwarting his urge to avoid this stranger, whoever he or she was—whom he could now make out, a figure squatted on a boulder that gave a sweeping view of the beach—and there for how long? Gazing down at what? Ships and gulls? The riders romping on their sea horses? A man and woman ringed by black rocks, making adulterous love with blind abandon under the bright sun?

"Oh no. Oh God, this is so sad." Erica sighed. "It's Ruthie."

The boulder turned into a golf cart, black in the twilight. A folded wheelchair stuck up jauntily from the back. Ruth Pryor watched the couple approach, saw their linked hands casually drop apart. When they were so close that speech was inevitable she composed a smile: cool welcome toward late or unexpected guests. "Gibbous moon," she said. Her arms were crossed tight. Her fingers twitched on her sleeves. "But I expect the stars will be enough to navigate by."

"This time of year," Erica agreed. For a dislocating moment Lex felt he was listening, without a clue, to an exchange of pass-words. Stiff wind pinned back Erica's hair. "You're not in the mood tonight to party?" she asked the girl. The party was audible: a buzz of laughter, the muffled steady thump of a bass.

Ruthie ducked her head. Her hair was wrapped as always in a bandanna, the jaunty protection grooms wore against the dirt and dust of their jobs. "Tried," she mumbled. "Trouble with the steps."

Lex had a flash picture of the entrance to the Big House: six-foot stone walls, an iron gate, mossy half-moon steps leading into the grounds. Hardly a wheelchair entrance. He had never gone in, himself. "Jeez, this wind cuts right through you, doesn't it? So, um—have you been up here long?"

"Earlier, I saw a bunch of kids." Ruthie was looking at Erica. "Took their horses swimming—no bridles. No hard hats."

"Brainless wonders, those kids. A miracle nobody got bucked off."

"I never had a chance to do that. Ride in deep water. I imagine it's wonderful fun. . . ." Statement of fact. No particular emotion in her voice.

Erica said, "Look, Ruthie—is something wrong?"

"Maybe." Her hands stopped scrabbling; they reached for Erica instead. "After the horses swam I went back to the barn—to make sure the kids had rubbed them all dry. No one was in there. Everybody's partying, I guess. But a couple of horses were acting—upset. Hyper, the way some do in a thunderstorm, except it's such a clear night. Probably nothing's wrong, but—could you come back there with me?"

They drove between the trailers, around the deserted roped-off courses. Erica rode perched in back, holding the chair; Lex sat folded like a jumping jack beside Ruthie. He had to admire her driving. The nervous hands became all business now, braking, steering, accelerating. Fifteen mph over the ruts and hummocks felt reckless as the Indy 500. Ruth, like Erica, apparently had excellent night vision.

They passed the entrance to the Big House: paper lanterns gyrating in the wind, a burst of music. The golf cart steadied in the sandy track that circled the stone wall. On its hundred or so acres, Seacrest Farm comprised enough buildings—greenhouses, worker cottages, hen coops and cow barns—to be its own village. Most, Lex had noticed, were empty but kept in meticulous repair. The farm had the gloss of a "living museum"—Sturbridge Village, say, or Plimoth Plantation—minus, of course, any sloppy tourist hordes.

For this week, though, the main barn was fully occupied. No Vacancy. It loomed ahead now, size of a hockey rink. Stone foundation, slate roof. Light spilled from the main aisle through double doors, open for ventilation, secured against equine Houdinis by two thick horizontal planks. As the golf cart slowed, Erica jumped out and dropped the planks from their brackets. Lex was caught half standing, trying to uncurl himself, when the cart rattled over the boards, straight up the center aisle.

"See?" said Ruth. "No owners. No grooms. Nobody."

Lex called, "Tino? Hey, Tino! You around, man?"

Erica bent to retrieve a clipboard from the floor. Tino's watch record, blank. "Here. I know whose ass you're going to want to kick."

The car hummed forward. Erica walked beside them. Moist curious eyes appeared at the stall grills, but there was no shying at Ruth's vehicle. They're used to her, Lex thought. The floorboards groaned. They were driving into a sibilance of horses chewing, shifting and scratching themselves, a sound that reminded Lex of the sea.

"At least they've been fed." Erica peered into each stall, pausing longer at her own horses. She shoved aside a wheelbarrow stacked with open feed bags and buckets, and Lex divined that in her own barn such temptations were stored safely away. "So where's the problem, Ruth?"

"You'll see. Or maybe not. I hope not. I hope I was—"

"*Wait.*" The car stopped. Lex climbed free. Erica was jerking at a door bolt. "Oh, *shit*—" Together they swung the stall door open. For a second Lex saw nothing. The horse lay below the shaft of light, half covered in a confetti of wood shavings. It was sopping wet, the hair swirled in all directions as if it had been licked. Every inch of its body was trembling. A leg kicked convulsively. The tail thrashed.

Ruth said, "What is it? What's wrong?"

Lex stepped back and roared, "Tino! Man, where the hell are you?" He ran a hand along the belt loops of his jeans. No beeper. He must have lost it, on the beach.

They found two more horses down and in the same condition: shaking, pouring sweat. "Honest to God," said Ruth, "they weren't like this before. They were excited. Screaming for company—you know. Revved up."

Erica, kneeling, probed two fingers under a horse's cheekbone to find its pulse. It didn't resist. "Real weak," she said. She lifted the black lip and pressed on the gum. "See how long his gum stays white? Damn." She stood up. "I need some Banamine. Pain control. Where do they *keep* stuff here? Lex, we need a *vet*—"

A wall phone hung near the entrance, beside a plastic-covered sheet of numbers. As Lex listened to the steady ring at the vet's his thoughts darted, choppy as the bats in the rafters overhead. Three down. One old hunter, belongs to the Urbachs, Ruthie tells us. But the Sherpin horse—my responsibility. And one of Coco's string—also HorseGuarded. Hah! Where the *hell* is Tino? Sacked as of now. Get my hands on him, I'll—no answer. Here, right, try up the house. Have to be natural causes. Try to take out three at once you'd be nuts, or? For what? Probably come through fine. Just sick. From swimming? Damn delicate brutes. Shit—where *is* everybody?

Now what the hell is *this* doing here?

He'd been staring at it all along, disturbed, not realizing why. An open matchbook, left on the shelf beneath the phone. Ordinary anywhere else, but about as welcome in a barn as a hip flask at an AA meeting.

Ruth Pryor motored up beside him. "Erica found the meds. She's injecting them now. Might help. Can't hurt. Any luck?"

"No. No answer at the house, either."

"Probably all tight as ticks by now. They invited even the grooms."

"Real democrats."

"I don't think . . ." She squinted. "What's that?"

Lex held out the matchbook. A grubby object, corners torn off as if a mouse had chewed the cardboard cover. None of the matches had been used yet, though.

Ruthie took it and turned it over slowly, frowning. "It's not yours?"

"My money's on Tino," said Lex. "On principle."

She didn't comment. From deeper in the barn they could hear

Erica crooning to a sick horse. Pocketing the matchbook Ruthie said, "What now? Should I give you a lift to the house?"

He slammed the receiver back on the hook. "Let's go."

Lying supine on the hammock-thin mattress that over-lapped a spindly camp bed frame, he watched brown moths flutter into the ceiling bulb and ricochet to the walls, where they clung tattered and heaving before flying back for more. Outside, the incessant surf pounded on a rocky shore. If he stood up, the curtainless windows would show the full glow of the Milky Way, and a ghostly handful of one-room cabins like his own, perched on the shingle of the east rim of the continent. But Lex didn't want to stand up. He had a champagne headache. With champagne there was no need to wait until morning for the hangover; it was instant payoff. Ordinarily, he would have thought twice.

He had thought twice before knocking back glass after glass of the yellow soda-pop-with-kick. No ordinary day. No ordinary night, even after he'd hoisted Ruthie and her chair up the steps and they'd eventually located the officiating horse show vet behind a stand of lilacs, entangled with the Technical Delegate, a crop-headed sprite of indeterminate sex. On hearing that three horses were down with what looked like acute colic, both the vet and the Delegate sprinted for the barn, drawing a half dozen of the more alert party guests in their wake.

When Lex turned around, Ruthie, in her wheelchair, had disappeared.

His next goal was to unearth Tino—one, to give the Colombian the verbal bone break he deserved, and, two, to quiz him about the horses' condition before he left his post. Anything out of the ordinary. Three horses down . . . There had to be a common factor.

A virus? Show horses, unlike schoolchildren, were kept inoculated against a raft of diseases—HorseGuard required the docu-

mentation. But shots couldn't ward off every disease. Was tonight
the start of an outbreak that would decimate barns everywhere, in
a wildfire contagion? He wandered between hundred-year-old
oaks and long tables littered with the leftovers of a buffet feast. Riders ate hearty. Lex had scavenged blindly from the remains.

Reggae blasted from loudspeakers: Bob Marley, hammering for
the revolution. Between cuts, the lubricious professional voice of
Owen Goodchild invited the guests to dance. In a lantern-lit clearing a few people *were* dancing—sort of. Their bodies gyrated and
jackknifed to a white-bread tempo not remotely related to Marley's
drums.

A gardenful of strangers. He had learned to distinguish riders in
their show uniforms by certain essentials: a prominent mole, quirky
teeth, an expressive nose. Here, these details were drowned in
makeup and mousse, luau shirts and swirling skirts.

He'd recognize Tino, though. Can't mousse-up that hair: snake
black, shoulder-long, bound by a red browband in which Tino,
five-four, looked like a fierce and prematurely wrinkled Navajo
teenybopper.

He saw Don Deluna, standing apart from the rest, stirring
slowly in a punch bowl as if trying to read his fortune in its depths.

He saw Mickie, Erica's equitation starlet, being chatted up by a
pair of tall, handsome New York trainers. Out of uniform, they
looked to Lex confidently gay; winks and ironic glances Ping-
Ponged over the girl's head. Odd that top trainers would detour off
their main circuit for the Urbachs' backwater show—unless they
were trolling for new clients. Mickie prattled on, flattered, her eyes
shone. For a moment Lex felt a sour empathy with old dad Sherpin: the dangers to these rider-children only began with the height
of the jump. But Vivvy Sherpin was gone from the show world
now. Leaving one horse hostage, which at this moment . . .

Lex glanced back toward the punch bowl. No Deluna. So
Ruthie must have told him.

He saw Ranger Boyd give a rough jocular squeeze to Coco's
remaining ice maiden. Either Ranger had never had a cavity or his

molars were capped. The girl, laughing shrilly, threw a neat punch to his belly. Almost a match for each other, Lex thought.

He did not see any of the Urbachs, or young Laura, or Coco Beale—by now presumably in the barn. He did not even look for Jesus, or Pino. They would be in the "boys" cabin—Pino snoring toward his early watch, Jesus maybe reading Samuelson's *Economics*, or laying down a solitaire.

His growing rage was part frustration, part anxiety. If he had to report Tino missing, along with the sick horses, whose job would be on the line then? For all their wide-eyed wonder at the generosity of fate and providence, this job was the one real, frail tie between Lex Healey and Erica Hablicht. His passport to her world. If he lost it, was there any other way to follow her? *No.* He'd spend the rest of his life trying to forget. He had a sudden bleak preview of years to come.

He thought of searching the house but the front door was locked; apparently the Urbachs' hospitality had its boundaries. After circling the garden twice, he headed for the gate. One hundred acres. Fifteen miles to the village. Find that shit Tino if it takes me all night—

"Oh God. Finally. There you are." Erica, climbing toward him out of the night, up the steps.

"Been looking for Tino. Why the hell would he bail out?" He caught her arm, not too gently, as she stumbled. "You must be starving. There's some food left. I'm going to get my car and—"

"For Chrissake, Lex, forget that jerk! Don't you even want to know how the horses are?"

"Sure I do! I mean . . ."

For a moment, she focused on him. Breathing hard, as if she'd just jumped a double round. "The Sherpin horse is up. Looks a lot better. Same with Coco's bay. Only . . . we lost the hunter."

It was then—after she tore away, nearly colliding with a boy attempting to offer a trayful of drinks—that Lex had thought twice, and downed his first champagne.

. . .

The music: it sifted into his brain like the spore of bad dreams, whenever he began to drift off. He opened his eyes to the lightbulb and one surviving moth, and ground his good ear against the pillow. The music came from the next cabin. Who lived there? The Urbachs rented these shacks to fishermen, twenty-five bucks a night. "For the love of heaven!" he yelled. "Turn it *down*." The moth dropped to the floor. The music played on, clearly. Every word.

No sleep now. He stood up. The cabin oscillated and righted itself as Lex sat down at the vinyl-topped table where his work sheets lay. He began to fill in the night's watch report, using the list of horses from his logbook and Tino's ID.

> *Are we gazing at stars, babe,*
> *Or the bright lights of hell?*
> *All we can promise is*
> *Too soon to tell.*

He wondered if anyone read the sheaf of reports he mailed every two weeks to a P.O. box in Boston. Maybe they piled up. Or ran straight through the shredder.

Fake it. One lesson he'd learned as a kid: don't pipe up with an unpleasant truth unless you want a clip on the ear. After all the decades it still irked him that he couldn't remember exactly what he'd *said* to his father a moment before the clip landed, that particular afternoon.

He marked all horses up and well at 20, 0 and 4 hours.

Then he pulled out another blank form and began to list a new set of names:

1. "Crimson Cadillac," deceased—owner: DiSenza (previous: Morton)—trainer: Ranger Boyd
2. "bay jumper," name unknown, colicked, recovering— owner: Coco Beale—trainer: Beale

3. "Thanks to Daddy," crashed, rider injured, colicked, recovering—owner: Sherpin—trainer: Don Deluna (previous: Boyd)
4. "aged hunter," colicked, deceased—owner: Urbach—no trainer

He leaned back, biting the pencil. A single thud outside made his heart leap in answer, drove him to the door. There was no one, only stars, wind, waves, the damn music. At the party he had gone after her, tried to corner and calm her, to reason. . . . *Just leave me alone,* she'd said. *You don't see who I am anyway. You think I'm this tough broad who's got it all sorted out. You think I'm using you. You don't* want *to know who I am—*

His cabin had no phone. . . . He hoped she was asleep by now. Forgetting. Forgiving, not that whatever crime he'd committed was the real source of her anger. Her pain. Well, he could take the flak, for her. He wished he could take this whole night too, from the moment they left the beach, and twist it in his hand till it vanished.

He knew exactly how she looked, sleeping: arms flung up, fingers open. Her profile relaxed in a soft amusement she would never see in a mirror. Her tender sleep-smile. Somewhere he had read that those who sleep on their backs have a basic faith in the goodness of the world; they can give themselves up to it.

Lex slept curled on his side.

He heard the mosquito whirr of a rewind. The song began again. What was this? Same trick they'd used to drive Noriega to surrender.

> *Does the money enchant, babe?*
> *Do you stab me for spite?*
> *Did you have to betray me?*
> *Will you love me tonight?*

Lex shook his head, picked up the pencil and stared at his second list. There had been other cases this year, he knew, but he'd never paid attention to the details. What was clear was that of the four top local trainers, this year only one hadn't been struck, only one had yet to be handicapped by the death or injury or illness of a valuable competition horse. Finally he wrote:

5.   ? ? ?

Tomorrow, he would take over Tino's watch.

Marion, Massachusetts, September 6

First she saw a landscape of white pillowcase; beyond were windows puffed with early mist. Music rose from a distance—piano and strings, Mozart—and in her head a dream phrase echoed like a stone plummeting through water: *he'll forgive me.*

"He." There were two "he's," and for a long time now if she hadn't dreamed about one it was the other, inevitably, who slipped and stalked through her sleep, caressed and raged, pleaded and consoled. In the morning when she woke their illuminating words fractured to gibberish. But occasionally they appeared together, or shared rooms in the same recurrent dream house—a rabbit warren riddled with staircases and doors that all opened inward—although in "reality" (life with less logic and cohesion than dreams) they had never met. These dream encounters filled her with nearly incredulous relief. Two summers ago, she had watched helplessly as an approaching tornado roared toward her barn, to spin up and away at the last moment. . . .

Forgive me. For what? Who should? Convention would say the husband had the most to forgive, but she wasn't sure. . . .

Too *hot*. Kicking off a sheet, she sprawled, legs apart, air-drying the film of sleep sweat. Not enough sleep. Her head and heart pounded, as if she were coming off a crying jag. Why not? After all the years of work and single-minded purpose and the astringent satisfaction of self-discipline, she had learned to cry again. In the last seven weeks she had cried more than in all the years since childhood. Single acid drops at first, then torrents of tears, as if a rich well had been struck open inside her. Mornings after, her face looked ravaged as a drunk's. She was thirty-nine: too old to cry, this crazy way. Too old, she told herself while she cried, to *want,* this way—

Lex. He lay beside her, long limbs, the light outlining his hips and ribs. He gave her his crooked slight smile, but the gray eyes, fringed by black lashes silky as a child's, stayed solemn and searching. Alone, she turned to him. Sank, surrounded. *I can't help it. I never felt this before. Believe me.* He held her close.

She strained to hear the low harmonics in the Mozart. A concerto, but she couldn't name it anymore. Music and horses: back when she was in high school those two had been the rivals, each demanding fidelity, reconciled only in dreams. Ascending arpeggios—counterpoint to the flight over jumps, in full gallop.

At seventeen she'd sold her cello for road money: her ticket from home. Long ago. Sudden decision. Never look back. Now her hands, held up to the light from the windows, were sun cracked and sinewy from the habit of gripping reins. She hadn't listened to music in forever; that was for winter, when snow locked high against split-rail fences and gates. The imbecilic hammering some called "music"—the amplified yowling of the party last night—that racket made her want to—

The night came flowing back, moment by moment. Now she remembered, completely. *Forgive me.* . . . She rolled over on her stomach and jerked her arms up tight beneath her. Against the blackness she saw the aged field hunter, lying with his hooves tucked under his chest. She still held the useless hypodermic. White hairs sprinkled his muzzle, and the flesh of his face was sunken and molded to the bone the way it is with very old ones, giving them a wise experienced look, and he looked up at her steadily, as he died.

The big oval table was crowded with breakfasters. Her boots rang on the polished floor, punctuating the Mozart that flowed from wall-mounted speakers.

"Bright-eyed and bushy-tailed, Coach?" Bruce Urbach stood at a sideboard, making waffles. The machine, as he lowered its heavy lid, hissed like a pants press. "C'mon, join the winner's circle. I've been telling these folks not to sweat. Wind'll shift. This fog'll blow off by nine."

Bruce was no horseman—*Me, I just berth here,* he liked to say, *putzing around with Trigger is* their *scene*—and he grinned vacuously at Erica as he took the orange juice pitcher from her hand and poured her a glassful. He had a large, jelly-jowled face and eyes so deep they looked screwed in. The eyes held a canny spark, despite his jovial babble. Normally she could take Bruce Urbach easily enough. Now she grimaced back at him. The orange juice wouldn't go down; she had to turn away.

Coco, with her remaining blond student, and Don and Ranger all sat eating with their backs to her. Opposite them were Laura, Suzy DiSenza, and Ned. Ned's pallor had a greenish tinge. His pile of waffles was untouched. With a rush of sympathy, shared desolation, she tried to send a message: It's okay, Ned. That old hunt horse was your buddy from way back, wasn't he? Ned, you're maybe the only sane guy here. Then she wondered, But will you be able to ride today?

Leaning over her son, Helen Urbach pushed platters of Danish and muffins at her guests. Helen's fleshy forearms trembled; most of her 180 pounds was swathed in a raucous caftan printed with an expensive Palm Beach logo. She wore no makeup, and despite the low light, sunglasses covered her eyes. Helen invariably partied till dawn and drank like a Cossack. Was that all the glasses were supposed to hide?

Mickie Travnicek and her wispy, steel-core mom shared the foot of the table.

The in crowd. The less-favored show participants—other trainers, competitors, even the judges—were quartered in motels along the coast road, or, with dubious privilege, in one of the Urbachs' "shacks." Sort of like culling a herd, Erica thought. Incessant vigilant division and subdivision of humanity into keepers and culls. The main societal function of the rich. She (as a child, scorched with embarrassment) had seen her father try his hand at the job, but clumsily, since the money he managed wasn't his own. The Urbachs, in contrast, had the ruthless self-confidence of pros.

No coincidence that the kids around this table were the Northeast Region's current best. One might well take a win in this year's finals. Like a band of select young thoroughbreds . . . In racing, a horse's owners, trainers, and so forth were simply called its "connections," and that's what she and the parents and other trainers were: merely the connections. And it was the nature of this particular game that instead of training in seclusion till the moment of competition they were thrown together all season like a big squabbling intimate family, right down to literally sharing bagloads of dirty wash—

She would bet that by now every man and woman in this room knew about her and Lex. Well, so what? Broken-off talk and bug-eyed glances could be ignored. . . . But not the imagined laughter at Roland, who still had no idea. Or did he? It baffled her that she couldn't tell. He was sweetly, unshakably, the *same*. That was why, two weeks ago in Haydenville, she had cut and run for home with him—another split-second gut decision. Running from the risk, from the sudden reality of his *being* there. He was like an innocent vacationer drifting over a pool of sharks—

Clink of spoons and cups. Except for murmurs between Laura and Suzy, no one talked. A strange, airless morning. Instead of the usual adrenaline-shot eagerness she felt as if a ball of ice were congealing inside her.

"More?" Bruce topped her glass of juice to the brim.

"Thanks."

"Sit, Coach. Chow down. Damn, how come nobody's buying my waffles? What am I, trying to sell IBM to you guys?"

She shook her head. Tapped her watch. "Getting late. Mickie? Ned? Finish up. We've got horses waiting."

Ned threw a vague, glazed look, as if he couldn't tell where her voice was coming from. Mickie, standing, crammed in a last piece of toast.

Coco Beale swung around in her chair. "At least your kids have something to *ride*."

Erica asked, low and quiet, "How is your horse doing this morning?"

"*Her* horse. I leased him to her. You know that." Coco briefly touched her student's coiled blond braid. "To answer your question, he looks like crap. All we can do is pray he'll be fit in time for regionals. Meanwhile she can scratch this show, unless I manage to rustle up another mount. But what's available this time of year is trash. I've put calls in to every trainer who—"

"I'd lend you something, if I could."

"Of course." Coco stared a moment, expressionless. "Too bad. Too bad you can't."

Erica looked around the table. For one reason or another, no one met her eye. "Laura? How is T.D.? Can he show today?"

"He's—well, he's like . . . " The girl faltered, as if she'd been warned against talking to enemy trainers.

Don Deluna broke in. "Wants a day or two off, Erica. But she's got her old horse here. So we'll manage."

"What *is* this?" Ranger threw down his napkin. "What are you doing, Hablicht, taking *inventory*? I mean, let's see. . . ." He leveled a finger at Suzy. "My best kid's got no horse. As of last night, *their* top kids have no horses. So it's your show now, isn't it? Candy from a baby. Easy pickings—"

He strode out, boots clacking. Suzy DiSenza scurried behind, dutiful and rabbit-quick, nearly colliding with Owen Goodchild.

"Well, howdy and top o' the morning to you too, Miss!" Owen swiped his hammy face, miming shock. He headed for the waffle stack and forked three at once with a bluff air of special privilege: he rented a cottage on the farm, as home base for the few weeks a year when he wasn't on the road. Suddenly Owen paused, peering into their collective silence, suspicious. "Gee. What's everybody here so gosh-darn joyful about?"

What the announcer said exactly didn't matter—his voice was a kind of miracle. Warm as a country Sunday, reassuring as kindness from a stranger. In this way, Owen Goodchild was blessed.

Helen Urbach lifted her sunglasses to press a sleeve against swollen, smeared eyes. Bruce Urbach was humming along with Mozart: a ghastly, keening sound.

Owen nudged Erica. "How 'bout you tell. Somebody win the lottery?" he persisted.

"Not that I'm aware of. Horse colicked last night, is all." She pulled in a deep breath. Only one thing left to do, only one way to get back to herself. "Pack it up, kids. I want our horses to see that jump ring *early*. Get the spooks out. Let's ride."

Fog, and choking dust. Quaking ground. Shouts of fear, and savage aggression. Horses looming out of nowhere, hurtling from all directions toward the practice jumps, swerving and cutting across each other's trajectories, freaking, bucking, and now and then smashing the jump rails skyward, like so many tossed pick-up sticks. On mornings like this, the center of a warm-up ring was a war zone, under fire.

At eight o'clock, in fifteen minutes, it would all end. Officials would clear the ring to set the day's first course. Meanwhile, everyone—equitation kids, adult hunter and jumper riders, trainers quick-tuning a fractious horse so its amateur owner could later sit more or less pretty—were taking every fence they could before the buzzer sounded.

Erica stood leaning against a standard, less for its slight protection than to be able to adjust the rails higher when her kids were ready.

"Heads up at the oxer!" she yelled. General warning.

Twin shadows in the mist suddenly resolved to Mickie on her gray, with Ned close behind wheeling through the corner on his monster German gelding. They cantered hard toward the jump, too tense, mouths gaping.

"Mickie, don't look down or the Devil will pop up and grab you! It's a long one, let go now! Ned—circle him, for God's sake! *Circle!* Ned, you're too damn close!"

The jumps happened. Both jumps. Clear. She swallowed the grit stuck in the back of her throat.

"Okay! Mickie, gallop around and come again! This time keep your body back and give him *room*— Ned, Christ, your horse nearly took her heels in the teeth, you've got to do *exactly* what I say out here—"

The boy pulled up and trotted back to her, breathing hard. "I didn't hear you say anything."

Horses whizzed past them. Mickie had vanished, lost in the fog. "Ned—listen up. I know what's bothering you. But for right now you better make your mind up to—"

"You don't know. For you, I'm a machine wearing spurs. All you care about is me *winning.*"

She looked up, incredulous. His lips and cola-brown eyes were narrowed to slits. She said, "All right. Get off, Ned. Give me your horse." She took the reins. "You're just giving him a bad ride."

She turned away as he dismounted, dedicating all her attention to Mickie's takeoff. Two feet to spare. "That's *better!* Now keep that rhythm! Come again, after I raise it one—"

"Testing. One, two, three. May I remind you folks that *all* riders, hotshots included, are required to wear protective headgear in the ring—"

She grinned. Waddle in here and make me, Owen.

Maybe nine minutes' warm-up remaining, as she pivoted up into Ned's saddle. The fog was beginning to shred, revealing the action in the ring to be not so much chaos as an unpredictably choreographed dance. The skilled riders looked out for the blind novices. The horses looked out for each other. This was why real accidents—like the crash that had sidelined Vivvy Sherpin—were surprisingly rare.

She jacked the stirrups up four holes and kiss-clucked for a trot. She liked to sit high and light, in almost a jockey seat. Given her size, she could never *muscle* a horse down to submission in a serious conflict anyway. The goal was to engage all six senses, get the animal to listen on your terms—to your mood, pulse rate, the deliberate shift in weight— *Canter, Monster. Ah. Good boy*—

Her thoughts kept going back to Vivvy's unlucky horse. "Thanks to Daddy." What kind of dumb name was that? First the crash, then coming down sick last night—a classy jumper, but he seemed jinxed. Well, some horses were. Maybe the name did it. "No Thanks" would be more like it now. There'd probably be a wrangle over the lease. One more headache for poor old Don—

She bagged the reins to let the big horse figure out the jump on his own. See, kids? Not a big deal . . . Slow-cantering along the rail she searched for her students, but only the forlorn freckled face of Suzy DiSenza stood out, intently studying the ride. All right then, Suzy, *you* watch. At least *some*body's paying attention. . . . Which was why Ranger had brought the girl along, even though she was grounded. A good rider learns plenty simply by watching. Of course. All trainers think alike.

Easy pickings, he'd predicted. Nasty. Cheap shot. And also *wrong.* When you enter the ring believing your name is already penciled on the back of the blue ribbon is when you're guaranteed to blow it. Not that Ned—or death-grip Mickie, either—were riding near the form they'd need for a win anyway. Despite the scratches there were still plenty of capable eq riders here. No easy pickings, for Stoneacre Farm.

Someone had rigged up a four-foot-high two-stride. "Hah!"

she cried, and the big horse flicked his ears. He sank on his haunches, then pistoned, carving the air over both jumps.

I like you, Monster, even if you are a thickhead Kraut. Course you might think the same about me.

What the *hell* was eating Ned, to talk to her that way?

She had a hunch. Until now, there'd always been a wordless connection between her and the boy. She guessed he'd felt the same shock she had, in the moment after Ranger Boyd's outburst: her mind wiped blank, because Boyd had broken a rule so essential and obvious that no one ever spoke it out loud. It was the rule of solidarity among horsemen, in the face of all the catastrophes and dashed hopes and random shit that chance can dish out.

Everyone in the room must have felt that shock. And Ned blamed her, because she hadn't fought back.

When the buzzer sounded, she and the Monster smoothly switched leads, and cantered out the gate.

"Drink, Erica?"

"Oh—great! Thanks." She took the soda can Suzy held up to her and gulped. Fizz dribbled down her neck.

"What's this guy's name?" Suzy swabbed under the Monster's breastplate with a clean rag. It was good to see a kid make herself useful, and hard to believe she'd learned her manners from Ranger Boyd.

"Graf tum-te-tum von hoop-de-doop. Or something." Erica grinned. "A.k.a. the Monster."

"He's pretty talented . . . I guess?" The question was Suzy's way of deferring to a trainer's judgment.

"Well, he'll make up to something good. That's assuming his owner ever figures out to ride even one side of him." Her little joke lost on the girl. Erica chugged the rest of the drink.

"He's imported, huh? Hanoverian?" Suzy's finger traced the brand, a large stylized *H*. "I guess he must have cost a mint. A horse like this. Oh, I hope that's not rude to say—"

Erica shrugged and handed down the empty can, avoiding the look in Suzy's eyes. That naked, horse-starved look. She'd probably worn it herself, all the early years. Years of catch-riding losers, and schooling promising horses so their owners could hop on and win. "Hey . . . Can't Ranger dig up something for you to ride? I mean, he knows God and the world."

"He's really trying. I guess it's complicated. To get the insurance straightened out? On my—my old horse." She paused. "But it's getting so *late*. I still need one more USET this season. And regionals are in two weeks. . . ."

"Yeah. I know." The Maclay Horsemanship Regionals. Otherwise known as the "Valley of Tears." A marathon of cutthroat competition and capricious judging, passion and politics, in which about two hundred preliminary qualifiers would be cut down to the fifty eligible for the Maclay Finals at the National Horse Show in November. "Suzy, I'm sorry—"

"It's okay. I know you have to go. Only, watching you ride him, I wanted to ask . . ."

"So, ask."

"Why don't *you* ever compete in jumpers? I mean, seriously, you're so good—like the way you took that combination? And you hardly even touch their mouths—I mean, if I can ever ride like you someday, *I'll* sure be out doing jumpers—"

Erica's face warmed again under the cooling sweat. She tried to laugh. "You're not me, Suze. Competing out in front is not my thing. Catch you later, okay?"

She let the Monster carry her away through the thickening crowd but rose up in the stirrups to wave at the freckle-faced girl. To take the edge off her words.

Suzy waved back. As did a man who had suddenly surfaced close behind the girl, as if about to tap her shoulder—a rounded individual in a pearl gray suit and glinting glasses. Erica dropped her arm and rode forward again. The queasy lurch she felt came from the shock of certainty, not surprise.

• • •

"Hi. Roland?"

"Hey, gorgeous stranger! I been telling Farah you'd call today!
How goes?"

"So-so. Weather's good." She moved the receiver a hands-
breadth away from her ear. Roland had a tendency to bellow into
the phone. "How is she—the flea factory?"

"Right now? Sitting on my foot, thumping her tail, drooling
and grinning. She knows it's you."

Always, before the marriage, Farah had traveled with her on the
circuit. Why had she agreed to leave her dog behind? Because
Roland insisted, or because she wanted a piece of herself to stay
home with him? "Hug her from me. Tell her I'll be there
soon."

"What's wrong, sweetheart?"

"Why?" Sweetheart: the nickname always had a tin ring to her.

"You sound low! Think I can't hear?"

"Well, I didn't sleep much last night. Three horses colicked—"
"Yours?"

"No. Guess that must be the good news. But . . . one checked
out. An oldster. I guess he was ready to go."

"Aw. Sweetheart, I'm sorry."

"I can't figure it, Roland. It looked to me for all the world like
all three ate something toxic. Something in the feed? But that
doesn't make sense—I mean, the rest of the barn had no symptoms
at all."

"What's the vet say?"

She snorted. "The *vet*. The vet was trashed. Urbachs had this
party . . . And another thing. One of the watchmen here—you
know, from this outfit called HorseGuard?—" She flushed suddenly, helplessly, and shifted the receiver to her other hand. "Well,
he went missing last night. AWOL. There could be a connection.
I don't know *what*." She stopped. Sometimes the censor in her got
confused, couldn't divide out what was safe to tell him from what

would give her away, and simply shut down. Why couldn't she mention the clash with Ned, or Ranger's snide attack, or the apprehension she felt, knowing the insurance adjuster was somewhere on the grounds? She had to hand it to Whitaker: for a suit, he got up early. Over an hour's drive from Boston. Who had alerted him?

But none of that was the low haunting in her voice. She waited while the censor blacked out Lex.

"Sweetheart? Earth calling. You there?"

"Sure. Sorry . . . I just have a feeling some people aren't going to let this rotten episode go away. It's more like the beginning of something. I mean, right before finals . . . people around here are already wired to detonate, anyway."

"Now listen. You don't sound like you've been practicing transcendental meditation yourself. No, sweetheart, *listen.* You've been on the road all summer, me and Farah have hardly seen you and when we do you're chasing around so much it's like we're hardly there, you're so skinny, you look like you've been running on empty since—"

"Thanks."

"Sweetheart . . . Why don't you just come home and let me take care of you?"

She sighed, loud and hard, fogging the receiver.

"What's that mean?"

"I *can't.* Regionals are the fourteenth. I'll take a break for a couple days, before. Okay? But after—"

"*After,* all hell breaks loose. After is this regionals shindig, plus those three supercircuses I can't even get the names straight on let alone which is when, where—"

"That's my job. To keep everything straight."

"So what's *that* mean? Butt out? See you in December? Home in time for a happy first anniversary?"

"Yes. Just about. Look, I explained how it would have to be before we— Look. This is my life, Roland. It is what I *do.* It also happens to be what pays the bills." She listened to his breathing, labored and tight. She thought she heard her dog whine. "Oh damn it. *Roland*—"

"Never mind. It's okay. Can you—just call me tomorrow?"

She nodded, dumb.

"I worry about you, is all. Will you *call*?"

"Sure. I promise."

"Love you."

She twisted the phone cord into a figure eight. "Yah."

He laughed, gently. "One of these days, sweetheart, you'll get to where you can say it out loud."

She hadn't even asked how he *was*. Whether the headaches were still bothering him, whether he was managing all right with the money left in the farm account, whether any job leads had come in. Slowly she set the phone down, without having heard his click. Now the only sound in the Urbachs' sun-barred, somnolent living room was the distant burr of the show announcer. She was re-membering April, near the beginning of the season, when neither she nor Roland had ever been willing to be the one to hang up first. Hanging on to the connection, joking, telling every incident of their respective days, nothing left out, as if enough words could merge two into one . . .

A family. She'd thought she was way past that illusion, when Roland walked back into her life. No: she had run back into his. Pulling up beside a construction crew on I-95, aggravated and late, she'd leapt out map in hand to double-check directions. All the crew were sun grilled, smoky red. In the shadow of his hard hat Roland's turquoise eyes blinked and flashed while he kept repeat-ing "Erica? *Erica!*" while they hugged and laughed and stared at each other. The air rippled with fresh hot pungent tar. Wow, you look healthy, she said. Where do you get off staying so *young*? Hey, he said, I've been sober *four years*. The other men laughed too, joining in a confused happiness, it didn't matter why.

Roland *knew* her. No one else did. Her sixteenth summer, he had even saved her life. . . . Maybe part of why she'd moved in with him, the first time. Total disaster. Stubborn mixed-up kids. Called *that* right. But all the pain of it washed loose by time, until after twenty years there was only the knowing left. . . . Before leaving the construction site she'd scribbled down her phone number and soon he'd moved in at Stoneacre. Three months later they married. For all those years, years drinking and scraping rock-bottom, he'd kept the unused pair of rings.

The curve of the Urbachs' swagged bow window cradled a baby grand piano. A fine black Baldwin but placed carelessly where sun and seeping ocean fog were bound eventually to warp the wood inside. She wondered, not for the first time, whether anyone ever played the instrument. Was it there only as decoration, for suggestive atmosphere? She lifted the lid of the keyboard and struck what should have been an A-major chord and winced. The piano was hideously out of tune.

Hunter divisions in the morning, equitation in the afternoon, jumper classes to end the day. A standard schedule but often blown by the minor delays—late entries, spills, mix-ups at the gate—that could stall and stretch a show out to where the judge needed a flashlight to see the final rounds.

By midafternoon Seacrest continued to click along like a train, thanks to its omniscient announcer. Pausing in the shade of Owen's booth, Erica noticed a lighter mood spreading through the crowd—the elation of winners, and the prospect of rest for those who were already packing up, or hosing down their horses. For all his aw-shucks delivery, Owen Goodchild was a brilliant organizer. No shortage of job offers for him. Palm Beach. Scottsdale, the California circuit in the winter, New England in the summer. She guessed he could have had a more conventional career, but Owen was one of those who fall in love with the show world whether they ride or not. He'd picked up the first moves and lingo, he confided to her once, from a brother who trained claimers for the track. Now Goodchild was worth every fee the show committees paid him. A happy exhibitor returns next year—with friends.

"Any possibility of a kidnapping here?"

"Oh, Lex. *You.*" In her relief she almost fell against him. He was unshaven, bristles thick in the grooves beside his mouth. He wore cutoff jeans, and the KidPower shirt that had been touched all over for good luck by sticky purple hands. "Where've you *been?*"

He thumb-pointed back toward the barn. "Working. Pretty thrilling, watching horses veg out behind bars for eight hours. Reminds me a lot of Deer Island."

"What island?"

"Never mind. Anyway, Jesus just took over. So. You coming with?"

"Where?"

Smiling, he scuffed his loafer through fine dust. "Hadn't thought that far."

"Did you know that Whitaker's poking his nose around again?"

"Sure. He tracked me down. He acts like I'm on his payroll."

Change the subject, she thought. "Any sign of Tino yet?"

"Wait a minute. Is somebody avoiding my original question here?" Lex spread his hands and studied them. "Okay," he said in a low voice. "Yeah, Tino came back. Around five this morning Jesus came banging on my door. Holding Tino by the wrist. I started reading the riot act, which was useless, but I was too out of it at first to notice the kid was higher than Kilimanjaro."

"Plastered?"

"No. Not drunk." Lex made a brushing gesture. A sweat mark like a Rorschach blot stained the front of his shirt. "He gave me lip. Mainly Spanish lip. Jesus kept shaking his head. I told Tino he could grab his gear and hit the road and he said, only with two weeks' advance. So I laughed in his face and like a jerk turned my back and next I heard this hissing sound—which must have been Jesus. So I looked around. Tino was down in a crouch, with a knife."

"Oh, my God. *Lex* . . ." She blinked, dazzled by the sun over his shoulder, half expecting him to break off now and apologize for spinning a story too far.

"Funny type of knife. Tino always wore it in this leather sheath but I never looked close. This morning I paid more attention. Plain wood handle, narrow blade about four and a half inches long, with this sort of inward curve—"

"That's a blacksmith's knife! For paring hooves . . ."

"Aha! The stuff I'm learning." He grinned. He glanced around quickly and then touched her arm. "Hey. This isn't fair! I shouldn't be telling you. Upsetting you in the middle of the show—"

"You're okay? Lex, you *are* okay?"

"Hey. Sure I am. Shh . . . Oh man. I *owe* Jesus. Either Tino didn't expect interference, or the kid was so dipped he forgot Jesus was there."

"Jesus managed to take the knife off him?"

"Well . . . we both did. Hey—really, nothing happened! That faint jangling sound is only my nerves. It's been a long time since anybody pulled a knife on me. Anyway—sayonara, Tino. He's gone now. Won't be back."

She closed her eyes, watching the hoof knife flash between three struggling bodies. "I feel crappy," she said.

"Too much sun. You need a slow walk in the shade."

She looked around to where Owen sat hunched over his microphone. His bulging back reminded her of Roland. "I *can't,*" she said. "They're setting up for the USET. My kids are waiting—"

"And after?"

She squinted at him, sideways. "Weren't you and I supposed to be having a fight?"

"Damn." Lex slapped his jaw. "Almost forgot."

"Me too."

"Boy, this is hard. Take a rain check on the fight?"

"Can I at least apologize?"

He glared. *"No."*

"Kiss," she whispered. "Lex? After USET . . . there's only the jumper division. I can afford to miss *that.*"

*   *   *

Not every kid, however talented, was up to USET. Today there were only eight entries, compared to the fifteen or so in the previous eq classes. As the eight filed in for the opening flat phase she gave a thumbs-up to her own pair, and a quick smile to Suzy DiSenza, tall and earnest on Ranger Boyd's big white thoroughbred. She had decided to give up trying to figure out Boyd. Where did his generous streak—offering this kid a catch-ride today on his private jumper—come from? The stallion was plenty of horse, but Suzy was managing well. Despite some hairy takeoffs, she had pinned third in the Open.

Walk, trot, canter. Counter-canter. Normally Ned's correct seat on the flat earned him an edge with the judges in the second phase, over fences—but today he switched a stride in the counter-canter, so no cigar. No second glance. Shouldn't have happened, Erica thought grimly. The counter-canter, in which the horse leads with his outside foreleg instead of seeking his natural balance to the inside, is much easier to hold on a German warmblood than a finicky thoroughbred. She concentrated on Mickie, whose stiff little fists pistoned at the trot. Next time we school, kid, I'm tying your hands behind your back!

For a smallish show, the fences were formidable. Erica approved. This was the point of the USET class—not to demonstrate an elegant position but to test the guts and intuition of kids who hoped to make the big time: open jumpers. In the USET, correct position was whatever did it for you. And speed counted.

Owen read out the order of go. She scribbled down numbers. The order of go contained a touch of coy mystery, in that the judge ranked according to the scores in the flat phase but wasn't obliged to reveal whether the numbers ran top to bottom or vice versa. Erica sighed. Mickie came in the middle, Ned seventh and Suzy DiSenza dead last. Top to bottom, then. *Easy pickings.* Sure, Ranger.

In the ring, the top-ranked rider tore hell-bent down the first line, popped through the diagonal jumps on a wing and prayer, and finally crashed the last element of the triple combination, smack under the judge's nose. Someone, presumably a mother, groaned.

If it were up to Erica, she'd make Suzy scratch this course. Too dangerous on a horse she didn't know well. And nothing to earn. She wondered what she'd missed seeing, what trouble had nixed Suzy on the flat.

The next round was clean but diffident. Then rider three went off course.

Erica grabbed Mickie's reins, outside the gate. "Now listen good. He's tired. Gas him in the opening circle. Wake him up. The first line's long—ride like you *mean* it—but take back before the diagonal line. Watch the triple, it's a tight three-stride to a two—but give his *face* room. Got it?"

Mickie nodded.

"Good. Now, go have fun!" She slapped the dappled haunch. To Ned, who sat slumped above her on the Monster, she said, "Pay attention."

Line. Diagonal. Double oxer. The better the round got, the harder Erica's heart knocked against the roof of her mouth. She rode into the triple with Mickie and at the last touchdown the crowd clapped and whistled and Erica's own victory hoot took her by surprise. Mickie trotted out, flushed and beaming.

"Was I all right?"

Erica rubbed the gelding's speckled nose. "Cricket always saves your ass."

"Don't I *know* it!" She toppled forward, hugging his neck and braided mane, tears of happiness in her eyes.

Coco Beale stood beside Erica, narrowly eyeing the lineup in front of the judge. "Who's your money on?"

Erica shrugged. Cool surface over warm hope. "DiSenza had an okay round."

"So did both your kids."

"Total crapshoot, isn't it."

The steward strolled out to hook ribbons on bridles. Yellow to

Ned. Red to Mickie. Erica felt all the tension of the day run out like water into sand. Over. Nothing counts but blue.

First place to Suzy DiSenza.

"Kee-ryst," muttered Coco. "Judge must've lost her contact lenses. Well. That's over, jumpers are next. My turn to tack up."

Clapping, Erica said loudly, "So Suzy's qualified now. All *right*. That should sweeten Boyd's disposition." She nudged thin air. Coco had gone.

Cautiously, Erica leaned back against one of the tall rocks. Its jagged spine bit into hers. Blue dusk filled the hollow; the damp salt breeze reached beneath her shirt, and the ache in her legs from the day's riding was too familiar to notice. Through half-closed eyes she watched Lex shake sand from his beeper and press the sticky buttons in vain.

"Give up," she said. "Your toy's busted." Her mind tracked back and forth over the day, the previous night, the day to come—showing, loading, departure. No, don't think about good-bye. She found something to laugh at. "Did you see Boyd, before we came down?"

"*Yes*. What happened? Guy looked like he choked on a goober."

Erica grinned. "Goober" was barn slang for a ball of manure. "Coco beat him by eight points in the jump-off. *After* his kid had just won the USET on that same horse."

"Ah. I see." He clearly didn't. He lay against his own rock, studying the overlapping cross of their ankles.

Close overhead swooped crisp black-and-white arrows, the terns whose last nesting grounds were preserved by these few last private beach holdings. But *you* don't know you're an endangered species, she thought. For you, now is forever. She stretched, glad to be in this place, this moment.

Lex said, "I guessed wrong. I just assumed it was Whitaker who'd pissed Ranger off."

"Why?" The jab of unease. She had nearly managed to forget Whitaker.

"Turns out he didn't come here because of last night. This profession was invented for him, he says—his bosses appreciate a tendency to be where lightning strikes. He only heard about the colic when he arrived. So he did check the Sherpin horse, which was chowing down fine, which made Whit all happy. Understandable. The critter's insured with his store for seventy-five K."

"Grade inflation." She yawned, the way a cat expells stress. "Wishful thinking. But what's seventy-five K to Papa Sherpin? Hotel tips."

"Are all your horses insured?"

"Some. Ned's is of course. . . ." Erica leaned forward. "Why *did* he come?"

"Talk to the DiSenza kid. And her trainer. Apparently there's been enough wrangling over that Crimson Cadillac case that they finally decided to dig up the horse. Brr."

"And?"

"Tell me—what do they even look for?"

Erica shrugged. "Gut content. Blockages. Traces of common stimulants or depressants? But the standard blood tests can't cover everything. And they usually can't find an injection site—especially after *this* much time. If they don't know what to look for . . . And there's plenty of stuff that either mimics natural causes or is too new to test for. The AHSA comes out with new tests every year, but they can't keep up with the state of the art. Doping's a thriving cottage industry, Lex."

"Cottage?"

"Well, more likely garage . . . Plenty of old garages around city race tracks. Make good labs. Imagine the payoff to some chemist if he can help rig a trifecta. A few years ago the big scandal was elephant juice. It's so lethal that it takes two vets to administer—one stands by with a needleful of antidote. Otherwise—if even a tiny amount is scratched into human skin—instant death." She looked up. "So. Did they find anything?"

"I have been asked not to discuss it."

"Lex—"

"Hey! It's not my fault the guy treats me like we're Brother Elks. Nothing conclusive, Whit said. The only thing he mentioned specifically, like I should comment, was some shreds of surgical cotton."

Erica shrugged. "Cotton in the ears, right? Standard show practice, when a horse is sensitive to loud noise."

"Not the ears. Between the teeth."

A shred of cloud reddened the last of the sun. She hated to think of the autopsy: the horse sawed open, a cadaver for alien human fingers and eyes to explore. "So what? He was probably chewing his bandages. They do that."

"On three legs? In a *sling?*"

"Lex? You're actually starting to believe someone got to that horse, aren't you?"

"And you don't?"

"*No,* damn it! Look—it's so late, suddenly—" She could hardly see his face. "We have to eat something, and then sleep, we both have to be up before dawn—" She fought a childish, grinding despair.

Lex pulled her close. He rubbed the crease from her forehead. His smell and the weight of his arm soothed her. "It's you I'm worried about."

"But why *me . . . ?*"

He went on stroking, in silence. Time slowed, like a sleeper's altered breath. He couldn't know the one valid reason he might have for worry—the danger of her cracking. Not being able to hold it all together. She pictured the cartoon: crack running down a cup and the pieces bursting away into nothing. Earlier today someone else had said he was worried about her—but she had not, deep down, believed him. She knew she had never attracted the concern of others, maybe even repelled it. I'm worried about you—at home that had been simply a code meaning toe the line, damn it. Behave. She remembered her father's glassy, slipping gaze on the day she told them she was leaving, and her mother's lips curling inward as she looked away. *Up to you, Erica. Do it your own way. You're a cat that always lands on its feet.*

"You know these people." His voice startled her. "I don't. Back when I used to box, there were plenty of guys willing to throw a fight. Buy or sell a fight. But not kill for a fight."

"Nobody—"

"Since I started this job, I think I have met people who'd sell their own grannies to win one of these finals—whatever they are. It's like nothing else matters!"

She smiled. "That doesn't mean—"

"Am I right that of the top four local barns, yours is the only one that hasn't been hit yet?"

" 'Hit?' " She laughed, a little. "Okay. So this is a sales push. I need protection. You want me to sign up with you."

"Too late, Slimbones." He lifted her hair. His thumb traced her cheek. "You *are* signed up with me."

PART 2

Regionals

Charlestown, Massachusetts, September 11

His MOTHER'S HANDS, SCRUNCHING HIS CHEEKS IN A VISE GRIP OF love, smelled of fresh garlic.

"Zandro! Why you didn't tell me you were coming? Look at me, my dress, the apartment— Everything's a mess. Oh my God. What should I care, what's the matter with me? I'm only the mamma, not the girlfriend! Oh, Zandro, you're so burned from the sun. *Paesano!* Come in! Give your suitcase—"

He refused to let go of the suitcase and trapped her in a one-armed, firm hug instead. He felt his mother quiver with pleasure.

"I should call up Leo! And your cousins. And Catherine? Oh I'm telling you, you won't hardly recognize Catherine, she lost twelve pounds, she let her hair go back to natural, she got a promotion with the post office. She's so calm and happy, believe me. Don't be afraid when you start to get old, Zandro. It's wonderful, wonderful to see these kids you know since little babies start to find a *purpose* in life—"

Rosie Healey, née Rosaria Buonagurio, talked on as she led

Lex down the narrow hall toward the comparative light of the kitchen/living room. She walked sideways, keeping her son in view as if he might otherwise vanish, with the talent honed in childhood.

Nothing had changed. Nothing, except that each time Lex returned the once vast room seemed smaller: his memory was collecting a set of diminishing apartment-boxes. The warped wood floor, its gray paint smudged in the kitchen zone by her house shoes, was dignified in the living area by a square of cinnamon carpet. To obscure the view to and from neighbors' porches, the two tall windows were shrouded with lace curtains. He'd never seen the room in direct sun.

On the ugly, comforting gas stove burbled a skillet of sugo. While his mother automatically stirred down the slow-popping lava boils, Lex wandered past the sofa set and his father's Naugahyde lounger and the twenty-six-inch Zenith that flickered and yapped with the urgency of all television sets, to the shelf wall. He couldn't help himself.

"Tell me the truth: did you eat yet?" The tinge of good-natured self-parody couldn't disguise her real concern.

"Mamma, it's only three-thirty."

"Lunch, I meant."

"Yes, Mamma," he lied. "I had a nice big lunch."

Nothing moved. Nothing missing. His father's pipe—the one he'd left behind. His father's Bible with its lush dangling gold, red, and purple strings, and the other six books: *Robinson Crusoe, Mr. Midshipman Hornblower* (both read aloud to him when he was too small to understand; never finished), *The Handy Guide to Fly-Fishing,* Albert Schweitzer, Dale Carnegie, *Profiles in Courage.* His mother's framed confirmation picture and his own, also fading as if trying to catch up to hers. An accordion-folded postcard panorama of the Grand Canyon. A plastic, illuminable Saint Francis, surrounded by the tiny blown-glass animal figurines he'd collected with almost shameful passion in third grade. His tooth-dented silver baby spoon. Finally, the Praying Hands: white plaster flesh, astonishingly lively, garlanded with his father's onyx rosary. He had never told her how this arrangement disturbed him, like a perverted switch of life and death. Sometimes the hands opened, beckoning or begging, in his dreams.

Through the television jabber, he heard his mother talking on the phone.

Then she was behind him, setting almond cookies on the coffee table. He had a vague impression she'd changed her dress. "Zandro, come sit down now. Oh my God, you look tired! I want to hear all your stories, all about this new business you're in—"

"Mamma . . . You think maybe first we could turn off the TV?"

She gave him a look: part angry, part hurt, part pleading. Day and night, even while she slept, the television played. She never *watched* it. He supposed she just needed these voices, to cover the silence of the place.

"Healey?"

"Speaking. Who is this?"

"Whitaker."

"No shit . . ." Lex sat on the edge of his bed, facing the old wooden school desk crowded with his sports trophies and an eerie photo progression of himself from baptism to graduation. The room was cramped. To lie down he would have to topple a pyramid of ratty stuffed animals, arranged by Rosie. "How'd you find me?"

"Routine data quest, Healey. Routine. Do you have a minute? Alone? Otherwise call me back, I'll be here in the office till midnight. Someday I want to hear how *you* manage the paperwork—"

"I'm alone." Lex jerked at the phone extension cord, which was stuck under the door. He had been about to make a call of his own. "What's on your mind?"

"Okeydoke! Right here in front of me now is the written au-

topsy report. Signed-off on. Tufts School of Veterinary Medicine."
A paper rustled in the line, as corroboration.

"Crimson Cadillac?"

"Correct. Now, what we have as the proximate *cause* of death
is extensive hemorrhaging."

"So, like we thought. Sure. From the knee wound." Lex nodded in relief: signed off. No drugs. No malice, no tampering, and
no link whatever to the three colic cases at Seacrest Farm. He also
felt a spurt of impatience, because Whitaker's ferreting out his
home phone number reminded him of . . . what? An unshakable
girl with a misplaced crush?

"You supposing along my same lines?" Whitaker asked.

"Huh?"

"You were there. When the wound was fresh inflicted, the animal did not bleed to death."

"He—she—bled a *lot*." Lex swallowed, remembering his sticky
shoes.

"But so why not until the next day? *After* treatment? Yes in-
deed, the stitches tore. But now add this: there were blood traces
in the lungs." Whit paused, as if to let Lex catch up. "In the *lungs*?
Now, I'm the first to grant you, Healey—seventy percent of racing thoroughbreds are lung bleeders. Which is why they're all shot
full of Lasix, your basic heavy-duty dehydrator, pre-race. But show
jumping is nowhere near that same physical exertion as racing. So
why the blood in this mare's lungs . . . ?" Another, longer pause.
"Ever hear of warfarin?"

Lex went blank, then snatched at something, from a shelf high
in his mother's kitchen. "Isn't that a rat poison?"

"Rodenticide. *Any-critter*-icide. Nifty versatile substance, and
very popular in stables, of course. Let me read you from this book
I have here: 'Inhibits a number of the clotting factors whose formation is dependent on vitamin K. Symptoms of overdose include
hema . . . hematuria, bloody stools, widespread bruising, hemo . . .
hemoptysis—' Heck. That's the lung bleeding. Rats stagger back
to their holes, and basically explode. Also—"

"Stop. A few days ago, you said all they found the least unusual was a trace of cotton in the mouth. Nothing in the gut. Nothing about any warfarin."

"Were they looking? Anyway, the animal is ashes now, can't keep them forever. We were lucky to get the one chance. Healey, suppose it was a teeny minidose. *Heparin.* You know heparin? Same type chemical, nurses squirt a little in the IV to keep the line from *clotting.* Another example of how everything's got its bad side and its good side. Go figure, Healey. For the mare, a minidose, local injection. Straight into that messed-up knee. Get enough blood flowing, the stuff mostly washes out."

"Whitaker . . . what exactly do you want? Why are you telling me all this?"

"Oh, *I* see." The insurance adjuster sounded insulted. "You're one of those not-in-my-backyard types. Healey, if the whole world took that tack we'd still be living in caves, wouldn't we?"

Lex sighed. Through the TV babble, he heard his mother's steps approaching and then discreetly retreating. The awful possibility occurred to him that she would invite Catherine-from-the-post-office to dinner. "It's a question of what I can *do.*"

"Help me out slightly. No big effort, surely. You're on the scene. You're going to that Maclay Regional next, right? Whereas I have twenty-two cases open here, one car, one pair of eyes. In addition I stick out like a sore thumb." This was true. "Whereas you, Healey, are definitely a low-key, fade-into-the-woodwork type of person."

"Thank you."

"Don't mention it. Only, you want to develop your proactive side more. You want to talk to people, draw them out. At this date, the individuals I have marked for surveillance are the trainer Boyd and the family DiSenza—including the girl."

"Suzy?"

"Girls that age, Healey. Knock your socks off, what some of them get up to. *Hormones.* I don't however mean to limit you. There's other trainers could have a motive to put that mare out of action—let's see, we have Deluna, Hablicht—"

Lex sat up straight. "No. Sorry. I absolutely don't have the time to spare for this."

"No time? Would that be because one of your illegals quit on you, little setback your company doesn't know about yet? Or is it no time for the twenty percent you stand to earn, if you can prove this claim was fraud? *Twenty-four K?* Peanuts, of course, to an individual with your earning prospects. Busy, busy! *I'm* busy, Healey. Here till midnight. Case you change your mind."

Whitaker hung up.

Lex's good ear was sore. His head buzzed. He disliked telephoning, but there were two more calls he needed to make before offices closed for the day.

The first went to a number he knew by heart: Gallagher and Stavropoulos, Attorneys-at-Law. While on the road he had called Ed Gallagher at least weekly; now it was a luxury not to sense the long-distance minutes ticking, when he was put on hold. He drummed his fingers through half of "Moon River" before Ed picked up.

"You could use a new tape, Ed. Maybe Vivaldi. Something up-market."

"There's a reason for that song, sir. Very personal. Do I know you?"

"Zandro Healey, Ed! I'm home—I'm in the neighborhood. I thought tomorrow we could get together, talk in more detail about my case—"

"Oh, boy. Oh, Jesus H. Lemme pull your file." Gallagher's long wheeze sounded like liquid being forced through a sieve. Lex pictured the fat man in his two-room "suite" over the Discount Druggist, smoking a cigar that turned the air so fetid no secretary would stay a day. Lex had been there, introduced by Uncle Leo. On the way out Leo had answered his question with *Nah, there was never no Stavropoulos, that's an invite for the Greeks. And don't be put off by appearances. Ed kicks plenty of butt, downtown.*

Again, he heard paper rustling through the line. "So is there news on my case?"

"Alex, lemme put it this way—because there's attorneys who would be happy to string a client along, on a retainer basis, you understand. And I can give you some names of these Councillor Feel Goods if you want. Whereas I and Leo—and you—agreed I'd put my time into this for zilch."

"Sixty-forty, on settlement." Lex's arm trembled from holding the phone. He wanted to hang up. He could already see Ed Gallagher dissolving, a wraith in brown smoke.

"Settlement? This complaint—" sharp slap on the papers "—won't make it to a *hearing*. For class action, first I need class. Plural. Now, not one of those nonprofits you listed . . . Let's just say it's a brick wall. Nobody's interested. Ones that aren't defunct are fighting to protect the little bone they've got left. Alex? Lemme put it another way. Since Third Street KidPower went under, which is over a year now, our benevolent governor has not been idle. He's slashed on health clinics, immunization, prenatal care, psychiatric care, meals and home care for old folks. See, nobody is grieving much about after-school playgroups these days. You hear what I'm saying, Alex?"

"I hear you, Ed."

"Give you some names of my colleagues if you want that."

"No. I don't think so."

"Yeah. Leo said you were nobody's fool. Sometimes we all of us got to cut bait, right Alex? Hey. I always enjoy talking with you. You stay in touch."

As he hung up, Rosie knocked. Dinner would be in a half hour. In case he planned to shave and shower first.

He found the next number in his address book, beside Horse-Guard Intn'l, P.O. Box 3116, Boston. A female-voiced machine picked up on the first ring, assuring that a message of any length would be promptly returned. Lex wondered in what form, and where, his employers existed. Then he wondered why he felt impelled to call in at all. It was not as if a live and breathing representative of HorseGuard ever came around to check up. The payroll money (most tagged as Expense Reimbursement) was deposited to various banks around the circuit in Lex's name, so as not to perturb the INS. So now why shouldn't good old Tino stay as a straw man on the books indefinitely—

He disconnected and stretched back, holding the phone on his stomach. A one-eyed baby squirrel and a moth-eaten antelope bounced head over heels to the floor.

"Zandro? You not gone asleep in there?"

"No, Mamma. Doing business. Be finished in a minute."

Her steps faded again, the click-scuff of mild sciatica. From his pocket he fished a scrap of an ad, torn from a horse-show program. Five-oh-eight was a long-distance charge, but not far enough out to run much of a bill. Assabet lay due west, on the ill-defined border between the affluent computer-and-software belt and the more distant pinched poverty of weed-riddled fields and abandoned mills.

"Hello." He held his breath. "You have reached Stoneacre Farm." Any moment, her real voice might break into its taped replica. "The office is open Tuesday through Sunday, seven to five. Or try the barn at 555-6465. Sorry, we do not rent out horses or give trail rides. Please leave your name, number, time, and day. And wait for the beep. Thanks."

He was smiling as he put the phone down. Stuffed animals avalanched on him like a soft hail. There had been a brightness in her voice, and he guessed it must have been a good day, maybe a sunny spring morning, when she recorded that tape.

He woke to the nail-gunning of rain on the window, and pounding feet, shrieks and groans.

As he opened the door, heavy hands grabbed him. "Alessandro! Lemme *look at* this kooky guy!" Leo punched his chest and kissed him. A surging crowd bore him along the dim hallway into the big room, where two card tables draped with a pink cloth were set for six, and the mingled sizzle of roasting peppers and rain on the fire escape almost managed to drown out the TV.

Around the table they were Rosie, Leo, Leo's two oldest boys, who owned the fruit stand in Haymarket, Lex himself, and a stunning, auburn-haired, black-eyed woman in a falling-off-the-shoulders dress, whom Lex failed to recognize. They ate radicchio in lemon dressing, and pasta asciutta, and saltimbocca with the peppers: they had two liters of Bordolino, and petits fours and grappa and espresso for dessert.

Leo talked about Ross Perot, little guy who sounded like he had all the answers but so did the devil. Perot was a union buster who should give any American the willies, a wanna-be Mussolini with more smarts. Lex agreed but said Perot was washed up now, a spoiler, the problem wasn't him but TV—with a glance backward at the screen—people didn't switch off their brains when they switched on the box, they soaked up the mush from the box like it was a big silver tit. There'd be another Perot. The balding cousins, cutting and chewing their food in tandem, signaled each other with swift, forebearing glances. Rosie said, "Can't we talk politics without using language?" But she was laughing.

The platinum sheen of Rosie's hair emphasized her dark eyes and upswung dark brows, vehement as a young girl's. For the special occasion she wore a navy blue skirt and white blouse with a gold pin at the throat. Elegant! Lex's admiration swung back and forth between his mother and the unknown visitor in whose creamy cleavage and ironic pout he pretended, for the sake of peace, to recognize post office Catherine. She would know *him,* she said, anywhere. How to forget a kid who in second grade liked to stomp your fingers on the jungle gym? Catherine's right dimple winked.

Was this a side effect of being in love? That exactly now, when he desired only one woman, all others were revealed to him as beautiful, each in her own essential way?

Late, he fell on his bed wine dizzy, filled with an almost teary affection for the people whose good-night hugs still warmed him.

For the cool, splashing, end-of-summer rain. For the constancy, the generosity of all things that stayed the same.

Tomorrow . . . hang out in the neighborhood. Day after, departure for the Maclay Regional, someplace in New York. Dicey, to be taking three days off now that Tino was gone, but Jesus had convinced him, had organized a relative to come help out, and Lex had faith in Jesus. Smart. Unflappable. Experienced as hell. There had to be a way to wangle the man a green card. Ask Gallagher. Then, when Lex left the job, he could recommend the Mexican as his replacement—

Leave the job. For what? Where?

The job paid four hundred a week. No bennies, except the leased Escort. After the hundred he sent to Rosie—her sciatica kept her from going cleaning, thank God Uncle Leo picked up the rent—he was still adding to his savings, but fifteen K total wasn't much of a retirement fund. Wipeout, if he got hurt again, or sick . . . You're forty-four years old, shithead. Fifty, in six. Pretty soon, *old.* What're you going to do, hawk pencils? Deep-dive the Dumpsters for soda cans and rags?

Sometimes he envisioned his father—somewhere—doing precisely that.

Sometimes he shook the picture off by rolling over and reminding himself he most likely wouldn't last that long.

But now he wanted to last. With *her.* Years ahead, together— no point in crying over the years lost, stupid precious evaporated decades, before. *But before, this wouldn't have happened,* she had said. *We wouldn't have given each other a second glance, because we weren't who we are now. You would have looked right past me.*

I just wish it was your fingers I'd stomped on the jungle gym. He grinned. She would understand, she would be flattered when he told her that.

But if they did have, take, steal, whatever time was left together . . . what could he offer her?

Old-fashioned question. Never spoken. But real. What did she imagine he had to offer? He remembered his mother's fond sig-

nificant look, the moment Catherine-from-the-post-office, face
flushed and shining, was safely out the door.

Into the rain he asked quietly, "Mamma, what have I ever been
able to offer a wife?"

PUDDLES CRINKLED IN THE GUTTERS. THE WIND WAS SEA SODDEN;
its punches made his eyes water and his nose run. The few rickety
trees wedged into the sidewalk were already stripped of half their
leaves, and he found it hard to believe that summer had ever paused
over gray Charlestown to break apart the rolling stream of clouds
overhead. He called up a vision of sunny fields and bare-legged riders, warm breeze fluttering ribbons and tents, like a dream he
wanted to return to. Summer, this year, followed the horses.

Here, aluminum tour buses squeezed through the narrow
streets, aiming for Bunker Hill.

Jackhammers, ground fog of gritty yellow dust, cars and trucks
broad-jumping potholes and torn-up pavement, explosions of
jolted steel. In the square, weird new structures betrayed no clue
as to function: concrete elephant trunks, pointed skyward? This
wasn't gentrification—that wave had gathered in the seventies,
raised the normal xenophobia of the neighborhood to fever pitch,
and finally broken in this recession, leaving behind shell buildings
and shell companies, and the flat low tide of bankruptcy. This was
worse: state investment. Corporation welfare. Make-work, to no
local worker's purpose.

He saw no one he knew.

Marrone's lay in the Hill's shadow. Flat brick front and one glass-
brick window, where a Bud logo glowed behind jail bars.

Inside, Lex paused, adjusting to warmth and gloom. A taffy cat
licked its hind toes on one of the empty tables. At the bar, two motionless early drinkers, a row of empty stools, and finally a big man

in suspenders and white shirt, whose oily grayish yellow locks overlapped his starched collar, who sat perched directly under the ceiling-mounted TV set hugging a phone to his ear and glancing up at the box as he talked, as if checking heaven for a sign.

The big man mouthed a welcome and patted the stool beside him. He nodded and shook his head, talking rapid-fire under the sound veil of the TV, jotting notes on a pad with a gold ballpoint that glimmered like a dragonfly caught in his hand. Next to the notepad were a dish of pretzels, drink, Casio calculator, a stack of opened envelopes, and a handful of loose sour balls. He hung up decisively and shoved the phone away.

"Hey, Uncle Leo." Lex grinned. "Still the same old office, huh?"

"You bet. What am I going to do, pay *rent*? Siddown, siddown." Submitting to the bear hug, Lex felt Leo's physical disappointment: he had never learned how to embrace men, he blamed the stiff self-consciousness of his Irish side. "Franny! Come out, say hello to my Neph! This a good-looking boy or what?" A wizened man in an apron appeared from the back kitchen to stare impassively at Lex. "He take after me or what? You eat breakfast yet? I don't need to tell you what a difference in Rosie, having you back home. *You* saw, last night. Beautiful woman, my sister. She could have had any guy she wanted in this town, maybe a city councillor, and instead— Aah. It ain't over till it's over. I keep an eye out for Rosie, but guys my age are all horny sons of bitches owing ten years back alimony. Fran, do up some eggs and fries for the kid, and I hope you got clean grease on the grill. What about you, Zandro? Now it's just us guys. Last I knew you were shacked up with that tall babe, college woman, social worker type . . . Help me out."

"Janice?"

"*Janice.* So I take it that's *fini*? Okay. Rosie never warmed much to her either. How many years she hang on with you? Jeez, are Protestant broads patient like saints, or what? A Catholic girl knows how to make a man make an honest woman out of her, *quick*. Hah! No fooling."

"Uncle Leo—"

The phone rang. "Pick that up and say I'm out." Lex did so. "Middle of the month. Some deadbeat with a sob story. I give two weeks extension on the rent but after that it's serious. There's parts of this business I like and parts I don't. There's a fine line between staying human and staying out of the red. Confession doesn't do it for me anymore. This priest we got now, he doesn't get it. All he wants to hear is sex, and how much did I give to Catholic Charities. So, you seeing someone new? Hah! Bingo! Look at you! Nice girl?"

"Yes."

"We get to meet her someday?"

"Leo, I need to talk a little about business."

The food came. Lex poked the wobbly egg white with his fork while Leo liberated stray fries. Lex explained that his case to have the 3rd Street project reinstated looked dead in the water, and Leo nodded, knowing, chewing. Lex explained that despite what he might have implied last night his current job was only a stopgap, grasped straw, no security, made no use of his skills or experience, kept him on the road like a frigging truck driver and besides—

"So what's so wrong with driving a truck?"

"Nothing. Nothing." Lex's throat and stomach closed tight. Leo's smile had vanished in deep folds of down-draped flesh. "I just thought—"

"You're saying what? I should provide you another job?" The phone shrilled. With a clatter, Leo broke the connection and took it off the hook. "You know what we got for unemployment here? *Seventeen percent.* That's the *real* number. Or what do you want, career counseling? You're what, forty years old, for some reason smart as you are, you never finished up at Community College, you still never started a family—and you don't know what you want to *be*? Hey, who said guys get a choice? I think, in that last cushy job you started hanging out with too many shrinks, Zandro. Shrinks, they'll suck the marrow juice right out of your spine."

Lex stood up.

"Shrinks'll get you so sorry for yourself, you turn down a good breakfast." He pointed at Lex's plate. "Holy . . . Wait a minute! What're you thinking, I don't *care* about you? Look. We're family. You got this job, *manager* for Chrissake, oughta be something you can make out of that! But worst case, you let me know. Probably I can fit you in with the boys over at the fruit stand. It's a very good business, clearing—" he tapped a manila file "—over four thou a month." He picked up a french fry and studied it closely. "Only . . . I don't know you'd feel comfortable around plums and pineapples, any more than with ponies."

He walked fast, pushing into wind. His teeth ached from clenching, back in the bar. *Leo was practically a father to you,* Rosie had said. *Paid for your school—with all his kids, he has such a soft spot for you. He respects you! Go see him again.*

He dove into the shadows under the bridge. Jerkhead: what's a guy your age want a father for?

Turn the corner. Any corner. A half block ahead, at the mouth of an alley, he saw a deal going down. No question. The driver of the idling silver Mazda leaned out the window, souped-up Coke can in his left hand, his right twisted into the shirt of a skinny kid who in turn was digging deep in the crotch of his jeans. Lex broke into a run. The kid froze, tore free and whirled for the alley. The driver yelled, "Get over here, motherfucker! What're you freaking out for? It's *no*body—" He threw Lex a black scowl that changed to a derisive pout as he sucked a hit of crack from the can. Or pretended to. The car roared, and careened squealing down the street.

Lex ran into the alley. Rain-soaked trash, overflow from the parked Dumpster. On a high picket fence at the dead end he saw the hands of the kid, just before they let go.

"Bungee! Hey, wait, I want to talk to you—" Lex reached the fence, got a grip, and scrabbled, trying to scale it. There was reason for the nickname: nothing the kid didn't dare get up onto or jump off. "Bungee, it's *me*, Healey, Lex Healey you stupe—you *hear* me?"

"Go back where I can see you, okay?" The soft, hoarse voice came from the other side of the slats.

Lex stepped back. Long silence. "Bungee, come *on*—"

Suddenly the boy's silhouette teetered, arched like a tailless cat, clinging hand and foot to the top of the fence.

There weren't many peaceful places to walk. They headed down closer to the river, where on a good day you could see across the no-man's-land of tracks and truck yards and warehouses to the Museum of Science, shining on its island like a white gold Atlantis, but today the visibility was zero. Fog steamed off the water.

Lex didn't lecture. He only asked where the bag was, because he didn't want to walk around with someone who was carrying, probably known to be carrying, and Bungee said, not *on* me, which meant behind the picket fence somewhere, so that was all right. Then Lex said are you nuts, dealing with a guy so far gone he's smoking on the street, in the open, what if the guy had a gun? Bungee gave him a look that said, so what, and anyway you butted in, same risk. But a little fear passed across his eyes, an afterthought, like the tiny reflection of a boy running.

Bungee wore a Bruins cap backward—the band bit into his forehead—and a *Jurassic Park* T-shirt, black baggies, and five-pound high-tops splayed open at the top. Lex wondered how he managed to jump in those shoes. Bungee was about five-five, with the bumpy stringy muscles that result from growing up eating mainly what comes out of cellophane bags. He looked closer to twelve than sixteen. He had been twelve when Lex first met him.

Bungee didn't complain about the spoiled sale. Lex recalled him as a quiet kid who liked to stay late and help out, who had evidently received some upbringing at home.

"School's started," said Lex. "Did you drop out or what?" Bungee shrugged, as if he wasn't sure. Lex inquired after the family. He had a vague memory of many brothers and sisters, the kind of rich noisy confusion of live-in and live-out relatives that can turn a kid helpful and quiet.

Bungee said now he was living with his grandmother, just the two of them. "She looks after me good. Right now she thinks I'm in school. You know last year she adopted me? She had to kick Mom out of the house. Mom kept bringing these really dumb guys home who trashed our furniture and, like, smacked her around, and she was, like, she didn't *care*."

"You see your mother regularly these days?"

"Nah." Bungee jumped a pavement crack. "My mom is my sister." They had turned away from the flats and were walking uphill again. Lex let the words echo in his head. *My mom is my sister.* He didn't want to ask Bungee to repeat himself.

Bungee looked up with a twist of his thin lips. "We have the same dad. Get it? It's not like I've ever seen the guy. It's like, the whole family knew but didn't tell me. I mean, my whole life, everybody lied to me! I only found out because of the adoption."

Lex pressed his hand to his lip. A clammy sweat, despite the wind. "Look, Bungee—it's not about *you*. You're just *yourself*. You're not in any way to blame—okay?"

"Yeah. That's what my grandmother says."

He arrived home late. The TV chattered, but the single lamp told him that Rosie had gone to bed. He had played pick-up basketball with Bungee and other ex–3rd Streeters, sprung for take-out pizza. More basketball had melted away the night.

In his own room he found a note. "Your dinner is in the oven I hope not too cold. A Mr. Whitaker called. Also another man who didn't want to leave any name. He will call again. Sweet dreams. I love you. PS—excuse me, but I forgot all about these." Three un-opened letters lay on the note, bound together by a grimy rubber band. He recognized Janice's slashing backward hand. Irritated, he looked around the small room. They didn't belong in here. To tear them up would leave telltale scraps for his mother to find. Finally he upended his duffel bag, tossed the letters in the bottom, and began to pack whatever was still passably clean in again for tomorrow. He unfolded his map. Roughly five hours' drive to the Regional, in Old Salem, New York.

When he had finished he brought the phone in. Lying on his boyhood bed, weary from hoop play, ageless and safe in the night, he listened to the recorded message from Stoneacre Farm, certain that this late, no one would answer.

The rain returned. Lex rolled over. The rain sounded harsher, like steel drums, once he switched on the light. He stood up, found a cigarette and smoked it, dropping the ashes into a 1964 hockey trophy cup. Maybe it was anticipation of tomorrow's drive that ate at him. Or awareness of how he had let his mother down tonight. Had and would again. He turned away from the window's wavering reflection of his thin naked body. Inside the rain Whitaker repeated, *Twenty-four K. Peanuts, to a guy with your potential*— Lex bent down for the phone and then dialed 411 and got the number of Global Insurance, Boston. The Livestock Division.

Whitaker picked up. "Healey? You keep surprising me. Mentally, I already sorted you out as 'Mister Not Available.' "

"I changed my mind."

Wellesley, Massachusetts, September 12

RUTHIE WAS DRYING HER PHOTOGRAPHS WITH A PILLOWCASE. She bumped her wheelchair around the desk, lunging for pictures which in her absence had been rearranged out of reach. The night before, she had opened her bedroom windows wide to let the stale heat escape, and while she slept rain had driven across her desk, soaked the edge of the pink carpet to scarlet, and clung still in scab-like drops to the silver-plate frames and picture glass.

She scooted to the window, clutching a photo of herself at sixteen on Brownie: a plain, brave mare who'd followed her without a lead line like a puppy, who'd had a sweet tooth for jelly doughnuts and ginger ale. If it had made sense to keep even one horse, Ruthie would still own her. In this photo, Brownie's legs were obscured by a banner that read "South Shore Open Equitation Champion." Ruthie tilted it to the light and caught her breath. Streaks of water glued the photo to its glass. She pulled apart the frame and the damp velvet backing, and with gentle concentration began to peel the photo free. Bits of color adhered to the glass. Biting the insides of her cheeks—a recent habit—she went on peeling, faster, unable to stop. The photo looked as if it had been raked by angry fingernails. A white gash glowed where Ruthie's face had been.

She hauled herself back up onto the bed. A hospital bed, a gift from her parents. Its steel side bars made the hauling up safer and eased her chronic fear of falling. She rolled on her side with arms crossed over her breasts, hugging the wet ruined scrap of photograph. In her mind her legs drew up in an infantile curl. Something she could never do again.

Was it because her legs lay stretched and exposed like the open blades of a scissors that she couldn't cry? She tasted a hot thickening in her throat, and the harder she swallowed, the more its pressure grew.

The room was dim. The last of the rain washed through gutters and dripped from the eaves.

Who are you? The old echo-question. But this time she was not asking Ruthie. *What kind of life do you have?* The question had turned in a new direction: she was asking the man. *Can you see me? Where are you? Don't you need to see me? You can't just leave me and never turn around, you can't just keep driving and leave*—

She longed to send him pieces of her. This photograph. That would feel like the right beginning.

All she had was the pronoun. *He.* No name, no age, no face. For *her* protection, they insisted. At first Ruthie had agreed, even grateful, too scared still to hear the humor: it was, after all, too late for protection from him. The lawyers settled out of court, out of the newspapers. . . . No case for criminal liability. An *accident.* Her shrink, with the embarrassment of a professional edging toward the bog of religion, dredged up the word "forgiveness." Ruthie, what does that word mean to you?

Ruthie held the photo away from her chest for one more look. It was warm from her skin. Finely wrinkled now—to anyone else, unrecognizable. She tore it in half, slowly, and laid the two damp pieces of paper over her eyes.

• • •

"Mom. Who's been in my room?" Ruthie sounded to herself like Baby Bear snuffling after Goldilocks.

"Not a soul. No *way*. Here, I rescued you the last croissant. There's scrambled eggs in the chafing dish—not *too* rubbery yet, let's hope. Did you catch up on some sleep?"

Now that Ruthie was able to laugh again, it came out abrupt and raucous, like a crow's caw. It often jerked her mother's smile out of place. "No way," that pathetic teenagerism, matched the sequined white sweatsuit her mother wore as if life were merely a series of quick recesses between aerobics classes. Ruthie wheeled to the table and pushed away the chair that blocked her place. "Somebody was in there. It's obvious. What's so hard about telling me the truth?"

"Oh. Probably Enrique . . . ? Darling, I *told* him your space is your space, but you never can be sure how much those people really comprehend."

It gave Ruthie a chill to imagine the Brazilian cleaning man, dry and slender and silent in his movements, working alone in her room. Handling and examining her possessions. Tucking smooth her sheets. She bit into the croissant. "If Enrique can't follow directions, you should fire him. There's plenty of people out there these days who bother to learn English, looking for work."

"*Exactly*. Oh, you're so sensible. You and your father. I'm totally surrounded." Ruthie's mother slipped behind the wheelchair. Before the accident Ruthie had grown three inches taller than her mother, but now she was small again. She stopped chewing and held her breath, knowing the hand was about to descend on her head, lift and fondle her hair, in a parody of care. "But you know me, darling. The terminal softie, right? No, I mean, seriously, don't you think people in our income bracket have a certain obligation? Not to think exclusively of our own convenience? Did you realize Enrique has a family to support? Last week he brought his wife to help out. Annamaria. Pretty as a Spanish doll but very shy. I heard them singing upstairs. I found them kissing in the hallway, standing in the coils of the vacuum cleaner. They nearly died, they looked so mortified. They were adorable. I—"

"Will you *stop* fussing with me." Ruthie was suffocating. Her hand, holding the croissant, flew up and struck her mother's wrist.

"Ruth?" Her mother stepped back. "Can't I even touch my own baby girl? Can't you understand how happy I am to have you home again? Please don't be mad at me."

Down the windowless hallway, shadowy and clandestine as a funhouse tunnel, Ruthie rolled toward her room. This was not the room she'd had through high school, but the upstairs of the house was now and forever out of bounds—unless she asked to be carried. She had not seen her old room in years. Sometimes she recalled it (the dormer nook and walls and sloped ceiling all splotched with green sunlight filtered through young maple leaves outside), stupidly, as a small one-person chamber in heaven. In school, they'd had to memorize the Chambered Nautilus poem. "Build thee more stately mansions, O my soul." That kind of junk. "My father's house has many rooms."

To add another ground-floor room to his house—a studio really, with its own separate entrance and handicap-fixtured bath—her father had remodeled the attached garage. Due to zoning and setback requirements there was no space on the lot for a new one. Now in all weather his gold Acura and her mother's red Saab and Ruthie's van cluttered the front drive, impeding each other, giving the impression of the beginning or end of a party. Upstairs, the house had three empty bedrooms, not counting her father's study. The house no longer made sense.

Essentially self-contained, her father had said. *Your own thermostat. Acoustic wall. Separate phone line. You should be able to live as independently here, Ruth, as anywhere else in the world.* They had tried to involve her in the garage's redesign, as if her showing interest would be as good as a signature on a lease.

She hadn't planned to stay. Only weeks before the accident she had secretly written to a few top-notch stables—in Colorado, in Virginia, in Illinois—asking about opportunities as a working student. Room and board and chances to learn and show, in exchange for grunt labor. A year she'd envisioned, maybe two, of gypsy life on the circuit, of testing her talent and her grit, before (maybe, maybe not) plunging into the dull unreality of college. That might have been only a daydream. Never know.

She pressed a button on the wall and the extra-wide, painted metal door to her room swung open. It operated on the same principle as an electric garage opener; her father had fought for this innovation with the contractor and was proud and vindicated when the door worked. But there was no lock on her side. *In case you need us.*

The room was spacious and low-ceilinged, a square minus the cutout cubicle of bathroom. Especially somber on this overcast day. Rhododendrons fingered the windows. Unmade bed. Desk, exercise machine, and a pristine, never-dented sofa-and-chair set "for company" arranged around a low teak table. Despite this furniture the large room looked half stripped, as if someone were in the process of moving. On the table her suitcase gaped, tongue of clothes hanging to the floor. She switched on lights, then the CD player, already loaded with Brahms. Her taste had changed; she no longer wanted to hear music with words, or even closed, comprehensible melodies. As a burst of uneasily yoked and straining instruments filled up the room, Ruthie bent double to pull off her shoes.

To go to the bathroom, to bathe, to dress herself properly, to dry her long hair. All this would take over two hours. With the aid of her crutches, and the bathroom hand bars, she was *independent,* but using the crutches exhausted her. She couldn't move far. In the hospital—months defined by their distance from operations, blurring to seasons while she forgot the taste of outside air—the staff in p.t. had said: Keep up like this and we'll have you walking! They praised her concentration, the sweat that dripped off her chin, her tolerance for pain. It was their job to find something to praise. Ruthie's goal then had been to build herself up as strong as the little kids she saw, even spastics, the born cripples who swung around on their crutches with marvelous, laconic agility.

She pictured her pain as an evil twin inside her. Instead of fading it thrived on the exercises the therapists prescribed. She was no child, the crutches refused to become part of her, she was too late. Her upper body trembled under pressure; all the exceptional strength developed from riding had been in her heart and lungs, and legs. Eventually, observing the others in the p.t. room—their buckling refusals, tears and grimaces and wobbling breakthroughs—she realized that while all healthy people are the same, every disease, every wound, is radically individual, a separate story with no predictable end.

No one argued when Ruthie Pryor decided to quit.

Naked in her chair in the bathroom, she set the tub faucets running. At the sink, she swallowed a Flexeril and two ibuprofen gelcaps. It was a good day: her stomach didn't hurt. She glanced down at her soft, creased belly bulged up against heavy breasts like a mock early pregnancy no matter how little she ate. Not my body.

The last thing she removed was her watch. Five to twelve. Plenty of time, the bank in town didn't close until four. I'd better call ahead, she thought. Make an appointment with the manager. Make sure.

The intention that had been forming in her mind, roughly since the moment her mother caressed her hair, was now nearly fully defined, with angle and detail. It occurred to Ruthie that she no longer made decisions the usual way, by doubting and debating alternatives and holding out for the shove of circumstance. Instead, she was in charge. No: she was an instrument, she was an eye pressed to a kaleidoscope that showed her the hidden, underlying design of the past and out of that, with a quick shake, what *should* be.

Biting her cheeks against the sting of hot water, she lowered herself into the tub. Her arms trembled. She was thinking now of another instance of intention: the letter she had written and mailed in Marion, to Roland Pettit. The letter mailed unsigned, not because she feared Pettit's reaction but because the informant's identity shouldn't matter to him. He might have received it by now. She tried again to sense the husband's emotions as he read—ripples of disbelief, hatred, remorse, desire for revenge, and finally powerlessness—but they came through less clearly to her now than during the writing. After all, though she had seen Pettit a few times, she didn't *know* him.

And certainly she bore him no malice. She was merely acting on what the kaleidoscope showed. And although both the blinding confusion of love and the complex claustrophobia of a poor marriage were outside her own experience, Ruthie knew one thing: infection needs air to heal. A deep, clean cut.

With both hands she slowly straightened her legs, under water. When she leaned back, her legs floated. She imagined swimming in the ocean, the sting of salt and the lift of waves.

Could she have swum there, alone? Why not? From the crest overlooking the beach she had been studying the depth and traction of the sand below, trying to gauge whether the golf cart could make it across, when the children coursed past her, parting around her as if she were a rock. Then, watching them skip into the flashing waves, she had waited for her turn, sure that she *would* go down, as soon as some other game claimed their attention and lured them away. She could swim in her underwear. Only, crawling the distance between her chair and the water would be awkward and strenuous and look ludicrous to children's eyes.

Her heart had beat slow and hard, filled with intention, waiting.

There was, arguably, some danger in swimming. But once the kids left she would still not be entirely alone, on the beach. The two figures sunbathing inside a rough circle of rocks (hidden from every viewpoint but hers) were Erica, and her new friend from the barn security service. Lex Healey had strange eyes—wide set like a grazing animal's, and bluish gray like quarry stone; he had a solemn stare that seemed unaccustomed to laughing at anybody. Once he had offered to carry her. She trusted them both. Perhaps she trusted them partly because she knew so much about them—about their "affair." Ambiguous word. It implied rule breaking and flouting; it also could mean a glamorous social event. In French, it meant serious business. *"Un homme d'affaires, par example. . . . Ce n'est pas ton affaire."*

Ruthie sank back farther, letting her hair swirl in the water, keeping a tight grip on the metal bars above.

Even before that afternoon on the cliff, she had often observed them together. Their heads leaned close, temples touching, like oblivious little children. Sometimes she had watched their cars pull out, ten minutes apart, and guessed where they went. Sometimes the unblinking, longing glances they sent each other passed through her, as if she were a prism that bent light but absorbed none. Though the glances made her giddy, even queasy, she welcomed them.

It was not her fault that she saw so much. It was not by intention. But she felt drawn close to the pair of them, drawn in. They were so unaware of what went on around them that sometimes she held her breath, or wanted to utter some warning.

After the children abandoned the beach, scrambling past her up the slope, she had released the golf cart's brake and headed for the path. She took a last look down at the beach—her goal—and stopped. Inside the rocks, Healey lay stretched over Erica. Both were naked. Their bodies, made small by distance, were the colors of seashells—his shining pale, hers rosy brown. They moved together, slowly. A dragonfly chirred near Ruthie's ear, but she was motionless, transfixed. She had never seen lovemaking, except the way it was fake-filmed in some movies. This was entirely different. Along with her curiosity—it frustrated her to be so far away—she also felt a kind of wave of peace, of simplicity. Only once did she look away from them and up to the sky, an intenser blue now, marked by one long white cloud. They were alone, the three of them. No one was watching.

Until after a while she heard the children return, this time on their horses. Bareback. Skittering hooves loosened rocks that tumbled down the slope. In angry disappointment Ruthie had retreated through the phalanx of riders to her higher post on the cliff. She saw horses breach the waves and buck and bob. As the air cooled and thickened, she knew it was too late for her to go down to the sea.

Was it there on the cliff that her intention to tell Roland Pettit the truth had begun? Or maybe afterward, during her brief first visit to the barn? (Not searching for any human, in fact, but only for the company of animals.) Or much later that night, after she and Erica and Healey had discovered the sick horses and worked together in the Seacrest barn?

Intentions, essentially imperceptible at first, grow not like plants but in all directions like crystals, hardening out of sheer water and air.

All she knew was that she could see clearly, more clearly than lovers could, the uselessness and misery of secrecy. Of deceit and chronic compromise. Though they were much older and so more experienced than Ruthie, she could see how passion both absorbed and confused them. She had seen a pair of lost children (their hesitant climb up the cliff path under starlight) faltering, waiting for a sign. And it so happened that she, Ruthie, could provide their courage: could simply write the truth: a letter that would free them.

All she knew was that she wished she had not come home, had never left summer.

"Miss Pryor! At long last, eh? I was delighted to hear you'd be stopping by. I do think a personal relationship, one-on-one, is still the cornerstone—"

"I need to know the status of my account."

He was, she thought, inappropriately young for a bank manager. Sausagelike: bloated mottled skin topped by thinning blond hair. A cabbagy smell filled his small glass-walled office. After a couple of jarring misses her wheelchair had barely passed through the door. (And the chair ramp was at the back of the building, trademen's entrance, hard to find.) She was not in a mood to say "please."

"No problem deciphering the regular statements, I hope?" He played, virtuoso style, with a computer keyboard. She craned to see the screen. "Here. Statements sent monthly, in care of George C. Pryor—how is your dad, by the by?—37 Woodbine Crescent—"

"Show me."

He drooped his face at her, shrugged, and swiveled the monitor so they could both read. She struggled to make sense out of blinking digits and strings of letters. "There must be more." He scrolled down. Ruthie tapped the screen. "Right there—is that number the *total*?"

"Exactly!" As if she were a bit less retarded than he'd expected. "Nine hundred forty-four thousand, sixty-two dollars and seventy-five cents. Invested for your benefit for a current estimated annualized yield of, hm . . ." The keys clicked, the picture flashed and changed. "Yes. Almost eight percent. Now, in today's climate I would say these funds are doing *very,* very respectably! Of course there is no guarantee of future performance. And if—considering your personal circumstances, Miss Pryor?—you feel it would be prudent to restructure your portfolio—do you understand what I mean by 'portfolio'?—to a more risk-sheltered strategy than the one we originally designed, I would be more than happy to—"

"Go back." He did. The same number glowed, yellow on green. One point eight million less over nine hundred thousand equaled . . . almost a million. Almost. "That's not all I have. Can't be. Isn't there some other fund, or something, a trust—"

"That is the full sum of cash accounts, funds and instruments to your benefit. In your name, Miss Pryor." He leaned back and templed his fingers. A thick wedding band flashed.

"Who can make withdrawals?"

"Why, you, of course."

"No one else?"

"Certainly not. Not without your countersignature. Not even your own parents." He looked at her narrowly, as if reading her mind and not liking what he saw. "Of course, you may wish to *authorize* another signature. But everything's been set up quite properly here, all for your protection." He chewed his lower lip, then released it with a moist pop. "Perhaps you're thinking of *mental* incapacitation, where laws and banking regulations . . ."

Ruthie was only half listening. She was dimly recalling pages of blank yellow checks held up to her at breast level in the hospital for signing. There'd been her van, the golf cart, and the remodeled garage suite—a year's tuition—not a million dollars' worth, though, so where has it gone—

"I trust our chat has cleared up any little doubts you've been having? Is there anything else we can be of assistance with today?"

Ruthie stared at the glowing number on the screen. "What I tell you is strictly confidential, right? I mean, this is a gossipy town."

He smiled, puzzled. "Of course. Strictly confidential."

"I want you to sell them. For cash. All these instruments and bonds. Whatever."

"*Miss Pryor*. Given current market conditions—! No. No. Now—have you talked to your attorney yet? You must. I really most strongly advise that you seek your attorney's advice. If it's a major cash withdrawal you're considering, there are tax consequences I'm not qualified to—"

"Not a major withdrawal."

"Well then. Good heavens, forgive me. For a moment I misunderstood."

Ruthie leaned forward. "I want *all* of it. Today is Monday—by Thursday morning at the latest, I want all there is left. One check."

Ruthie, before and after. Since the accident, nothing in town looked, felt, or even tasted the same. Before, a free hour to stroll down Washington Street was a minor taken-for-granted pleasure—the remodeled shops sang out with harmonious displays of English sweaters and Italian boots, books, antiques, sports equipment, silk flowers, imported coffees and cheese. Even the traffic slowed for the song of abundance. It was a mostly female street: tanned, tailored proprietresses catered to smooth-coiffed young wives pushing baby carriages, and to college girls, and to Brahmin matriarchs who still had the knack of judging a fabric's quality by rubbing it between thumb and forefinger. In Ruthie's no-longer-reliable memory, the sun had always shone over Washington Street.

Today, she froze. The wind blew, the sky boiled with clouds. Maneuvering a wheelchair through pedestrians didn't warm her the way their brisk walking warmed them. She sat outside an ice-cream parlor, wondering what idiot impulse had driven her to buy the blueberry-cheesecake flavor-of-the-month cone. It tasted like kindergarten paste, but despite an ice-cream headache and stiff fingers Ruthie went on licking, slowly.

The idiot impulse had been . . . *celebration*. She had succeeded: all the bank manager's posturing, patronizing bluster crumpled against the strength of her intention. It had been—almost—easy. Inside the warm ice-cream parlor, where in childhood she had celebrated such milestones as new party shoes, dental checkups, and honors report cards, Ruthie had felt a rush of elation, an urge to smile at strangers. But then the waitress had stretched flat on the broad counter, so low that her little gold crucifix tinkled on the glass, to hand Ruthie her cone. And when the girl's pastel features squinched in a pantomime of sympathy, all Ruthie could do was scowl and pivot for the door.

She touched the puffy furrows between her eyes. Maybe this was the true source of her headache: the dull beat of unwanted anger forced on her from outside.

Someone paused behind her. A chirpy woman asked if she needed any help crossing the street. Ruthie clenched her teeth. "No!" Deep breath. "No, *thank* you."

She pitched the tasteless cone into a sewer grate. Good aim. Twin gobs of ice cream stuck on the grate like a fat white mouth. Ruthie thrust her chilled hands in her pants pockets, and met an object that her fingers, for a moment, couldn't identify. *Matchbook*. Her fingers closed on it, exploring, pressing the rough-soft curves of torn-off corners. These were the same pants she had worn that night at Seacrest Farm, when she and Erica and Lex found the sick horses. . . .

And the old one died—

Though she hadn't yet known that when she left the party and returned to her motel, to write a letter to Roland Pettit.

And until now, she had utterly forgotten the matchbook. Why had she saved it? Because it *reminded* her . . . Of finding one oddly like it, with the corners missing just so, somewhere before. And the old one died . . . Now she remembered when and where. Back in August, at the Haydenville show, the morning after Crimson Cadillac's leg injury. Matchbook, lying half buried in the dirt under the edge of the mare's stall door. Ruthie had called to Suzy to pick the thing up, an automatic precaution. Her attention then had been focused on the mare, who dozed in the slanting dawn light, bandaged and drugged, in her makeshift sling. Suzy DiSenza obediently handed over the matchbook, then returned to her vigil, sheet white and sweating. She climbed up and crouched on her tack box nearby. She didn't speak, hardly seemed to register Ruthie's presence. Ruthie remembered thinking that Suzy looked as badly off as her horse.

What had she done, then, with that first matchbook? Tossed it away, probably, safely outside . . .

"Well, hel-*lo*. No one told me you were back in town."

Ruthie jerked around. The voice was smooth and low. Ruthie's eyes met the speaker's blue-jeaned crotch. She looked quickly upward, to a softly stubbled chin and soft smile, flared commas of nostrils, crinkly hazel eyes. "Brett. Hi."

He squatted in one fluid motion down to her level. "You've got ice cream on your chin, Ruthie." Ruthie wiped it. "All gone. So how's things?"

"Fine, Brett."

"I see. Yeah. You *look* good." His tongue flicked across his upper lip, just the way it used to. "I heard you were in school. Skidmore?"

"Skinner. No." She stared up the street to where cars were jumping into infinity over the trestle bridge. "I quit." She said it for the first time. "It didn't make sense."

"No shit." He bounced, narrow buttocks on heels. "Know what you mean. I dropped too. Four years ago."

"Brett, I have to go. I'm really late." She kept her eyes on the bridge.

"You home with your folks? Listen, I'll *call* you."

"I'm leaving in a few days."

"For how long?"

"Long. Definitely long."

"Come *on*. Hey, Babe Ruth. Where's the fire?"

She shrugged.

"Well. None of my business, I guess. You know, I think about you. Honest to God. I really think you're—" His tongue flicked again, but the word wouldn't come, or he wouldn't say it. "You're all right, Babe Ruth. Hey, you know what I mean." He stood up. She glimpsed the tight jeans again, a thick black belt, motorcycle boots. "Take care of yourself."

"You too, Brett."

"No kidding."

When he was far enough away she could look straight at him again. His hunched rolling walk toward the bridge. She wasn't cold anymore. Wind tears warmed her eyes. Brett wasn't exactly a friend—simply a guy she used to know. A cool guy at school, a popular guy because he truly could dance. The one night Brett for some reason decided to dance with her, she'd let him slide his hand inside her blouse. *"Just checking your heart rate, Babe Ruth—"* She had never liked him.

"I need to know who did it. I have the *right* to know."

"Ruthie, darling, are you still so upset about your room? Now really, isn't that being a little rigid? I thought we settled . . ." Her mother cocked her head for a moment, listening into the phone she cradled in one hunched shoulder. She had exchanged the sequined sweats for a turquoise warm-up suit. She had been put on hold, Ruthie could tell.

"I don't mean my room. Stop acting like you've got amnesia."

"Darling, I am *on the phone*. Could I please finish this phone call? Please?"

"It was a man. Okay. Young or old? Does he have a wife? Kids? Does he live—anywhere near here? Have I *seen* him? I want to know now. It's the only way to get him out of my mind! Either you tell me—or Dad does—or if you won't, I'll go talk to Shumway—" This was the attorney who had handled her case. She did not want to talk to Shumway ever again. Even to speak his name was like twitching the curtain that covered bad memories. Very bad memories.

Slowly, blinking at Ruth, her mother hung up the phone. "Darling. When did you last make an appointment with your therapist?"

"Ah. *Ah—!*" Ruth gripped the wheels of her chair and half rose from it, then gave the wheels a push, and pivoted, and pushed again. She was chair-pacing. Her mother looked anxious. That was not what Ruth wanted. It occurred to her that fear often stemmed from guilt: that her mother might have some intuition of where she had just been and what she had discovered. But Ruth did not intend to confront either of her parents about the missing money. In her imagination she had already listened to the stream of excuses, apologies, and irrational counter-reproaches that would not bring her money back.

She wanted to leave very quietly, without disturbing them.

Ruth wheeled close to her mother. "Look. I'm not going to *do* anything. It's too late, I know that, I won't even go near him— Trust me. I just need to know who it was. It's as if, it's more like . . ." She stopped and smiled at her own thought. "Let me try an analogy. It's like the way adopted children need to know the identity of their real parents. You agree with that, surely?"

"Please, Ruthie. I hate when you take this artificial tone with me."

"Damn it! Damn it, Mom! I need to know who *made* me the way I am!"

Assabet, Massachusetts, September 12

THE AUSTERE SPLENDOR OF THE PLACE ALWAYS TOOK HER BY surprise. Not of *her* few acres, particularly, but Stoneacre Farm lay on an immense sweep of hillside that plunged down to a narrow bluish valley to touch its twin: the steeper wind-scoured ridge that rose like a magnified reflection on the other side. These old hills were sinking; their granite bones gleamed through the fur of hemlock and pine. Up here, strangely, the sky receded. Cloud shadows prowled across miles of forest like the silhouettes of animals. Year by year the holdout patches of fields and orchards shrank, their stone walls breached and swallowed by the resurgent forest.

Her second surprise, coming home, was how much work needed to be done. The farm was always, again and suddenly, on the verge of falling apart.

The morning was chilly, a mixture of sun and rainsqualls from a low pressure system stalled eastward, on the coast. Wind ironed the pale grass, the horses crow-hopped and jigged as she led them out. Moving in the rhythm of chores between barn and paddocks,

Erica stopped to drink coffee from a thermos balanced on a fence post. She gave the post an inquiring shove; it waggled in its socket of earth. If one post was loose they all were, and once the deep frost set in to buckle and shift the ground these fences would sag badly enough to snap the board nails free.

The night before, after driving in, she had registered only the ruddy streak of Farah, cannonballing toward her in lunatic canine ecstasy, and later the plate of warmed-up stir-fry that Roland, bustling and talking nonstop in his own version of euphoria, had set before her. Now she saw tiles on the barn roof lifting like a fringe of bangs in the wind. Downhill, the lower turnout paddock was a black pit of mud and floating rocks that only a new ditch could reclaim. The house itself—narrow, two-storied, with a zigzag metal woodstove pipe—was still covered with the leprous asphalt siding she had sworn to replace on the day she bought it. At least the house can wait. Most likely it always would.

A trio of gleaming Cherokees splashed up the unpaved drive toward the barn. Women clambered out, tailored and helmet-haired and waving, and as if she had expected them, Erica lifted her arm in laconic return. These were her "adult beginners," chronically jealous of their teacher's time away during competitions, for whom she felt a sort of hopeless protective affection. Why hadn't she remembered scheduling a lesson for today? What was happening to her *head*? Farah—the bitch she'd bought for a watchdog in the days of living alone—bounded off barking, plumed tail helicoptering welcome. Erica's grin faded as she glanced down at herself: baggy brown britches. The snagged wool sweater, saturated with smells of lanolin, liniment, and manure.

How the farm looked couldn't be helped for now. How the *house* looked didn't matter a damn. But how she and her animals appeared to the world was a different subject, it began with vanity and pride, of course, but went deeper, to a proof of discipline that transcends all the advantages of rank and resources and luck—perhaps especially luck—in or out of competition, it was a kind of *staring down*. . . .

"Oh, Erica, God, you're so tan, you look fabulous! We've missed you—"

"Hiya. Tell everyone to tack up?" She glanced at the woman's high-gloss boots. Custom boots, new wheels . . . But this lady, like most of them, squealed blue murder if the board bill went up five percent, and her check was always late. "And I think you better take those spurs off."

"Oh. They won't *help* me, a teeny bit?"

"Help a lot, if you plan to eat lunch in the next county. I've got a call to make—ten minutes? Meet you all in the ring."

She strode toward the house. Farah trotted ahead. With the insertion of this lesson, the day she had planned rearranged itself, tasks tumbling like the picture cards of a slot machine. Order feed. Consult vet. Double-confirm groom and transportation and braider commitments for regionals. *Pay* the bloody grooms. Ned and Mickie trailering in for jumping session. Scrub out her own trailer, even though she wouldn't need it at regionals, because urine rotted the floorboards—

The fencing, and the barn roof, absolutely had to be repaired before cold weather set in. But there was Roland now. Lean on Roland, a contractor for Chrissake, let him work out a solution—

She wasn't used to the free-fall sensation of leaving her jobs to somebody else.

Reschedule lessons, for the umpteenth time. What she needed was a clone, a clone who could *teach,* so the lesson income wouldn't be lost. But no way to pay a salary, until the business grew, and it would only grow because of reputation, and the only road to reputation was *the* road, leading to the finals, this year with Mickie and Ned, two genuine prospects more promising than she'd ever had before, though still some rough edges, but tougher and deeper-trained than plenty of the kids out there who maybe had two-hundred-thousand-dollar mounts and all the flash but no *spine.* And the incredible pressure of the finals worked like an X ray, even the most biased judge couldn't help seeing who still had spine—

"Stop." She spoke out loud. Farah, halfway up the porch steps, glanced back at her, panting. "It's just a pair of long shots. Crap-shoot. It's just a game."

And maybe down to one long shot. What the *hell* was wrong with Ned? Two days to the first round in New York. Forty-eight hours for him to pull out of whatever hormonal tailspin he'd locked into. Because that was the only explanation, she'd decided. Boys were no easier to focus than girls; right at the turning point, when all the work was starting to pay off, these teenyboppers went ballistic—maybe what she *really* needed to succeed was a degree in endocrinology—

Overhead, the clouds tore apart. Erica gripped the porch rail, facing west. She was completely distracted by the blue-gold chasm of the valley, and the spangled rush of the sky. Tiny horses pranced soundlessly inside fences that lay threaded like a cat's cradle on the hillside.

A few times, maybe three or four in her adult life, she'd had a certain dream: that she was driving on an unfamiliar road with a steep drop on one side, and as she rounded a corner the car's accelerator sank beneath her foot, stuck at full throttle. As the car sped faster all she could do was steer, until one belated reflex sent her crashing through trees over the road's edge, knowing this was the end. In those seconds before dream death, certainty blotted out fear. She felt a terrible howling regret for all the things left undone behind her, as leaves and branches whizzed by the falling coffin car, clacking on glass and metal—because this was a realistic dream in its detail. She saw never-answered letters and horses languishing forgotten in their locked stalls and friends she had let disappear, and her mother and father joined in a moment of warm easy laughter that other memories had sifted over till now. So she must love them in a way, had loved them after all—

And then, in the dream, she was lifted up again, with blue air streaming past her. The car was gone. She rode on a massive cloud white horse, bareback and bridleless, high over the depth of the precipice, up and out of sleep.

Farah whined at the house door.

"You hush. Someone's been spoiling you."

Of course there had been a real incident. That was why the dream kept returning. And six years ago, when she committed all of her "inheritance" to a down payment on Stoneacre Farm, she must have realized on some level that the lure of this place, her sense of *possibility,* was connected with the dream. But she hadn't *thought* about it. She had been fed up with traipsing around properties for sale, and even more fed up with the hassle and uncertainty of renting stalls for her students on other professionals' farms. Back then, thirty-something and parentless and childless, hooked on bute for the shooting pains in her joints (no insurance, too busy to bother with doctors), she was grappling with a secret phantom: herself, turned old. She trained and rode hard, she competed and won, and mirrors showed her a bold, still youthful face with only minor sun damage. But the apprehension of what she would necessarily *become* haunted her, it didn't let go. In time past she had worked hours each day to improve: to gain an edge in strength, balance, reflexive speed. Now all her effort would, at best and for a while, keep her the same. And though it was nearly impossible to imagine not-riding, her body was all she was: sinews and bones, eyes and heart and nerves. When her body could no longer take the pounding—what then?

It was her father's money. She almost wished her father alive again, to applaud her plan: buy a run-down farm and build it into a showcase—something a romantic city family would eventually pay a bundle for, as the city crawled outward. *Plus, the land's subdividable,* the agent had said, addressing the devil in Erica's mind. *You wouldn't believe the smart money that's rolling in here. Invest and hold, time flies, well look at me still slogging in the traces, but of course I love my work. . . . Honey, can you guess how old I am?*

So the arguments in favor of buying Stoneacre had been overwhelming. No need to brood about what it might mean to move to a place that every day would offer the dispassionate glaring light and plunging slope of her dream.

Down below, stick figure students coaxed horses into the exercise ring.

She kicked open the house door, which always stuck. Farah

bolted in, tail slamming the tight-wedged furniture, hers and Roland's.

"Roland?" She hadn't noticed whether his truck was parked in back.

Silence, except for the cackle of TV from the kitchen. She went there, shucking off the sweater, grabbing her ratcatcher jacket from the back of a chair that was piled with bridles and martingales waiting for cleaning.

The kitchen woodstove, in a halo of spilled ashes and bark chips, radiated sauna heat. She tripped on a dirty cat saucer that frisbeed off the fridge. More unwashed dishes filled the sink and counter and formed an overflow turret on top of the TV. The table was spread with yesterday's newspaper, open to help wanted pages circled by random coffee mug rings.

Erica killed the TV and sank on Roland's chair; her elbows crumpled the paper. The ache in her hips asserted itself, but inertia kept her from getting up to take a bute. "X-Windows Xperts wanted . . . Peripheral sales to 60 K . . . Oracle wizards wanted, the sky's the limit . . . " Coffee mug stains. How did he feel, reading this mumbo jumbo week after week? Farah flopped against her possessively. The newsprint wavered, hazy ballooning letters. September 11— Today's the twelfth, she thought. This day has barely begun. It's too early to want to run away. . . .

Roland was most real in his absence. His brown plaid shirt hooked on the back door. His gaping toolbox in the corner, this warmed chair . . . He surrounded her now. A mix of tenderness and regret and desperation welled up inside her. If he were *here,* reduced to himself, she could more easily look away from him.

Next to the TV was her answering machine. The red light winked. She pressed MESSAGE, and caught the brief departing skid of a hang-up call.

Should she try to reach Lex now? Later, there might not be another chance.

She waited for a wash of guilt to pass. Her hands were still cold, swollen tight around the wedding ring, but under the jacket she was sweating. Here in the house her guilt was like a low-grade nausea, a background unwellness she could more or less tolerate. Guilt wasn't exactly the right word but close enough: she felt disguised in her own skin, a guest plotting a crime in this unlocked house.

And at the same time, once she was home, part of her ceased to believe in Lex. Nothing had changed here, she didn't want it to, she was *safe,* there was no space for an idea like Lex in the geography of her life. Who was he? How could anyone make her feel what she thought she remembered feeling?

On the drive home, she couldn't stop remembering. Flash images of Lex had erased the road in front of her. His smile—why did one person's smile matter so much? She'd seen the long wing of his bare shoulder and the arrow of fine hair above his full erection. And then their narrow pelvises joined, rocking the cot by the edge of the sea. Driving, reliving her surrender, she had felt her belly melt and tighten—it was almost a faint, a blackout. Only pictures in her mind, but at sixty-five miles per hour they could have killed her.

She started to punch the carefully memorized Charlestown number. A shadow spread over the back door window. Farah, claws scrabbling linoleum, leapt up with a yip.

"Well hey. Roland."

"Well, *hey.* Go on, you finish your call! So how're my two beautiful girls?"

He elbowed the door shut behind a crisp gust of air and simply stood there. Farah rammed his thigh with a dog hug, but his vague soft smile was for Erica. She forgot, always, how dense and how broad he was; he took up a quarter of any room. She could see where he'd been: a fresh newspaper rolled under his arm, along with the mail, in a heavy rubber band.

"Is that today's mail?" Dumb question.

He plopped the mail packet on the table and then stayed, propped on his knuckles. "You don't know how good it is," he said. "It's so *right.* All the mornings I walk in here praying for a miracle. For you to be sitting right like you are." He blinked.

One of the envelopes in the sheaf was postmarked Marion, Mass. Erica frowned. She thought she had settled all the bills and fees from Seacrest before she left.

Roland kissed her forehead. His lips were dry as wood. "Sweetheart. You know you got students waiting in the ring?"

"Um. Doing what?"

"Tiptoeing mincy circles. Looking petrified, like any minute a bomb's going to go off under their asses."

He made her smile. Did he know that there was only this one full day? Had she made clear last night that she was leaving tomorrow, or did his disappointment still lie ahead? "I'm sure not being very responsible, am I?"

"Featherbedder." He leaned close again. She shut her eyes before the wood-kiss pressed against her mouth. She smelled coffee and eggs, a sour oiliness. "Speaking of which," he said. "Tonight we turn in early, huh? I'm just *so-o* tired. Something tells me you are, too. All that driving. . . ."

Erica didn't breathe.

His tongue was chilly from outdoors. It probed her lips, and then her ear. Licking, in and out. "Mm . . . Don't let me keep you from duty, now. Guess you better get a move on."

LIKE THE PEALING OF BELLS IN A CATHEDRAL, THE EXTRAVAGANCE of sunrise and sunset over the valley made her drop whatever she was doing and turn to the sky, too limited by her senses to take it all in. Beginning and end seemed reversed: at dawn Stoneacre's slope lay in semidarkness, hoar and mist, while the western ridge ignited to fiery rose and green-gold. Evenings (they fell quickly now in September, as if the valley itself were contracting with the approach of winter) the far ridge flattened to a jagged black gash beneath the fantastic racing colors of the sky, and the wind vanished, and her own fields glowed with a transparent warmth. No matter how fractious the horses might have been all day, at sunset they quieted, grazing slowly or daydreaming wherever they stood.

"Erica? You want me to jump that again?"

"What? No . . . don't. Drop your reins. He's blowing. Let him walk a minute."

As the Monster ambled by, she studied Ned. Even the peach reflection of sunset didn't improve his pallor much. He wasn't sassing her today, on the contrary—he was almost pathetically polite, swallowing criticism, apologizing for every rail he knocked down. But he wasn't *right*. Her adults in the morning lesson had done better at finding the jumps.

At least Mickie had schooled well. After half an hour Erica told her, *Nothing to fix. See you in New York. Is there one good reason you can't ride that clean with a number on your back?*

Now she and Ned watched the loaded Travnicek trailer bump uphill and curve south on the road out to the highway.

Ned said, "Permission to take the oxer to the in-and-out again? I know what I did wrong before."

"Permission to take . . ." Even his sense of humor was uptight. Private school, she presumed, was to blame. Ned went to an all-male academy where the students dressed up as junior naval officers; it was not, she gathered, a haven for the best and the brightest. But bill-paying parents there could set their own priorities, and when released to the custody of his mother—now sitting in her truck at ringside, as if judging the lesson—Ned cut out, absent with leave, to ride.

Taking Erica's silence for assent, he had picked up a trot along the rail. Monster dragged his huge hooves, hypnotized by sunset. Ned's shirttail billowed loose. His bony boy wrists jutted raw and red; he had forgotten his gloves. He didn't know what a disorganized, vulnerable picture he made. He looked almost happy— and for the moment, determined. Why did she have to be so hard on him?

Because somewhere in Ned, from the beginning, she'd seen the unformed talent. A genuine chance to win. Long hard road, with no shortcuts. Does he want to win? she wondered. Want it bad enough? Am I helping this kid or am I using him?

He rolled back to the small crossrail before the oxer. Half-asleep, gravity-bound, the Monster missed. His lazy hooves sent both hundred-pound rails spinning.

"Pull up! Ned! *Leave out* the next jump!"

Most accidents happen in the schooling ring. All crashes are slow motion. You run toward the horse that is flailing, trapped inside the twin poles of the oxer jump, and the rider whose smooth trajectory high overhead is ending in slow motion. A rain puddle shatters to spray as he hits the earth.

The Monster plunged and twisted above ground, his chest suspended across a creaking four-foot-high pole. Ned scrambled to his feet. Moving crabwise, approaching his horse with one hand outstretched for the dangling rein.

"Back *off,* Ned. Don't be a jerk hero! Stay *away* from him—"

Under a ton of live weight the pole cracked. Rifle blast. From only three feet away Ned watched with enormous eyes as the Monster seemed to crumple to the ground, then shot straight up, to clear the second pole of the oxer, and galloped, bucking and squealing and farting, stirrups and broken reins flying, to the far end of the ring.

"Wait." Erica grabbed Ned's muddy sleeve. "He's all right. Your horse is all right." She wasn't sure. "I want to look at you first."

"Not a scratch, Erica. . . . Maybe one scratch but Jesus Christ, it's not like I never got dumped before. . . ."

"Don't swear. Hold still."

She ran through the tests. Range of motion. Reflexes. Neck, shoulders, lower back. As her hands moved over him she found only minor scuffs on his jaw and one elbow. And blood blossoming through his shirt, where the last rib met the spine . . .

"Breathe deep. Good. Can you walk?"

"Can I—? Sure." He stepped out, wobbly and confident. Short term, the adrenaline produced by a fall is better than morphine.

"Now, wave to your mother, so she can see you're okay." And they both turned, waving, smiling broadly as politicians, to the woman who had descended from her truck. Impassive in her pyramid of flesh, Helen Urbach leaned on the fence she could neither run around, climb over, nor crawl through.

Ned was weeping.

In the wash stall, the barn's only source of hot water, he sat slumped on an oak bench. Erica's first aid box lay open on the floor between his stockinged feet. Helen Urbach, after a quick head-shaking glance at the stall's tight dimensions, had returned to the warmth of her truck, but Erica had heard her parting thought as clearly as if it were radioed: *This won't boost his confidence much, will it?* Safe to bet Ned had heard it, too.

The Monster, untacked, rubbed and checked over for major damage, stood steaming in a stall farther down the aisle, munching hay.

She had sponged Ned's jaw and slathered it with rust orange Betadine, but the other side of his face remained dirt streaked. He looked like a clown in fright makeup. He didn't wipe away the single tears cutting deltas down his cheeks. Perhaps he wasn't even aware of them, like certain grown men when they cry.

"Your Monster's fine," she said. "Knucklehead Krauts don't bang up easy."

He nodded. His lower lip vibrated when he tried to smile.

"Time to have a look at your back. Stand up, now. Off with that shirt."

He glanced at her, then looked away. She had no idea what his black eyes were seeing.

She hunkered on the floor in front of the boy, studying his face. He'd been a baby of eleven when he came to her. Two years from now he'd be entering college—and from then on she would never see him again. That's how it was with the kids, she reflected. Teaching them to ride meant teaching other things from scratch: self-discipline and self-forgiveness, patience, the unnegotiable re-sponsibility of human to animal, how to win without apology and take losses in stride. They brought their dolls and puppies for you to mend or name. You traveled with them, and nights when the motels were booked full, laid them to sleep in the hay of the trailer. You tried hard not to admit the fact that many of them trusted you more than their own parents. But after all, you knew their *bodies*— the angle of hip, sinuosity of spine, which was the inevitably weaker side and which the strong. You watched a pudgy baby face lengthen and hollow. One day like any other, with no more fuss than a swift hug and honestly meant "I'll come back to visit, next summer," that face would disappear.

"Want to talk about it, Ned?"

"About what?"

"Whatever. Whatever's got you so stressed out."

His shirt tightened across his chest. Deep breath. He pressed his hand to his jaw and then discovered the wetness of tears. "*Shit.* I'm going to make a frigging mess of regionals, aren't I?"

"Don't swear. We'll see. Maybe you won't even ride." Harsh threat, intended to rouse an argument.

He stared at her and merely nodded.

Crouching on the damp floor was uncomfortable. For balance, she rested her arms on Ned's long thighs. "Trouble at home?"

"I don't know. Ah, there's always trouble. 'Sell the farm, keep the farm.' Dad wants to sell it. He can't, though, without her signing. He throws his weight around but Seacrest is from her family. Mom wants to keep it when she's sober but sell it when she's drunk. Dad's got a girlfriend—you probably know already, who doesn't—which I could care less about except it's a great excuse for Mom to get drunk more often." He pressed a hand against the dirty, uncut side of his face and examined the result. "Know what I am? A totally lousy student, that's one thing. Not such a great rider, either. But at least this way I'm learning the animals. Since I was little I've had this picture, that when I grew up I'd really take care of the farm, you know, work it, make it pay for itself, I mean it's not just a pipe dream, I've got a lot of ideas—" He leaned forward, voice diving to a whisper. "If they *do* sell it— I don't see what there'll be left to care about. For me, nothing. There wouldn't be any point *left* to . . . being *me*. You know what I mean?"

"Damn it. Ned, that is a really stupid, exaggerated, irrational—" She understood completely. "Now, you listen to me a minute. . . ." She made a move to stand, but he grabbed her arms with surprisingly strong hands.

"Don't worry. Right now the farm's not even the main thing. All that garbage has been going on for ages."

"What then?"

"Something that just happened. Last week, at home, that night, same night as my folks' party and when— Anyway, there was this guy, he tried, he—" Ned swallowed hard. "No. I can't."

"Okay." She patted his knee, trying to ignore the cramp of crouching. "Wasn't a very good night all around, was it? You don't have to tell what you don't want to, Ned. Christ. Your age—hey. I wish I had a buck for every night I wanted to forget."

"But I have to ask you something. Right now. Can I?" His grip shifted, higher up her arms. He leaned closer, so close that the garish streaks faded and all she saw were the clear glittering young eyes.

"Ned, it's time for you to—" Her mouth was caught slightly open as he kissed her. Hadn't she understood, the second before, that he would do this? But not believed. His lips were satin smooth and warm. She caught a bracing tang of Betadine, felt the moth-wing brush of the boy's never-shaven trace of mustache as he probed harder, pressing his question. She allowed the asking. She was torn between laughter and crying for him. For the moment, it didn't feel wrong.

They both sat on the floor, side by side, backs against the cement wall.

"If you ever do that again—or anything *like*—I'll clock the living daylights out of you, Ned. I mean it. Crazy or not, get that much through your head."

"I'm really sorry, Erica."

"Sorry? *Sorry*'s about as useful as wet Kleenex in a tornado."

They were on the floor because in the force and bewilderment of the kiss, Erica had lost her balance. Ned, grappling to save her, also tumbled, with an agile aerial roll so as not to crush her. Unforeseen benefit of lessons in how to fall.

The damp from the floor seeped into her britches. At least she could stretch her legs full length.

"I want to tell you the story," he said.

"Maybe we should—" A horse whickered, then another. Past feeding time. The bare-bulb light of the washstall showed a high flush on Ned's cheeks, the first color there in weeks. She bent forward, to knead her calves. "Maybe you'd better."

"It was, like, before the party started. I went to the barn. I was in sort of a rotten mood—"

"Rotten mood? *You?*"

He flashed her a look, stern and impatient. A glimpse of Ned as an adult. "This isn't *easy*. Okay? Anyway . . . There'd been this fight, while I was helping them set up the tables. About Seacrest. Dad—*I* basically think his girlfriend—sussed out this developer who says he'll draw up all the plans for condos and not charge anything until they get approved by the town and stuff. Mom said the guy's a sleaze by definition and anyway Conservation won't ever okay that dense a subdivision and the land's really hers to do as she sees fit including burning it down if she feels so inclined. Then she latched on to me and said to Dad, You're a bully always making Ned feel so insecure, at least everything stays like it is until he's done with juniors and this year's and next year's finals are over."

"That's a step," said Erica. The story both bored and depressed her. She thought of the Urbachs' farm as a huge creature, radiantly alive but vulnerable to the whims, jealousy, and greed of humans.

"Mom said, Go get dressed. So I cut out. I went to the barn. I wanted to talk to Monster, make sure he wasn't cold after the swimming."

Erica said automatically, "You probably should have walked him more."

"There was only this one guy in the barn. One of the Hispanics who work for Mr. Healey."

"Tino?" Erica straightened.

"I wouldn't know. . . . Looks like an Indian sort of? *Tino?* Kind of short, he's not a *big* guy—" For some reason Ned covered his face with his hands, then flung them down again. "He was feeding. Well, the wheelbarrow was out in the aisle, with all the buckets filled for the different horses, you know. I said, That's not your job, or, Is that your job?—something like that—and he gave me this funny look and I felt like I was being a bossy jerk. So I started helping. Partly to make sure our horses at least all got the right stuff. This guy—Tino—clapped me on the back and called me his amigo. He was all smiles. He doesn't speak much English, so I was trying out my school-Spanish on him. I guess I felt . . . cool."

"Then?"

"Okay. He had some coke. Powder. You know. He had a ton of it, in this Ziploc baggie. Kids at school brag that they snort when they get out on weekends, but I never did."

"So did you?"

"He showed me how. We were just standing there, in the open aisle, with the horses nickering that hadn't been fed yet. Then I hardly heard them anymore. It was—*incredible.* You ever do that stuff? It's like when you come off the last jump *knowing* you just put down the trip of your life. I told him I was going to win, next day. I was speaking Spanish like I'd swallowed a Spanish dictionary. Then—I don't know how—he had his arm around my waist, hard, and he was . . . he was kissing me—but for a minute I really thought this was like they do, in Latin countries—then I pushed him and some of the stuff from the baggie spilled, and I thought he was going to freak but instead he started laughing, pinching the coke off the floor and tossing it into feed cans. 'Make your horses want to jump to heaven,' he said. I said, 'Stop it, that might be bad for them.' Then he put the baggie down real carefully, and he grabbed me. Real fast. He grabbed me—*there.* It hurt. God, it hurt. I couldn't move. He had a knife in his free hand. A blacksmithing knife. He said, 'Make you a nice quiet gelding, boy, easy.' And I,

I—then he let go a moment. It was like he thought he heard some-one coming. He let go. I ran."

"Oh, Ned." She wanted to reach out and surround him with her arms. She didn't move.

"It wasn't very late. It was still light out. I ran out the back, into the woods where it was dark—and I kept on running. Don't know how long."

"Ned, are you all right?"

He looked at his hands, which were shaking. "*Am* I all right?"

"*Yes.* You are. Believe me, kiddo." She willed him to turn to her. Her sense of lateness, in the gray cell of the wash stall, had pro-gressed to timelessness. Where was Helen Urbach . . . dozed off in her truck? Why hadn't Roland shown up yet, to help with evening chores? She watched Ned trace figures and lines with his finger on the cement floor: the pattern of an invisible jump course.

"Erica? When I ran I completely forgot about the horses. For-got the stuff in their feed and how—dangerous it was. I didn't come back for hours. By then I was too late. . . ."

It was after nine by the time she dragged up to the unlit house, picking her way by star shine. Dizzy, as if she'd missed a night's sleep. So that's what happened, was all she could think. That's how it happened. Tino, the little shit. He was high, whacked out. . . . He probably didn't even realize what he was doing to the horses. Probably thought he was giving them a treat. That's how it happened, and that's why the old hunter died, but I can't tell anyone without betraying Ned—

As she reached the front door Roland's truck clattered up be-hind her, and as she flicked the lights in the kitchen he came in through the back, meeting her. Farah torpedoed him. He pushed the dog down gently and began unpacking white cartons from the grocery bag in his arm.

"I got Chinese."

"Great. I'm ready to eat dog kibble. Starved."

She sat with a sigh. Unlaced her boots. The message button on her machine was blinking again, but she didn't press it. Not with Roland right there. He slid the new and old newspapers away and trashed them. The mail had already disappeared, and she thought with a spark of gratitude that this meant he would take care of the paperwork for her this month. They were still working out the homely details of who did what task—still working it out, she thought, in a marriage that had already almost stopped breathing. She watched him crease two pieces of paper towel for napkins, and set two plates on the table.

She said, "You're quiet."

"Don't mean to be." He put her favorite Sam Adams beer and the opened boxes with spoons stuck in them on the table and pulled up a chair and began serving her plate. He slipped a curl of pork to Farah.

"Roland, *don't* teach her that. Honestly . . ." She stuffed in food and swallowed. Hunger sometimes took her this way. "Is something wrong? Where were you so late?"

"What should be wrong? Actually . . ." He dumped enough soy sauce over his rice to make a black pond of the plate. "Actually, I stopped by to see a guy in town about fixing some of the fences. You know how it is. Guys get talking."

"The fence? Gee, Roland. Oh, that would be *great*. He can do it?"

The warmth of food, and her expanding sense of safety. A gift only Roland had ever brought her. His hand squeezing hers for a moment, his stubby dirt-creased thumb stroking. Anchor, holding her down to the ground.

She reported Ned's crash. Described Helen sawing wood in her truck under a lapload of *Town and Country* magazines. Some mother. Hope they make it home all right. Hope Ned's not bruised too stiff to ride come Saturday.

It was like old times, retelling the day. And you never did tell everything, else there'd be no end, no story. She only wanted to see him laugh.

Roland tilted the beer can up and drank, eyes slitted. "If your boy's too banged up to ride, that makes you a member of the bad luck club, doesn't it? Least they can't harass you anymore. For escaping the whammy."

Had she told him so much, about the other trainers, her sense of isolation? Maybe she hadn't. Part of the link between her and Roland came from his anticipating her, knowing her in some ways better than she knew herself—

It was why he had been able to save her life, when she was only sixteen. She'd taken her father's car. Middle of a July day. Never drove before. Turned the stolen key, ground the gears till one lurched into place and the car shot forward over a curb—many curbs—amazingly heavy and rough to steer, her heart pounding and hand pounding the gear shift. One stall-out with horns blaring outrage but then she got the thing going again, up to third, way too fast almost flying one street another no idea where she was going, part knowing the crash coming, rehearsing it for calmness the way you rehearse a challenging jump, approaching a house under construction where the carpenter stood on the sidewalk as if on watch waiting for her, older guy from the neighborhood her mother said had no business *snuffling* after a youngster like Erica *it's sick behavior*—she waved at the carpenter, steering one-handed, showing off, foot raised from the accelerator but the car didn't slow down he sprinted closer ran pumping alongside then tore open the passenger door the car swooped and shimmied when he crushed against her grabbing the wheel. His work boots scraped down her shins, to finally hit the brake.

She was sixteen. She stood free in the sun, finger-swiping her bangs off her forehead. Nothing had happened. You didn't have to do that, she said.

I won't ever let you hurt yourself. Understand?

"So where are you?" asked Roland.

"Huh?"

"*You.* You're a million miles away."

"Oh. Know what?" She laughed. "I was remembering you teaching me to drive. . . ."

"Yeah. You learned good. So when's the next grand departure?"

"Tomorrow. I told you. I need time there, to set up and let the horses settle in."

He crackled the empty beer can, grimacing at the sound. "I could help. I could come with. Me and Farah both! How would that strike you?"

Panic. Don't let him look into your eyes. Control it. Find a voice. "Great. I mean it. Only, isn't it late to find someone for here, and I'll be busy every minute, I don't think you'd really want—"

"Okay. It is too late. Real dumb idea."

She flinched as the bent beer can snapped loudly in his hand. It wasn't fair for him to frighten her. Or to make her pity him. "Whatever's wrong, Roland, will you please just come out and *say* it, don't make me guess—"

"Tomorrow's soon. That's all."

He's lying.

What right did she have to think so? Or did she have to begin to mistrust him, because she had lost her own compass about lies? Deceiving him over and over, reflexively, snipping the lines of promises assumed and unspoken. The one you choose to lie to becomes less and less real, less credible, because his beliefs are based on nothing—based on your lies. It's a way of destroying someone, in your mind.

"Sweetheart? *Hey,* you come on now." The pity in his voice shocked her, and then he was standing, righting the chair that almost fell, folding his arms around her from behind. The pressure of his head against her bowed head, his low voice filling her ear. "Look at Farah. Silly dog's all upset over you!" His arms tightened. "Sweetheart. You and me, we'll be fine. We are going to be all right. One way or the other. Believe me."

She nodded. She suddenly saw Ned, his slack flushed expression after she returned the kiss. So hard to console someone, so hard to be consoled.

Roland murmured, "Long day. Let's get you some rest. I'll clean up this mess in here tomorrow."

SHE FOUND MORE DRUG SONGS ON THE RADIO THAN LOVE SONGS. Especially on the jammed-up stretch through Hartford, where even lane-hopping without the drag of a trailer she couldn't push the Bronco over a steady fifty-five. She punched twice through the station buttons, switched off the radio, then rolled down the window to let in a crescendo of traffic and damp city wind.

You ever do that stuff?

No. Never inhaled. Not a morality thing—live and let snort, or shoot, or whatever does it for you. No lack of opportunity; plenty who take advantage. Ranger? Coco Beale, for sure, had earned her nickname. For the jump riders a natural temptation. Point of view: every workday you're giving your horses a chemical cocktail, legal and illegal—Acepromazine to wipe out nerves, say, bute and Banamine to block out pain. The vet's your buddy, writes you what's needed, whether for your critters or yourself, you're handier than hell with the needles, the whole arsenal, and your animals perform. So what's the difference?

Step up. Matter of increments, erasing barriers. The gradual progression reminded her of hunting—little kids BB-gun fat robins and squirrels, big boys move up to rifles and deer, and next there's some middle-aged card-carrying NRA guy with a homeowner's shotgun blasting his family to eternity from the back porch.

Not all hunters, of course. Her father and his cronies had stuck with deer.

Drugs. Can't knock the jump riders, doing what you haven't had the guts for since you were sixteen. Entering the ring on an animal that's already half crazed by what it sees coming. Crowd pressed against the rails, tiny sober figure of the judge. Forest of crayon-colored obstacles up to six feet wide, five feet high, too high to see beyond so it's all on faith, on the staccato rhythm of the canter and your *eye,* that split-second moment of finding the magic distance, the one point of takeoff from which your horse can fly clear, *flee*—then his jolted gasp on landing and drumbeat stride to the next hurdle—

It's the flight instinct. The exhilaration of escape.

Lose the rhythm, over a course that high, and it's over. No second chance. Pull up or crash. Think about a ton of somersaulting flesh, rump over shoulder.

Not that anyone out there does think about it. No space for physical fear—otherwise, you'd stay home, shell peas or walk the dog, get a normal life.

She knew exactly what had cost her the rhythm that day when she was sixteen: the watchers. Judge, parents, trainer, and her peers, some of them jealous as hell. All incredulous that grubby little local Erica Hablicht who couldn't afford a single trip to the finals was leapfrogging the system here, riding jumper division today and *winning:* carrying a four-and-a-half-point lead now into the final round. The timed jump-off round.

Descending off the first good fence, she'd felt the pressure rush in on her. No room to gallop, or even breathe. The watchers held silent, tense and knowing. For the first time she was stripped of the spell of the rhythm, trapped naked in the ring, with no music. Spurring to where the next jump should be she saw a hundred different distances, and none. Her overwhelming memory of those last seconds was the black hole of failure. Of shame.

She never decided to pull up. It was pure reflex, despair, so late and so sudden that the horse continued forward, skidding on sleigh-runner hooves into a cardboard brick wall.

Not that the crowd cared much. After the collective gasp for Erica they drifted, having other rings to watch, other riders to root for or against. And the consequences afterward—her father without warning dropping the lease on that horse, so that when she returned to the barn the stall lay stripped and empty—might have happened anyway. *I've supported this silliness too long, young lady. It's gotten way out of hand. . . .* Deadened with anger as she was, she might have stolen his car anyway.

She had a hang-up about jumper competition, that was all. Too many eyes on your course, too much at stake. Never went back. Though maybe a timely dose of chemical courage would have helped her. Maybe it could still.

To trust in that shortcut was tempting: it took a different kind of courage.

Get it? That's why you're worried about Ned.

Ned was like her. Control freak, she called him, and one reason their partnership worked was that his weaknesses echoed hers. Out on course, she could read his mind: before the visible false move came the sudden wrench of ambition, the belief that *this* time, he could force it by sheer will.

You can never force it.

From now on, she meant to keep a closer eye on Ned.

When she focused, the scenery was unfamiliar. Arched yellowing oaks, a humped two-lane road. In the rearview mirror, the white gates of Old Salem Farm winked from half a mile back. Erica swore happily, hit the brakes and swung a U-turn. On the grounds ahead now riders were training, and long aluminum trailers dazzled in the sun, bright as a gypsy camp. She started singing the last dumb thumping song from the radio—

> *You can't always get what you wa-ant,*
> *you can't always get what you wa-ant,*
> *but if you try sometimes—*

This was her real homecoming, after all.

Old Salem, New York, September 14

JESUS PUSHED THE SILVER BUTT OF A RIDING CROP DEEP INSIDE HIS paddock boot to scratch his left arch. "So," he said. "This Mr. Whistler—"

"Whitaker."

"Sure thing. He wants you to come out and play his cops-and-robbers game. He don't like the way that nice Crimson mare died."

"He doesn't buy it."

"Eh. Me neither." As Jesus zeroed in on the itch, his look of introspection intensified. He and Lex sat on sparse grass, shaded by an eighteen-wheeler with Ocala County plates. Despite a moldering odor of early fall, the air was so warm that Jesus had shucked his shirt; he wore it tied around his waist, the sleeves knotted in a limp embrace. "Only, Alejandro, you told him where he can go, right? I mean, that's some joke. The man's problem is his business, correct? You got your own business, and you don't get no risk premium bonus pay neither. Be a joke, for you to get messed up with those guys. For what? He think you're some kind of fool?"

"What guys?"

Jesus puckered his lip. Then he glanced up abruptly toward the stabling tent, where a clean-shaven young Mexican stood under the canvas flap holding a clipboard. The boy made a finger-and-thumb okay sign, Jesus nodded approval, the boy ducked back inside. To replace Tino, Jesus had hired two new workers, who split the wage. Despite the recent addition of twenty new equine wards, HorseGuard was humming along with the efficiency of a Honda factory, and Lex felt it would be churlish to ask much about where their eager and competent new recruits came from.

"What *guys*?" Lex repeated.

"Eh." Jesus twirled the riding crop one-handed, thumb to pinkie and back again, with the skill of a Dallas schoolgirl. "Whoever, right? What I mean, it is not personal. It is the law of supply and demand. These days, there's way too many horses—and always a big demand for cash. Owners going broke, *but*—they got to still look rich, save face. Now plus, maybe nobody gets a kick from killing horses—or maybe somebody does, you know? But anybody can do this quick-death job—you, me, anybody—it is simple. That is what you call no barriers to entry." Jesus shifted the baton crop to his left hand, which worked more slowly. "Now, plus, what is the bad news? What is the downside? Tommy Burns, for example. He is now home in his house in Chicago, on bail pending trial. If convicted, Tommy gets probably eighteen months. *Only*. For me that looks very bad, that is deportation; for you it is maybe bad, I don't know—that is what you call a subjective disutility position. I think. Plus you have working here the price umbrella. By this you mean, Tommy got paid maybe five, ten, even twenty grand for an animal, and you know everywhere people every day kill other human people for very much less, so there is what you call a big margin, an opportunity incentive—"

"Jesus. How the hell do you know all this?"

"Reading, Alejandro. Not only Samuelson, neither."

"No—I meant about Tommy Burns."

"Reading. Newspapers, Alejandro. It's a magnificent library system in the United States of America, in every little town—"

"You're saying you don't believe Tommy Burns worked on his own?"

"Eh, no man. He maybe preferred to. It's not the point. See, there's plenty of folks—maybe working a job like we do, you know? Who are easy to be tempted. And so many, many ways to make a horse be dead. Mr. Tommy Burns, he's not even so smart, first he tried to suffocate with a big plastic bag. Alejandro, you ever try to hold a garbage bag on, over a horse's head? So later he went to the electrical method, better. But there are many other ways for accidents to happen, no? For example, you can overwork in heat like here today and then not cool the horse off properly, so he cramps all over, even the heart muscle. Simple? Plus there's all the poison weeds, like yew, locoweed, fescue mold, that might come from bad hay. Who is to say? A horse cannot—what do you call it? He cannot vomit."

"You make this whole world sound like a loony bin. A lottery in a slaughterhouse . . ." Along the trampled path between tents, juniors were leading their mounts toward the indoor arena. The big well-fed horses' coats gleamed from a last-minute brushing with silicone. Sun winked off bits and spurs. Although the riders walked with bowed heads, as if the course to come were inscribed on the ground, their high boots strode nearly in tandem. Black velvet caps. Tight tailored jackets. Lex saw an elite child calvalry, from an earlier century. Black gloves holding the looped reins just so. Too many horses these days.

Jesus' smile crinkled. "Such pretty girls."

"Did you *know* Burns?"

"No. Never exactly." He opened his hand, the baton fell.

"Do you know *anything* you haven't mentioned? About what happened to Crimson Cadillac?"

"Alejandro, I was sleeping, remember? Pino had the watch. He hears the noises, comes into that aisle, he finds the mare kicking the devil out of the place, like she been bit by a tiger—"

"He didn't see anyone else around? Who had the watch before him? You?"

"No. That watch . . ." Jesus looked straight at Lex, frank and reflective now. "I remember, sure. Was Tino."

"*Shit.*" A passing girl turned in surprise. She had pinpoint pupils, dazed eyes. Lex waved an apology. To Jesus he hissed, "So what are you *thinking*?"

"*Nada.* Forget it, is all I think."

"Listen. Explain one thing to me. You've been working the shows how long? Ten years?"

Jesus shrugged. Not telling.

"So how can you stand it? You're a very smart guy, you could do some other work. . . ." Lex paused, wondering and not for the first time why Jesus had never made it to a green card. Again: not telling. "You care a lot about these damn horses, hell, anybody can see that from the way you handle them, so how can you stand seeing this stuff happen, or knowing what you say you know—"

"Listen." Jesus picked up the crop and tapped it for emphasis on Lex's sneakered foot. "*You* listen, Alejandro. You look at those nice animals." The last muscular round rumps were descending the slope to the arena. "Even now, hard times, they got a good life. The world they live—it's a very good place! They got grain three meals a day and soft wraps and sweet, clean stalls. They feel so safe and sure—hey, that is why they can win, right? Where I come from, even the children don't know how to dream of such a happy time. You understand this?"

Lex pictured Bungee, teetering cat style on the fence. Though irritated by the tapping of the crop, he nodded.

"So. Don't say I have no dirty job, Alejandro. Me, I rather shovel horse manure than do somebody's *dirty* job."

"Okay. Maybe. But just now, you were talking about the danger—"

"Danger to *me*? What, I get a nip, maybe my foot stepped on?" Jesus poked Lex's sole, hard, and laughed. "No, man. No. All I try to explain is: there is not very much risk here, if some folks want to kill horses. For us, we have a quiet job to *care* for the horses. We write down what they eat, when they sleep, who has a little tummy

ache. The danger is, a person steps out. A person interferes. He
will be caught—" Jesus flipped the crop high in the air, where for
seconds it hovered spinning, the silver butt tracing a circle of light
"—be caught dead in the middle."

The Rolex/Maclay Northeast Regional was a different kind of
horse show. It didn't feel like a show at all. There were no strolling,
day-tripping spectators, only grim parents and purposeful professionals—the "connections." There were no chatty vendors hawk-
ing logoed mugs and sweatshirts, slush cones and patented training
gimmicks. Leaning on the fence of the warm-up ring, Lex watched
the contenders tick back and forth over practice jumps, their silent
concentration underlined by the occasional bark of a trainer and
the horses' bellows-breath. Periodically, a fuzzy, dehumanized
voice boomed out from the p.a. system of the indoor arena, a hundred yards away, listing numbers up and numbers to stand by. At
each announcement, certain riders would halt in midcanter and
turn for the gate, where others stood waiting to enter.

It was near noon. No one was eating or drinking, but plenty,
scattered along the fence rail, were smoking. Lex had been trying
to pin down what these regionals reminded him of. Now it came
to him: an examination. An institutional ritual of suffering, like,
say, the SATs. Many called, few chosen. The huge windowless
corrugated metal arena was the exam hall. Students straggled out,
exhausted, with livid stunned faces crumpling toward tears or ex-
ultation. The results wouldn't be posted until later: they were only
guessing their eventual grade.

Nearby, a few feet down the rail, Erica also observed the ring.
Wispy Mrs. Travnicek flanked her on one side and Helen Urbach,
gaudy as a Rose Bowl float, on the other. When Erica was baby-
sitting clients, Lex knew better than to greet her with more than a
slight lift of one brow.

Still, he liked to stand near her.

"Hurry up and *wait,*" Helen grumbled. She sucked on her cigarette as if it were a clogged straw. "Wednesday, Thursday, here it is Friday—for *what*? Shouldn't Ned be out here, warming up? Well shouldn't he? He rode one lousy class yesterday, which he tells me doesn't count. Good thing too. You know I've forgotten what real food tastes like? That spaghetti bender in the village is probably financing a villa in Capistrano on the profit he's raking off all of us. For what the Rangadang Inn up the road is gouging per night we could all have suites at the Ritz. With room service, gratis." She smiled, sourly, around her cigarette.

The value consciousness of the very rich. Normal people— Lex's kind—considered it part of civilized etiquette to swallow numbing bills without a murmur. If anything, they blamed themselves.

"Could be they figure in the boot polish," piped Mrs. Travnicek.

"What?"

"Last night I was on my hands and knees trying to scrub it out of the carpet, after Mickie did her tack. Now the carpet still looks like subway graffiti, and all the white towels are black as sin. So I stuffed them in a suitcase. I arranged the suitcases on the worst of the carpet and pinched fresh towels from a cart in the hall. We had nothing to dry ourselves with! I'm sure we're not the only ones. Normally I'd die but I'm too nervous about what's going on *here* to care."

Erica gave a half quirk of a smile.

Helen Urbach wheezed, blasting smoke through her nostrils. Then her expression sobered. "One mother told me this morning that her kid couldn't get the toilet to flush right. So they jiggled around and opened up the tank lid and found—what?"

"Drowned rat, probably," said Mrs. Travnicek. "Am I right?"

"*Needles. Syringes.* Does that take the cake? Half a dozen, just floating there."

"Oh. Oh my Lord . . ."

"No wonder the john didn't work. I'm telling you: the motel from hell."

Impatiently, Erica pushed back from the fence and glanced at each of them. "This show breeds rumors. Same stories every year. Do your own kids a favor, all right? Don't listen."

Baby-sitting, she was. Ridiculing their anxieties, bullying them to take hold of some sane perspective. Explaining the mechanics of competition to distract them. Her task reminded Lex of his former line of work: for kids to have a prayer of overcoming obstacles, you had to neutralize the parents first.

"One hundred and thirty-six," Erica was saying. "Think about it. That's how many qualified to be here out of the *whole* region. Each of these kids should be proud just to *be* here. Forget this mystique about making it through to the national. Used to be if someone could say they rode at the Garden, that was it—halo time. Hey, *I* never rode at Madison Square Garden." She hugged the fence again, missing none of the action. Her gaze flicked to Ranger Boyd, demonstrating moves on his powerful white jumper. Suzy DiSenza stood grounded, waiting her turn to mount. Ranger, as even Lex knew, *had* made it to the Garden. And he had won.

Why not approach Ranger for interview number three? In his role as moonlighter for Global Insurance, Lex counted his talk with Jesus as the second interview—for what that philosophizing chat was worth. The first had been a phone call to the vet Ianuzzi, who confirmed that after Crimson Cadillac's first injury her prognosis had been "Recovery: good/Return to use: doubtful." Time to move closer to the main players. Mark down Ranger Boyd, the dead horse's trainer, as the third.

Erica was saying, ". . . few years ago, when they switched the national from the Garden to the Meadowlands, the fogies took a fit. 'End of the sport, end of equitation,' blah-blah. Christ, the Garden was structurally so rotten we had horses falling through the floorboards. Anyway, Meadowlands is up like a daisy. Still a big deal. No question. All the hoopla . . . But it's not the only final, and for pure *riding* . . ." She eyed Ranger, who seemed out of patience with his horse. "Well, some years it seems like getting through regionals is too much about pretty-pretty."

"And," said Helen, "too much who you know."

"This course is easy! If anything, our kids are overtrained. You'll see the difference I mean at the USET next month. That course always separates the sheep from the wolves."

Both women were now nodding, to the drawl of her words.

"One hundred thirty-six," Erica repeated, "is, on the other hand, a boggling number of rides to judge. Three judges. They average the scores. Out of those, they'll call eighty back to test on the flat. The top fifty qualify. Simple."

Mrs. Travnicek said, "Honestly. Was Mickie *so* bad yesterday?"

"I told you, warm-ups don't count! Basically a way to get the horses in the arena, work out kinks. Look. The kids who win the warm-ups—they give their best ride too early."

Good point, thought Lex.

Helen fumbled for another cigarette. "But where is *Ned*?"

Erica pointed to the arena. "Inside. He better be. *Studying.* Look. We don't compete till tomorrow morning. I want them both here by five-thirty A.M. I'll also school them again tonight, after this ring empties out. And please, no offense, don't *you* be here. Take yourselves out to dinner or something."

Easy, thought Lex. Don't blow it.

"The best you two can do is—see the kids get plenty to drink. And enough sleep. No slumber parties. And if *you* can't stay calm, at least stay away from them."

Great.

Behind Erica's back, the two mothers traded looks. Helen fanned her wrinkled cleavage with a wrinkled class list. They would, they announced, go watch the rounds themselves for a while. And find their children.

Mrs. Travnicek strode away on stick legs. Helen Urbach pitched like an aroused rhinoceros. Erica watched them go, before edging closer to Lex.

"Hi." He touched her wrist. Her face looked drawn, skin clinging directly to bone.

"I hate regionals," she said.

•   •   •

The face so changed from when he'd found her, three nights before, wandering through the dim half-occupied stabling tents. Searching for him, as he was searching for her. She had fallen against him with such sudden force that the nearest horse pressed up against its stall gate, muttering in curiosity. Burrowing her arms under his jacket she had held on like a sailor in a gale. He smelled and tasted her—apple odor of shampoo, tang of salt on her upper lip—before he could see. Then the long hello kiss, after a long time. When he turned her face up to the stingy overhead light it was slack, almost puffy. Her eyes shone. Is something wrong? he asked. Were you crying?

No. *Singing.* I missed you. I've been a bitch, haven't I? But I was singing all the way. These hokey radio songs—

You? He pressed his finger gently, twice, against the glistening corner of her eye.

She caught his hand, gripped it. Please, let's go somewhere, Lex. Where can we go?

He kissed her again, thinking of the poverty of those with nowhere to go, and wishing for a rock-screened hollow on a beach.

They'd gone to his motel room, of course, and there had made love with a ferocity that left them trembling and translucent. At dawn he'd lain beside her weightless with happiness, wondering first why it came so late in life, and then why it chose to come at all, and promising all the powers that be that if this happiness never came again once would be enough. . . . But that was three nights ago. Since then Erica hadn't returned to his room.

Roller coaster: at moments he imagined she wished him away. This damn show consumed her. Now her wrist felt hot to his touch. Unlike a sunburn, the heat didn't fade beneath his fingers.

"I think you might have a fever."

"Silly." She finger-combed strands of pecan brown hair back

from her forehead, and frowned at the ring. "When the *hell* is he going to give it up?"

She meant Ranger, who still hadn't turned the jumper over to his student. Suzy stood nervously twisting her watch, eyes flicking from her trainer to the shimmering metal arena. No one looked more naked, Lex thought, than a rider deprived of a horse.

Ranger's bruised plum complexion did not go well with his yellow curls. He sat his jigging, twisting horse in a style even Lex found unorthodox: leaning back balanced on his tailbone, with legs lifted forward around the horse's shoulders in a weird embrace. His left long-spurred heel pounded. Whenever the jumper—its white coat ruffled by spur jabs—leaped forward, Ranger reined him back. The mouth gagged open, scarlet and foamy.

"What does he *want?*" Lex whispered.

" 'Shoulder-in.' It's . . ." She shrugged. "It's a lateral move, to improve suppleness. Obedience. Past the point now. That horse's brain is fried."

"But Suzy has to *ride*. In the arena. Soon."

"Yeah. And Ranger deserves to be shot." She turned her back on the practice ring and stared out at nothing: a million dollars' worth of high-tech trailers. "What's gotten into him?" With the sun behind her, her face was gray. "He's lost his marbles. He's ruining that horse."

At noon they drove to the village, to the spaghetti bender's. Most of the lunch eaters were show people; he spotted Don Deluna and a trio of New York trainers squeezed around a Formica table. Another tilt of the roller coaster: Erica's old distinctions (Jesus and the boys were safe to be seen by, Ruthie Pryor was safe, clients and colleagues emphatically were not) seemed hardly to matter now, at regionals.

Not that she would introduce him. In conversation she gazed through Lex so convincingly that more than once he had jerked around, to see who might be behind him. No one.

"Hablicht! Over here! How's the home team scoring?"

They paused at Owen Goodchild's table. Erica clapped the announcer's hammy plaid shoulder. "Coco's girl laid down a killer trip this morning. If she doesn't get a callback—"

Lex read from the wall what he knew by heart: pizza four-way, pizza two-way, antipasto, grinders . . . .

"I saw that trip! Kid rode cute as a ballerina on a seesaw."

"Owen, you're such a dirty old man."

Owen laughed. He had strong white teeth—teeth, Lex figured, that never missed their quarterly scrape and polish. In laughter, Owen's black nostrils flattened and flared.

Erica asked, "So why're *you* here anyway? They've got some other marble-mouth on the p.a.—"

"Gee whiz! All year I'm announcing for these kids—yours in-cluded—and busting their swelled heads for them when they win and playing Bozo the Clown for them on disaster days, *you* know—think I don't want to be in on the showdown? The gay-la victory gallop tomorrow?"

"Huh." Erica's grin softened. She tapped the plaid shoulder and moved off. Invisible, muttering apologies to the chairs he bumped against, Lex followed.

She ate fast, as if food was nothing but an energy source, while scanning the crowd. Now and then her eyes settled on someone with specific interest. More than the loud clatter and buzz of con-versation all around, her faraway focus made Lex not only invisible but dumb.

He thought, why can't you look at me, for once?

Despite a propped-open door, the small space of the restaurant was suffocatingly hot. With a plastic toy fork, Lex poked into an obese meatball. From its center rose a nauseating thread of steam.

He thought—this was the comfort thought, the one which for the past four days he woke with, fell asleep with, rubbed against other thoughts to spread the glow—about what he could do with twenty-four thousand dollars. Enough for a down payment on a condo—he saw the polyurethaned wood floors, a fireplace, sun-light. Erica stepping into his condo rehab loft overlooking Boston Harbor. Enough to buy a piece of a business. A gym franchise . . .

Buy a fast car. Take the courses to finish his degree. Wasn't that the trend—baby boomers back to class for a last sit-in? Or, he could surprise Rosie with the ticket for a Mediterranean cruise. Present Leo with a season pass to the Celtics. Kidnap Erica—to that gringo brochure paradise, where ripe fruit falls on the beach blanket, no problem— Get real. Bribe some bastard on Beacon Hill into resurrecting 3rd Street KidPower—

Twenty-four K was not much. The more Lex thumbed twenty-four K in his imagination, the smaller it got. Amazing, ridiculous, and indisputable fact. He almost sympathized with the parents of the rider-children, with their jealousies and stingy insecurities. Once you got trucking, even a million—or two million?—might not seem much either.

The *hell,* he thought. He wanted that twenty-four.

He could look at Erica. The sinews of her forearm shifted under brown skin as she took a wedge of bread from his plate. A tiny constellation of freckles—like Cassiopeia—on the roundest part of that arm. Physical attraction was a net tossed over him and tightened. Besotted. Can't have enough— But what did it mean—would it mean—to "have" her? No answer. No definition. Sex wasn't having, sex only sharpened the longing, bared the longing that drove the act—

What can I buy for you? A good-enough jumper horse, for twenty-four K?

The rational Lex, able to put down twenty-four K as not much, realized that not everyone in the world or even in this restaurant saw Erica Hablicht as he did. The peculiar blindness of others. It reminded him of the slivers of philosophy a Jesuit father had tried to slip him when he was twelve and as greedy for faith as he would later be for lessons in sin. "What is 'green'?" Father Aucoin had asked. "Can you presume that what you call 'green' bears any relation to my green? To what others denominate as 'green'? What is the soul? What is a state of grace? Think about these things. Remember the story of the three blind men patting the elephant. We all perceive an aspect. Is there an essence? Is an absolute intended?"

He saw Erica. Others might see a fortyish woman who moved with a long impatient stride, whose laugh lines scored her cheeks when she grinned. He guessed so; it didn't matter.

"About tonight," she said, gnawing bread.

"Yes?" He smiled.

"It's all right, isn't it? If we don't get together? I wouldn't be good for much anyway. You can understand, right?"

What the hell am I for you? Just good enough for *that,* and only when you need it? Just useful enough to take off the edge?

"Lex?"

"Yeah, sure. I understand."

She did look at him directly now. Her eyes had turned violet in this indoor shade. His anger had about as much impact on the attraction as a stream running against full tide.

"Are you done with lunch? Can we get out of this hole now?" he asked.

"Hey." She gazed past him, again. "Look who's in town."

He turned. There were many people behind him. Then, in the hazy glow at the open door, what at first had seemed to be a squat child changed into Ruthie Pryor, in her wheelchair. Ruthie was leaning forward, peering in. As Lex stood up, to help maneuver the chair, she jerked back. Through the lettered plate-glass window he saw Ruthie's hunched shape glide swift and level, out of sight.

"Funny." Erica was standing now too. "Why'd she all of a sudden leave?"

"Could be the smell in here changed her mind."

"I don't know." Erica laid four quarters on the table. "It looked more like she saw someone. . . ."

"Who knows. Let's *go.*" This time Lex held her arm, firmly, piloting her through the crowd.

Erica murmured, "She likes *you.* I feel bad for her. Not because of—well, more just because she seems so damn lonely—"

Lex thought: this must be your day to feel sorry for almost everyone.

On the street Erica hesitated, looking around. But the sidewalk, only two blocks long, was empty.

THE NIGHT WAS FILLED WITH CRICKET SONG, GNAT SWARMS, AND an occasional whiff of ripe sweat, both horse and human. Halogen lights on twenty-five-foot poles cast cones of artificial moonlight into the practice ring.

"Five. Four. Two— All right, not bad! But I want to hear you *count*! Yell those strides out! Both of you!"

Erica's jump lessons reminded Lex of a mystery story—the initial predictable exercises built up through quirks and coincidence to a shocker finale. Tonight's plot had peaked in two tall oxers, the strides spaced so wide that to avoid adding an extra "chip" the horses had to gallop full speed and then somehow gather all their forward momentum into the effort upward and over. Erica's strategy was to train over towering bogey jumps like these that would make tomorrow's actual competition course look to both horse and rider like "a dose of Sominex."

"Three, two, one—*kick his ass*! Gallop on, don't let *him* decide when he's finished! Okay. That's the rough idea. *Good.* Now drop your reins."

The horses stretched their necks long. Mickie and Ned snatched light wool blankets from fence posts, spread them like droopy skirts over the steaming hindquarters and ambled on. Whispering to each other. The cooling-out walk.

"How'd it look?" Erica had joined him at the rail.

"Sweet," said Lex.

"Not what I wanted. No rhythm. But I have to save for tomorrow. Every horse is born with X number of jumps in him. Once you spend them . . ." Her breath came quick, as if she'd been the one jumping. "Helen Urbach could *damn* well afford a practice horse for Ned, but she doesn't get it. I can't find the right button to push to open her pocketbook." She ruffled her hair and leaned back, grazing his shoulder. An invitation? No one was looking. Lex bent lower. Erica murmured, "So tell. What was Ranger buddying up to you about?"

Damn. Lex straightened. "Oh—not much."

"You could get a reputation, Lex. I saw you two sitting together inside, in the bleachers. He was asking stuff about my kids, wasn't he? God, that is so *low*. And what's he need dirty tricks for after the trip Suzy pulled off? He doesn't deserve that kid. What is the matter with him—male PMS or something?"

What is the matter with *you*? As the weight of her head settled firmly on his chest, he felt a sudden pang of aversion. What was in that head; who was speaking? The words sounded nothing like her words.

"Randy Ranger." Low bubbling laugh. "My God. Coming on to you, of all people."

"Cut it out." But he couldn't defend Boyd, not without admitting the deal with Whitaker, whom she detested. And his own willingness, for the sake of twenty-four K, to view everyone in her world as a possible horse killer. He was looking for someone as cocky and confident as the Sandman had been—

It was Lex who had slid across the bleacher bench, intent on striking up an "interview." Ranger's first reaction was standoffish, then nervous, affable, morose, and charming: his moods flashed and overlapped like dealt cards. Eventually Lex had worked up to a mention of Suzy's loss—that nice mare, Crimson—and in the dusty dimness of their high corner of the arena, before he had finished speaking, he saw a sparkle of tears widen Ranger's eyes. The trainer's lips had twitched, and a flush shaded his high cheekbones. No question: Ranger Boyd was a handsome guy.

Sorry, Ranger had said. I just wish to hell—it's hard, though. Being a pro. Keeping up this façade . . . See, you get to *know* the horses. Better than any person. When I was a kid I never could make friends. But there was a rent-by-the-hour stable in town where drunk teenagers played rodeo on old broken-down trail horses. It was crummy but to me, wonderful. I worked there after school for free. I had friends, I'd found the horses—

I'm sorry, Lex had said. Thinking: Bag it, Healey. This is no fun. And you are no kind of detective.

The metal clank of the gate latch startled him. Ned and Mickie were leading their horses out, up the path toward the stable tents.

"You coming? Or turning straight in?" asked Erica, moving away. A cool circle on his chest now, where her head had briefly rested.

"Wait—" He couldn't leave yet. Not to spend the rest of the night alone with this sense of betrayal—*her* betrayal, her fault for his moment of sudden complete emptiness. Her awful laugh. Tonight something else had to happen, to erase that. "Wait. I'll keep you company."

She lingered at the gate. They started uphill slowly, an arm's length apart. The kids were already out of sight.

Blame the trouble between them on the deal with Whitaker. First time he'd ever been less than open with her—but she seemed to detest the insurance man, as she detested the talk of horse killings for gain. Maybe she was right: there was a kind of salaciousness, a dirty fascination in the talk. And what did Whitaker expect him to ferret out anyway, almost a month after the mare's death? Cold trail. Something Erica had said, back at Seacrest: Most of us would starve so our horses could eat, Lex. Why would any rider—any real horseperson—inflict ultimate harm?

And all he'd learned today was that if anyone had wanted the mare dead, it surely wasn't her trainer, Ranger Boyd.

They neared the first tent. A grizzled black man and two deeply tanned girls—grooms—sat out beneath a single lightbulb, framed by their stable's string of ribbons, talking, laughing, pulling pizza slices from a flat cardboard box. Lex sniffed a sweet homey drift of marijuana in the air. One of the girls bent down over a portable radio, its thick fuzzy layer of grime visible even in the night.

Does the money enchant, babe?
Do you stab me for spite?
Did you have to betray me?
Will you love me tonight?

"Oh shit," said a deep amiable voice. "Caroline, find us something real."

The dial whirred. The voices faded. Erica's own tent was still a hike away, the very last.

The song, complete with walloping guitars, ran on uninvited in Lex's head.

Burns had killed horses for money. No question. Jesus reported that at the arraignment Burns defended this purity of motive with injured indignation, as if normal red-blooded Americans were raised to grasp such opportunities, risk and reward, that's what made the system great—and where did the fat-cat hypocrites who hired him get off, ganging up on him now?

Crimson Cadillac had been insured for 120 thousand. Maybe overinsured—plenty of these animals were, whether wittingly or not, as the prices fell through the floor while face-value policies were routinely renewed for the high premiums they brought. Maybe that was what still held up the settlement. But suppose money for once was incidental? Had nothing to do with the mare's death?

Love, he thought, and his imagination failed. In euthanasia, the cure of last resort, love might figure as motive. But Crimson had stood a good chance of mending. She hadn't needed to die.

Spite. He glanced at Erica, who marched with hands jammed into her britches pockets, scanning the ribbons displayed on competitors' tents. At times—after midnight, when insomnia inflates paranoia—he had seen the murky outline of a conspiracy aimed at Erica, the successful loner. Framing *her* as the ruthless engineer of a series of "accidents"—no proof, but enough ugly suspicion to frighten off clients, to wreck a career on the verge of national recognition—

Who would do that? Who could hate her?

You had to betray. Compulsion, he took this to mean. An inner compulsion to inflict suffering, to destroy. However mundanely the killer Tommy Burns presented himself as a small businessman, surely a streak of warped compulsion had to be at work there as well. Lex recalled a brief but stomach-turning lecture from Whit Whitaker, the walking encyclopedia of animal morbidity, back at Seacrest Farm. "There's people—I call them 'people' for want of a more accurate word," said Whit, "who raid farms at night to kidnap or attack the animals. Sole purpose of which is, in order to abuse them. On the one hand you have your religious-motivated abuse—that's mostly your throat slitting, bloodletting, and ceremonial drinking, sometimes the extraction and burning of organs from the live victims. Then you have your sexual-motivated abuse. That's where usually though not always the female animal is incapacitated and then violated with implements such as pitchfork handles. There's frequently a lot of cutting. Extremely aggressive. That animal's likely to be a hundred percent loss. We've had trouble in the bovine section, the pig section, and recently on horse farms too. Florida, Maryland just last year . . . Of course these are isolated acts of perversion, you might say, as committed by depraved, ignorant dreck from the bottom of the human barrel—" he had gazed around at the dapper children ambling on sleek braided ponies "—nothing like these educated individuals here. Therefore not to worry, Healey. We never had a horse show incident of that type. You're in fine shape by comparison, working the shows."

Still, Lex thought. Spite. Around him now, at this Maclay Regional, he felt the first jagged cracks of temporary insanity. Finals fever, as she called it. What would someone *not* do, to win? Or to see their child win? Were these parents any more civilized than the cheerleader's mother who had made national headlines by contracting to have her daughter's rival murdered? How intimidating a rival had skinny pigtailed Suzy DiSenza been, paired with the chestnut mare?

"Now where's Ned got to?" Sighing, Erica slowed her pace.

Their tent was the very last. Up ahead, in a yellow apron of light, Mickie was toweling her horse's fresh-washed legs. The animal dozed with an expression Lex couldn't help reading as bliss.

"Probably still out in back walking Monster." In the deep shadow behind the tent, the few pickups and vans parked on a strip of field gave off glints of chrome. Beyond rose a black wall of woods, and the hazed aquamarine sky. "Listen, can I ask you something? Back in summer, when Suzy was still competing, was there anyone in particular whom she—"

"Lex, *don't*! For pity's sake!" Erica blocked the path. Her face broke into anguished lines. "Can't you see I've had it? I've still got to clean up here, I have *got* to get some sleep, I've got to get *out* of here—"

Mickie looked up, startled.

"It's okay," Lex whispered. "Forget I asked. . . ."

"Oh, God. I wish you could just hold me."

"I know. Me too." He tried to match her sadness but was hiding a crazy relief. The anger was gone. Her sadness redeemed them both, made him want to sing out, laugh, lift her right up off the ground and dance.

"My fault. Oh, Lex . . ." She mumbled so low, he had to bring his good ear close to catch each word. "There's stuff—a lot—I haven't had a chance to tell you. No. Or just wanted not to think about. Not spoil things. It—"

"Shh. We'll have time. Soon."

"There has to be one person you don't keep anything secret from, doesn't there? Because otherwise . . ."

"I know." He nodded, giddy with tenderness and deceit.

From behind the tent, somewhere in the makeshift parking lot, came a strangled cry. A beat of silence, then a long harsh groan. Erica gripped his arm, and Mickie jumped for the lead shank of her spooking horse.

"Put Cricket in a stall, quick," ordered Erica, and after the girl went in there was nothing, only ink blue night and a rustle of grass—and then Ned burst into the light, running, hauling the Monster behind him. The ground resonated like drumskin under the big horse's trot.

Erica started to lay into him. "Dumb stunt—yelling your head off like that! You know better. What're you, totally flipped out? Seeing ghosts?"

Ned swallowed. He appeared deaf. His lips moved. The Monster nudged him, and he swayed slightly, then caught his balance. "I saw a guy," he finally said. "I think—I saw Tino."

"Just now?" Lex exclaimed. "Tino is here? So what did he say? Where'd he *go*?"

"Nowhere."

Erica frowned. "Ned. Talk sense!"

"Tino's still laying in the grass out there. I think he's dead."

But Tino was not out there. After stowing the Monster in his stall, with a hasty excuse to Mickie, Erica had grabbed a flashlight from her barn kit. The light bobbed, illuminating a palimpsest of horseshoe prints on the ground. Night birds cooed from the wall of woods. In Ned's sobbing breath, Lex recognized a watery suffocation, the border of hysteria. Alongside a pickup truck, Ned stopped. "Somewhere right over here." Erica swept the light forward, past the cab, over the long grass, over nothing. There was, perhaps, an indistinct depression.

Ned babbled, incoherent. At that moment Lex fought an instinct to clip the boy one, hard and swift up the jaw. Act of mercy.

HUNCHED HIGH IN THE BLEACHERS, VULTURELIKE, HE HAD PLENTY of time to remember that moment.

It was nine-thirty-eight, on the morning of the last day of regionals. The oval jump-studded arena below looked distant as a canyon floor. Between rides, a buzz rose and bodies shifted on the benches, but with the entrance of each new rider an instant hush descended. No one came here as a casual spectator. Everyone heard, and counted, the soft concussion of each single stride.

Lex wiped slick palms against his jeans. His focus wavered, eyes hot and gritty from sleeplessness. He remembered how Erica's decision—to tell no one, to take Ned back to her room for a few hours' rest, to go on with today's competition—had both stupefied and convinced him. It had a logic: the weird indisputable commitment of a dream.

Mickie had already had her four minutes in the ring. The round looked good to him—he'd slammed his sweaty palms together furiously as she rode out—but the dull patter of clapping everywhere else told him: no callback. Not good enough.

Ned was on standby, three rides off.

You imagined this, understand? Erica, leading Ned away by his limp arm. They had searched around other trucks. Nothing. Dips of crushed grass everywhere, from hooves, boots, and tires come and gone. *You probably imagined it because—look, it's not hard to think why, now is it?* It was hard for Lex to think why. *Probably you saw something—maybe a dog lying there? Things can look so different in the night. Wake up, Ned, was it a dog, maybe wearing a bandanna for a collar?*

And then, in his monotone, as if he were the only sane one there, Ned had described his vision. Of Tino, curled on his side. Tino's same headband, for sure. Dead because his eyes stared wide, wide open. Because. Ned could see. When you have been out in the dark awhile, you can see. Because a line—jumper cables—led from Tino's body into the open hood of the truck. One alligator clip fixed to Tino's upper lip. The other clamped inside his unzipped fly.

Lex had spat to ward off nausea. Wishing he had slapped the boy sober while it still might have done some good.

They had walked Ned around the perimeter of the tents. Lex recalled nights forcibly walking friends who were sick drunk. Ned's sobbing stopped and started. *I'm sorry, I'm sorry,* he cried. Crystal-clear snot hung from his chin. *I'm not a head case, I don't want to be crazy—what about tomorrow? I have to be okay. I am. I have to ride—*

It was a poor set of choices. Not one of them, including Ned, ever made a choice. They just left the possibilities—a boy's obscene crack-up or an obscenely executed, vanished corpse—lying out there in the field, untouched.

Still. To allow Ned to ride the course, this morning . . .

He heard the number announced: one-twenty-nine. He prayed, purely and simply, that Ned not crash. He prayed for the Monster. That through four minutes, both would survive.

The hush, as Ned entered. He saluted the trio of judges with a tug at his velvet cap. Tall, slender, from this distance a man. Touch of spur to the Monster's broad ribs. Lift into canter. Lex froze, his heart barely beat. Safe, through the diagonal. Safe, forget about clean. Picket to the single narrow oxer, then outside combination—Lex had forgotten the sequence he'd watched over fifty times: now each jump came as a surprise and a miracle. On a never-ending course.

He realized it was over when the uproar broke out. Monster circled, tucked into the bit as if he knew the meaning of praise. Whistles and bravos and, from somewhere far below, Erica's wolf howl. Lex got up on shaky legs, looking around at the crowd, grinning like a fiend. He figured it was all right to clap.

PART 3

The Finals

Gladstone, New Jersey, September 24

THE POWERLESS BET LONG ODDS; FAITH IS THE MIRROR IMAGE of frustration. He entered the mock-Tudor lobby of the Hunters Courte Inne shortly before noon, certain that after a week's separation she would arrange to arrive early too. The desk clerk gave his duffel bag, shouldered like a saddle, a glance of sour complicity. Here for the equestrian event? Unfortunately, the special-rate rooms were not yet quite . . . The gentleman might enjoy waiting out in the garden? Stayed with us before? No? Ah—many guests returned *mainly* for the garden. Unique.

The gentleman aimed as directed for the rear French doors. He hunched under the burden of his bag and also to avoid whacking his head on phony oak beams. At each step his size-twelve sneakers—ochre-brown, with a pale memory of former whiteness under the laces—shed flakes of desiccated manure. The clerk's dismay skittered up and down his spine. Snazzy place.

Outside, the gummy envelope of warmth. Low gray sky, eighty degrees. For the past week, working a series of shows in New York and Connecticut in the first mellow downpours and cooler nights of autumn, he'd found it hard to credit reports of Montreal express winds roaring a few hundred miles northward. And here, down in New Jersey's woodsy-wealthy northwestern pocket (so much for Uncle Leo's "scratch-and-sniff map of Noo Chersey" joke), summer hadn't budged. No great distance. More like time travel. As if summer lingered wherever the horses were: just follow the horses.

He dropped his bag on flagstones. The Hunters Courte (its truant apostrophe distracting as a lost button) straddled a hillside: gray, white-shuttered buildings on sloping terraces, all subdivided by pebble paths and linked by stone steps descending to the loop of road. No flowers but plenty of trees. Maple: one leaf he could identify. Maple leaves sheeted the surface of a swimming pool narrow as a hospital gurney. There were iron chairs and benches, perforated to let rain drip through. So this was the garden: dank, dreamlike and somehow relaxing, like a graveyard.

He walked, searching for a lookout post over the road she would drive in on. Rounding a corner, he stumbled on a client of his. The client sat slumped on a bench, one leg cocked up, the other pole-straight across his path.

"Morning, Miss Beale."

"*What?*" Shading her eyes against the steel sky. "Oh, it's you. Funny! For a sec I didn't know *who* you were talking to. Sit down, Stretch. You can't call me Coco?"

The bench commanded a good enough view. She shifted sideways, and he joined her.

They discussed the weather, no casual subject. How springy the footing would be, as long as the next rain held off. This humidity, on the other hand . . . but the kids could cope. By now, these kids were tough as borium shoe studs. But the horses were delicate always and especially near the end of a long season. USET courses— Coco tilted her profile, musing, and he found himself admiring the high bow of her nose—USET courses were something else. He knew the scuttlebutt, no? This new course designer, an ex-Olympian convinced that American kids had gone soft as burger buns, was out to prove his case. She, Coco, couldn't wait to see the final course unveiled—what bummed her was not being able to ride it. Such a bummer, to be *old*.

Without the harsh lipstick she could have been eighteen. No bulge to her stomach at all. The long designer-blue-jeaned leg rested carelessly across his thigh.

Multicolored Jaguars prowled the road below. He veered back to the subject of animal welfare. His job, after all. (Her leg began to jiggle, as if marking the beat to a pop tune.) Looking back, he suggested, it had been kind of a hard-luck year, no? Though didn't it seem like every so often the gods singled out a major sport for their wrath? Boxing, say. Skiing? He remembered reading about accidents, whole planeloads of athletes going down. The difference here being that half the athletes involved were dumb critters who couldn't call in lawyers to bust their contracts, couldn't begin to calculate the risks—

"Dumb?" Coco challenged. "Horses *know* the risk." She was braiding her hair into a rich, bleached-wheat plait.

He was thinking, he said, of freak losses he'd heard about, early in the year. Not to mention the Sandman case splattered all over the media, with Tommy Burns's finger smearing some of the top talent in the country—not good for the sporting image, no matter who you believed. Major corporations scrambling to withdraw their sponsorship of events. (Coco rubbed her left nipple thoughtfully. She wore no bra.) He was thinking of Coco's own student who got her leg smashed so bad she had to withdraw—and later that same horse colicking. And of that poor kid Becky Hedgepeth, *her* fall. And then there was Suzy DiSenza losing her mare, what's its name—

"Becky's horse walked away from the crash sound," Coco informed him. "And as for Becky—well, most kids would hock their Nintendos to be where she is. She *placed* in the regional's jump-off. She's got a crack at *winning* the Maclay!"

He winced. Coco's blond clone had made the cut for the Maclay Final, so had Suzy, so had Don's kid. Despite a clean performance on the flat, Ned wasn't called to the jump-off, and when the list was posted, "N. Urbach" stood in fifty-first place. Out. One Grand Canyon notch away from the cut. Erica had simply ruffled the boy's black hair, saying, *What counts is that you rode great.* (Her one false smile, the practiced digestion of bitterness.) *It's politics here, Ned. They'll know you next year. Never mind.*

But no trip for Stoneacre to the national this year.

Becky might have a crack at that win, he admitted to Coco. On the other hand, after her head injury young Becky Hedgepeth still couldn't *talk* right.

With a dismissive, impatient thrust, Coco tore up her braid. He wondered by what trick, in her line of work, she kept the nail polish from chipping.

"And as for Crimson," she said. "Care to hear my take on Crimson Cadillac?"

Sure. He brushed her knee.

"Somebody got to that mare. Now wait. I can't prove somebody *did*. But that whole situation was fishy as Gloucester Harbor. Wasn't it? *You* were there. Stinky, stinky! *You* know—the payment thing."

Payment thing.

"DiSenzas' bought that horse off some couple named Morton. I ran across *her* once, they're not genuine horsey, just wanna-be fence decorations in Hermès and Burberry who bought into the market when it was exploding out of sight. Fools rush in—into tax shelters, right? When they went to unload Crimson, the deal was *not* what they'd banked on. DiSenzas' were strapped because they took a bath selling Suzy's *last* horse. Dominoes. The deal was a small down payment, monthlies, plus a balloon. When Crimson Cadillac died, that balloon was already two months late."

Ahah.

"Ask any rocket scientist. DiSenzas' didn't have it. Even though Suzy was cleaning up on Crimson by then, I heard Papa DiSenza wanted to return the mare to Mortons'—wash his hands, even if it meant walking away from what he'd already paid in—"

Not good from Suzy's point of view. Nor from her trainer's.

"But, no deal. So. You follow my drift, hmm?" Her lacquered fingers drummed on his thigh, which was half numbed by the weight of her leg. The perfume he inhaled was not the sweat and liniment mixture that girl grooms called "Eau de Cheval"; it was the real Parisian thing, Joy. He felt a stirring, the pulse in his groin. A sort of excited misery: he didn't *like* her. "I gather they're in a legal wrangle now, over who gets the gold egg. The insurance. DiSenzas see the chance of getting Suzy a new mount, cash on the barrel, after all. *If* they can argue something was goofy with the mare to begin with—for her to bleed like that? Hah. It's the kid's only chance. Ranger sure as *hell* isn't going to let her ride his own horse next year—not the way *this* season's going." But wasn't Suzy doing remarkably well? asked Lex. "Exactly." She laughed. For a moment her face was sweetened by glee. "And Mortons—they expect their stake back. Some highfliers. For Pete's sake, if you want to play big time, you've got to roll with the punches, hmm?" She squeezed his leg muscle, a rough twist. He was grateful: it hurt.

When Crimson died, the Mortons had been hundreds of miles away. He'd spoken with them on the phone. Suzy and her mother, at least, had been on the grounds.

"I like you, Stretch," Coco said. "You're outside this circus. You're sane."

He replied, sincerely, that he wished they'd had a chance to talk like this before.

She flexed her hand, as if intrigued by the pain it could cause. "It's funny. How people talk to me. I end up hearing things I absolutely don't *want* to hear, but I understand why. I don't have any axes to grind."

You don't need the money. "An impartial ear," he nodded.

"And I'm not hung up on money." She laughed, again sweetly. "I *have* it because I don't *need* it. Isn't that always the way? There's actually not much I *do* need, really, except . . ." She peered at him, lips parted for the thought about to come. "What am I saying? The truth? I don't need a man. Who needs the hassles? Give me a box of chocolates, and a vibrator. . . ." Her small golden eyebrows drew together. "By the way. Speaking of money. Since you seem interested. The price on that mare—the paper price—was ludicrously inflated. To match the insurance value? They make it look like an arm's-length amount in case of a claim. It's done every day."

Every day.

"*One* more little thing. Regarding my friend Ranger. Ranger, he and I go a *long* ways back—"

Please, don't laugh again.

"But his proboscis is deep in the candy jar. Recently. I mean, too deep. You've noticed? More than is healthy for him, or anybody else."

Have I noticed? Surprised, but not surprised. And you, Coco Beale? Do you like a taste of refined sugar now and then?

"Whatever does it for a person, right? But you have to stay on top. Control the stuff, don't let it start to control you. Listen, when they ask why some well-heeled Grand Prix star would cash in his soul for a lousy hundred-thousand-dollar settlement—search me. But Ranger is not so well heeled. I worry for him. He used to ride like an angel, *but*— Besides, times are hard. A couple of lines cost the moon these days. . . ."

Gravel crunched. They both jerked upright and slid apart, like a startled pair of parked teenagers.

"Miss Cornelia Beale?" The woman, in tight-waisted navy blue, held up a key attached to what looked like a hand grenade. "Your room is all set now, miss. Manager's sorry about the delay."

Coco stood up. "Hallelujah. Lead on." As the maid turned, she bent down to whisper, "Stop by, Stretch. The Peregrine Suite, I think? First star before midnight, last cottage on the left. Only, give me an hour's head start. I need a *bath*."

Lex slumped on the bench. What was he supposed to do, charge after them, bully the woman, demand his own room *now*? Yes—but too late. Some people just take the treatment—padded bills, needles in the toilet tank, deadpan stares, and nudges to the end of the line—and blame, if anyone, themselves.

The road was empty. Coco's words spooked in his head, suggesting, proliferating. Coco's invitation, no damage to his ego, confused his mood. The scene in which he'd intended to costar here—his faithful vigil, *her* arrival, dank motel grounds transformed to the lush private garden of reunion—was turning stale.

Erica, it's time. Where are you?

She'd made no promises. There'd been no chance. After regionals, with no more qualifying wins to "chase," she'd returned to the local circuit with her novice students. Meanwhile, Lex and HorseGuard worked "A" shows (the next season beginning even before the current round played out) in New York. Days strung together by a haze of dull irritability, while he tried to settle the question of why a good mare died. And whether a boy's mind could crack open on a single grotesque vision. But Ned had gone home, and no one was eager to recall the mare. Each day brought an abrasive loneliness he'd never felt in his years alone.

Once, near midnight, Erica had managed to reach him on the phone. He'd babbled, laughing in an explosion of relief at her voice. As if pressed for time, she'd interrupted: "Wait, Lex. Listen, the only place to stay in Gladstone is Hunters. So looks like we'll be together." That was all she said, her tone uninflected—for fear of listeners, he had guessed.

He looked around the garden, then uphill, and brightened. Vivid as a cherry cough drop, Ruthie Pryor's car stood out against the gray and green.

Flash of aluminum, as Ruthie saluted with her crutch.

A curious comfortableness had developed between him and Ruthie Pryor. In the long idle hours of the job he'd found himself ambling in the direction of the red golf cart, juggling an extra Coke and cone of fries. Was this simply the bonding of two wallflowers, he wondered, sidelined at the dance? (Picturing Ruthie's legs, shrouded by black sweatpants even in the summery heat.) No—there was also some change in her. A light in her brooding eyes as they followed the action in the ring. A new energy when she applauded a round. A hint of a smile as he approached. At moments, Ruthie seemed almost happy.

He watched her motor on, into a veil of pine. Good to know Ruthie would be staying at Hunters Courte too.

Young Ruth was bent on educating him. "Jumping," she'd explained, "is all about seeing. Seeing distances. The takeoff, ten strides out . . . When I did freak after a fall—it's strange how you freak out afterward, not during—I was scared for my eyes." Ruthie had his number: "Anyway, my eyes are still fine. I can see what you're doing, Healey. You're looking for someone." With a laugh he had brushed this off, spilling Coke. "Seriously, Healey. I'd like to help. I might be . . . If I can—or, well, whether or not—see, I'm looking for someone too. In general. Not here. I'm not in the habit of asking for favors, but you, you have connections, don't you— files and records, all the insurance agencies—and of course I would pay you—"

Forget *that,* he'd said. Whatever, he'd said. Any little favor. But for Chrissake not to go imagining things about him, or sticking her neck out—

Later she began to confide in him more: about the accident, or rather the catastrophic blank like a skid mark in her memory that connected driving to her regular lesson at Deluna's barn and waking, two days later, into a world of pain. About her increasing longing to meet the other driver, for no particular fathomable reason other than to complete the circle, complete the course, to go out the gate she'd come in by. (Understandable, Lex agreed.) However, no one trusted her. You'd think she was a mental cripple—as if the main injury was to her *head.* She merely wanted the driver's name. Theoretically her lawyer could tell her, presumably he kept all the depositions (Lex nodded again, of course the information had to be available), but this Shumway refused to talk on the phone, he insisted that Ruth come in person to his office—and she had reasons for mistrusting *that*—

In their last conversation she had launched a different subject, asking mainly about Lex's previous work, with KidPower. *You did that all on your own?* she said. *I think you must be incredibly brave.*

Hooting out loud, slopping more Coke, he'd earned a glare from the rider just entering the ring.

Not a suite, but still a generous room on the second floor. Profoundly quiet. A catwalk veranda ran outside; inside he kicked off his sneakers and high-stepped a few aimless figure eights for the pleasure of the lush trampoline bounce of the rug. Brocade curtains, matching wing chair—and none of the furniture bolted to the floor. Mint patties pillowed on the turned-down bed. How a rented room could make you *someone*—while others stripped you down to their level, where even hanging your clothes on the theft-proof hangers made you feel like something not worth stealing, an anonymous piece of dreck.

He flicked on sixty-watt bulbs. Instant blackness outside. Almost five o'clock. Any moment now she had to arrive, might be down at the desk already, signing in, asking whether, by the way, a Mr. Healey had arrived. Bed-test time. He flopped backward, rolled, pounded the mattress with his elbow, grinning. Three nights. Already the time apart—time for his irrational jealousy to swell like a jackhammer toothache, all right, admit that, now, face it and forget it—was over.

He showered. Shaved. Dressed in stiff clean jeans and a new T-shirt. He placed three phone calls: one to the desk, one to Whit Whitaker (out of town, leave message), a reassurance call to Rosie. Then he filled the sink with a cold bath for the wine he'd bought. Settled in the wing chair, facing the door, to wait.

So quiet . . .

But for a long time, someone had been tapping on the door. He blinked and roused himself and went deliberately to open it, aware that he was expecting a visitor but unable to remember who. A boy-man, wiry and quick, slipped into the room. His shoulder-length black hair was bound in a twisted red bandanna. When he turned, grinning, a pink worm of tongue bulged through the gap in his front teeth. Offering clenched fists, the man asked, *Which hand?* His nails were black and torn as if they had clawed in dirt. The right fist opened. On his palm lay a painted toy horse. A show souvenir. A chunky bay with the *H* brand, like Ned's horse. *You forgot this one, didn't you?* Lex answered: *No, that one's not mine.* He backed away but wherever he went the visitor's hand moved with him, only inches from his chest. Lex realized that the horse although tiny had real hair, real hooves, moist flickering nostrils. Then the hand darted against his heart. Touched. The room roared, convulsed, flashing black and red.

He opened his eyes again and again there were the lamps and the room as it had begun. No one else. His duffel bag open on the floor. A cramp ebbing slowly from his chest. He sat motionless, absorbed by the slight whistle of his own breath, waiting to find out whether he had woken into reality, or into another dream, or back into the same one.

A knock on the door struck straight through him.

And the telephone rang.

"Mr. Healey?" He nodded, blinking, with one hand holding the door ajar, holding the phone with the other. "Here's the corkscrew you called down for, Mr. Healey. And mail. Manager must've overlooked giving it to you when you checked in." The maid's face and uniform blended with the night.

"Now let me guess," said the phone. "Tsk, tsk. You. Fell. *Asleep.*" A nasal, teasing tone.

"Sort of. Could you just please put it on the table?" said Lex. The phone cord was stretched to its limit.

"Who are you talking to? You're not alone."

"What time is it?" he asked.

"Nine-forty-five, sir."

"Ten, roughly roughly. I'm on my way over to the exhibitors' party. Thought you might like a lift. But I take it you're otherwise engaged."

"To be honest, I don't think I can stand another exhibitors'—"
He fished in his pocket for money but the jeans were freshly
washed. "I'm sorry. I can't find any—but thank you. Thanks very
much. Sorry to have bothered you—"

"I'm not *bothered!* Christ, how desperate do you think I am?"
That irresistible free-flowing laugh. "You faked me out, Stretch.
Fast operator."

"G'night," said the maid. "If there's nothing else?"

"Nothing else. I have everything I need now. Much appreciated . . ." He closed the door.

"You said it, I didn't. Well! Congratulations. Can I guess who
the chosen damsel is? One guess?"

"Damn it, Coco, please listen—"

"Hey, I'm easy. You two enjoy the evening! Isn't that what
we're all here for? See you ringside, Stretch. Down the road,
there's always another show."

He watched the last half of a movie on television. It appeared to be
about a voracious enchantress bent on destroying the well-ordered
life of a righteous man. But he wasn't sure. He had missed the beginning. He speculated that the righteous man might be the insa-
tiable one, might have seduced the enchantress because of a need
to see his conventionally lucky life—wife, child, brick colonial
house, golden retriever—which he had sucked all the juice out of,
had outlived—blown to smithereens.

Music, but minimal dialogue. Lex lost the thread. The actors
stalked, writhed in and out of bed, tortured the dog and then each
other. When bloody mayhem broke out he pressed POWER, and
watched the star in the center of the screen contract like a sigh.

This had always been his weakness, his moral failing: an inabil-
ity at certain times to distinguish good from evil, to sort each into
its own pile—no. To *believe* in evil. He had a sense of what good
was: a Dreamsicle orange winter sunrise over the Charles basin, for
instance, or wading into a fight with strangers for a buddy's sake,
or Thanksgiving with Rosie and Leo, eating glazed turkey stuffed

with horrible bland chestnuts. Evil, on the other hand, looked like
a blank black patch. Wherever he looked long and hard enough, it
faded. *By denying evil,* Father Aucoin had argued, flushed with ap-
petite for an argument, *we trivialize the good.*

I said, Father. I can feel what good is. So doesn't that come from—

*Your aesthetic reflex. A higher order sensory response. Whereas true
goodness—*

Why he'd finally quit going to Mass. Along with the usual reason: the Saturday night/Sunday morning problem. Losing his vir-
ginity was revelation enough to deal with. It was *good.* No kid
wants to be a hypocrite.

At five before midnight he began to undress. He wasn't angry
with her anymore. And the lost evening—one whole evening—
hardly mattered now. All his energy went to not imagining what
could have happened to her, could be happening, on the road.

He would leave the lights on. Glancing around the room (just
a room, it had lost its sheen; a patch of old stain, wine or coffee,
marred the carpet), he pursed his lips at the corkscrew. Playing pa-
perweight, it lay across a small square envelope.

The return address, ink stamped, was Stoneacre Farm. With the
corkscrew's tip he ripped open the flap.

Mister Healey,

This is to say I know who you are. And where.

Maybe you don't know what you are doing to people or maybe you
don't care. For myself I'm no saint but it is extremely hard to
understand something I could never do myself.

Please, don't do this to us.

Is this the first time? I guess probably not. But I'm asking you this
question because I need to get an honest answer.

To write this letter is the hardest thing I have ever done. The facts
have been clear for a while. Once I tried to call you and it's just as well
you were out. Since then I have been thinking about what to do.

You are the last person on earth I care to meet in person but I think
we had better. She has enough problems right now so let this stay

private between us. Call me here at the farm. Otherwise I will have to
leave here and come find you.

> Yours,
> Roland F. Pettit

Lex held the letter for a long time. The laming chill of the nightmare had returned to his arms and legs, and he thought about how
limited the range of physical response was to a wide array of emotions. Guilt felt like fear, for example. And fear for one's self—as a
sensation, a physical symptom—felt like fear for another, though
the emotion was entirely different. And dread imitated anticipation. Limits of chemistry. Without the context, nothing distin-
guished a laughing human face from one howling in grief.

At the first knock he jerked awake. He *hoped* awake—at least his
hand stung where it had just slammed the headboard. He lay
doggo. That was what his father had called it, when he walked in
"to have it out with the kid, here and now" about some damn
stunt. There'd been a lot of damn stunts pulled, although now as
an adult he found them harder to recall than the unvarying after-
math. "Lookit him, Rose. Laying there doggo." And the click and
businesslike slither of the belt coming off. And Rosie behind,
pleading, which did no good, he could have told her . . . sometimes it seemed exactly because of her pleading that the belt had to
come off.

Another single knock. He sat up, naked, squinting. Past two
A.M. "Who is it?"

"*Me,* Lex. Who else? Let me in—"

He flew to open the door. She looked terrible: bruise under one
eye, bruises on her neck, matted hair hooked behind her ears. And
silently, aware of other sleepers, she laughed at the sight of him.

He pulled her in and hugged her hard, while turning the lock.
"What the hell happened?"

Her eyes were huge from night driving. Nothing, she insisted.

Nothing worth telling. Late start. Then the rig broke down. Pay-back for shipping one's own critters to save money. But telling about breakdowns was like telling the story of your uncle's gall-bladder, forget it. She held out her hands: "Grease, see? Yuck. I'm probably covered."

And grease, nothing else, marked her neck and face.

She had found the USET grounds and settled her anxious, hungry horses and caught a lift to the motel with a straggler from the party. And it was selfish of her so late but she had wanted to see him. Sleep was out for tonight anyway. Tomor-row— Her wide eyes took in the room. "Were you sleeping with the lights on?"

He led her to the shower. He undressed her. She felt brittle in his hands: an overcharged wire, metal at the point of fatigue. But this is how her days are, he thought, this is nothing so unusual. He climbed into the steamy glass cell and scrubbed her body—her back, loins, neck and, most carefully, the grease smear beneath her eye. You're being nice to me, she said.

They turned out the lights together. He glanced last at his bag where the letter lay buried. Clearly, whatever the week at Stone-acre had been like (but he hated picturing her there), she had no idea. "Private between us," as Roland demanded, and that was right, she *shouldn't* know, not now, not till the season was over. That letter—Coco's information—even his threatening dream visitor—these were all snares he had to protect her from, from now on.

For a moment he felt Roland's presence in the room: as an ally.

In bed he meant only to hold her and pray for a few hours' sleep for them both, but in the dark she searched for a kiss and pressed close, she arched and stretched long as if every inch of her needed to connect to him. Their bodies, he realized (as he answered, moved with her, took command), had by now a separate language, and a fluent, eager, continuing conversation that paid no respect to the days and nights apart.

THE MOIST GREEN SUN SLANTED WITH A PRICKLING PROMISE, AS IF there were a deity after all and She cared about nothing more passionately than a weekend of competitive games on horseback in the hills of New Jersey. Stepping out on the catwalk, Lex watched trainers, kids, and parents drift down toward the parking lot. They lugged saddles, bridles, jackets in dry-cleaner bags, lumpy bags of gear; they merged like passengers leaving ship for a new port. Don Deluna glanced skyward, saluting. Coco, her hair a platinum helmet, jogged past. Mickie Travnicek and Suzy DiSenza walked arm in arm, prim schoolgirls in their high-collared, long-sleeved riding shirts. Mickie blew a kiss up to the catwalk and both girls sagged against each other, giggling and dimpling. Lex wafted two courtly kisses back.

He had an unexpected, inexplicable sense of family. Of generosity and warmth. His troubles of last night—the dream visitation; even Pettit's accusing, belligerent letter—seemed equally insubstantial, their sources far away as the single pennant of cloud fixed near the northern horizon. All that mattered was *here,* today and tomorrow—and he wanted every one of these kids to win.

The boards of the catwalk swung as Erica approached from her room. "Ready?" he asked.

"Already way late." Disheveled and frantic ten minutes ago, now impeccable in her uniform. White shirt, britches, the tall black boots. Lex had a thing about her boots. Fetishism, he thought cheerfully. The leather molded around her calves, the spray of creases inside each knee. Close up, no amount of Kiwi could disguise the thinning and scarring of years' wear against horses' sides.

"I love you," he said.

Her eyes caught and stayed on his as if he'd gone on speaking and she had to concentrate on every word. Then she faced down

toward the parking lot. "What a morning. Just an incredible morning . . . Let's go."

It's a freaking Camelot, he thought, wheeling through a wrought-
iron gate at the nod of a guard. A Gatsby thing. Mile-long driveway through glades too natural to be natural, vistas of close-shaved
emerald meadow. They crawled, pinned in a procession of Jags and
pickups and BMWs and caterers' vans. A chance now to look at
Erica, who sat bolt upright beside him, in full view to those who
walked or rode past. She was explaining the USET's structure.
What to expect, what would happen, in these two days.

He only half heard. What mattered was that she was here, his
passenger, in the car lettered HORSEGUARD INT'L. A public decla-
ration. All his fears about the week apart—he wanted to laugh out
loud. Through the open window she waved to a man passing by
on horseback, traded a wisecrack, as though there were no reason
why Erica Hablicht should not be driving in the early morning
with Lex Healey. The rider—florid, squinty, on a swaybacked
palomino—was a judge, his boots chafed even browner than her
own. Lex thought about the uniform and about how, no matter
how loused-up these riders' private lives might be (and most were),
wearing the uniform they appeared stripped of all entanglement.
The past, one way or the other, not mattering a damn.

He'd guessed right: a castle, for Chrissake. Round stone turrets
popped over treetops. Medieval stone arch and a cobbled court-
yard.

"Oh, Lex . . . *Look.*" Erica clutched his arm, leaning across
him, pointing to the side. Along the shoulder of the road, through
a haze of shrubs, stalked a cock pheasant: gold and crimson and
copper and bronze. Its long shining burden of tail feathers parted
the bleached grass. Horses' legs blurred past, then the cock
reemerged and paused with one claw suspended. His eye, light
melted in a shallow gold bowl, beamed on Lex.

Hey, bud. Bring us luck?

• • •

He had caught the gist. This dressage business came first, later a phase called "gymnastics" (mental image of thoroughbreds doing splits and cartwheels), and tomorrow the climax, the jumping phase, but this year over solid obstacles and in an open field instead of the protective arena both kids and animals were used to. "Thrills and spills," the kids were calling it. There would, of course, be a jump-off, and with a twist: the top four riders would exchange horses. Round-robin.

But meanwhile, by ten-thirty, the dressage dragged on, slightly less pulse quickening than a quilting bee. Nearly identical horse-rider pairs performing identical prescribed figures, over and over . . . and over. If a polished hoof ever slipped out of line, Lex couldn't see it. The ringside hush under green-and-white-striped pavilions irritated him, as if there were a joke going around that he didn't get. He prowled through the barns (no Porta-Johns for the U.S. Team headquarters, instead vaulted stone aisles and the spacious cells of privileged prisoners in wings extending from the castle). He checked in with Jesus, and gorged on too much free food, and returned to ringside again. If there was an afterlife, he figured, he'd probably spend purgatory watching this excruciating monotony called dressage.

An inflated pigeon, a dove gray ninepin, was rolling toward him through the tables. Lex shook off his daze and whisked crumbs off his T-shirt.

"Well *hey*. Whit! I'll be—" But no, he was getting used to how quickly the insurance man moved, materialized from place to place. "So you got my message?" He'd left a sample of his fresh insight into the Crimson sale on the man's answering machine.

Whitaker grimaced. His eyes popped, directing Lex's attention to a tiny elderly woman pasted like a shadow behind him. "Have the pleasure to introduce a lady," said Whit, as the shadow stepped forward. "Who traveled on your account all this way from Boston!"

The lady was draped in lace and purplish gauze, and a grab bag of jewelry latticed her wispy chest, but from below the scalloped hem jutted a practical pair of rubber mud boots. She quick-pressed Lex's hand and trilled, like a small bird choking on a seed: "Thripp!"

Lex smiled uncertainly.

"Miz *Viola* Thripp," said Whitaker. "One savvy business cookie and may I say always a *dee*-light for yours truly to do business with?" He looked satisfied, cunning, and guilty. "Miz Viola is the Founding Mother, and president and chief executive officer, of Horse-Guard International. There you go, Healey. She's your boss."

Gradually, as she talked, he recognized the voice. On the company's Boston answering machine, this same voice had sculpted for him a flirtatious twenty-year-old temp. He had a sense of tectonic plates shifting beneath him. Minor adjustment. Others evidently recognized Miz Viola Thripp as well: an aproned man hurried over with drinks and whispered something that bared her silver-edged teeth in a soundless laugh. As she quizzed Lex, her gaze stayed riveted on the dressage tests unrolling behind his back. "Up until last year," she volunteered, "I used to do a bit of that myself." He guessed *she* could see every slip of a hoof. No glasses, no telltale bulge of contact lenses on her damp colorless eyes. Though she seemed never to look at him, he also guessed she had the trick of observing at least two things at once.

She approved of Healey, in general. Healey's reports came in on the button and made sense, unlike the scrawls of his predecessor. ("That wishy-washer. Always in women troubles— *You* recall that boy, Whitaker?") Healey's client base was up eighteen percent, seven percent net over the other crews. (Other crews? The company had substance then, a solid existence beyond the P.O. box?) Quite the sales talent, Healey. Appreciated. (She broke off, slack-jawed at some error in the ring, before continuing.) And no major misbehavior from the help? Apparently not. No nastiness from the red tapers—IRS, INS, those busybodies? Thank goodness for that.

Lex nodded solemnly, as if they were discussing not himself but a third person. Still waiting for the exception, the "but." The reason for Viola Thripp's personal descent. His fingers slid into his jeans pocket to meet a crumpled half pack of cigarettes. He wasn't smoking much—wasn't *remembering* to when Erica was around—but now . . . No. Not in front of Thripp. Suddenly she raised and windmilled her arm vigorously. Lex and Whit turned to see Ruthie Pryor motoring away, snail's pace, along the ringside path.

"Lovely girl," said Miz Thripp. "Wasn't she gifted, had such a lovely tight leg on a horse. . . . Why do these wasteful things happen?"

Whit tore off his glasses, polished, and replaced them.

"*Except*—" she said, tapping the table for a return to business. "I'm quite satisfied, except for that hanky-panky about Tino Varez."

Ah? Ah, yes. Tino Varez—

"You apparently didn't see fit to report. To bother me. Never worry about *bothering* me, Healey. Oh, you do look sheepish. Well, I already know the situation, that he quarreled with you, ran off and so on. I had a letter—quite outrageous, in fact—from the lad."

Lex leaned forward. *"When?"*

"When what? The silly letter? Oh . . . Thursday, that will have been. Thursday last."

Under Whit's reproving scowl, Lex's uncontrollable grin of relief. To hide it, he twisted abruptly to the ring. And there was Mickie, midway through her test. And Ned, at the in-gate. *Thursday*—over a week after Ned's nightmare at the regionals. Only a waking nightmare. Well, he'd seen boys crack before, under stress, though maybe with more warning. Pray that Ned can hold together from now on. And Tino, bless him, was still out on the road somewhere, undead, a dog turned stray, still nursing his grievance.

Decent applause for Mickie.

What was Thripp saying? Hard to listen while following Ned's test. Something about reorganization. Needing a general manager, back at HorseGuard headquarters. End of season. Profit share.

Counter-canter left, halt, rein-back. Full benefits. Sitting trot, twelve-foot circle. End of an era. New brooms at the INS. Counter-canter right. *Beautiful*. Let all the illegals go—you close your ears, Whit. No room for sentimentality, is there? Hard work, long hours. A single-minded . . . preferably, a *single* man. Decisive self-starter. You needn't answer now, Healey. You may think about it. Halt, salute, exit working walk, on a long rein.

Whistles, applause like brisk wind. Ned at the far gate, bending low, shaking his head in jubilant disbelief, dismounting into Erica's back-thumping embrace.

It's all coming together, Lex thought. It's *about* to. (He and Whit were escorting Viola Thripp back to her car. Her enthusiasm extended only to the dressage, she said. Over the decades she'd witnessed too many horrors at the jumps; viewing jumps made her indigestion act up.)

General manager. Hah— Hey, Leo, get *that*. The condo within grasp! And Ned in *tenth* place after dressage. Goddamn it . . .

Not that now he couldn't still see problems, but real, graspable problems were all. Jesus, and the boys. No more illegals . . . But some solution they'd find. And . . . Roland. So who is he? Not exactly a saint either. He doesn't own her. All right then, *meet* Roland. This time, no running. Tell him . . . the truth. How it has to be. What can he do?

General manager. Hah. Still no more an expert on horses than on aardvarks but moving up to the executive office. Desk job. So what the hell. Maybe about time.

Viola Thripp, at her car, offered a slender wrinkled hand.

"Tell me. No wishy-washy, now," she said. "Do you eat meat?"

"Meat. Oh no." Nothing but hot dogs, for days. "Brr."

"You do own a suit?"

Somewhere. "Blue pinstripe."

"Really? Wonderful. Well, that takes care of everything, then, don't you think? Bye-bye."

•   •   •

Walking back, Lex skipped every few steps, Whit bobbed regularly beside him, pointing out the powerful influence of his recommendations to Miz Thripp. Seeing a familiar figure rush past, Lex hailed for a light. "Your coffin nails," joshed Owen Goodchild, patting his pockets, distracted. "I quit. Still keep a fire on me for the ladies, even so." He had to rush, the announcer said. Short lunch break. This was a sixteen-hour day, a cracker's mule's job. The grousing sounded false in his mellow country-boy voice. Lex inhaled and the smoke after so long tasted odd too, moldy and complex.

"Now we're alone? About our little project," said Whit. "That was a mighty fine piece of work, you coming up with the Morton info."

"But that gets your ass—that changes the picture, right? Now you know the mare was overinsured, I assume you can deny the claim?"

"Nice fieldwork on your part, Healey, yes. Of course nothing I didn't already have in my own notes but gee, it's sure great to see you're on the ball."

You sleaze, Lex thought. First impressions, he thought. Healey, you sucker. He'd disliked Whitaker at first sight, and now all the bastard had to do was say "I already knew" to dump their deal.

"Hearsay." Mournfully, Whit shook his head. "On hearsay I can't subpoena bank accounts. Or maybe you can provide some evidence?"

"No."

"Or document your source?"

Lex dumped the cigarette with a shake of his head. Coco presumably had mixed feelings toward him, and no incentive even to admit their conversation.

"Well, there you go. So now you know and I know why, and pretty well how—you do still like my thinking there, don't you, Healey? About the warfarin? Pretty nifty shtick. But who gave the injection? If it was for the folks we're thinking, who'd they hire, who'd they pay off? You got any little notion?"

Lex shrugged. "Might."

"Good. Stay on it. Geez, Tommy Burns left a trail wide as the interstate—you get us a little smidgeon of evidence on this new fellow. Chop-chop. Now it's all coming together, let's close this baby. Gee whiz, Healey, you don't want this individual carrying on operations-as-usual amongst all these fine animals you're responsible for!"

Lex looked up at the shimmering noon sun. Riders rushing toward the arena buffeted past him. He nodded. There was that problem too, he had to admit. Not to be forgotten.

Gladstone, New Jersey, September 26

Dust boiled up in purplish brown clouds. In predawn the practice ring was alive with young riders, but she paced the fence, useless, clutching a Styrofoam cup of black coffee. Her stomach in revolt against any form of food. This day's rule that competitors work independently—trainers banned inside the ring, and forbidden to tune up their kids' horses—set the USET above and apart from other finals. The rule was an equalizer: under an uncertain rider even a seasoned jumper would begin to hesitate. Self-doubt was contagious.

She set the coffee hastily on the ground in order to yell through cupped hands: "Mickie, *left* rein! And give Cricket *space,* for God's sake ease up, *trust* him—or you think you're going to *lift* twelve hundred pounds with those scrawny chicken arms?"

Cantering by, Mickie threw her a blank, puzzled look. Impossible for a rider to sort out words from inside that rush of air and hoofbeats. Erica watched her take back reflexively over the next jump, stiffing the horse in the mouth. A scrambled landing. Touch-and-go. "*Why,* Mick? The poor guy didn't *deserve* that!"

Then why? She squinted through the haze, analyzing, as Mickie cantered the far side. There—the hint of an early buckle in Cricket's lead leg, as for a fractional second it took all the weight of the stride. And again, three beats later. Definitely. Not a stumble, but the prelude to a stumble, and the rider's natural instinct was to pitch her own weight back and yank rein: to try to hold up that horse.

If she, Erica, could just get on, she'd gallop Cricket no-hands till he learned to carry his own front end, even if he had to fall on his face a few times to get the message.

Cricket, you lazy— But when did it start? Yesterday? Even earlier? Had she seen and ignored the symptom, wished it away? Guilt mingled in the back of her throat with the bitter oil of coffee. She hadn't been giving her kids what they deserved. She was there but not there, her attention absorbed by the mess that was her so-called private life, which she could anyway no more direct or decide— here, now—than she could control what went on in this ring.

And no sleep. Dragging her tiredness like a blanket through the day, while at night . . . Even now a memory of last night erased the present. Under lamplight, sharp and clear compared to this dawn, Lex had unbuttoned her shirt, smiling. *I want to spoil you.* His changed smile, triumphant and secretive, like someone hiding an extravagant present. She believed him. His new mood, whatever its source, refreshed her more than sleep. She had looked down at the foreshortened perspective of her flushed breasts, erect nubs of nipples, and her long thighs pressed together, right angles to his. He knelt barefoot, belt open, the top of his faded jeans undone. On sudden impulse, she'd kissed the palm of each of his hands. Inhaling the nameless spice from his skin and from his breath against her cheek.

But now, today, the kids needed her completely. She had no *right*—

She bent down to retrieve her coffee, found it covered with a lens of dust, and kicked the cup over, coffee trickling beneath her useless boots.

The impact was an explosive sigh. Sound of air knocked out of a horse's lungs. The beat of silence that followed was shattered by shouts of "Whoa!" and "Loose horse, you guys, heads up!"—a

more immediate danger, for the moment, than anything else. Erica
lunged over the fence rails. Landed running, boots slipping in sand.

Cricket seesawed to his feet. Mickie lay rolled in a ball, moan-
ing, on the far side of the jump. Her small monkey face looked suddenly wizened and the eyebrows whited out by dust. But she seized
Erica, hauling on her trainer's wrist, shirt, and belt, to pull herself
up. There was no stopping her.

"M'okay," she croaked. She spat mud. "No big damage. Honest." Clinging for balance. "Crick must've tripped, huh? You saw?
He jumped fine—the jump was clean. You saw. Where is he—?"

Cricket had been caught. Led away through the gate he shuddered, letting fly his own layer of dust and sand. The loose stirrups
clanged. Erica recalled where his name came from: when bored,
this pony took quirky pleasure in running his bared teeth along the
bars of his stall, to hear them sing like the insect.

"I think—" she said. *Navicular* was the word in her mind. De-
generation of the hooves' nerve and bone. Dreaded, common, and
incurable fate for a jumper horse. "I'm going to have him X-rayed,
okay?" She paused, to gently remove Mickie's skewed hard hat.
"Best to be cautious. But I've been thinking anyway, it may be
time to find another horse for you."

SHERPIN. ALOIS SHERPIN," SHE REPEATED. "IS HE THERE OR NOT?"

"And whom might I say is calling?"

Madonna, you might say. Gennifer. Whomever he'll go for.
Tapping pencil on Hunters Courte notepad, Erica waited for Sherpin to pick up. A radio station wormed into her ear.

"Are we gazing at stars, babe?"

Dumb song. Always bothered her.

"Miss Habick? *I'm* so sorry. He's tied up on a conference call.
Where can he call you back?"

She read out the number on the phone. "Tell him, if it's within fifteen minutes. Otherwise, I'm gone."

Great. She slumped, stretched her legs, glanced around the room. Boot smudges on the floor, clothes everywhere, but the bed after two nights still undisturbed. Noon. A sulphurous threat of rain, wasps batting the window, throbbing air conditioner. Some risk of falling asleep here.

And fat chance Sherpin will call.

She had some time. Ned's ride was posted for two-ten—and Mickie now was a scratch. *Sweetie, please understand, no way can I let you out on that course.* The kid had taken disappointment on her square little chin. Both she and her mother, having seen the outside course, might even have felt a touch relieved that the decision to withdraw fell this way: by a stroke of fate and with honor intact.

But Erica, last night, had dreamed of riding that course herself, on the Monster, in place of Ned. With grass and trees streaking away, the garish walls of jumps rose up again and again before her. She was hitting every distance with the suspended sureness of perfectly sight-read music. (To look down, to become conscious of the fingering of the notes or the solid mass of the jumps—to *know*—would mean the end of the rhythm, and prove the impossibility of completing, even of having come that far.)

Turning toward dawn inside the silky weight of Lex's arm, she'd felt the exhilaration of the dream still running light in her veins.

And later on the grounds she was startled to discover that the actual course, with its fifteen fences, nearly mirrored the one mastered in her sleep. But then, she'd memorized and analyzed hundreds of courses. . . . And it was such random echoes, coincidences, that gave life a kind of transparency at times. A hint of underlying structure, like a play arrived at in the middle but not too late to get the central—

Don't fall asleep—

She rubbed her face, ruffled a hand through her hair. Only minutes since the call. So wait it out, on the off chance. A snap decision: to borrow Lex's car, return here to phone about the Sherpin horse. But Mother Travnicek was ready to buy *now,* aching with her daughter's frustration and infected by the competition fever of this USET. Ready and eager. Next week, at home with the bills and younger kids and husband, her financial priorities might become a tad confused. Tended to happen. A trainer had to seize the moment.

Not that she intended to screw a colleague or maneuver behind Don Deluna's back. She'd located Don in the USET's dungeon-like stone barn, mucking his own stall. You go ahead, he'd told her. Snag the nag. Laura's parents are cheaper than string cheese, they won't *buy* T.D. So make an offer. My loss, your gain. Anyway, he added, he was about to scratch Laura. Couldn't let her loose, out there. For some goddamn reason, she'd lost all confidence on that horse.

Funny how that happens, Erica commiserated.

So Thanks to Daddy was available. Sound. Not a *bad* horse—although maybe a hard-luck horse. Hard-luck horse for a hard-luck rider. And the trainer?

As Erica's laugh broke the silence of the room, the telephone rang.

"SAY THE MAN SAID *WHAT*?"

Lex's voice so sharp—edged with anger—in her ear. They had been walking side by side (pacing was all she did today) until he gripped her halfway between the announcer's booth and the start gate to the outside course. Owen's raw-carpentered announcer's booth mimicked, too cutely, a wishing well. The gate was merely a break in the looped white chain that defined a field of galloping ground studded with inventive obstacles. They kept far enough from the gate not to be trampled by contestants, who trotted in blind—rigid, thin-lipped children, mute or muttering to themselves and their horses—and exited blindly, soaked in tears and sweat as if they'd left a lifetime behind them out on course. Not all rode out; some walked, a few were carried. There had been falls. The jumps weren't light rails balanced in shallow cups; they were logs, ditches, stone walls. Nothing that gave way.

"*Well?* Erica, for heaven's sake, if you expect me to believe—"

"Oh, don't. You heard me. Don't blame the messenger." Only twenty minutes until Ned's start. She kept her gaze fixed on a hummock thirty paces away where Ned, ignoring a smear of grass and horse drool on his own sleeve, was obsessively rubbing his gelding's copper coat.

She could feel Lex glaring. Were his moods more volatile because of their long separation, or because of something that happened while they were apart? Late the night before, after the lovemaking, she had crouched on the floor of his room naked and happy and dripping from her shower and reached into his duffel bag. Searching for his hairbrush, but what her hand met first was paper. A letter—more than one, perhaps. Furiously, Lex had grabbed the bag to himself, as if she had no right, and then had coldly handed her the brush she needed. His irritation evaporated instantly, and she was left unsure, doubting herself because the notion of someone else in his life was fantastic and absurd. *Was* he hiding a surprise for her? Somehow she couldn't ask. She felt tendrils of secrecy and silence growing over them, like the fast-spreading bindweed that strangled healthy hedges and flowers on her farm.

At this moment though, after her talk with Sherpin, Lex's resurgent anger almost comforted her. It was familiar. Any habit can comfort, she realized. She suddenly realized how often this edge, the thin, precise blade in his voice, slipped free. For no reason. No sufficient reason that she could imagine . . . This time, though, the anger made more sense. It was, like her own sickened stupefaction, a natural response.

"Did he tell you *who* offered to do it?"

The edge braced her. "Of course I asked. But Sherpin didn't *care*. Probably a groom, he said. He assumed, because of the Spanish accent . . . That's why I—Lex, one of your boys? Will you quit *breathing* on me like that. Lex. Come on . . . Tino? *Tino,* damn it! You know that's what you've been thinking, for a long time. *I* didn't!" And why, she now wondered, had she so stubbornly clung to the belief that the season's string of disasters must be random bad luck? Not because she gave a shit about Tino, but because to suspect anyone meant buying into the paranoia. . . . And why buy in, as long as the Burns case dragged on with no solid proof, only lurid accusations shredding the careers and futures of people she'd worked with for most of her life? The Florida killing had to be a bizarre fluke. The rest a sour-grapes bunch of lies. Burns had confessed; weren't the others innocent till proven guilty? Ever since the rumors about Crimson started up, she'd felt like she was in a struggle, with Lex her only tangible enemy. A silent battle, though, never admitted between them. Even when Ned's gruesome night vision shook her conviction she hadn't let on, had taken charge and heard herself lie like a Bible Belt wonder-huckster, one lie unfolding into the next— Until yesterday, when Lex told of a letter his boss had recently received from Tino. So *Tino was alive.* And yesterday Ned rode the dressage like an angel. How reassured she'd felt, vindicated, the world not a vicious crazy joke after all—but that hadn't lasted long, it was gone now—

Behind her, Lex backed off a step. She interrogated the sky: smoking clouds like a welter of bruises. But still no rain.

He was nagging about Tino. His voice measured now, irritatingly sane. How could she be sure of Ned's story about cocaine in the barn at Seacrest, knowing what the boy's mind was capable of fabricating? And, by the way, weren't they in over their depth on him, wasn't it time to alert Ned's parents, let a doctor take on the responsibility—

Doctors. Christ. She did wish Tino dead! Wished Ned's vision (truck, body, jumper cables) true, if that would make Sherpin's story untrue. Though it would not. Of course not.

"When? *When* did he hear from this guy, exactly?"

"Lex—once he'd said it, he barely wanted to talk to me! It just came out. First he told me he'd let T.D. go like a shot, but only against a cashier's check. 'I've learned the hard way that horse-show people are all trash,' he said, 'and I don't extend credit to trash.' I thought he was still nursing a grudge toward Coco, but then he blew up about this other call he'd had, from a man who offered to 'solve his problem with the sick horse, permanent, for ten percent.' Sherpin apparently hadn't known about T.D. colick-ing last month. He said he didn't know what 'sick' meant and couldn't figure if it was an offer to rub out or a setup for blackmail. He talked as if I had something to do with it—as if he'd almost ex-pected to hear from me. 'If that beast croaks,' he said, 'it better not croak under *my* name.' He wasn't too naïve, he said, to see what he was being railroaded into, and I could have a hell of a discount but to leave him and his family out of it. He didn't want ever to hear how I solved my problems."

"Hey."

"Hey, what."

"You need to pull yourself together. Now."

Erica nodded. As Ned walked toward them she gazed far over the field, to clear her sight, and then leveled a firm smile.

"So. Carpe diem, huh? Guess this is it?" He flipped the reins high over Monster's head; they fell in the bristly mane.

"Guess so. Ready on three?" Erica squatted, to cradle the shaft of Ned's left boot. "One, two, *three*—" Ned sprang up, then eased down in the saddle. She wiped sweat from her lip. "Ned, before you go in, canter a few. But don't worry about waking him up. He will wake up out there, trust me. He knows his job. You'll be fine. Only please remember—"

"We *will* be fine." He stopped her, with a funny, deprecating twist of his face.

As they moved off, her arm jerked. It wanted to reach for the rein, his boot, the Monster's rippling tail. Not a chance. Ned struck a canter, dwindling.

She felt empty.

"Everything all right there?" Lex's hand covered hers.

Empty. No fight left. Wherever her mind circled, only this dull oppressive sameness. Sherpin's right, she thought. It's a sham. It's a cruddy business. Glory hype to sell fancy cars and watches. Takes no more than a phone call, a jolt, or a needle, to turn the meat back into money—abracadabra. Nobody takes any real risk—or only the dupes out on course, the kids. . . .

"Erica, listen. You look—not well. Please go sit, take a break—Ned's about to go in, but can I watch his course for you? This once?"

"*Damn* it." She widened her eyes at the rippling green field and jumps that shifted and flickered in a sultry light. "This is my *job*. Okay?"

THEY'D FOUND A RAKE AND, HOLLERING AND SHOVING, HAD scraped the rotted black leaves from the pool. The last light poured from a gash of orange between clouds and gilded their bodies, all in bathing suits and startling white except for the browned faces and forearms. Becky Hedgepeth, as victor, was the first to be thrown into the pool. Ned cannonballed in after her, grappling, hooting, plunging the girl's shoulders beneath the surface with a laughing crazy aggressiveness that Erica, in all the years with him, had never glimpsed before.

"Twelfth *place*. It's fantastic. Good for him." Lex nudged the rim of his plastic cup against hers. " 'Gratulations, coach." The tepid wine he had finally uncorked in his room tasted to her as nourishing as bread. Freshly showered and changed, they leaned on the catwalk rail, overlooking terraces, parking lot, and the pool frothing now with swimmers. "You proud?"

"*I'm* not," she fibbed. "Ned sure is. Look at the show-off. It's the Monster who *should* be. God. He pranced over the fences like an old foxhunter. He was having a blast out on that course. . . ." She sipped, exhilarated and exhausted, trying to push the night drive ahead out of her mind. The Monster and Cricket were still stabled on the grounds, waiting for her to come load and take them home. Watched over meanwhile by the kindness of Jesus and his crew, since she had already paid off her grooms. "Monster is a great horse. He could be. Know that?"

Lex rested low on the rail. Their heads were even. "I'm thinking, Erica. I think I'll just beef up the guard on him. Won't charge you."

She murmured, "If you can. Till after Harrisburg. Sure." Her mood slid a little. So, they shared the same anxiety—but unreasonably. Because who would want to harm the Monster? Everybody loved Ned's big gentle guy, and now he was a success story. . . .

So was Suzy's mare, remember? Everyone loved Crimson too. "Love." Well, *that* was stupid. Horses weren't slaughtered like people, in some fit of passion or jealousy. Horses had dollar signs branded across their haunches.

"Hey. I didn't mean to start anything. Rejoice, Hablicht! Stop biting the nickel. If you can't be happy now—" He swiftly kissed the corner of her mouth, eyes slanting sideways to be sure that no swimmer happened to witness. She smiled, sloshed the wine left in her cup. Lex lifted it away from her. "More?"

"Yes, please."

He turned back into his room.

The parking lot was two thirds empty. Losers departed early; the winners, celebrating, stayed on. (Paying extra for emptied rooms, to keep this day of the year, perhaps day of a lifetime, from ending.) Erica saw a drop of rain fall on the wood rail, to be joined, after a long, indecisive pause, by another. Below the catwalk strolled two women, one a blonde cased in sausage-skin jeans, her companion gargantuan, multilayered, like a pile of rugs topped with a head. Coco Beale and Helen Urbach. What could those two possibly have to say to each other?

Coco's girl had actually made the jump-off, for a fourth-place finish. At the show, Coco, gushing praise for Ned, had embraced Erica like a hard-muscled sister. A strange, though not unpleasant, sensation.

Then Helen (pinning Ned's twelfth-place ribbon between her breasts, adding to her colors) had loudly praised Erica's uncanny ability to pick good, young horseflesh. And wondered, by the by, whether she ought to up the insurance . . . ? A justifiable question. Why not? And the Urbachs are fighting about money. Watching huge Helen sway along the path below, Erica tried to cut away the canker. One should pity this woman. And also remember her grief, after the old family hunter died.

"Don't you want it?"

"Oh—" Erica took the cup. "Thanks. . . ." More drops were falling but no one below seemed to mind; the rain felt warm as air. As the light in the cloud gash dimmed, only the bodies clustered around the pool stayed clearly visible. Almost all were girls, adolescent athletes with hollow waists and narrow buttocks. Girls as long and sinuous as minnows. A separate species, no relation to Helen Urbach or any other grown woman. It seemed suddenly obvious to Erica why so many girls refused food to the point of starvation: their instinctive defense. The drive of any species is to survive, to persist as itself. She might have tried to remain one of them once, if she'd known how.

"Thinking?"

"Thinking total nonsense." She laughed, sipping.

"Good." He rubbed her spine, releasing a shiver. "That's better."

Engines revved. Mothers and a few fathers dashed along the paths, calling, and as the last reluctant swimmers emerged from the pool the rain pattered applause. Down in the parking lot the wheels of Ruthie's chair glittered like cobwebs, spinning to and fro as she directed a housekeeper's loading of suitcases into her van.

Erica crushed her empty cup. "Time we both hit the road." The second drink a serious mistake.

"I don't want to go."

"Me neither." There was a question that always hung over

every hour, put off by cowardice until the last moment. But it was the rain on her face, the suggestion of seeing him through wavering water, that tricked her with the sensation of tears. "So . . . When will I see you again?"

"Well. There's Harrisburg, soon."

"Soon . . . Lex, that's over two weeks away." She turned her back on the commotion in the parking lot, wiping rain from her nose. "I don't guess— I don't guess you could take some days off in between? For once, you come see me? Somehow." In the dark and the rain she could hardly make out his reaction. He looked grim. Or startled, or even alarmed. "Sorry. Never mind."

"See you where? How would we work that?"

"*I* don't know. I said, forget it. Never mind." Why did she have to act so desperate, destroy the chance of a civil, gentle good-bye? Just hating the thought of the long, hard drive, is all. Just the damn wine.

"Erica—I'd rather not ask the company for days off right now. Listen. I didn't want to jump the gun. But with this job, there's a genuine possibility—"

"*I said, never mind!*" Screeching, like a crazy slut. Well, everyone's shouting at each other, down in the parking lot too. And how appalled he looks. Don't be scared of me, please, I'm not losing my mind. Only sad. Why so desperate? Everything's falling apart now, disappearing. . . . I'm scared of everything. Scared to leave you, to go home, scared of what can happen there— Please, Lex, I need you to *make* me love you. The way you did in the beginning. Love streaming up from inside, beyond my will. Because for once to feel so much and keep giving it all away to you is the miracle, that's all, and I never believed I was able before— That's what you gave me. But now can't you feel things closing in? The danger that we aren't so strong, that we won't last? You stand there so sure we'll be all right, you *have* me, you don't ask how it is for me away—who I turn back into—when we're apart. Or you don't care, not enough.

"What did I do?" Lex swayed, as he sometimes did from no discernible cause, as if his height alone disturbed his balance. "This won't be forever. Hey. We have to have faith."

"Faith in *what*?" Oh no. Oh why am I doing this? Ugly to you now. Bawling. It's not your fault, is it? Sorry for myself. For us. Maybe—because I've been using you. I know. Never tell. Say we tell everything. No one can. Not the truth underneath. Not how I've been using you—just to feel somebody want me, really want me—

"Look. You hang on a second." Lex touched her arm. "Stay up here. Go in, get out of the rain—"

"But what—?"

He was running away from her, along the catwalk, skidding on the slick boards. Erica felt the whole rickety structure vibrate beneath her as he pounded down invisible stairs.

She followed him.

The paths glistened, broad snail tracks. Dusk had triggered sodium lights over the parking lot, they cast bronze bells spangled with rain and one trapped a clutch of small dark figures. It took her a moment to recognize a voice from within this bell as Ruthie Pryor's because she had never heard Ruthie so shrill before, octaves higher than her usual distinctive monotone. What was it about the timbre of a voice that made it unmistakable?

She felt much better, running. Breathing deep. Strong. Rain trickling across her face and into her ears, blurring the voices. Sharp, reassuring shapes of pebbles pressing up through the soles of her sneakers. As if there were somewhere to go. People run to arrive somewhere, whereas horses have a gene that makes them run for joy. She heard herself give a funny, shuddering gulp, the final sound babies make after recovering from tears.

"Let go of her. Now." At Lex's voice, Erica slowed to a walk. "Let's all just calm down here. Take your hands *off* the *chair*. Let's all try to talk—"

"Who the dickens? Butt out, mister." A man in a plastic raincoat was wrestling for Ruthie's chair. "Butt out! All right—that's it. I'm calling the police. I am goddamn it this kid's father. Hon, you heard me. You march in there and call nine one one." A ginger mustache: the only hair on his wrinkled shining head. A walrus, up from the sea. His wife—clearly a wife, wearing jewels on her fingers and only a sodden sequined sweatshirt over spandex tights—turned openmouthed to Erica, as if an ally had arrived.

"*Erica—?*" Ruthie half pushed up from the chair, as if the instinct to stand hadn't left her. "Please. You tell them. Tell them I've been taking care of myself. I can! I'm all right. This is crazy. He wants me to come *back*—"

"I'm not giving you a choice, Ruth. You're not safe on your own. We can't expect you to understand that at this point." Ruthie's father's foot fumbled to lift the brake on the wheelchair. Lex kicked it down again.

The wife, with an ingratiating smile, whispered, "We've been—basically irresponsible, I think. You know, sometimes it's real hard, to know what's the right thing to do. My poor baby. Will you just look at her?"

Erica said nothing.

Ruth's bandanna hung limp, black from rain. Wet, black tendrils clung to her cheeks. She balled her fists. "I can't believe—they were here, all *day. Inside,* waiting for me. Hiding. Until everyone else left." She twisted in the chair, trying to see the two men behind her. Her voice dropped. "I can't believe this is really happening. . . ."

"Sweetie pie," said the wife. "You're very confused. This isn't an ambush! We came all this way because we *care,* we simply can't stand by and watch you self-destruct! Sweetie, listen: I spoke to your doctor—"

"Oh my *God.*" Ruthie jammed her fists against her face. "Healey. Don't let them. *Please* don't let them. They have no right—they can't, I'm an adult, no one can make me go back—"

"Young lady." The walrus man's raincoat squealed as he leaned over the chair. "You have about pushed me to the end of my rope." Ruthie arched backward. Father and daughter, each upside down, locked eyes. "I drove six hours to get here, and it's six more back! I've had as much of this as—" Her father gripped the handles of the chair and shoved. Lex held one wheel. The chair stayed. "Son of a *bitch*. Out of my way. *Move*. I'm warning you."

"It's raining pretty steady," said Lex. "How would it be if we all go inside? Dry off. Calm down. Talk this whole problem over."

"Who *are* you?"

"Friend of Ruthie here."

"More like the guy who's been brainwashing my little girl! Ruth Ann, *baby*—"

"Really," the wife confided to Erica, reproachfully, "this really is more sort of a family matter. No offense."

"No offense," Erica replied, "but we can't leave her."

Ruthie Pryor, standing, would have been taller than either of her parents. The father's shiny head barely reached Lex's shoulder, but he was stocky in the way of men who enjoy hard physical labor in their spare time. Now, without letting go of the chair's handles, he rammed sideways, swiftly, with his head.

Lex swayed. "*Don't* do that again," he murmured.

The father gave a chuckle. His head swung again, and Lex crowded close against him to break the punch. The raincoat flashed as one arm released the chair in order to grasp Lex by the neck. Lex ducked and pivoted in a reaction almost too quick for Erica to follow. She saw his arm shoot free of the crouch and she heard the delicate crack of bone on bone. And then over the father's bellow of pain and outrage came Ruthie's shattering scream, as under the weight of her thrashing father the wheelchair listed, wobbled, and completed its fall.

The father stood gaping. Lex with automatic solicitude propped him up by the arm. The wife sobbed, luxuriously, like someone who's been waiting for a good, solid chance to weep for a long time. Erica, cross-legged on the puddled pavement, glanced up at her, in mixed sympathy and disgust, and then leaned low again. She held Ruthie, cradled head and shoulders in her lap.

"Think you can get up okay?"

"Up—" Ruthie choked on a laugh. "Are you kidding?"

Erica smiled. This was the trainer's reflex: to smile, if possible, whenever one of her kids took a tumble. Show them how to take it in stride—

But Ruthie couldn't see her now. Ruthie's hand moved toward her smeared wet forehead. "Hurts. I'm okay. I know this body. Nothing's broke. I mean—" She had started to tremble. "Oh God. I was so frightened. Falling. Something happened. It was like—it was like *before*."

Lex had righted the wheelchair and hunkered to inspect it. The father patted his wife's back. Someone might, suggested Erica, go ask for a doctor.

"No. No doctor," said Ruthie. "No need—"

"Shh." Erica hugged her tight. "I know you're okay. That's not the *point*. To play for more time—so we make sure you stay." She hesitated. "That is what you want?"

Ruthie nodded hard and winced.

"Hey. Your parents are real shook up now. You've got the moral high ground. So trust me. We'll work it out."

"Erica. Oh God. You don't know how it is—to be that frightened. And something *happened*. I saw the road—I remembered right before—it was like—"

"Shh. Shh." Erica's mind drifted to the horses, waiting to be taken home. She stroked Ruthie's tangled hair, her curved back.

"Be careful. You don't really want to touch me."

"Why not?"

Ruthie twisted and pressed against Erica's leg. Hiding her face. Her words came up muffled, barely audible. "Because . . . I must have . . . I'm sorry, Erica. Don't tell anyone. I wet my pants."

Harrisburg, Pennsylvania, October 9, Morning

THE PETA PESTS SWARMED LIKE A GENERATION OF CLUSTER FLIES hatched out of season by the extended summery heat. They harangued against such perversions as foxhunting, gelding, horseshoeing and horse meat in dog food. They chanted and pumped signs and spooked the children's horses. In Ruthie's view all do-gooders were potentially dangerous; these ignorant enthusiasts were bent on literally killing with kindness. Earlier that morning she herself had come within an inch of being bludgeoned by a demonstrator's pole as it hoisted a spray-painted sheet: StOP the TORTuRe NOW! BAN ShOW JUMpiNG! Since then, motoring around the grounds outside the Agricultural Hall to pass the time until the Medal competition started, Ruthie had sideswiped every batch of interlopers she could find: tilting the golf cart's left front wheel toward their splayed, sandaled feet.

A bowl of haze sealed the hall and its surrounding acres of parking lot, and the drab highway-sliced town and tired-green hillsides beyond. On a back strip of the tarred-over acres squatted a farmers' market. Ruthie could feel sweat soaking into her bandanna as she patrolled the stalls, trying to summon an impulse to buy. Wilting dahlias lolled from mason jars. The tomatoes were split and overripe. Her covered, immobile legs itched. She envied the strolling riders in the crowd—buying, haggling, also killing time—in sleeveless tops, bare-legged. She did not envy the farmers: work-weary men and women with heavy bellies and washed-out eyes.

But neither the heat nor the demonstrators could spoil Ruthie's essential mood. She felt *good*. Trouble—trouble she could act on—exhilarated her. Fact. Let trouble come. This was the same mood—conviction, excited release—that she'd felt when she wrote to Roland Pettit. This was something about herself no shrink had been able to penetrate, let alone manipulate. Now let trouble come worse, fiercer, out in the open—she couldn't see the design of what would come yet, not clearly, but she tried.

The previous night, after gulping her bedtime mix of Flexeril and ibuprofin, she had inventoried the remaining pills in the lineup of plastic root-beer-tinted containers. The reserves added up a third higher than expected. Grace time, before the anxious campaign to obtain new prescriptions. The odd fact was that since her last trip home, she'd hardly touched her hoards of Percodan and Seconal. And of course the less medication she needed for the pain of the day, the more clearly she could see ahead. Cold rage and resolve turned out to be finer, better-calibrated drugs.

She still needed help at night. There were bad dreams; since the confrontation with her parents one in particular, which woke her sweat drenched and struggling to let out a soundless scream, with jolts running through her like knives turning inside her legs. The dream didn't replay the night of the brawl; it was another form of memory. Awake, with her sense of place and the present returning, she commanded herself to lie completely still again, to try to extract more images from the borders of the dream. What she saw: fluffy summer clouds. The descent from the overpass. White guardrail ticking past as a book slid from the seat beside her to the floor. The book's title, gold-lettered on green, *Riding to Win*. A loan from Deluna, whose place she was heading for now . . . Glimpse of dashboard and below, her two summer-bare sturdy legs balancing the pedals of the machine as she leaned over sideways to retrieve the book. And surfaced to find the world vanishing: a flash of chrome, a brown shade blotting out her windshield left to right—and as she spun the wheel (into the guardrail, the last landmark she remembered) there was only the briefest irrelevant impression of brightness returning and an ordinary brown van—pulling away on the road that was pivoting behind her as she crashed and spun, in a long weightless moment of shattering glass. . . .

She woke again. Three times she'd let the dream run through her. No more. Better the hammer-fist sleep she was used to, and the codeine headache in the morning.

There had been one pure deep sleep, though—on the same night her parents came. The local GP, after a tentative examination (the fool had hardly dared touch her, as if she were some rival's *property*), had prescribed another sedative (unexpected windfall) and immediate rest. Travel, he'd warned, blinking at her father's swollen jaw and lip, was not advisable. Her father waved him off. Then had come the ugly pointless "discussion" with her parents and, later, real talk alone with Lex and Erica—and finally her friends had tucked her, drained of fear and indignation, into her motel bed. Erica slid in beside her. Lex lay on a raft of cushions on the floor. Into the stale, comforting dark, amid the rustles and slowed breathing of her friends, burst the sudden realization that she had forgotten her medication. But then she had simply slept. . . .

She used to have many friends. Hadn't she? Ruthie considered this question again while driving from the market toward the trailer encampment where Don Deluna's patched and ancient rig should have pulled in by now. It was noon. "Hunter competition" day, the relatively easy and straightforward course that preceded tomorrow's tough AHSA Medal finals. She'd ridden medal finals twice herself; at shows like this one even strangers had called out to her by name. Not this year. No one knew her anymore.

What you need is a friend, Lex had said. *Someone your parents trust.* (A contradiction in terms.) *Probably someone older—*

That's you, Healey.

He'd made a face and grabbed at her nose, while she ducked, laughing. *I mean it. Your money—if you could appoint your own trustee, someone they can't possibly object to, not legally, or . . .*

Erica had asked, *Ruthie? What do you expect they'll do? Come back again?*

Sure. Soon as they can mobilize the little white men. No laughter.

Her joke sounded too true to be funny, Ruthie had realized. The standoff wouldn't last. The threats still echoing in the motel room—her father's bluster about assault, Lex's cooler speculation on "coercion" and "financial exploitation"—had only temporarily neutralized each other. Her parents had stormed off (humiliated, livid, tugging up their shredded righteousness), but once they were back at home they would begin to pull the levers of the machinery. Shrinks and lawyers. They would come back.

Erica had trickled the last of the tea into Ruthie's cup. *Then listen to Lex. It's good advice.*

No, she'd thought then. Well meant but terrible advice. A step away from surrender. But as the days went by in ominous silence, the advice looked better. An act, a barricade against interference that would let her move on with her decisions. What mattered. Still, Ruthie didn't like the emptiness that swelled around her when she tried to picture this "friend." (Healey, it *should* be. Or Erica. But they brushed her off.) And then, as if he had been waiting patiently for his turn, Don Deluna came to mind.

Deluna had an incorruptible reputation. When she'd switched from Coco's barn to Don's, her parents had been "ecstatic." (Her mother's word. Coco she'd always termed "a cold fish.") Don had at least once confided in her, as an equal. He had been a good teacher to her too, when she was her other self.

Ruthie drove slowly. Fresh manure piles steamed on the pavement. Horses were being backed off the vans to be led into the stables—an all-purpose cavernous maze behind the arena, built more with pigs and cows than hyperathletic horses in mind. Now steelshod hooves clattered on the slick asphalt, and she stopped frequently, respecting the nerves of the animals that trotted and skidded in front of her. They were bug-eyed, crouched for flight as if, in this strange and treeless new place, fearing a blow from the sky.

Tucked in the shadow between two gleaming eighteen-wheelers stood an ordinary green van. The back doors were stenciled SOUND IDEAS, O. GOODCHILD, PROP.—this was Owen's vehicle, his jumble of amps and microphones and wires lay all humped inside, but for a moment a shudder rose through her. Ruthie swallowed against it and closed her eyes. She'd had this reflex frequently in the past two weeks: the world was full of stubby, loaf-shaped vans.

"Don? Hello, Don? Are you up there?"

She switched off the golf cart and waited, wondering whether he could hear her through the din of trucks, shouting grooms, and whinnying horses. No point in getting out of her cart, she could never scale the steep step up into the cab of his truck. Deluna's four-horse rig was custom-built in the sense a sharecropper's shack is: the animals traveled in a massive wood box bolted to a flatbed, while the ancient dented extra-large cab served Don on the road as bedroom, tack room, kitchen, and office. In the dim, messy interior she made out a pile of boots, the corner of a table, a minifridge. He would hardly go off and leave the door open.

"Don! Can you spare a minute? It's Ruthie!"

Someone was speaking inside, or else a radio had been left playing. She listened, uncertain, while re-rehearsing her offer (an offer, not a plea): to pay him a proper fee, merely for taking on pro forma this trusteeship which she would do the work of setting up and managing. An arrangement to benefit both. It excited her, to be about to spring on Deluna (who had once pinned his hopes on her winning here, who was always short of money) her generous solution.

"Hello? *Deluna!*"

Abruptly, she switched on the cart and backed and drove up tight against the cab, but now she was too close to see inside. She listened again. The voice, though not Don's, had the cadence of a real speaker.

"—Nobody. Heck, what's got you so frazzled? I can *see* right out the door from here." She recognized the sunny baritone of Owen Goodchild. "Or want me to shut it so we both can suffocate?"

A mumbled buzz. Scraping sounds.

"Here. Final delivery," said Owen. "Looks like shop closing time. Now hold on! Nobody's sorrier than me, old buddy. Got a call from the grocery boy up north. Makes it sound like a Gestapo raid. Boston's finest, shooting fish in a bucket. Revere, Charlestown, Billerica . . . *Twenty-two* they pinned. Not just punks either. It's all a big fat mess so don't ask me why I'm laughing."

"But you didn't *warn* me. You know I'm counting on . . ." Ruthie bowed her head, leaning closer to the cab, trying to decode Don's thinner, unsteady voice. "Four *years*. My God. You can't just quit—"

"Excuse me? And why not? Now listen, good buddy: you had a long, easy ride with me. I have gotten next to nothing out of this. Did it all to help you along."

"That was only because—"

"*Please.* Will you shut up about that? Ancient history. I swear, you lean on me again, drag that up one more time— Listen: you have to know when to hold them, know when to fold them. Right? So, I am folding. How do you think I feel? Good golly, you think this is how I had things planned to turn out for *my*self?"

"All right. Tell me who to contact instead."

"*Don.* You're kidding."

"You don't understand. It's for her. She *needs* it—"

"What your wife needs is what you should have given her twenty years ago. Swift belt in the chops. It's never too late."

"Please, Owen—"

"Now just what's the awesome ole problem? Look here. What I brought you here in the brush box ought to last her, probably even till things loosen up again. Right? And hey. I'm out of here tonight, *tonight,* so don't come looking—but I'll be back in touch. Honest. Only right now I have to get a wiggle on, understand? So this time it'll have to be cash on the barrel—"

"I can't, Owen. Not until I sell some first, here. One *day*—"

"Not jerking my chain, are you? No. Shoot, good buddy. Sometimes I wonder can you zip your own Velcro."

"Wait—"

"Steady down. Don't get fussed. I got an idea. You could help me out, be to both our benefits in actual fact. Because here I am up to my ass in alligators and needing to hit the road—but there's a favor I promised a friend, which I'm supposed to take care of tonight. I don't *want* to, it's a royal pain in the butt, but I sure can use the travel cash. . . . Tell you what. You do the favor, and we split the commission. Fifty-fifty. Which buys you at least, oh, say, a third of what's here? Now how's that strike you?"

"What kind of favor? Oh Jesus . . . Oh no. No."

"You can handle it great. Your type of thing I'll bet. Having your special touch with the critters and all. Darn—in fact, I wish I'd thought earlier—"

"I don't want to hear any more about it! Get the hell out of here!"

Ruthie heard the sharp impact of something thrown, or fallen, inside. Her hands felt stiff and bloodless as she struggled into reverse. *Get the hell out of here.* She heard the weepy helplessness in Don Deluna's voice as she obeyed him. The golf cart lurched backward, made a drunken pivot, stuttered along the length of Don's rig, and climbed cockeyed through a dump pile of straw. She didn't see much of anything until she looked back over her shoulder. Owen Goodchild, toting an ordinary wooden brush box, filled the door of the cab. As he bounced from the step to the ground, the whole rig shook and lifted.

Owen looked different. She registered, automatically, a recent clownish growth of beard. He set the box down and pulled a matchbook from his pocket, tore a scrap from its corner and with the scrap began to pick his teeth. He seemed to stare in her direction with no expression at all—but by then she was already in the next alley of the parking lot, where anyone had a right to be.

She could find no trace of Healey.

The whole show world had turned into a maze, agonizingly slow to search. She might not find him until nightfall, when the hectic turmoil of the day's competition ended. She might not find him at all. There was the maze of the acres of parking, filling rapidly now with spectators' cars. The PETA protestors scuffled with guards, stole behind the guards' backs to litter windshields with their fluttering pink leaves of propaganda. There was the maze of the indoor stabling, ill-lit rows and aisles of stalls draped like medieval battle tents with the various appliquéd cloth colors—some rich and flashy, others worn and bedraggled—of the barns that had taken up temporary residence there. The moment she entered the stables flocks of sparrows and pigeons whirred into the lofty dimness, and all her sense of direction dissolved.

Linked to the stables by a gated, upsloping ramp was the arena itself. Ruthie knew it well: the oval of fine-harrowed cushiony dirt, separated by only a low wooden wall from the looming tiers of seats, hundreds of seats forming a steep funnel up almost to the top of the dome. Her memories of riding here came flooding back. On medal day (tomorrow, again), when the seats were all filled, she'd entered the arena with the sense that one gigantic murmuring thousand-eyed animal encircled her and her horse from above. To ride, one had first to perform the prodigious mental trick of blotting out this huge suspiring creature, the funnel of watchers. She could not recall how she—how any of them—had done it. Concentrate to a pinpoint. Reduction to the essence of each movement, each moment. Concentrate into oblivion. That's what riding was about.

Even her mother had said, *Oh, Ruthie, I nearly died. It's so scary, looking straight down. You kids look so alone, like gladiators waiting for the lion.* The funnel was scariest, though, for the horses. Horses are born knowing they are natural prey; no coddled barn life can erase that wary instinct. What they fear most is the predator from above—the jaguar, the mountain lion. Her second year she'd had to take her chances here on a green horse, a talented youngster that had never experienced finals before. The gate opened, he marched three obedient steps—and saw. Her clenched urging legs could tell him nothing. He froze, paralyzed, and she heard the animal's heart stop.

Now she braked her golf cart at the base of the ramp. The arena was yet another maze, rising vertical; there was a rickety elevator in one corner tower, but without her wheelchair she was banished. From within came a light drift of applause that ushered one contestant out from the hunter course, a hush to welcome the next. The exiting horse paused to sniff her cart.

"Good round? He still looks nice and fresh," said Ruthie.

"Oh yeah. He eats courses like that for breakfast." The rider, fondling her horse's ear, still looked fresh too. Under the helmet, not a hair had escaped from its net. Barely a crease in the tailored, pinstriped jacket. A new face, no one Ruthie had ever seen before. "*I* don't, though." The girl laughed. "He was being so good but I missed the distance at the oxer. Tight. We won't *get* anything."

"Don't worry. It's only a warm-up. For tomorrow."

"*Oh* yeah." The girl rolled her eyes, then said, "You're, um, Ruthie Pryor, aren't you?"

Ruthie stared at her.

"I saw you ride here once. When I was just a little kid doing novice! You were so fantastic. Really. You should have—" Her horse pawed. Another rider waited to pass. "Oops. Guess we better move on—"

"Wait. Do you know if Ned Urbach went yet?"

"Ned . . . ? Oh, definitely. Hours ago . . ." But she had to move on. Over her shoulder, with a bright smile, she added, "I'm so jealous. It's like, the judges adore him. But he really did nail the course."

• • •

She returned to the stable maze. Healey had no reason to linger in the arena; Ned was done for the day, and Mickie was scratched from this show. (Her three-hundred-dollar deposit a loss, unless a vet certified her horse unsound. But that would practically wipe out any chance of selling him.) Cricket was here now, to be sold, but how could Erica offer him without mentioning the stumble? What would *happen* to Cricket? Erica was maybe too straight-arrow for her own good.

If she could at least find Jesus, in here. Or Erica. They'd probably know where Healey was. And Healey had that beeper thing, she remembered, as her own watch peeped. Two o'clock. How much time left? What did "night" mean? Seven, ten, midnight? Not that she would tell either of them what she'd heard. Especially not Erica. (Not unless she, Ruthie, wanted to guarantee that Ned would blow tomorrow's ride. She considered this possibility a moment, gnawing the flesh inside her cheek, and shrugged.) How could she even be sure about what she had heard? The sense of each single sentence—to her frustration she couldn't even retrieve them exactly now, not word for word—wasn't necessarily ominous. Not at all. Clear enough that Goodchild and Deluna were together in some kind of partnership, dealing stuff—well, so what, if not those two, someone else would. For the older jump riders especially, coke was just a routine preparation, like the bute they numbed their horses with. Goodchild, constantly coming and going from Boston, traveling up and down the East Coast with his loaded van, had the ideal delivery system. Deluna, the loner acquainted with everyone, trusted and respected, made the perfect retailer. Her initial astonishment over Don had faded rapidly. Why not? Especially if he needed the stuff to placate his addicted wife—perhaps that had been his link to Owen in the first place. The shadowy Mrs. Deluna: always "sick," in and out of expensive "clinics"—Ruthie touched the bulge of a vial in her sweatpants. Waste of a life. I could never live like that.

But the rest of their talk? A favor . . . What kind of favor? Nothing, nothing clearly said. And then Owen had jumped down from the rig and paused, the way you do to collect your thoughts. What next? Maybe aware of her, maybe not. He had pulled the matchbook from his shirt pocket and tweaked a corner off the cover. And proceeded to shove the invisible bit of cardboard—a makeshift toothpick, she realized, what a revolting habit—deliberately, rhythmically, between his large white teeth.

"Kee-rist, Ruth! You trying to run me over?"

"Sorry! I didn't see, half the lights are out in here—"

"Tell me about it." Coco, who'd sprung backward and nearly fallen, steadied herself on a stall pole. "Hate this dump. Worse every year. Pig shit in the stalls. Firetrap. Dozen accidents waiting to happen."

"Coco—have you seen the guard manager around?"

"The who?"

"Healey? Tall, skinny, kind of bristly short hair—"

"Ah. Our Ichabod. Mister Weird, the fast operator."

"What?"

"Mamas, don't let your girls grow up to be riding instructors. You know what's missing around here . . . ? Water water all around and not a drop to drink. Of course you can try to make do with the grain rep, or your friendly neighborhood blacksmith maybe, or if you truly luck out the night watchman—" Her forehead bunched up in wrinkle waves.

"The night watchman. Have you seen him?"

"Sorry. Not that I've been looking. What is it with these losers? Most never made it past the eighth grade. Whereas the ones who do turn you on, swaggering around in their britches, showing off their tight little buns—they only have eyes for each other. Don't mind me, Ruthie. I'm in a funk. One of those days when you wonder what the hell it's all in aid of. Do I look as awful as I feel?"

"No. Not awful at all."

"Oh, diplomacy. You've grown up a lot, haven't you?" Coco crossed her arms; she gave Ruthie a sweet, fading smile. "Not

Ranger though. The everlasting boy charmer. What do you think? He's not one of the *boys'* boys though, is he? God knows where *he's* coming from. Acts like butter wouldn't melt in his mouth. Inspires the little girls' riding, I'll give him that much. Look what Suzy pulled off today—on *his* horse. Beautiful. If her nerves hold, is she ever set for tomorrow. Damn. *I'd* like to hop on that horse. Dream on, Beale. Ranger won't even speak to me now. Not after yesterday—did you watch? I beat him out of the grand prix. That's four in a row. Were you there? What was I supposed to do, pull *up*? Today when I tried to talk to him he looked at me like, like—" she twisted her long fingers with their meticulously polished nails together and her face twisted at the same time. "We used to be friends. Pals. We even—never mind. Now he makes me feel . . . like nothing. *Old*."

"Coco? I, um, really need to keep going."

"I think he's in love with himself. Warning: don't anyone try to come between Ranger and Ranger."

"There's a couple of things I have to do now—"

"Oh. Sure, honey." With a graceful thrust of her back, Coco abandoned the pole she'd been leaning on. She bent over Ruthie, who felt the reassuring hard scratch of calluses as her former trainer stroked her cheek. "You're absolutely right. You keep on going on. Me too."

LITTLE MISS MUFFET SAT ON A TUFFET.

Whose voice?

Light, confident, with a thrill of indifferent intimacy. Ranger Boyd's voice, of course. Coco's fault, that it sang in her head just now. Coco's problem was not hers. How anyone could waste a moment's regret on Ranger—

She sat on no tuffet, but in her golf cart, on the bottom of the Susquehanna Valley, under a vast metal roof invisible in the darkness overhead, surrounded by rows and aisles of straw-bedded stalls, wooden cages. No outside air penetrated from the wide entrances that shimmered, miragelike, at opposite ends of the barn. The relative coolness here, a blessing to animals, was constant as a cave's.

If anything, Ruthie thought, she was the spider, and this was where she had to wait.

Her golf cart almost filled this alcove between stalls, the green-and-white-draped "headquarters" of Stoneacre Farm. Tack boxes, class lists, soiled saddle pads and leg bandages, feed bags and pails, and one gaudy new ribbon from the morning, all piled in back. She had leveraged herself far enough to swipe a half-dried doughnut from an open carton and was ordering herself to bite and swallow, bite and swallow, despite the chemical aftertaste, which blended with a pungency of liniment from unrinsed wash buckets. It was after four and she'd had no lunch.

In his stall on her left, the Monster nickered a gutteral plea for a treat.

On the right, Cricket was swaying like a jazzman, zinging his bared teeth on the iron grill bars.

Which horse was marked for tonight? If she could only know that . . .

Tonight there would be over two hundred horses stabled under this roof. Healey's crew would make their rounds, with hours between each visit. The schedule was easy for anyone to predict—simply read the check sheets posted on each stall.

Powdered sugar dribbled in dashes like tiny snow tracks down her front. She brushed them away, reminded of cocaine.

The old hunter died. At Seacrest. Probably cocaine in the feed—Healey had surmised this, in one of their talks. But he wouldn't say where that idea (typical show rumor, she'd thought) had started. Who would want to? For what? It couldn't have been Don— Don had sounded completely surprised. Horrified at Owen's proposal. But you could remain horrified as well by a memory of something you had once done, yourself.

Cold here in the cave. Suddenly she craved light, and the last of the day's heat.

Not Don. But Owen—

And what about Crimson Cadillac? Back to the beginning of August, midpoint of this never-ending summer. And there'd been unusual deaths before—in July, in June—they'd drifted like summer clouds across the season's sky. . . . You had to put the losses out of mind. A horse will live only for fifteen good years or so. Often not. Even the youngest pony rider soon learns to deny being in love—learns from the first loss, when the beloved is shipped off to a sales barn, or discovered stiff in a field, or is put down by a vet's slow, remorseful injection. If you risked your neck to ride, you also had to risk your heart.

But Healey just couldn't forget about Crimson. There been an autopsy—surely cocaine would have shown up in an autopsy? Anyway, what a clumsy, unreliable way to attempt to kill a horse. Ruthie herself could think of a half dozen superior methods. . . .

Owen Goodchild was at least as smart as she was. He'd created his business, the whole concept, from scratch. He was a city person—though there was, she recalled, a cousin or brother somewhere who worked at the track—who'd never so much as sat a horse but still made you believe he'd been born on a farm. Owen's knack of foreseeing snags before they bloomed to catastrophes earned the loyalty of all the volunteer ladies who organized the shows behind the scenes. Funny: as a kid Ruthie had been part of his Pied Piper band (vying for the bear hugs and peppermints he bestowed whether you won or lost)—but now that she was older, she had a different sense of him. His smooth smile reminded her of certain hospital nurses: the ones who either couldn't see people as such anymore or else secretly despised what they saw. Under Owen's tupelo honey voice was a chill that made her head hurt. Recently, without knowing why, she had changed her path, even changed her plans, to avoid him.

Not stupid, though. And if he had happened to drop a matchbook with torn corners outside Crimson Cadillac's stall—and to misplace another, at some point, in the barn at Seacrest—what did that *prove*?

The Monster rattled his empty feed bucket, pawed through the straw. Her head pounded. She ached, stiff and chilled. No drugs.

Gooseflesh on her arms. Nearly five. Stay here. Don't go running in circles. Someone had to come, soon, if only to feed Monster and Cricket. Then, for a while at least, she wouldn't be alone.

She was thirsty now. Misery made her sleepy in a fitful way. Her thoughts tripped on each other and scattered. A panic thought broke the surface, about her money. How to protect it now? Numbers flashing on a screen, microimpulses on wires—tap the keys and it's gone. *We only reimbursed what your riding cost us, sweetie pie! Now, isn't that fair? With your father about to retire— All those years, I swear we were all on some irresponsible, lunatic binge, we borrowed against the house, life insurance, everything, so you could campaign and win, win, win—*

That made her wince. But it's impossible, thought Ruthie. They would never have gone so far.

The kaleidoscope shook, and she saw herself wrapped warm in a quilt on her own bed, not in the gloomy garage but upstairs in her small, sun-bubbled room above the buzz of the house, happily, confidently planning her escape—

She saw Lex and Erica twined together, whorled brown and shell pink against the sand, inside a circle of rocks.

She jerked. Where *was* her letter? Roland must have it; what had he done? Or did he not believe her? Or was the letter lost? To-morrow, send another . . . ?

No one ever escaped quite the way they planned.

And here came Brett again. His clever lips glistened from the kiss. Though she hardly knew him, after the night of the dance she had walked many times to his house—a shutterless duplex it was, vinyl siding and toys left out on the porch—and passed without stopping. This summer, more than once, she'd dreamed about him—or made use of his name in dreams, maybe that was all. She hardly knew him. When she woke her hand still pressed between her legs, as if pressing on a flowing wound. Tears spilled clean and cool, not from shame, but release.

Brett faded. She heard a few last horses returning from the arena, their iron shoes ringing slow four-four time.

Someone real would come to her soon. Ned, or Erica, or Jesus, or even Healey. So thirsty. And while they watered the horses she could take a drink too. . . .

To let herself go, to drowse, Ruthie realized, was safer now than later. Because unless or until Healey came, she had a long night ahead here in the huge dim barn. Nothing to do but keep watch, among the innocent, restless horses.

Harrisburg, Pennsylvania, October 9, Evening

THE PLANE WAS A SEVEN-PASSENGER PROP. NO SHOCK ABSORBERS. It chucked and bounced over solid ruts and boulders of air with an old-timer's antic vigor. It reminded Lex of a ratty, bewitching MG he had once owned, long ago and much too briefly.

The air was clotted with haze. Under the plane's wing, through yellow striations, shone the flat metallic snakeskin of the Susquehanna.

His was the last, rearmost seat. Legacy of a blessed no-show, on the last connection to Harrisburg. He'd felt fantastically lucky to get it, after sprinting through the terminals at Logan with a premonition of presealed doom. One hundred and eighty-six dollars: the full-fare price of first having ducked out on his job to detour northward and then giving in to Rosie's pleas not to set out driving Boston to Pennsylvania, in lashing rain, on no sleep. He'd stayed the night—to polish off a bottle of sticky Lambrusco in celebration, though his mother couldn't know why. The trip north had turned out wildly different from what he'd expected. He had not even managed to see Erica. But there was no way—no matter how his most cynical side bit the coin—that he could regret it.

Now he sat hunched in the narrow fuselage like a hog-tied convict. Any attempt to lift his head for a glimpse of his fellow travelers set off a twanging series of cramps. It was easier to glance out the window; easiest to contemplate the bony geography of his own knuckles and knees.

Snatches of conversation pierced the laboring racket of the engines.

"—had to decide. Her ballet teacher . . . lowered the boom. Riding destroys the turn-out, apparently. She was losing her pointe. . . ."

"—my Jennifer, the visitation rigamarole. And she was in *tears*. Her so-called father's sacred schedule—"

"—and zero social life. Look what they sacrifice! You wish you could *help* them—"

Sacrifice. He spread his palms, to study their mottled hills and etched branching rivers. *Sacrifice* was the kind of word Roland Pettit was able to use out loud without flinching. Right along with words like *fate* and *commitment*. Lex could still hear the surprising high pitch of Pettit's voice, as if his burly chest were merely a medium for a nearby ventriloquist—perhaps their waitress, or the toothpick geezer in a fedora who remained perched at the counter of the diner, gazing at the wall, while Pettit's words streamed on. Pettit's hands had clenched and scrubbed the table between them. His plain rounded wedding band put Lex in mind of the brass curtain rings he and some fourth-grade accomplices had used for after-school games of "married people." (A hectic solemnity. Anyone giggles, they're out. Take turns being "priest." Then, in a closet, with a flashlight, the first dedicated exploration of a girl's simple secret: the chubby mound, single dimple and cleft.) Pettit's ring glowed, the one object of any value in that place, catching light from the window. Lex had mostly kept his head turned toward that window to avoid seeing Pettit—later, he knew, he would not want to remember clearly the other man's face. The Assabet Diner looked out on a strip of minimall in a valley town scarred by chronic depression, even its few fine old colonial houses sagging into the rain-soaked ground, clocks in the church towers without hands. Not what he had imagined as *her* town. Pettit's stubby fingers looked permanently inflamed, the nails chewed below the quick. He found it as hard to avoid seeing the ring as to stomach the embarrassment he felt for Pettit, for Pettit's sickly, advice-column phrases.

He imagined those swollen fingers moving across the landscape he knew, her body.

"She's sort of like an artist," he had heard Pettit declare in that strained, light voice. "She *is* one. You know she could've even gone to the Jewel Yard?"

Lex looked up, startled.

"Jewel Yard. The conservatory, that's how good she played the cello. And what she does now, that isn't art? You didn't know about her music, did you? You've been—you've maybe known her since how long? You don't have the slightest idea. What it is, is . . . see, there is this fantastic pressure on her right now. With these finals. She's like—a sleepwalker. Well, you're there! Isn't she? She *needs* to feel like she's totally free. But what she *wants*—"

Lex had picked at the rash of bubbles on his side of the Formica. This age- and heat-blistered table had to be at least four decades old; a fifties-style baby jukebox rested on its window end, coin slot gagged with tape. What *he* had wanted right then was to flip forward in time, as nimbly as he was flipping through the jukebox cards. So why had he agreed to come? When he called the farm, reciting her name under his breath—why hadn't he replaced the receiver, immediately and quietly and not for the first time, when Roland Pettit answered? Because it was *time*, period; he was sick of dodging the inevitable. Probably (the truth flashed at him between Dion and the Everly Brothers) the grand notion of driving up to surprise her was only a smoke screen to himself, a booster for the courage needed for this meeting. He was here out of a sense of obligation, of owing Roland Pettit, once and once only, the ceremonial confrontation his honor—his loss—demanded. Pettit knew that, so they had this understanding together. In this one way, they were alike.

"Healey—are you even *listening* to me?"

"Of course. Every word." With a genuine spurt of guilt Lex had let go of the jukebox. He saw a cold rain stitching down again, ending its midmorning intermission. This—their "talk"—was a mere formal preamble. Pettit presumably knew his own town, knew a discreet place to fight. Not out there in the main street mall. Somewhere with decent footing, Lex hoped. There'd been too much scuffling in the rain recently. It was one thing to sucker punch Ruthie's father, a blowhard half his size. Pure reflex: he had not been proud of that. But Roland Pettit would expect the real thing. Their "talk" only served to wire him up. Reaching for his coffee mug, Lex noticed a fine tremor in his own hands. He flushed and jammed them down under the table. Anticipation, he thought. Stupid goddamn nerves. He tilted his good ear back to Pettit.

"One thing I'm not doing is leaving her in the lurch. Understand?"

Lex said, "I can't sit still anymore hearing you talk about her like she was some child. *Your* child. The two of us—you can't hear how ludicrous this is? It's disgusting. Christ—Roland, I don't know where you get your . . . What have you ever *done* for her?"

Let's get on with this now, he thought. Let's just get on with it.

"Healey? Maybe you don't understand. I'm gone. Leaving. After the finals, that is. It's time to get on with my life, Healey. And for her the same. I know that. I'll always love her. There'll never be nobody else. But that's my own freight—maybe good, maybe bad. Whatever you decide is yours."

Lex had looked up at Pettit. A stranger who meant zip to him, with cut-glass blue eyes and infected fingernails and a reddish angry bloom on one side of his massive neck where he had gouged too deep that morning shaving. Lex nodded slowly, to cover how the amazement and relief drained all the strength out of him.

Lightheaded, he asked, "Where is she now?"

The stranger sniffed his coffee and set it down. "Up to Rowley. North Shore. For a two-day. But she's all packed, all set for Harrisburg. I got all the stuff under control." He shifted sideways. "Guess for her this one's the last inning. Didn't make the National show. Cripes. All I want is for her to get what she deserves. She deserves to win." The bench wheezed. Pettit yanked out a worn-out billfold, curved in the shape of his buttock. "My invite, remember? Forget it, Healey, I'm paying here. This one's on me."

The engines shrieked like tortured souls. They were landing.

He saw the slow-twirling lover's knots of highways and toybox Monopoly houses. The occasional turquoise cyclop's eye of a swimming pool. Hieroglyph malls and cars moving with the impenetrable purposefulness of insects. The holy signs of baseball diamonds. America, from the sky.

"There it *is*," exulted the woman in front of him, jabbing.

They were nearing the ground. The sun also had dropped low, so the plane's shadow glided well ahead of them over a system of sprawled warehouses, city blocks' worth of parked vehicles. The place could have been an industrial park, except for the startling oddity of spidery horses crawling here and there on the pavement.

They landed like a cup of rattled dice. After a moment's silence, the grateful survivors cheered and clapped.

The instant Lex entered the terminal his beeper shrieked.

It was a new, upgraded model, issued by Viola Thripp. He had clipped it onto an equally new silver-buckled belt, a present from Erica, and not given it a further thought. As he fumbled to switch the noise off, passengers hustling around him turned with expressions of alarm congealing to irritation. Who's this bum, making himself important? Evidently his overnight beard and the Kid-Power T-shirt didn't meet their specs for a professional in high demand. So *what*. The guy downstairs from Rosie, who worked for Rudy's Towing, wore a beeper too.

The digital strip blinked a local number.

There were lines at the phone wall. He joined the shortest and then watched all the surrounding lines melt forward while his remained frozen in time. At the phone, a woman barricaded by luggage teased a credit card through the slot, shook it, and tried again.

The man in front of Lex suggested she use the pot or get off.

Lex could think of no one who would call him. Who even knew he'd arrived? He figured beepers were probably subject to misdialed numbers, and he wondered how often Rudy's Towing got called to a cardiac arrest.

Apologizing, tugging a string of green suitcases, the first woman barged past him. The line oozed forward three steps.

—bright lights of hell?
All we can promise is—

His consciousness had been hijacked by terminal Muzak. Though it only played a sugary instrumental version of the tune, he couldn't help silently adding the words. A kind of interior karaoke:

Does the money enchant, babe?
Do you stab me for spite?
Did you have to betray me?
Will you love me tonight?

"All yours, Bud." The man in front of him handed off a warm, greasy receiver. He struggled to recall the number, and dialed.

Heavy static. "Hyello!" it cried.

"Uh, this is Lex Healey. I—"

"*Commandante!* Where the devil you hiding?"

"Airport. I'm sorry, Jesus, I got held—"

"Man, no problem. Everything copacetic here as usual, right? Hey. Right next to me is a lovely young lady who is impatient to talk to you. Okay? Lemme see I can make this cord to reach . . ."

Reach whom? He rubbed his stubbled jaw, frowning. Ruthie

. . . Had to be. And if Ruthie was calling him, there had to be something wrong.

THREE OF THEM, IN THE SPARE STALL. JESUS LAY UP AGAINST THE wall, snuggled in straw, embracing his knees like a Hollywood lazy Mexican.

"Pedro," Erica whispered. "All you need's a sombrero."

"¿Qué?" Jesus peeled open one eye, playing the part. Suddenly his face changed completely. "Hey. I watch *all* the time, missy. That's my job, no? The best way I watch is I open my ears. Anyway, no one is coming around here tonight. I don't think so. That girl. She has difficult nerves—like my oldest. My Carlita." He settled back. "What time?"

Lex checked. "Quarter to one." His voice came out low and scratchy, like Erica's. Only Jesus spoke in a normal tone. This same Jesus, whom Lex depended on enormously but hardly knew, had a daughter somewhere. A Carlita, a high-strung girl.

"Oh, God," Erica moaned. "Why *tonight*? I'm going to be a zombie tomorrow. Ned rides at—"

"Today. It's after midnight, so *today* your boy rides," Jesus corrected.

She stared through the receding sets of grill bars. Their post gave a good clear view of her tack area, flanked by Cricket and the Monster in their boxes. But she was looking farther, past Ranger Boyd's stalls—Equiprix Enterprises—and a lurid orange Florida outfit, all the way down the empty, clean-swept aisle to the far door, where hazy yellow light spilled a few feet into the night. "Lex. I could use a smoke."

"You go out now, you warn him off."

Jesus said, "*Commandante,* this is not really the optimal—"

"We have to *see* him. Otherwise—he can come back. We have to finish this."

Erica hunkered down beside the Mexican. "Fuck *Owen,*" she muttered. Only Lex was left standing.

He had sent Ruthie away, back to her hotel. But Erica was not so amenable to good sense. When she returned to the barn for a final check on the Monster and discovered two humans camping in her tack stall, he'd for the first time not felt glad to see her. He and Jesus were already deep in whisper-argument. They had no faces prepared. She looked from one to the other, her own face drawn and determined. Her questions came clipped and direct. After only a cursory glance at Cricket she had hurried in to the Monster. Gently and thoroughly she stroked all four massive legs, his stifles, the broad twitching back, the long grooves of his crest. Lex watched through the grill bars. It wasn't a way she had ever touched him. He felt shut out, almost jealous of the slow probing attention. "Well?" he'd asked. "Find anything?"

"No." She must have had recently showered; the pecan brown hair swung like heavy silk. "He's normal. Do you think he's the one?"

"Why the Monster?"

She straightened and for the first time looked at Lex directly. "Because the Monster . . . Because he's favored for tomorrow. That's what I'm hearing. The talk going around . . . Maybe I'm turning superstitious."

Jesus had tapped his arm significantly. Earlier, alone together they had leafed through the roster of HorseGuard charges, the listed insurance companies, and insured values. Global—Whitaker's outfit—had the lion's share. Global happened to hold the Monster's policy as well. A value recently revised from eighty thousand to one hundred sixty-thousand dollars. Clean doubled. Amazing what a few good ribbons could add up to.

No one, then or now, wanted to draw a conclusion out loud. Slight variations, Lex guessed, all leading along the same lines. Erica, too, presumably knew about the updated policy. She would be aware, too, that Owen Goodchild kept a cabin in paradise, somewhere on the Seacrest land. So Ruthie had told him, adding (with her monotone flattening further to express her distaste for rumors) that some said Owen was a "special" friend to Helen Urbach, general Mr. Fixit and comforter, particularly when Bruce Urbach was out on his boat. One hundred sixty thou: however heavy the mortgage burden on paradise might be, that would go a long way toward lightening it.

Following this particular line left Lex feeling dirty, as if he had discovered a taste for decay, for the complex attraction of filth. Jesus had merely tapped and raised the black quarter moons of his brows. No one spoke. But there'd been no real argument when Lex proposed taking up station in this aisle with its view of the Monster, while Jesus' two other boys were sent to patrol the farther reaches of the barn.

A flimsy arrangement. By now his count of ways the night could go wrong was up to nine. The least of them was Jesus' prediction: that Owen had changed his mind. Simply reneged on the favor.

"*¿Qué hora es?*"

"Two . . . Two-ten."

Erica with face buried on her knees, hair spilled forward to reveal a wan wedge of neck. She might have been sleeping, except for the shiver that passed through her now and again. The barn air was dank—with urine, water, the exhalations of animals—and the ground cold despite the straw bed. Once, on a beach, she'd boasted, *I don't have the nerve to feel cold.* No? Then this must be the shiver of exhaustion.

"Look." Lex sighed. He wanted to touch her, but in front of Jesus felt unaccountably shy. "If he doesn't show in the next hour, you two both pack this in."

"Shh." Soundlessly, Jesus slid almost upright. Erica raised her head, questioning.

"Alejandro, *down . . .*"

His lousy ears had picked up nothing. Still didn't, but he half crouched just in case, and the tremor took hold in his thighs with a vengeance. For support he gripped the ledge of the grill.

A slight clicking, faint as rain. Gradually . . . a more definite sound. Footsteps, in brisk, irregular percussion on the cement aisle. Someone alone. Not the job-dulled scuffing of a groom, he thought, nor the patter of one of Jesus' boys. Weight of a man. A man in a hurry, but who faltered or paused before spurting on.

They were so used to silence. A memory resurfaced in Lex from decades back: of hanging out with some buddies outside Charles Street station, on the slab-stone parapet, a no-man's-land of beer-bottle shards and blue-flower weeds. Waiting for a train to come shooting out of the tunnel. Though he'd forced his eyes to remain wide open throughout the train's passage, in the end the wind and noise—and fear of falling—had always blinded him. He remembered that sweet explosion of fear now as the steps drew close, amplified and ricocheting off the cement and wood walls. Boots? Farther down the aisle a horse nickered. Strange, he thought, to come wearing boots, indifferent to the echo they'd make.

The footsteps clacked past. Ignoring a movement of Jesus' arm, he raised his head. The night visitor's back was still nearer than he'd expected, less than ten feet away. A slower walk, on long bowed blue-jeaned legs that ended in the high-heeled swagger of cowboy boots. Loose shirt. Head hidden by a wide-brimmed Australian outback hat.

He was well beyond the Monster's stall when he stopped, turned profile, and with a smack of his palm shot open a stall door bolt.

Lex ducked, wobbling. Jesus blinked the question at him. Lex mouthed "Ranger," and Jesus nodded, as if his bet had been confirmed.

In the poor light Erica raised an unblinking slate blue stare.

Lex counted from memory: the stall Ranger had entered must be one of his own, most likely the extra-large box of Boyd's white stallion. From that direction came a series of homely sounds: crackling straw, the soft thock of haunches shifting against the wallboards. In sudden bursts they could hear Boyd's voice—incomprehensible and intense. Urging, arguing, or pleading. It was not the tone humans use to soothe a nervous horse.

Jesus drew with his finger on the wall. Meds? / for tomorr—

A reasonable assumption. Of the over two hundred horses to compete tomorrow, over half would have found their edge through the point of a needle. The judges rewarded that tranquilized, semiconscious look. Forward movement, but dead broke.

Erica whispered, "Come on. *I'm* going to ask him what's up—"

She was right, he supposed, though this was hardly the crisis situation they'd planned for. Lex unfolded to full height, felt his body snap all over like a piece of stretched aluminum foil. Then he saw Owen.

Owen stood at Ranger's partly opened stall door, one fist clutching the grill. He leaned in. He wore sneakers. A red sports bag, crossed by a two-foot stick or pole, lay at his feet.

"Well, I'll be blued, screwed, and tattooed. What the *hell?*" Owen said. For all the quietness of his approach, the announcer's voice carried. "If I'd of thought *you'd* be here—"

He stepped back, as Ranger pushed through the door. "I've been waiting for you. The deal's off." His right hand gripped Owen's shoulder, with the other he swiped his own nose. "Thank God. I made it here. Before you. In time. Oh God. All day I was paralyzed. I couldn't stand to think—think about it—but I woke up, *somehow*—only then I was afraid, almost sure I'd get here—too late." The fancy hat was gone, and Ranger's wavy hair gleamed like a stained-glass angel's. "So. Now you can forget the whole thing. Go on! It makes me puke to look at you! Pick up your crap and get *lost.*"

The peculiar high shine of his cheekbones: for the second time, Lex was seeing Ranger Boyd in tears.

"Calm down. Take it easy, son." Owen nudged the hand on his shoulder, which didn't move. "You shouldn't ought to even be here. Shucks, nobody said doing it's a picnic, that's why you need a buddy to help you out. Person's feet tend to get cold—" He glanced down at Ranger's cowboy boots. "But real soon you get over it. You scoot along, now."

"I swear to God, if you so much as *breathe* on my horse I will . . . Now, you listen to me, Goodchild. As far as I'm concerned, I never talked to you. I never *meant* it. I don't want that kind of money. The fact is I've been in a lousy depression for a long time, I can't imagine what possessed me—"

"Spite," said Owen. "You meant it all right. Critter didn't deliver for you, did it? Plus that little girl got your goat. Suzy? Winning on him like she does? Whereas you yourself can't halfway ride your own horse, so what the devil you want to keep feeding it oats and hay for?"

"Shut your stinking *mouth*." Ranger gave the shoulder a hard shove. Owen stiffened.

The strain of complete immobility made Lex feel he was swaying. He sensed more than saw Erica and Jesus, also on their feet now. They all breathed in shallow unison. The grill might veil their heads, he thought, the way a screen veils someone behind a window—but it wouldn't hide them. There was something comical about their chance imprisonment—if Ranger turned his head once from Owen and focused, he'd receive a serious surprise.

"Well, you're the customer, son. Whatever you say's right. Only now where I've taken considerable trouble on your account, one way or t'other, you owe me."

Ranger booted the red sports bag into the aisle. The pole rolled with a clang onto cement. A length of drainage pipe, Lex guessed, something like that—not the newfangled PVC stuff but solid old leaded iron.

Ranger grabbed it up, almost dropping the weight. "What the hell's *this* for?"

"Only backup insurance. Case of a problem with the main method. Like I told you—"

"You were going to use *this*?" He held the pole in both hands. "The way Burns did on that mare in Florida—?"

"They'd think it *was* Burns, or somebody close. They sure as lambs in springtime wouldn't think *you'd* ever get up the nerve—"

Ranger raised the pole. Owen bobbed in a waltz dip, backward. "You be smart to put that thing down now—"

Lex was wrestling with his stall door. With a screech it slid open. He was barely aware of the others scuffling out behind him, or of pins and needles jabbing his legs, as he ran toward Ranger, who glanced toward the interruption in pure disbelief, still brandishing the pole. A ninja cowboy.

Owen turned, too. He flashed a brilliant grin. Astonishment, and comprehension. He ducked sideways for his bag, and at that instant the pole came down, its tip thudding and then sliding from the announcer's barrel ribs before it rang, striking sparks, on the anvil of cement.

Owen groaned. But it had been only a near miss, nowhere near the man's spine, Lex thought with relief. He ran forward, hand outstretched to take charge of the weapon.

With an athlete's reflex Ranger kicked the bag again, harder, sending it twirling toward Lex. Owen, in a low scuttle, followed its path.

Lex was already between the two of them when the pole fell a second time. He felt its swift cool sigh pass along his body.

Erica cried out.

Her cry froze them all. It exploded high and inchoate and soared higher, above audible reach. Horses shuddered and stamped, muttering in their stalls. Only Owen Goodchild kept moving. A bloodstain the size of a handprint darkened his back. He leaned across Erica who lay doubled, a sudden supplicant with her forehead pressed to the ground, and he snatched up his bright red bag.

Lex kept a last, distant snapshot of Owen as he neared the open barn door, feinted past two Mexican boys who'd come running from their posts, and merged with the remainder of the night.

As if he'd been in the vale lodge before, perhaps in this very room, Lex could anticipate the quirks of personality underlying its surficial blandness. The oblique twists and turns of the corridors, which they slowly negotiated. The code sequence in which light switches had to be flipped on and off in order to make the ceiling fixture respond. The left bottom drawer of the bureau where an extra—and extra-thin—blanket lay stored.

"I'm not cold," she said. Her teeth chattered.

"Good. But humor me?" He spread the flimsy flesh-colored wool over her legs, and tucked it, very cautiously, under her free arm as high as the base of her breasts. He stood above her, hesitating, at a loss. The emergency room nurse had scissored to shreds her shirt and bra. Now, despite a skewed rag of a johnny, the sling, the back brace, and a diamond of bandage taped over a section of her left collarbone, Erica's upper body was bare.

"Let's see. I could . . . maybe lay the blanket up over your good shoulder, and then very, very lightly bring it across—"

"No!" Her eyes darted, left to right. She wanted to shake her head, but didn't dare.

"Okay." He moved toward the window, certain of where the pulley rope to open the curtains would be.

"No sun. Too bright," she said. "Please, Lex." A calmer voice, almost apologetic, and a touch slurred, either from lingering shock or the codeine. In the ER he had expected them to give her a slug of morphine. He didn't see why not. But they'd given her nothing, not even the water she craved. Nothing when they palpated and X-rayed her fractured collarbone. Nothing when—after ordering him out of the examining room, down a long corridor, well out of earshot—they had reduced the fracture: manually realigned the ends of the bone.

A *good* break, they said. Stabilized. Suddenly she was released, no ceremony beyond an imprint of his credit card, and with Lex supporting her as best he could they shuffled out into the unreal commonplace of another warm sunny afternoon. He drove to a nearby drugstore to fill the scrawled prescription. She washed a tablet down with Coke from a can, her hand shook, he caught the dribbles. To drive was excruciating. He had ground his teeth over every bump and pothole, while her groans escaped against her will and traffic honked and swerved around them.

He hung up some pieces of her clothing, jumbled on the one

chair. He placed her boots in the closet. Maybe later he could polish them for her.

"Could you eat something? If I went out to scrounge?"

"Maybe. Later," she said.

He, too, was past the point of hunger. The dull artificial light gave the room the general timelessness of any sickroom. She wasn't sick, he reminded himself, only hurt; and she would eventually recover. Eight weeks, plus or minus, the doctor had predicted. (A doctor maybe half Lex's age, stethoscope dangling from his scrawny neck like a kid's toy.) Eight weeks? December, then. Winter. Hard to see forward as far as winter. The vertical ribbons of daylight around the closed curtains reminded him of other afternoons, of other motel rooms, of her whole and wholesome nakedness, of making love. He felt a sudden absurd and childish impulse to weep. They would not, after all, make love in this room.

"Do I look that awful?" she asked.

"*No*. You look much better already. Erica . . ."

"More water?" she begged.

He foresaw that the cold tap would gush and blurp before it settled to a flow. He let it run clean for a while. When he returned, her eyes were closed, so he perched on the cleared chair holding her glass of water.

She lay propped on pillows, almost sitting, her neck so straight it arched. The sling was navy blue with white piping; along with the back brace it suggested a military freshness. The bandage was not so fresh. A mix of blood and yellow antiseptic had seeped through. She looked now, he thought, both better and worse than before . . . at dawn, wheeled on a gurney out of the barn. Incredible, to realize they were still living in the same day. She had never lost clarity. Her voice from the gurney had surprised everyone: firm and melodious, as if in conversation. *My own fault,* she'd remarked to the sky. *The horse kicked out behind while I was bending down—* Ranger, grasping that she meant to protect him, had grunted a meaningless exclamation. His eyes were red and puffy, his face white as the setting moon. Lex hated him. Ranger trotted awkwardly on one side of the gurney, Lex on the other, Jesus behind. It did not occur to the ambulance crew to wonder why these people were all there at that hour. In fact, grooms were already arriving for work, and grooms watched from a distance. *Don't worry about anything,* Ranger had told her before they lifted her into the ambulance. *I'll coach your kid all day. Trust me. I'll take care of Ned as if he were my own best chance.*

Then, what had been hard to look at was her face: grit embedded in the lacerations where her cheek and temple took the fall, and shiny, congealing crusts of blood on her chin and mouth, where she had bitten deep into her lip. It was from this mouth the calm voice came.

Now her face was still swollen but sponged clean, and a butterfly bandage compressed the torn lip. (There might be a scar, the kid-doctor speculated. She didn't seem to care.) Now it was her body he forced himself to study, to get used to, against the icy weak thrill he felt in looking.

Her torso, cropped and illuminated as ever by the tan lines of arms and neck, was stained from beneath the skin. From the edges of the taped bandage (it bulged from the pressure of bruised tissue, he told himself, not the broken bone) the stain radiated in changing colors like oil spilled on water. Angry purple to bluish green to an outer border of yellow. It had spread below her heart, beneath the sling, past her cradled, curled hand. He thought, sitting there, that he could see the colors blend as the stain progressed, imperceptibly, into her right, intact and unblemished side.

The last notion of time left him. The lines around the plastic curtains dimmed while he sat motionless, praying for her to sleep. For sleep to continue. Once, a frown shivered across her forehead. Her lips parted; in sleep she licked them, as if to taste the cut and its bandage, before her face fell smooth again. Something in him seemed to break open, then heal, then break again. For the briefest moment he saw all the random pieces of his life merging to a luminous and necessary design. There was a story after all. He had never loved anyone before. He had never before loved her, this way.

He jerked so violently when the telephone shrilled that water splashed across the carpet.

"Healey," he whispered in fury.

"Healey—is that actually you? You don't sound right."

"Ranger. Hello." He stood, pulling the phone as far away from her as its cord would reach. "This isn't the greatest time for a chat." There were stronger ways he might have put this. For some reason, the need to whisper kept him civil.

"Well, excuse the intrusion, but I thought I ought to tell her—"

"No. Tell me."

Lex half listened to a rundown of the day's events while twining the phone cord around his free hand like a *garotte*. Was he wrong, he wondered, to loathe Ranger completely? Ranger had summoned Owen to execute his horse, and Owen had ducked Ranger's raised weapon—but who could predict that Erica would take the blow? Didn't matter. Moralistic hairsplitting. Having seen her harmed—seen her broken—Lex was brimming with a rage that mimicked fear in the way it melted his insides, and was far more than Owen alone could absorb. Although Owen wouldn't escape him. As soon as she could be left safely on her own he would track Owen down—

"So what do you think?" Ranger asked. "Kid could've done worse."

"Great. Sure. I'll tell her." Utterly indifferent to the narration of the boy's day. All Lex had registered consciously was that Ned hadn't fallen. And the monster was intact.

"Well! If Erica has any questions, or needs anything else—"

"Right. Bye."

He replaced the phone, wondering why in hell, even after taking the blow, Erica's instinct had been to cover up what Ranger had done. And almost done. Was it simply tribal solidarity?

They are a tribe, he thought. The riders—they might as well be

Gypsies. All kin, all blood related. Thicker than water, and they close up against the outside.

"Who was that?" she asked.

"Oh damn. I wanted not to wake you up—"

"Was it Ranger?"

"Yes."

"About Ned?" She pushed up on one hand, her swollen face twisting against pain. *"Say."*

"Well. Ned took eighth." He paused, not sure whether this news sounded good or bad. "Well, so at least he for once made it to the jump-off—"

"Oh. My *God,* Lex. He won *eighth*? His first time ever riding Medal?" She was grinning. He saw her lip gleam where it threatened to crack open again. "Tell me. Come on!"

"Well, let's see, on the morning course I guess they looked completely in charge—" He smiled in the sudden reprieve of hearing his literal memory kick in. "Real aggressive, only there was, was a, a kind of a weak approach to the narrow gate—"

"*Yes.* Shit, I knew it. Gate of hell for the Monster. Not the narrowness, it's that damn left-angle approach." Her words made sense but she sounded like a drunk, thick-tongued and blurry. "I told the kid use spur but not too much, or he freaks and loses it— what else? How was the jump-off?"

Lex tried to recall more phrases. "A bitch of a course," he quoted finally. "Okay—very technical distances, with a tight triple at the end that came up out of nowhere. Rails flying like tiddly-winks all day. The pair in front crashed, so our pair had to wait an age for the jumps to get reset. Which can wash out nerves, lead to disaster, right? But that didn't happen. Ned went in and laid down a dream trip. 'Dream trip,' is what Boyd said. Boyd was still *all* excited. Ned looked like a winner, rode like a winner. I guess some people thought he should have pinned higher, afterward there was some grumbling—"

"Ah. Forget it." Beaming, she waved her good hand to dismiss all cautious judges. "They don't know him yet. They will, next year."

Next year.

"Oh. My God, Lex, aren't you *ecstatic* for him? The little jerk must be shit-faced, I'll bet he's full of himself now! Oh. I hope he calls me, soon. . . ." She did not dare laugh. Her head rolled back on the pillow. "I am so, so glad. My God. Lex? Now, can you bring me some water?"

With the freshly filled glass, he brought her the next dose of codeine.

When she woke again he was chewing a slice of previously delivered cold pizza and watching TV with the sound turned down near zero. He'd found one of the black-and-white star-vehicle oldies he liked not so much for the story as to see the graceful, self-possessed way both women and men used to move.

"Lex?"

"Hi, you." He pressed OFF. "How's it going?"

"Um . . . Lot of dreams. Strange. Awake. Watching you. Thinking . . . So long we didn't talk. No chance . . ." Her lips were gummy. She gestured again for the water. She looked definitely worse but he tried to keep a steady smile, not to let her read from his eyes how the swelling and discoloration had triumphed, how her face seemed a stranger's—ravaged and piratical, with one squinting eye.

"Everything's changed," she said.

"Well. They say things do." He took back the glass.

"Where is Owen?"

He shrugged, glanced at the curtains. "I don't know. He bolted. Probably halfway to Panama by now. He won't be back around here."

"Might be. See . . . Anyone could be Owen. I never realized. It's the big secret, isn't it?"

"The big . . . ? Hey, now. Shh . . ."

"Everything's changed. Used to think it couldn't. Riding, just sun and rain and luck, hundreds of years the same. Not what you call real life. That's *why,* I guess, huh? My choice. Now there's nowhere to go back to."

"Come on. It's all still there. You need to give yourself time. You're *hurt.* And I'm going to take care of you."

"Been hurt before. Worse. Only not like this. Not feeling sorry for myself. Am I?"

"No, silly."

"Yes. There's one day—" Tears slipped along her cheekbones, catching hardly a glimmer from the dull light. He wondered how long she had been crying. "One day I want to go back to. It shouldn't be over. Not finished. Sometimes I think when you die that's what happens—there's the one day that's your whole life and you return to it forever, and eternity is to keep living in that day, it never ends. . . ." The pirate face gave a self-mocking pout, asking indulgence.

"Erica? What day?"

"At Seacrest. On the beach with you there."

"Ah. Well yes, sure. I remember . . ."

"I still wish you could hold me!"

He stood up quickly. Careful not to jar the bed, he reached for her good right hand and held it. He saw her tears suddenly running freely in broad bright paths. What kind of craziness was the mix of pain and painkiller putting into her head? What thought had she woken to and watched him with, before?

"Lex?" It was almost a cry. "I've been trying to remember us— from the beginning. The first time we kissed. How it felt almost too strong to stand, like a drug's first hit—what fainting must be like. We said, this has to mean something. I don't think we ever lied to ourselves. We really were in love, weren't we?"

Her cold hand. "Listen . . ." he said and twined his fingers through hers, willing warmth to flow into her. He looked down at his left hand clasping her right. "We still are."

November

THE REPLACEMENT OFFICE-SUPPORT PERSON LOWERED A SLOSH-
ing mug of tea to a clearing between briefs and files on the blotter,
saying, "*Achtung,* Maury, hot! I nuked the dickens out of it!" He
nodded, swabbing the spill with his palm, reflecting that he'd already spent too much of his life on confrontation. The door left
ajar revealed a slice of barren waiting room. His one-thirty was
eight minutes late. When the replacement person went out, the
door whooshed shut like an air lock.

Maurice Shumway sliced at his mail with an antique glass knife
(graduation memento from his mother), stacking emptied envelopes on one pile and their pale meat on another. He had a problem with the economy: witness the leased, tubular-steel, empty
chairs outside and the downward spiral in the quality of office staff
his billable hours could justify. In this, Maurice's forty-sixth year,
what had seemed heretofore a purely abstract bloat and contraction
of the flow of goods and services had caught him in a personal
squeeze. Always, in fatter years, he had been insulated by an asso-

ciate professor's dribble of salary, augmented by steady public sector work; now, since his launch into private practice five years ago, he sat fully exposed to the whims of the Beast. Abysmal timing, in retrospect. Maurice Shumway's metier was immigration law, and the hordes of green card seekers who used to phone, plead, waylay him with mind-boggling life stories, improper inducements, and wads of cash extracted from the heel of a shoe had dwindled to zip. There were no *jobs*. . . . The agile illegals were decamping faster than the INS could scoop them up for deportation. In fact, all that had kept Maurice Shumway, Esq., afloat thus far was a single windfall contingency fee: from the Pryor case, hardly his metier and a siren song from entrepreneurial easy street if there ever was one. A one-off, comparative no-brainer, picked up like a winning lottery card, merely because he'd once helped Elspeth Pryor put a couple of terrified young Brazilians on the tortuous straight and narrow toward citizenship. . . . In fact, the Beast Economy (he stabbed into a subscription-only, private-intelligence investors' newsletter from Washington) was by now completely out of control: a raging, self-devouring, anorexic Beast. Utterly useless (he scanned headlines) to go on force-feeding cheap money, lower interest rates. *Reductio ad absurdum,* on the backs of fixed-income widows and orphans. The Beast simply refused nourishment.

What it needed, he knew, was a transfusion of *real* blood. Open the floodgates. Let them all in, the best and the worst the world's gene pool has to offer, in the great national tradition of periodic ethnic free-for-all. Let *everyone* fight it out, rattle the cages of the moribund establishment. Let heads roll. Maurice Shumway (glancing at the desk clock, a miniature silver-plated Big Ben tower, graduation gift from his father) felt consumed by a fiery indignation he hadn't experienced since junior year at B.C. He snapped open another newsletter. He wished he had someone—other than the replacement-person—with whom to share his ideas.

The light blinked on his phone and then glowed steady as she picked up outside. When it died, his number buzzed. His one-thirty, she told him in a tone reeking of commiseration, had canceled.

"Thank you," said Shumway, his lips hardly moving.

That left Elspeth Pryor, scheduled for two-fifteen.

The newsletter was called *International Immigration, Refugee, and Asylum Policy TrendWatch*. What his father would have lambasted as a "pinko broadside." But *TrendWatch* came gratis, whereas the right wing—*Kiplinger* and so forth—made you pay through the nose. Still, he had to keep a balance of views and information, if only in his own head—balance was what he *was,* the end goal of his training, his one hope for a meaningful function in this entropic so-called society. A redemptive unit of balance.

Shumway's eye dropped to a sidebar news article in the lower right column. "U.S. INS Nets 120 in Sweep of Equestrian Industry—Grisly N.Y. Find." What find? Grisly enough, to think the Immigration and Naturalization Service could field enough agents to cover all the racetracks in North America simultaneously. Scanning, Shumway learned that "industry" referred exclusively to horse shows, private stables, and the like, and the "sweep" was limited to a few states in the northeast. Usual hyperbole. Still, 120 illegals . . . Here: the grisly bit.

". . . course of pursuit, agents discovered in wooded property of multimillion-dollar N.Y. farm the partially clad, severely decomposed body of unidentified young Hispanic male. Occupation presumed groom or farrier's assistant, based on blacksmithing tool found in deceased's pocket. Coroner's report cites cranial contusion as well as burns at body orifices, cause of death given as cardiac arrest. Continuing energetic investigation by State and local police authorities—"

Energetic like hell, thought Maurice Shumway. The poor nameless bugger. "Authorities" wouldn't waste a taxpayer's dime. A life and a death too cheap to rate mention in a regular newspaper. And what, exactly, was the implication here? Inconveniently deceased illegals simply tossed out by the employers, like junkyard rats? Or tip of the iceberg: violent vendetta among the undesirables? But that was hardly the *TrendWatch* slant. Or might an INS agent in his zeal have blundered, taken the mandate to crack down on black-market labor a step too far. . . . Cover-up. An intriguing supposition.

One of those little things we'll never know, he thought. The phone buzzed.

"Yes?"

"Maury? I have Mrs. Pryor here to see you."

"She's early." Jowling the phone, he squared his stack of fluttering newsletters. "Tell Mrs. Pryor I'm on a conference call."

"But nobody even—"

"A *conference* call, understand? I'll be tied up for at least ten. *Tell* her that."

His preparations were automatic. Replace the file of the no-show one-thirty with the thick depositions from the Pryor case. Swallow cold tea dregs. Dump trash mail in bottom left-hand drawer—Ruthie Pryor, he thought, watching the drawer slide shut over fine print. Also one of those horsey girls, before her accident. In fact, that had been the reason . . . Stuff shirttails deeper in trousers. Scrape pocket comb through thinning copper wire hair.

Four and a half minutes. How long since he'd last laid eyes on Elspeth? Well over a year. Undeniably attractive woman. Not one of those increasingly prevalent *noli me tangere* types. Perky breasts, and she appreciated having you notice. What could he help her with this time?

Not a lot, he feared. Elspeth Pryor was a genuine mother, more heart than head. He understood how her child's misfortune had unleashed the full force of her protective instincts, a natural if belated reflex. He had acquiesced to her insistence, buttressed by a psychiatrist's two-pager, that the case be settled with a minimum of conflict and delay, and Ruthie spared exposure to the full details of events surrounding her accident. *What she's lost is awful enough, isn't it? Nobody meant this to happen. Why rob her of precious memories, her good feelings about a sport she loved?* In this, if anything, he had admired the mother's empathy, her wise forbearance, and her insight.

But now? He'd assumed, up until the recent spate of phone

calls, that all was reasonably well *chez* Pryor. . . . *Now* his evasion
with Ruth verged on deception. So he must make clear to Elspeth:
that Ruth Pryor was no longer a child. . . . Unquestionably, as Elspeth described it, the girl's behavior was erratic. The fact that she
hadn't been heard from in weeks might be grounds for concern—
but to have her declared legally incompetent . . . ? Extremely un-
likely. And unethical, to fan the mother's expectations. One would
need rock-solid evidence of some flagrantly self-destructive action,
behavior beyond the bizarre. . . . Otherwise, not a chance. It was
time to let go of the kid. So he must tell Elspeth.

He rose and pushed open the door.

For a moment, the fresh dazzling light made him think he was
in the wrong room. Outside, he realized, it had begun to snow. A
woman leaned in profile against the window, wearing a nylon sea
green jumpsuit which clung to her, neck to ankle, like a veil of oil.
He had been in this profession of ambiguity too long, he thought
suddenly. He no longer knew where he himself stood.

"I'm sorry," he said. "Elspeth? I hope you weren't waiting—"

"Oh no. Not long at all. But you are free now?" She turned,
indelibly appealing, hands outstretched. Her rings flared. "Maurice.
Finally," she said.

Fɪɴᴀʟʟʏ, ᴡɪᴛʜ ᴀ ꜱᴜᴅᴅᴇɴ ʜᴜꜱʜ, ᴛʜᴇ ᴅʀᴜᴍᴍɪɴɢ ɪᴄᴇ ʀᴀɪɴ
changed to snow.

Past four, and already the house was dim. Dusk spread from the
middle of rooms, while the windows glowed with a fresh silver
sheen. She didn't want any lamps on to spoil this moment. The
blue hour, she thought. Hello, young lovers, wherever you are.
Skirting the long dining room table, she fiddled with the CD player
until whatever music had been left inside began to play. Violins . . .
Beethoven, or else Mozart, she was certain. In the gloom she
poured herself a double scotch with a sure, firm hand and carried it
through the hall to the parlor. There she sat down on the piano

bench, sipping, facing the bow window, contemplating the season's first contredanse of snow.

Snow flattened all perspective, absorbed distance; she could hardly see as far as the rose border, winter-bedded with grimy straw mulch. But she knew exactly how and where her land lay, its rises and fallings until it slipped under the sea. In her imagination she watched snowflakes drop and melt into the gray eddying foam and glassy backwash of waves.

Far off, the back door slammed.

She listened to his steps. The chock, chock of boots, tapping through hallways and rooms and eventually closer.

"Mama?" He hadn't called her that in years. "Everyone's fed and blanketed. I poulticed the mare like you wanted. Mama, what the heck are you doing sitting here in the *dark*?"

Ned snapped on the brightest lamp. His cheeks were reddened, melting snow crusted his lank black hair. He'd carried the smells of outdoors—hay, ice, tang of wool and sweat—in with him.

"You're a handsome guy," she said. "Remember where you heard it first."

His hand snaked for her glass; she held on tight. "Booze. A mingy little token," she said. "For the blue hour." She laughed. "Cross my heart. I'm on a *diet*."

He said seriously, "I noticed. Way to go, Mama. Just go for it."

She stood up: a sigh escaped. The diet was only since he'd moved in at home again, and she hadn't shed much weight yet. But already her flesh felt, somehow, less a part of her. She had a vision—by spring she'd have lost sixty pounds and they could go out and ride together again. She smiled. "So, what kept you so long?" No reproach implied, and he knew that, knew what a gift it was to have him here, helping with the horses, wonderful simply to have him home.

"Nothing. Walking around. Checking out the place." He slicked back his hair. "How's it going—with all that stuff?"

With the divorce, he meant. With the lawyers. Since his win at Harrisburg—well, not *the* win, but a precise and skillful and coura-

geous ride, and everyone who mattered knew it—they seemed to
share a new understanding. Each anticipated what the other one
meant. Ned was different now—or else more himself. The way
she'd always wanted him to be. He'll find his own way, she
thought.

"It goes, it goes. Not exactly a *picnic*." She shook out her skirt.
Her only child didn't need to know the cutthroat details. "I was up
in Boston—you know, meetings, all the blah-blah—all morning."

"And will we?" Keep the farm, he meant.

"Oh, we will keep it. Absolutely." She drained the glass.

"When I was walking I went down to Owen Goodchild's
shack. That guy . . . do you think that guy is ever coming *back*?"

Something quivered inside her. She shook her head.

"Good. I mean, we're not like, obligated? He's a total pig. He
left things incredibly gross in there. It's not worth—"

"Wasn't the shack locked?"

He shrugged, as if locks were irrelevant. "What occurred to me
is, it's started snowing."

"True."

"We could get a burning permit. Like you do for brush clearing. I mean, in case anybody from the village worries about the
smoke."

She lifted the piano lid and depressed a key. It sounded terrible.
She wished someone in the house knew how to play.

"I mean," said Ned, "I'll *do* it. Kerosene? The trees are far
enough off to be safe. I can handle it. I'll rig a long fuse. How long
does getting a permit take?"

Torch Owen's shack, she thought. Well, then he'll never come
back. She felt queasy from the effort of not remembering what the
announcer had done to her, made her feel, and what they'd done
together.

"Mama? You okay?"

"Of course!" She closed the lid. "A week? Maybe three? I'll call
Town Hall. Depends on the weather. And while we're on the subject, will you remind me—" now she could look again at her tall,

self-possessed son, who was taking a break this year to work with the horses, to decide whether his future would be with the horses—"remind me, first thing *tomorrow,* to call a piano tuner?"

SNOW WAS FALLING. AN ICY PATTER, NOTHING MEGA, BUT THE BIG guy had told Bungee that up here on the frigging mountainside they generally got inches more than the weather report had a clue about. Now the big guy was crawling around on the roof, hammering. It made the whole ramshackle barn, huger than a gym, quake and echo. With each hammer smack, hay dust drizzled from the loft. Horses were freaking and kicking, pissed off at the racket, and Bungee was supposed to be calming them down. How? He figured the smartest he could do was stay away from the stalls so they wouldn't smell fear on him. Animals could snuffle you out, for sure. *Campagnolo,* you wuss, he told himself. The big guy, on the other hand, was a maniac. Nothing and nobody could've dragged Bungee up on that roof. He might be losing his guts for climbing, he thought: a sign of getting old. But Bungee kept flashing on his cousin Vince, who was in the wheelchair, who threw stuff and talked amazingly specifically dirty about women even when the women were right there in the room, who used to be a roofer before he fell and pulverized his spine. Here the barn roof had to be glazed with ice, everything else outside was, he'd almost lost it a couple of times just bringing in the last of the horses, feeling noodley-nervous but looking straight ahead the way the wife had taught him, while the two animals he led slipped and struggled uphill in their treacherous steel shoes. Now as the hammer cracked in gunshot bursts Bungee's stomach felt shrunk and frozen, the way it did when he was gearing up to run. It was only him and the big guy here today, alone on the farm. He was listening for a slithering sound, for the sudden free-fall shout of astonishment. If that happened, he'd run out and—do what? *Jesus.*

Bungee spat. Puny spit, not much juice left. Two weeks ago

he'd been at his gran's in Charlestown, packing the two-tone suit-case Gran bought new from Lechmere while the old lady bumped around stuffing in more junk, telling Bungee what an awesome chance this was. *See, God's giving you a chance, and next time you see Mr. Healey make sure you thank him again, so he can hear you mean it, for helping you get away from this neighborhood. From all this danger. How you feel now? You gonna learn a good clean work, live in a fresh air. Okay? You deserve!* Then she'd grabbed him so hard he choked.

He'd been laughing, he'd felt warmed by a streak of serious sadness and proud to be moving out of the neighborhood this way, of his own free will, taking Healey up on the idea of working for these friends of his who needed a "with-it, athletic-type kid" to help out—instead of him shipping into jail like he'd pretty much started to count on. It wasn't just because his main supplier got ambushed and busted in the raids that he couldn't wait to move on. Not to have to lie to Gran anymore, that was the best. . . . But what nei-ther of them realized back when he was packing was that, com-pared to Charlestown—or compared to about any other normal life you saw on TV, maybe even compared to jail—the farm was wild, full of traps and hazards, a constantly dangerous place.

"Like for example," he said out loud to this one spotted gray horse, who kept zinging his bared teeth on the stall bars, making a sound like a high-speed train, "look what happened to the wife."

The hammer slammed overhead, faster than you'd believe an arm could move. The big guy could drive a nail home on one hit, he was a real carpenter, he'd shown Bungee his union card, he was wicked good at a lot of things. But Bungee couldn't get that pic-ture—slide, grapple, and fall—out of his mind. He slipped into the windowless grain room, shut the door, switched on the light, and fished his Winstons out of a coffee can on the top shelf. The rich sweet smell in here, a mouthwatering mix of oats, corn and mo-lasses, was plenty to mask the occasional smoke.

As long as the hammer boomed—muffled now, less nerve jan-gling—he was safe.

He pinched off the filter and lit up and inhaled openmouthed, hacking mainly from the grain dust he'd sucked in. This was better. He thought ahead into the rest of the day—it still felt different here, being able to see the whole day ahead, instead of blindly letting whatever was out there come down—how when the big guy climbed off the ladder they'd go back to the house and grab a bite, and then whether or not any owners hauled ass out to ride in this frigging weather he'd brush the horses, a job he didn't mind because the horses got off on all that stroking, stayed pretty laid-back. After last feeding rounds, pizza and TV with the big guy, and crash. He crashed so hard here, night felt like it lasted two minutes. Maybe it was because he was learning so much new stuff. All his dreams were about reality: the right knack to cleaning a hoof, how to piece together a bridle.

He missed the dog, he realized. From day one Farah had acted like he was something super. The wife mentioned how Farah even slept outside his bedroom; he wondered if the wife felt kind of jealous. *He* would have. This weekend she'd taken Farah with her and some friends down to New York, New Jersey . . . wherever. Some high-powered major action national horse show, he gathered, the "Maclay finals," sort of like the NBA play-offs. She was only going to watch but the big guy obviously hated the idea of the trip. The wife said stop fussing, her busted bone was enough better; Bungee hadn't decided yet whether it was the big guy she never listened to, or was she one of those people who never listen to anyone? Still, he liked her. She taught him the ropes like she *knew* he'd catch on soon, like mistakes starting out were normal. With her one free hand she hooked her straight brown hair behind her ears, same way a girl his age would. She had the bluest eyes, sun crinkles at the corners, but a few times he noticed her looking at him with a kind of blurry, far-off, sad expression, like someone trying not to cry. He thought it was probably because her shoulder still hurt, and she wasn't used to hurting.

A jolt ran through him: the barn was totally quiet. He punched out the butt and field-shredded it, pocketing paper and filter, toeing tobacco shreds down between the boards of the floor.

"Yo! Roberto!" That was his name as far as they were concerned. A name still fresh from the wrapping paper, as good as new. He reached fast for the light cord, squeezed out, and shut the door.

The big guy was already in the aisle, stomping work boots, swiping ice from his sleeves. "Got that bitch done," he said. "Guaranteed for six months. Looks like a patchwork quilt but she won't *leak.*" He was talkative and grinning, always, after finishing any unusually dirty, or risky, or at first look impossible job. "Once our girls get back we can all hunker down for winter. Batten the hatches. Play checkers, pop corn, get fat. I love winter. Hey. You ever snowshoe?" He paused. "Up on the roof, I wondered how the horses were taking it. Down here must've sounded like inside a cannon."

"Nah." Bungee shrugged. "Nobody minded too much." He looked around behind him, at the shadowy heads of horses, some with ears perked, some dozing. "I like, just talked quiet to them."

"See? All there is to it. Next thing, we'll have you up in the saddle. You've got the rider's build, she says. . . ." Then something happened that made the back of Bungee's neck prickle, made him let go in a kind of shy, incredulous smile. He felt the big guy's hand on his head, ruffling his hair.

T<small>HE SOUND FROM OUTSIDE CONVULSED HIM; HIS EYES SHOT OPEN</small> and then he lay still. Deer, he told himself. For days he'd been hearing them, slamming through the brush in their habitual brainless state of panic. Already light for hours, he sensed. The days swam together, color of tarnished silver. Even inside the shack with door and windows shut tight, today—whatever day it was— smelled like more snow coming. He had the shivers, he looked down his body and saw the flesh wobble, and though he didn't hurt any worse than yesterday (every raw nerve on alert, strained to the

limit), it scared him to be gripped by shivers when he was trying to
take the right care of himself, to control how he moved.

There was the woodstove, soot-streaked block of ice with one
log from last year molding underneath. Supposing by some miracle he could drag in more fuel and get a blaze going without re-
injuring himself? The big house was over a half mile away, beyond
a thick band of pine and scrub oak. And the Lard Lady *if* she was
home had no cause to take a sentimental stroll down here, not in
this weather, not after the truths he'd told her (it stung his cracked
lips to smile) about how the only way he'd been able to get his tool
up was to snort a hit and then make believe he was jerking off
alone, on the world's biggest water bed. . . . But even so. Forget
about fire. He'd be crazy to chance the smoke being seen.

Both his blankets were stiff with dirt and puffed out a sour ex-
halation of mouse droppings when tugged higher. In the farthest
diagonal corner his own human droppings (painfully eliminated,
with outbursts of sweat and obscene prayer) lay under a few sheets
of newspaper. The cold did dry them. He wondered if a person
might be immune to the impact of his own smell, the way a speaker
is deaf to the timbre and color of his own voice. He, for example,
realized his voice was golden, a velvet persuader, but mainly on the
say-so of others. Deaf to his gift, he worked on improving its effect, always wishing he could be on the receiving end of the magic.
For once, completely hear himself. But it sounded like any old
voice to him.

"Freezing. Shithole. Haul my ass *out* of here," he croaked.

His luck, he thought. In ten years, he'd never known the cold
to invade this stretch of coast so soon. Recent winters had been
"open," nothing but rain and welcome concealing fog for Seacrest,
in Marion, hugged by the good old Gulf Stream. So there was
nothing wrong with his head, or with the inspiration to hole up
here, to recuperate. . . . But in ten years his luck had also never run
so rotten. Lying here (and before, too, at brother Scotty's place)
he'd gone back over everything and still couldn't see why. Not that
he expected *fairness*. Some sons of bitches got breaks, other sons of

bitches didn't. In his life he never so much as got to lick the silver spoon. (Unlike pie-face little bro Scotty, who with his wife's land and money could afford, even as an unsuccessful race horse trainer, to play life Sunday school style, by the book.) He, Owen, had always worked his butt off to develop his businesses. Had a rep as tough but good on his word. He was an entrepreneur, took all the risk, no paid vacation, no insurance. It was his kind that invented America in the first place and still kept it nose over water level despite the down-suck of politicians and lawyers and welfare queens and foreigners swarming in to chase the quick buck. He'd read the autobiography of Lee Iacocca and wondered if Iacocca and Scotty hadn't been switched at birth: Lee and himself apparently so on a wavelength, *they* ought to be brothers. Got to force it, he thought, got to strong-arm your own luck into happening. That was Lee's philosophy, and his too. He was doing it now—by lying here still, listening to his body. He had the experience, he'd followed death into bodies and the payoff now was how he could follow the same path backward, into healing.

Sleep was scarce. He couldn't force sleep. He dreamed plenty, but awake. Here, too often—like before the sound hauled him out of it—he dreamed of *her*. The kid, with her luxuriant black hair wrapped down in a bandanna like she was ashamed to show it. She came zooming at him in a wheelchair with her white skin still ribboned with blood like he'd once seen her. Like a cracked carnival doll. Dreams were nothing but pasted-together bits of reality, he knew that much. This dream came mainly from the night at Harrisburg, when she—having waited outside the barn and not in the wheelchair, but in the cripmobile golf cart—chased almost silently after him, zigzag, till she got stuck when he pounded across the high road, uphill into the woods. That was a freak-out dream. His favorite dream was being on a raft, floating backward down the same Gulf Stream that guided up keel-heavy sports boats in the intracoastal water freeway, delivering fortunes in coke. Him floating free of this shithole, down to sunny Florida—

It was too soon. He knew that. He had to stay put. Not so

much because of the pain—that he could tough his way through, *had* toughed out for the past six weeks, even when it grew so savage it chewed straight into his sanity. He had to stay because he still couldn't breathe right yet. Because it wouldn't be any dream raft he'd be steering eight hundred miles south, but his van, stowed now in frost-blackened scrub and vines a few steps off the back access road. How long till he'd be safe to drive? With half-healed ribs, and the fresh scar tissue on a punctured lung.

"*Bitch.*" He meant, he pictured, the trainer. Erica Hablicht. It was her, and her gangly goggle-eyed boyfriend, who'd set Ranger off. Those jerks. Alone, he could have soothed Ranger, convinced him the way you soothed a needle-shy, on-the-muscle horse.

"*Suckass.*" He meant Scotty. Who'd flipped out, threatened to shop his one and only bro to the cops after snooping where he had no right and finding the business equipment in Owen's red bag. If Owen could have breathed, he would have laughed! It was from brother Scotty, with his sanctimonious ranting about what other trainers got up to, that he'd learned some of his best tricks. Horses were delicate as lacework: all you had to know was where to snip a few threads.

Food, he reminded himself. He wasn't hungry. But the job of taking care of his helpless body was absorbing. It demanded sympathy, authority, and tender persuasion. Slowly, he shifted and inched toward the edge of the bed, to reach down into the backpack stuffed with fruit and yogurt cups and peanut butter crackers: health food. The cold kept it fresh. In four or five days, he hadn't made much of a dent. He wasn't sorry for himself, but he pitied his body.

He'd shaken her off, for the absolute last time. Now he was flooring his van on I-81 in a maroon sunrise, hearing the deep pain tuning up louder every mile as the adrenaline seeped away. Florida bound, finally, new I.D.s in the glove compartment but still not the way he'd always planned this to be, with a condo view of the eighteenth hole and a Keogh fund, but instead to start from chicken scratch like a half-assed no-name—and the pain was suffocating him. Nothing looked right. The sun didn't climb like it should and the road signs hounded him, flashing mirrors, familiar and wrong. Where was he when he figured out he'd driven an hour, maybe two, in the wrong direction? *North.* And by then the pain was so weird, so many different sounds shouting at once, he knew it was too late to turn around, but how could he get off? He was going to need *somebody,* soon. He checked the radar and floored it again, *north.* He was aiming toward Scotty's place, where he hadn't been in over fifteen years but now all he could see in his mind was the gate and fence line and blue-sided ranch house, proper and dull, where nobody would find him. . . . And long before he approached Albany he was clawing and squeezing his face to keep from passing out, but it was only as his van jounced up Scotty's rutted driveway that he started screaming through bared teeth, in the seconds before he mercifully blanked out, pitched forward onto the horn. . . .

"Okay. That didn't go so bad." He meant the reaching down for a yogurt. It slid cold and tasteless along his tongue.

Another crackling crash outside. He dropped the spoon. Yogurt splattered the blanket, and a spurt of anger warmed his fear. What if it *was* all his head? Why hadn't he had the wits to turn south, pulling out of Scotty's place, and make the run for it? Wimping out . . . He wasn't *sick.* He coughed was all, he could stand it, not much came up anymore. Who said he wouldn't have made it? Instead, he'd incarcerated himself here in freezing solitary four—wait—five days now, *why,* when he was somebody always used to having people around, companionship, who'd always accomplished his best by his influence on other people. . . . He smiled, lips moistened with yogurt. He was thinking of the Lard Lady. He was thinking of how neatly he'd managed Don Deluna. Get myself out of here! Slowly, slowly, he lifted the stinking blankets, and went to work, pivoting his feet toward the edge of the bed.

The door opened, almost without noise.

"So you are here," she said.

How did you—

She leaned back, allowing her chair, with its footrest bumping the door, to propel her closer. Gusts of ice wind splashed over him. "Funny, Owen. I thought you would be here, but I didn't expect it."

What in hell do you want?

She looked like always, only this time her face shone clean white. Smidgen of pink on cheekbones and nose, but not a trace of actual blood. "You did it, Owen. You were the driver, weren't you?" she said. "I can remember."

I knew you would remember.

"Why didn't you stop, Owen? Why not try to help me?"

I did stop. And then it was *you* inside there, and you looked— oh Christ Jesus. What could I do? You think I could have hauled you out? It wasn't my fault. I signaled. There's not an accident on my record. What was I supposed to do, wait right there till the cops came? I had twenty ounces in that van!

"You used to drive a brown van. Not green."

Wait. Listen, *listen.* I did the right thing. Drove straight on to Deluna's place, where I was heading to make a delivery anyhow. Moved the whole stash into his barn and we called 911 from there. Nothing else would have made any *difference*—

"You're shaking. There's a disgusting smell in here, how can you stand it? Do you have a fever, Owen?"

You ruined me. The settlement cleaned me dry. Know that? I signaled to pass. Why the hell weren't you looking, paying attention? I had to settle—else I was looking at court, a complete investigation. So I gave you *everything*. All I'd saved. Insurance wouldn't nearly cover. And then came the deal with Don, cutting him in on the business to keep him quiet, make sure he wouldn't flap his mouth—I shouldn't have bothered. Four years, with Deluna skimming and stuff getting harder to come by, the cartel squeezing the margins—you think I made anything, made what I should have? With *you*, with you not paying attention—that's where the trouble started.

"Are you afraid of me?" She leaned forward. Her eyes turned

hazy, tender, like the eyes of a kid magnetized by a longed-for but unexpected present. "Owen? Was it you who killed the mare? Crimson—was that you?"

Morton called me. I'd sold them big time on investing, I sold them that mare, they resold it but the buyers wouldn't ante up. Fix the situation, he said. I didn't want that kind of job, but I was broke. See, if it wasn't for you—and then you turning up at every single goddamn show, you *following* me—

"I wonder. How many horses have you killed?"

The spic was supposed to do it. My *idea*—horses can't mouth breathe, so you shove a couple extra-strength tampons up the nostrils, pull them out easy afterward by the strings. Only the stupid spic botched it on the mare, so clumsy she broke loose and cut herself. At which point she was only a few hundred bucks' worth of dog food, so I had to come back next day with the warfarin. Hung around talking to Suzy, said I'd watch while she went out for a second, which was all the injection took, straight through the bandages. . . . After that the spic was always on my case, thought he had me in a corner, sticking his filthy little hand out for candy, for cash—

She reached out to him, far enough for her fingers to graze the blanket. His heart stopped. Suddenly she drew back, staring.

The spic was garbage. Worthless. Worse than an animal, he had no common sense, he popped up from nowhere, kept on jabbering, pushing me. Self-defense. Tino went for me first. He even had a knife. After he was down I had the idea to hook him up to Deluna's truck, you know how Deluna always leaves the keys in—

For a moment her eyes closed. A tiny blue vein ticked on one eyelid. He felt shut out.

I'm no quitter. Way things were going, that spic *had* to show up, right? He lost his senses but I never did. Finished the job clean like I had to and later I made some calls, you know how I can do all different voices, and wrote some letters, so there'd be folks saying they'd heard personally from the spic, so everyone would figure he was still making trouble, still in the neighborhood—

Her glance traveled around the shack, to the yellowed newspapers in the corner.

A strange hot wave of embarrassment joined his fear. She had been his favorite, he remembered now, a quiet standout among the rider-children. Willing to ride any horse. Never mentioning her wins.

No quitter. I'm like you, Ruthie. The two of us are—

"I have to be going, Owen."

He didn't believe her. Going where? She'd never said that, before.

"They'll start to wonder, up at the house. I only came out to Seacrest for a short visit. Ned invited me. He's cooking the dinner." She rolled backward, becoming smaller and darker against the open door. "I assume you don't want them to know. Don't want anyone to know you're here."

What are you going to *do*?

"Why don't you cover up more? You should. You're shivering." Now she smiled; and now her eyes turned sad. "I have no idea yet what I'll do. I'm still waiting to decide. Right now, Owen? Right now, I really don't care what happens to you."

The door slammed tight shut. Later, the wind stopped. He pulled the blankets up over his head. Now at least he was invisible. He couldn't leave for Florida yet, not with this fire in his left side. Maybe it was true: he had a fever.

"So, exactly what type of mount are you in the market for, mister . . ."

"Healey."

"That's it. Green? Broke-to-death? How very important is eye appeal? On this, I always ask prospective buyers to search their souls. Because if you are not into a beauty contest I have some ex-

ceptional talent. . . . Now, here. Have a look at this big boy. I like
the depth of shoulder, the gaskins on him. Came in only this morning. If you can handle a manageable, technical unsoundness. . . .
Do you need a *very* big animal? Would this be for yourself or for a
client? What is your price range? Realistically. No sense in my
showing the Porsches if you have a Ford budget. We can save us
both a lot of time."

"Sure." Lex loped down the aisle behind the proprietor, who
didn't make five four, who sported a feathered Tyrolean hat, and
flared twill cavalry britches on shriveled legs, and was well beyond
the biblical age of man. He, Lex, felt the blind snare of a misunderstanding. He'd called the sales barn merely for directions—
somewhere near Deerfield, was all he remembered, a nameless
place Erica had mentioned as a kind of semisecret wholesaler to the
trainer trade, and even with directions he'd gotten lost on side
roads and had turned for home before he found it—and now the
old man thought he'd come to *buy*.

"Well." Lex smiled. "I guess you've seen my car."

"So I think ten might be in your comfort zone?" The proprietor's whirligig limp didn't slow him down. Where were they
headed? The aisle was long and wide and chaotic. They dodged
horse traffic and wheelbarrow traffic, skinny middle-aged wran-
glers and buxom young women, all wearing oversized plaid shirts
with the tails hanging loose. No Latinos, though. Lex had caught
clips of the INS raid, background flashes on the motel TV on the
final, gala grand prix day at Harrisburg. After the dragnet sweep,
where had all those paperless, illegal boys gone?

"Shall we say top, twelve thousand?"

Lex stopped. "To tell the truth, I wasn't . . ." But the old man
was weaving forward, so Lex hurried on. Impossible in any case to
explain his reason for coming here. Because there was no reason:
only, in the monotonous drift of another flat gray weekend, after
another week of pencil pushing for Viola Thripp, a sudden over-
powering urge to be among the horses again, to hear and smell and
maybe touch a few of them.

In a way, he admitted, he was enjoying the misunderstanding. It made him feel more genuine, more alive than he had been in weeks.

Twelve thousand? He shook his head, half smiling. A half century or so of dealing horses had given the old man an uncanny sniffer. It was as if he'd exactly sniffed the check, still folded in Lex's wallet, that discharged Global Insurance Corp.'s gratitude for his part in saving the mortality premium on Crimson Cadillac.

Now and then they paused at a stall. Lex would enter and greet the occupant, run his palms over haunch, knees and pasterns, nodding, ruminating. The way to show one's deep understanding of horseflesh was to say absolutely nothing at all.

Twelve thousand. Not the whole twenty percent kielbasa, after all—*team effort,* Whit had said, *want you to know I went to bat for you this much, upstairs.* He better have. It had been Lex's laboriously handwritten, cowitnessed testimony that clinched subpoena of the Morton's bank records, revealing a wire transfer to Goodchild on 20 August of a lousy five K. Perjuring himself as to exactly what he'd heard the announcer say was not so hard. Harder to lie about Ranger. To whitewash Ranger, who then cosigned the statement—

"You like this young fellow? Tell me," urged the old man. "Be no trouble to take him out, run him around for you. I can be flexible, on terms."

"Thanks. But not this one." In apology, Lex patted the horse that was nibbling his sleeve and moved on. It's leaving time, he thought. Can't spin out the masquerade forever. He had a sudden cheering vision of Jesus, flanked by three of the boys, just as he'd seen them last—on the motel TV screen, pumping People for Ethical Treatment of Animals signs in a chorus line of granola-head demonstrators, whooping and stomping to beat the band. Right up front with the masquerade, while the INS raiders swept by . . . He'd laughed till he cried. He could have sworn he saw Jesus wink straight into the camera. . . .

"Whoa, there! Heads up!" The proprietor's wizened arm shot

back and pinned Lex against a wall. Out of nowhere a black horse
came thunder-dancing past. "You! Charlie!"

The girl hauling on the lead shank turned.

"Put that one away, and go throw your tack on Lancelot for our
visitor here!"

Yanking her charge's chain for an instant of peace and quiet, she
gave them both a dubious squint. "On *who*? Seriously."

There was no indoor arena. Sent outside to wait, Lex discovered
an oval of ice-laced mud behind the barn. Chilled but relaxed,
even a little curious as to what the proprietor intended to match
him up with, he leaned against the fence.

This wouldn't last long. Dusk, soon. Long nights of November.
Papery flakes speckled the blue air, in no hurry to hit the ground.
Only one individual—so muffled and hard hatted, he couldn't tell
age or sex—was still out riding. The horse, with a lovely arch to its
neck and a free-swinging stride through the slop, trotted up to a
single high pole in the center of the ring and jumped it as cleanly
as anything he'd seen at Gladstone or Harrisburg. Halted square on
a dime, wheeled, and came back over again. The jump was three
foot, at least. In mud. Taken from a *trot*.

Erica, I'd say you're missing a terrific prospect here. Want to
bet this is your type of horse?

He never much stopped thinking of her. And went on talking
to her, though in fact since Harrisburg they'd only spoken twice
together, by phone, formally and mainly about the arrangements
for Bungee, with everything unsaid left aching in the long pauses
between words.

Six weeks and change. Please understand. For now, I don't
have anywhere else to go. I miss you but I need time, she had said,
till I get over this. Last words, with the everyday pain of injury
making her voice thin and remote. Since then, he'd been waiting
for her next call. To look back on the time passed apart from her
made him dizzy, like someone starved for food or unpolluted air.

He would pick up the phone and just hold it, wanting to dial, to hear her careless brisk message on the machine. But if Roland answered—even if Lex then said nothing—Roland would know. He didn't want to upset or anger Roland, not while she was helpless there, a voluntary hostage.

The lifeline—his stroke of luck and inspiration—was having managed to put Bungee in place at Stoneacre Farm. To support her with the work. To alert him, in case anything went wrong. Still, he worried, imagining all that could go wrong. It didn't help that on the last call she had mentioned a fire at the Urbachs' estate, Seacrest, down in Marion. . . . *But according to Ned no serious damage. Some outbuildings burned to cinders but never any threat to their horses, their barn.* Now his imagination kindled fire on her farm, in the stick-frame stove-heated house she'd once described. His imagination also raised storms, cut off power lines, infected her with fever, morbid despair, or worse, the germ of forgetting. . . . Sometimes his imagination panicked him most by its failure. He strained to see and caught only the brown curve of a cheekbone, sand grains in a glint of gold down, rough, tanned fingers whitened by his grip. He had no complete picture.

Hey, you're almost well, aren't you? Another week, two outside, and you'll be well and we can begin to forget all this. . . . Even a chance that tonight, when he got home, Rosie would give him that look: Zandro, a young lady she called for you. Could be. And could be that the reason he now perched shivering on a fence with the snow and the darkness falling was because it felt much better to wait here, far away but closer to her than the phone could take him.

In the ring, the jumper horse snorted and shied.

"Meet Lancelot," said the old man from close behind him.

Lancelot. What a joke of a name for this horse. Miles high, slab-sided—a pallid dun, with a bowed Roman nose and the primitive black streak down his back. Charlie rode him into the ring and set up a shambling, disjointed trot. Lex tried to smile. He avoided the old man's eyes.

"I like *that* horse," he said, as the jumper was led out. "For sale?"

"What is not? But he has a price. Beautiful, yes? Talented. Not entirely easy. Now, this solid fellow—"

But Lex wasn't listening. Reaching back to touch the flat outline of his wallet, he watched the elegant jumper vanish into the barn.

"To decide which horse to buy," remarked the old man, "is to choose a future. A long road ahead together to ride, full of adventures and discoveries. So, which horse? Which road?" He's said this a million times, thought Lex. As Lancelot stumbled and caught up to himself, the proprietor said, "Believe me, that was only the footing. This horse is sound. But no honest dealer pretends to give guarantees."

And then Lex found himself being hoisted into the saddle. A sudden exchange, a sleight of hand, there was no way to stop what was happening—no words came. His numb feet fumbled for stirrups, his hands for reins. He had never held reins. Everything moved, the animal that bore his weight never stopped moving. Lex felt his head bob, swaying for balance. The force of snow in his face increased as the ground uncoiled beneath him. The saddle was liquid, slippery, he grabbed its cantle, then twisted a hand into Lancelot's greasy mane.

"Trrr-ott!" yelled the proprietor.

Great slamming jolts. His teeth clattered, the universe clattered, he heard his bones grinding together. Stay on. The snow stung his eyes like an endless swarm of bees.

"Lancelot! Caan-*ter*!"

Shock drowned fear. The universe smoothed to a single high repeating wave. Fence posts and white faces zoomed close and swirled away. Sweat streaming: he would never be cold again. Nickel taste of snow in his throat. Tears whipped free from his eyes. I'm with you. I love you. Here we go.

About the Author

Born in Chicago, KAI MARISTED has studied and worked in Tokyo, Berlin, and Munich. She has written extensively for German broadcasting. Her first novel, *Out After Dark,* was published in 1993. Recent stories have appeared in *The American Scholar* and *American Voice*. Currently she lives and writes on a farm west of Boston.

About the Type

This book was set in Bembo, a typeface based on an old-style Roman face that was used for Cardinal Bembo's tract *De Aetna* in 1495. Bembo was cut by Francisco Griffo in the early sixteenth century. The Lanston Monotype Machine Company of Philadelphia brought the well-proportioned letter forms of Bembo to the United States in the 1930s.